THE COMPANY OF DEATH

THE COMPANY OF DEATH

THE IMMORTAL JOURNEY - BOOK ONE

ELISA HANSEN

Cover Design by Natania Barron

For Cookies

1

TOWN DUTY

Killing something undead wasn't the same as killing a real person. That's what Emily told herself for the thirty-first time since her morning meal, the same as she did dozens of times every day she served town duty. It never got any easier. "This isn't who you are," she said to herself, to the hot gun between her hands.

But that was some bullshit. It's who she was now.

"Upstairs is clear!" Emily tested the body at her feet with a steel-toed nudge. Not so much as a flicker of the dappled eyelids. The clean bullet hole above its bushy gray brows revealed more purple than red, and its slack jaw exposed blood-blackened decay in perfect teeth.

No, not teeth. Dentures.

A wistful smile touched Emily's lips. "Hey, look at you. How'd you manage to keep those in? Feisty grandpa." Her smile faded as the image of her own long-gone Grampy shoved into her mind. And then her long-gone everyone.

One more down, millions and millions to go.

With a sigh, she slid the Glock 18 into the holster on her thigh and dragged the body by the armpits into the dim hallway that smelled of overcooked dust. She begrudgingly thanked the last seventeen merciless months of combat training for the muscle to lift him, because he was heavy for an old guy. How many pounds of human flesh weighed down his stomach? Or would it all be digested by now? Did they digest? Questions that just didn't matter anymore.

"Clear!" Sherice's voice shot up from the house's lower level. "Hurry it up, bitches."

Seriously? Not like she had places to go. But Emily was not about to get started, not with Sherice. Not today. Emily's last chance to ask for reassignment, and today was almost over. With a burst of anxious energy and a grunt, she heaved the body to the staircase.

"Sorry about this, Gramps," she whispered even though he probably couldn't hear her. Probably. A solid kick sent him somersaulting past the landing to join the others in the foyer.

Thwack went Sherice's axe. Decap done.

Emily jogged downstairs as the front door swung in to shroud the sprawled corpses in the unholy light of California afternoon sunshine. Rosa pushed through with the wheelbarrow, and Other Joe loaded it up. Emily joined Sherice, aiming her gun at the oozing faces. Just in case.

"The fire's going." Rosa's wiry hair stuck to her round cheeks. "Let's get these over there. Everyone else is done."

Emily blinked. Already? How had the day gone by so fast? Her team usually lit the fire a couple hours before sunset, but by Emily's count, she'd shot fewer than three dozen people since coming down into town that morning.

Not people.

Undead. Flesh-eaters. More than two years since the Ecuador Explosion, why couldn't she get over it? Almost a year and a half since she joined the LPI and spent most days between missions shooting and torching them. She forced her eyes away from the pearly white dentures in the framed family photos on the hall wall. *Not people anymore.*

Town duty was the worst.

Well, second worst.

Today.

"Good work, Em," said Rosa while Other Joe donned the gauntlets and navigated the wheelbarrow out the front door. On the driveway, the three of them fell in around him, Sherice taking point.

"We're not doing the next block?" Emily triangulated with Rosa a few paces behind the wheelbarrow to cover Other Joe's back.

Rosa shook her head. "Ramon says that's it for today. We've been cleaning here what, like two weeks now?"

"More like three." Twenty-two days exactly. Not that Emily was counting compulsively or anything.

"Not many of them left in this place." Rosa shrugged. "We might even run out before Mission 12 starts. And then what'll we do while we wait?"

"More drills?"

Rosa rolled her eyes. "That'll make you-know-who happy."

Imagining their trainer's sadistic pleasure made Emily twitch, but it would beat the way they spent the last three weeks of duty going door to door, clearing out the little desert town. And anything would be better than the imminent Mission 12. Thinking about her assignment made dread grumble deep in her guts.

Sherice led their group through debris-scattered residential streets. As they passed into the shadow of craggy yellow Suncrest Hill, Emily let a few extra paces fall between her and Other Joe's wheelbarrow. Rosa slowed, glancing at her with the curious-concerned expression that made Emily pretty much love her from the moment they met. She was only a few years older than Emily, and about six inches shorter, but she made Emily feel safe.

"Did, um, did Ramon say anything else?" Emily asked.

"About cleaning?" Rosa shook her head.

"No." Emily hesitated. Rosa always had her back, but Emily hadn't told *anyone* yet. "Never mind."

"What never mind? No never mind. You got that constipated look on your face like when you don't want to do something."

Any other day, Emily might have laughed. "I just..." She lowered her voice to keep Other Joe—and especially Sherice—from overhearing. "It's Mission 12. My assignment."

"You're one of the three infiltrators, right? I do not envy you that."

"Yeah. Me, Sherice, and Brion. We're supposed to pose as refugees so the commune will take us in. But it's almost funny, you know? When I was a kid, I used to play spy all the time. It was like, the awesomest of career paths, right?" Almost two dozen people left in their unit, but Emily landed the only assignment she couldn't do. It was Michele's call, but they lost Michele last month. Now Ramon was basically in charge, but Michele's plan would go on. As far as Ramon was concerned, the plan was perfect. "But I can't do it."

Rosa stopped walking. "Say what?" She gave their surroundings a quick visual sweep then caught up to Emily. "You're actually serious."

So serious, a ball of acid spent the last month eating through Emily's stomach lining. "I just…yeah."

"Damn. You better tell Ramon."

"I know, I know." Emily should have done it weeks ago. Putting it off to so close to the mission's start made it all the worse.

"Damn, okay. Just talk to him, I guess? He'll give you a different role."

"You think?"

"He can't exactly make you do it if you don't want to."

"Yeah." Ramon needed someone willing on the assignment, but he would give Emily that look. The look like he thought she could do anything. The look that made her want to prove him right.

It wasn't that she doubted the cause. She was devoted to the cause. The communes must be destroyed. She would do anything for the cause. Anything, except… She pictured it a thousand different ways, what it would be like to infiltrate the commune, to pretend to need their protection from the flesh-eaters and be willing to sell herself in exchange.

No way in the universe was it going to happen.

Emily groaned and rubbed the tense spot between her eyes before doing a visual sweep.

"You don't want to disappoint him." Rosa watched her with furrowed brows.

"Right."

"What about me?"

"You're—" Emily blinked at her. "Am I disappointing you?" Heat rose behind her nose, making her lips prickle.

Staring past Other Joe's back, Rosa frowned at the undead bodies in the wheelbarrow as if they held the answers. But she didn't say yes.

"What about the rest of the team?" Rosa asked without looking at her.

The change of subject cooled the flush in Emily's face but made her neck itch under the film of sweat. "I'll be disappointing everyone."

"Well, that's not the word I was thinking."

Right. They'd be, what, disgusted with her? Worse. But Emily would rather die than give herself to a commune. Literally. She would kill herself first. Her fingers tightened around the G18's grip, and she clenched her teeth against the acidic rise accompanying the thought. Her brain had taken a bleak turn since Michele first gave her the assignment, but it didn't feel dramatic. It felt like the simplest, purest truth she knew. Her teammates' derision would happen; Emily would find a way to swallow it.

"You'll lose your chance at promotion." Rosa shrugged, but the movement was stiff, and she wouldn't meet Emily's gaze. "If you actually care about that."

She did, damn it. Graduating out of the field team was always the goal, into a position of safety at LPI headquarters, across the country on the fortress island of Manhattan where she'd never have to think about being near the undead again. Either kind.

The Life Preservation Initiative's goals were simple. Preserve life. Keep people *alive*. Make both kinds of undead dead-dead and keep the living from their gruesome grasp. Wipe out the flesh-eaters and take down the blood-drinker communes. And every part of Emily's being wanted to make that happen.

Any other way but this.

It might be another week before Mission 12 would officially begin, but it might not. It could happen the day after tomorrow, and she wouldn't get another face-to-face opportunity with Ramon for days. Today was her last chance. She couldn't care about disgusting everyone, not if she wanted to live. As long as she had Rosa, she'd get through it.

"Now." Emily pushed past the last of her hesitation with a rough exhale. "I'll talk to him now."

"Sure." Rosa gave her a tight smile and turned her attention to their perimeter.

The smell of the smoke reached Emily before it rose into view over the low houses. As they followed the wheelbarrow around the corner of the last block, her eyes zeroed in on Ramon by the bonfire in the center of the street. He stood with his arms crossed over his broad chest, frowning at the flaming stack of undead body parts as if he could stern-face them into burning faster. He'd shed his reinforced jacket, and the tense lump of muscle above his elbow twitched. The sweat on his warm brown skin reflected the flames as he watched the blackening limbs and torsos writhe and wither.

Emily let a few more steps fall between her and the wheelbarrow. Of course, he would have to look so intense right when she needed to ask for an entirely selfish favor. She had worked so hard to prove herself a strong recruit, as efficient as the guys twice her size, and the thought of Ramon thinking less of her in any way snarled her guts in knots. She glanced to Rosa, but Rosa focused on the job.

They parked the wheelbarrow, and Emily worked with the others to heft the bodies and heads onto the fire. When they finished unloading, her team retreated to relax on the shady porches across the street with the dozen others of the day's town duty squad. Emily lingered in the halo of heat with Ramon. A trail of sweat snaked past his eye from the thick black hair at his temple.

"Hey," she said. "Can I talk to you?"

His gaze flicked to her. "Hey. Yeah." The tension in his square jaw softened at the sight of her. "What's up?"

She ignored the dryness in her throat prodding her to reach for her water bottle. Ignored how the sweat in her hair made her scalp itch. "About Mission 12." She stared at her black boots. Even through the caked dust, she could make out the bloodstains.

When Ramon didn't say anything, she made herself meet his eyes again. Brown, but not like hers. So dark, almost black. The kind of eyes you could get lost in, maybe, if things were different. He watched her patiently. She told herself it was her imagination, but he always seemed more accommodating with her than anyone else. Usually, it gave her a secret sense of confidence, but this time, it made what she had to say so much harder.

"I don't think..." She swallowed and set her jaw. "I can't be one of the spies."

Ramon's brow knit, and he cocked his head as if he misheard her.

"I'm wrong for the assignment."

His eyes narrowed. "You're perfect for it."

"No, Ray." She took a breath. "I'm not."

He relaxed, warmth coming to his gaze, and he laughed softly. "Most vampires are old white guys, right? Old white guys like women who look like you." Right. *Exotic.* The unspoken word hovered like a cloud of gnats. "They'll want you to join them, no questions asked."

Emily flinched. Did he think she was fishing for compliments? "That's—no—" Getting *into* the commune wasn't what worried her.

"And besides that, you're perfect."

The knots in her guts tightened. "No. I'm not."

"So fake it," he said, and to Emily's dismay, he smiled. "Em, you could sell ice to a penguin, when you turn it on. You'll have Sherice and Brion in there with you, but come on, Em. You're the one who always wins at Bullshit."

"But that's a game, an act—"

"And this is your job."

"I know, but that's why—" Her breath shuddered. "Look. I've given this a lot of thought." In truth, she'd known it in her core the second she got the assignment. But Ramon's expression was darkening. Emily pushed on. "And I have to be real with you. When it comes down to it, Ray, I'll blow it. I know I will. I can't...I can't let them *use* me."

The short scar in Ramon's left eyebrow wrinkled, and the corners of his black mustache sank as his expression slid into the one she dreaded. "I trust you, Em. Michele trusted you. It'll take you only a few days in there to gather the intel for the rest of us to bust in and destroy. You can do this. I know you can."

And how many pints of her blood would they take in *only a few days* in exchange for their "protection" from the flesh-eaters? One drop was more than she could allow. Emily's face felt hot, too hot, even so close to the fire. The way Ramon frowned made her feel like a chastened child. She didn't want a pep talk.

Stop. Just stop.

How could she explain it? What it was like growing up being told to be ashamed of her own face while at the same time encouraged to use her looks to hook a white husband? *Mixed girls like you have an expiration date, Emily. Use it.*

How could she make Ramon understand the undead wanting to bloodrape her was like that but a thousand times worse? How to make him get that her refusal to let it happen was the one thing keeping her sane? From spiraling into the creeping blackness that wouldn't stop hovering at the brink of her consciousness?

If Emily could control nothing else in her unraveling life in a dissolving world, this resolve—her *self*, her body—was the one thing she would cling to until the grave. It kept her worthy of existing.

She took a shaking breath.

"I'll do it." A voice cut through the noise of the fire.

Emily's breath abandoned her, and she whipped around to see who.

Rosa.

When did she come out into the street? Sherice stood a couple feet behind, and the rest of the team hovered at the curb, watching Emily and Ramon. How much did they overhear? The odor of the burning bodies turned stifling, clawing its way down Emily's throat as Sherice glared at her over Rosa's shoulder.

Ramon uncrossed his arms, bewildered. "You'll take Emily's assignment?"

"Sure, yeah." Rosa glanced at Sherice before offering Emily a grim smile.

"Rosa's not afraid of vampires," snapped Sherice.

"I'm not—" Emily clamped her mouth shut and gave a little nod. Arguing wouldn't help her case.

Ramon looked back and forth between them, started to say something, stopped himself, and then turned back to the fire. "Fine. Whatever. I'll brief you tomorrow."

"Sherice already told me everything," Rosa said. "I got this."

"I will brief you. Tomorrow." Ramon's back was to Emily, but she could perfectly picture his expression of disgust.

She turned to Rosa, but what could Emily even say now with Sherice scowling at her like that? Like she was a pathetic waste of existence.

What was Rosa *thinking*?

As her teammates' eyes all bored into Emily like thumbscrews, a burning sick feeling sloshed in to overwhelm the bonfire's heat.

Sherice fist-bumped Rosa, but when they turned back to the porches with everyone else, Rosa caught Emily's eye. What was in that glance? Pity? Frustration? Goodbye? It almost made Emily wish Rosa would go back to refusing to look at her.

Emily's gaze fell to the blood on her boots. She didn't want this. Not at all. But what did she think would happen?

She lifted her face, staring hard at Ramon's squared shoulders, her heart stuttering. What was he thinking now? That she was a coward? He needed to know it wasn't about fear; it was about strength. Power, control. The thought of letting a blood-drinker so much as *touch* her filled Emily with frustrated rage, made her want to flip tables, smash windows, punch in faces. The thought of allowing one of them to taint her blood, to *take* from her body—

She took a shaky breath. "Ray…"

"What?" The muscle in his jaw twitched. "Is there more?"

Emily winced and shook her head, though he couldn't see it.

The wind picked up, the way it always did when the desert air cooled before sunset. A clutter of paper blew along the sidewalk. In every town her unit cleaned, so much paper lay strewn everywhere. Newspapers, receipts, homework. Full of words, testaments to lost civilization. They scattered across artificial lawns, swirled in mini tornadoes, clung to telephone poles. Tons of other junk too, of course; trashed furniture and electronics, toppled solar panels, garbage cans rocking in the dead air that was always awake, rolling up against stripped cars like sad dogs hinting for head-rubs. But the paper outnumbered the rest exponentially. Was it because it flew farther in the gritty wind? Emily never realized people still used so much paper. It was a relic of her grandparents' generation. But it was what remained.

And now her LPI unit used it for kindling.

"Thanks," she whispered to Ramon. Turning from the fire, Emily walked through the paper and found a place to sit alone.

Rosa's laugh rang out from the porch two houses over. It sounded off, fake. The heels of Emily's palms ground into her eye sockets until stars spattered across the darkness behind her lids. She kept grinding until black overtook them again.

2

MUERTE

According to the plaque in the entryway, the visitor's center atop Suncrest Hill was set up as a concession to protesters who once thought the factory site in the valley ought to remain protected land. The little museum compound once made it possible for families to take picturesque hikes and feel at one with nature, so long as they didn't look down either side of the hill; to the north, smoke continually filled the sky, and to the south, the stucco town hugged the single endless highway.

Within its chain-link fence, the visitor's center now made itself useful by providing the perfect vantage point for Emily's LPI unit to stake out their target's route. The huge nomadic commune with the Amargosa hostages would pass through the factory valley any day now. When they did, Mission 12 would officially begin.

Inside the museum, Emily's teammates went straight for the windowless back gallery they used as a hangout/food room. Antique portable generators powered the hot plates, and their hoard of cans and tins would be popping with botulism long before the team could eat them all.

For the hike up the hill, Emily took rear, avoiding Rosa, not knowing what to say. Now she hovered in the gallery entryway after everyone filed in. It had been a hot day of heavy work, but she didn't feel much like eating. Ramon settled onto the floor with the others to dine among the taxidermy dioramas of local fauna. When his gaze fell on Emily, he locked eyes with her for a long moment before looking pointedly away. Any vestiges of her appetite withered and rotted.

Take a hint.

She stepped backward but yelped as she collided with someone coming into the room.

A strong, small hand grasped her waist. "If you wanted to feel me up, all you had to do was ask."

Emily cringed. Daisy, the drill sergeant. The title wasn't official, they weren't military, but as their physical trainer, she was merciless. The team had Daisy to thank for making them deadly, but that didn't mean anyone had to like her. Emily twisted out of her grip and shook her head. "Sorry."

Daisy smiled and eyed Emily up and down. "Obliques are feeling a little soft there. I think we need to up your reps."

Emily fought the urge to roll her eyes and stepped aside. She didn't have the energy to deal with Daisy and her Daisy smile. With her tight blond ponytail and ice-blue eyes, she looked like she could be perky, and while running their combat training, she never stopped smiling. She even smiled when she screamed. But perky wasn't the word for it.

Emily twitched. Today had sucked, but at least it had been Daisy-free. She turned down the hall, hoping to keep it that way.

"Hey," Daisy called. "Where are you going?"

Emily paused. Where was she going? She shook her head. "Not hungry."

"Really?" Daisy patted her sculpted midriff. "I'm always starving after a day of killing zombies."

Emily made a face. "Don't call them that."

The Daisy smile disappeared. "Why the fuck not?"

Her mouth opened, but Emily only shook her head again. Where had all her words gone? It was a valid question. Other terms for them existed—the undead, the infected, the violent, the ravenous. But blood-drinkers were all those things too. How to differentiate the two types of undead without saying exactly what they consumed? No one really called them flesh-eaters, though, not without sounding like a tool. Everyone used the Z word, but it just felt too meta for Emily.

"Zombies are like…" She made an empty gesture. "Like long-dead people that come *back* to life." And only existed in myths and movies. The image of a rotting CGI arm bursting up through a soundstage grave brought a nostalgic smile to Emily's face. The former-people she butchered every day were something else. Something immediate, real. Something never considered cheesy and fun.

Daisy's eyes narrowed, and she stepped up to Emily. "Seriously? Semantics? They're fucking zombies. Deal with it." The smile was back, so close Emily could feel Daisy's breath on her lips. *Ugh,* it smelled like black licorice. "Besides, if they're not dead, how come they get up and walk a day after you cut off their heads?"

Despite the black licorice, Emily held her ground. "That's not what I meant."

"Oh yeah? And what did you mean, hmm?"

Behind Daisy, everyone in the gallery stared at them through the doorway. *Again?* Heat flared across Emily's face.

"Well?" The Daisy smile spread, and she brushed a fingertip down Emily's cheek. "You're super cute, you know that?"

Clenching her teeth, Emily pulled back. "Thanks."

Daisy batted her yellow eyelashes. "Oh, sweetie. Sarcasm will get you twenty extra in the morning."

Emily turned before Daisy could see her wince. She was exempt from drills tomorrow due to scout shift, but Daisy wouldn't forget for next time. As Emily rounded the hall corner, she was sure the surge of conversation at her back was all about her.

Goddamn, how deep was she going to dig this hole?

The worst part is over. She could focus on the positive; now she stood in a place to be the best member of the team she could be. She'd had no choice, really. She needed to set herself up for success, for the good of the team and the cause they fought for. And Rosa seemed fine about stepping in? It was the right thing to do.

So why did she feel like such an asshole?

Being hung up on semantics wasn't like clinging to bodily autonomy. Emily could only control so much. Maybe it was time to let that one go if it would make people like her again.

"Zombies," she whispered to herself. "Vampires." Blood-drinkers had called themselves vampires long before the world learned of their existence two years ago. It made Emily want to reject the term on principle. Like they thought they were so fancy? She didn't want to give them the credit. But if it would make Emily come off like less of a snob, then time to wave the white flag on her one-woman war on terminology.

"Zombies. Vampires." Her mouth felt dirty, but it was a start. "Selkies," she added, hoping to make herself smile. It didn't work.

The central gallery dimmed as the last of the day disappeared beyond the tall grimy windows. Emily leaned in close to the shiny defunct water fountain by the useless restrooms to squint at her reflection. Yes, she looked even crappier than she felt. It was an effect of the dry climate and hell, the bonfire, but what did everyone else assume about the redness in her eyes?

She rubbed at the sooty streaks on her cheeks, then wished she hadn't. Underneath, ten years had been added to her twenty-five. After the last two years, she should look a hundred. Though maybe if she did, Michele never would have chosen her for the assignment in the first place. Emily made the grossest possible face at herself, then pushed away from the fountain.

Doing something useful would make her feel better. There had to be weapons to clean or stuff to put away. Anything to get Ramon's words from the bonfire out of her head. *They like women who look like you.* No way he could know how deep that knife cut.

Many people assumed Emily was white until they spent more than a minute studying her. The shape of her eyes, with their medium brown color, and her ability to tan deep golden in ten minutes were the most obvious traits she inherited from her half-Filipina mother. She had her white dad's buxom mostly-German genes to thank for her five-foot-seven frame, but she probably got her straight, heavy hair from her mom's side. Not that Emily had never known her mom with anything other than a bleached-out perm, like a cartoon flame on a short, stubby candle.

Pulling her hair out of its knot as she plodded down the hall, Emily ran her fingers through the bottom inches of two-year faded eggplant color. She let it get long because she hated the thought of cutting off that last length of artificial pigment, a lingering reverence to the modern world before it was flung back into the dark ages. The foot or so of growth since remained the ashy brown her mother always dreaded. *Pretty girls have blond hair.*

Emily lost count of the pots of dye she bought to cover the bleach once she first escaped her mom. The night she moved into her college dorm, a rainbow saturated her scalp. The next week, she joined the Filipino Students' Association. And even though she didn't look like anyone else in the club, by sophomore year, she was its vice president.

Emily turned into the museum's little movie theater, but she stopped just inside the door at the sight of Carlos, hunched on the wide, carpeted step seats. Though they used the semicircular room for sleeping now, once upon a time, it showed educational nature videos. A single camping lantern under the front wall's dead screen cast long arsenic green LED fingers up the shadowy tiers, but Emily could see Carlos clearly enough. He was alone, his shoulders tight, his face in his hands. She backed to the door, but he noticed her before she could disappear.

"Emily?" His voice was raspy. Tired? Or crying again?

"Hey. Um." She glanced to the hall to imply she'd give him his privacy. Lately, giving Carlos privacy served best for everyone involved. "Sorry."

"No." He turned to her, his big dark eyes bloodshot and beseeching. He was Emily's age, but she felt much older around him. Like he was perpetually the kid brother with a booboo needing a kiss-make-better. Emily supposed she might be sensitive too if she lost the love of her life a month ago. But Carlos was moody even before then. And now his grief took him to extremes, often made him useless in the field. Most of the team wondered why they kept him.

The answer, of course, was his eyes. He had those implants. He could see miles farther than most humans. Only a couple people on the team had them, and they justified any failings. Emily got regular old laser surgery when she turned nineteen, a gift from her dad to make up for his nearsighted genes. If they had waited a couple more years, and had a few extra grand to spend, she could have had implants too. But she was just grateful caffeine withdrawals comprised her biggest physical handicap when the world ended.

"Emily." Carlos took a shaky breath. "Have you ever seen someone die?"

A sharp laugh of disbelief broke past her lips. "Is that a trick question?"

He grimaced. "No, I mean *really* die. The actual moment of death."

What? She frowned as a slide show of all the...the *zombies* she took out flickered across her brain. Bullets, then decap, then fire until they became ash. The moment of death had to fit in there at some point.

She held in a sigh and crossed the carpet to settle beside Carlos. "Tough day?"

He eyes fell to the ratty red bandanna wound between his fingers. "Bones in the shadow." His lips barely moved.

Emily blinked. "Huh?"

"That's what I saw. In the shadows on him. Bones." The bandanna slipped to the floor as he rubbed his eyes.

"On who?" She bent to pick it up.

"Emily." He grabbed her arm so abruptly the bandanna fell again. "Do you think this is it? Do you think Mission 12... It's..."

"Dude, calm down." She patted his hand, then pried up his fingers. "It's been planned out for weeks. It isn't going to be like the Dragon Mart."

Carlos slumped, exhaling an exhausted joyless laugh. "That's where I saw it."

"Saw what?"

"When Alaric, when he..."

When he fell. Off the Dragon Mart roof. A month ago. Emily didn't see it; she was behind Carlos, covering his back, but she heard the smack. She heard the cry seize in Carlos's throat. She could swear she felt him go cold even through their layers of black insulation. Alaric had been hanging by Michele's hands, but Alaric wasn't the only one they lost that day.

"Alaric." Carlos swallowed thickly. "And then, Michele." His fist clenched.

Emily bristled. "Look, it wasn't her fault. It was *them*. Fast ones. They got her."

Michele had dropped her gun to grab Alaric's hands. It was either let him fall or let them have a chance at getting her from behind. In the end, both happened anyway. When Emily could finally turn around, she had plenty of time to see them ripping her leader apart.

Michele didn't have to grab Alaric. No one made her. She could have saved herself. She should have. *For the greater good of the team,* Emily told herself repeatedly. But every time she imagined herself in Michele's place, she felt her heart start to unravel from the edges, and she pummeled the thoughts away before they had the chance to drive her toward the abyss.

"I screamed," Carlos murmured. "She wouldn't have noticed him falling if I didn't scream."

"You reacted. You didn't know what would happen." Emily scooped up the bandanna and pressed it into his hands. "What could you do? Alaric was lucky, really, compared to Michele."

"No, that's not what I mean. I mean, it's exactly the difference, you know?"

"No." Emily barely restrained a tense laugh of confusion. "Not at all."

"When he fell, when he hit, I saw him *die*. And I saw...*it*."

"The shadow bones?"

"But not with Michele. Not with any of the others. That's what I mean, you know?"

"No!" Emily's anxious laugh managed to escape her. "Carlos, what the hell?"

"Not shadow bones. A shadow *with* bones. White, white bones."

Bones decorated Emily's landscape plenty of times over the past months, but she didn't remember any at the Dragon Mart.

"A shadow out of nowhere." Carlos took a jagged breath. "Right there. It was bright, remember? High sun. No shadows, nothing in shadow. But out of nowhere, it jumped on Alaric. Like, like it would stop his fall. But it blended with him and disappeared. But I saw the bones."

Emily stared at him. *Is this a prank?* No, Carlos was too upset to be messing with her. But how could he be serious? "A shadow jumped on Alaric. Out of nowhere. With bones."

"Do you think this is it?" His eyelashes fluttered at her like a five-year-old's. "Is Mission 12 the one that will kill us all?"

Okay. He needed to snap out of this. How could she reassure him? She opened her mouth to give him the first canned response that came to mind, but Carlos pushed on.

"Was it because he fell, Emily? They got Michele: no shadow. They got my little sister: no shadow. They didn't get Alaric. Alaric fell, he hit: shadow. Bones."

Emily went for the hand-on-hand technique. His was clammy, but she managed to keep the exasperation out of her voice. "But that has nothing to do with Mission 12. We're sending spies into a commune. Then when we attack, it'll be just vampires and humans. No *zombies*." She gave his fingers a press. "No one is going to be falling off any roofs. Why even bring this up?"

"I dreamt about him this morning."

"Alaric?"

"No, him. It. *La Muerte*. The bone shadow."

"What?" Did he really just say *Muerte*?

"In my dream, it was the same as with Alaric. *He* was the same. It was only for a second, less than a second, the instant Alaric hit, the shadow was suddenly there. It came out of nowhere and poured over him, so cold. I could feel it from across the lot. And the bones like a hand stroking Alaric's face. And then Alaric lay there, alone, broken, his spine coming out his neck. But his bones weren't white, Emily. They were dark…dark red. Michele on the roof…screaming."

"Dude! Stop this."

"I think, Emily, it's an omen."

"There's no such thing as a shadow with bones. You—you'd just seen Alaric fall. You were upset. You were, I don't know, hallucinating, or—"

"No, he wasn't."

Emily jumped. She twisted to see Sherice in the doorway, giving Emily the same curled-lip glare as down by the bonfire. Emily's stomach tightened. Sherice was a SoCal recruit, like Emily, like Carlos. Like almost everyone in the unit, actually. Rosa and Ramon were the only ones left from the original team Michele brought out from New York. When Sherice first joined them, Emily was a little star-struck by how pretty she was. She had dark brown skin and full lips and long braids with cherry red weave, but one day she made a very public show of chopping the braids off. She shaved her head and proclaimed, "In memory of my parents!" She was still beautiful bald, but Emily's admiration wore off for other reasons.

Carlos sniffed sharply and squared his shoulders. "Sherice. Hey. I didn't realize anyone was listening." He shot Emily a glance, his cheeks splotchy.

"I know what you saw." Sherice let the doors fall closed behind her. "You weren't hallucinating. That's what happens."

"What?"

"When you die." She crossed the carpet to him. "It takes your soul. Like what you said, shadow and bone. Like smoke, right? But thick and, and, what you call it. Like ink in water, like melting. And the bones, they come out of it. The death hands, reaching. Nothing holding the bones together, but they're solid, like there's someone trapped inside the dark parts, needing flesh, stretching to get out. Like he's only got to touch one more person, steal one more soul, and he'll finally be free. But he never is."

Okay, was Sherice drunk? To talk that way to Carlos when he was so upset? But the conviction in her dark eyes made all words of protest go cold on Emily's tongue.

The color fled Carlos's face, his mouth gaping. But then his expression crumbled, and he shook his head. "Sherice, you weren't there."

"No, not then. That's not when I saw it. When my moms and dad… When they…"

Emily's shock almost made her laugh. It was the first time she ever heard Sherice at a loss for words on the subject of her parents. She was usually the my-tragedy-is-worse-than-yours type.

Emily had her own tragedies. They all did. She'd only told three people what happened to her dad and brother, and that story slipped out in what she regarded as her weakest moments on long, black, haunted nights, with whispered voices the only things masking the howls in the distance.

Carlos grabbed Sherice's arm. "Did you dream about him—*it* last night?"

Sherice screwed her mouth into a frown, shook her stubbly head. "No, but I saw it. Back then. When I saw my parents die. Right before my eyes. Like you saw Alaric."

Carlos's face pinched. "Just me, then." He turned to Emily. "This is it. He's coming for me."

"Alaric?" Emily couldn't help herself. She should feel bad, but the two of them had gone beyond pitiable straight into ridiculous.

"No! Him. It. The shadow." Carlos sank to the step, his eyes on the floor, his fingertips brushing his chapped lips. "In a way, I'm glad. I'd rather *he* take me than get bitten. I'd rather die like Alaric."

Not like Michele. All ridiculousness aside, Emily didn't disagree in the slightest. If she ever found herself between a four-story drop and certain bite, she would take that fall in a heartbeat. And if no roofs to leap from presented themselves, other ways abounded. Ways to keep *them* from using her body to increase their ranks.

Sherice pushed past Emily to kneel beside Carlos. "Dreams have power."

Carlos shivered. Emily snorted.

"What?" Sherice snapped at her.

"I don't think you're helping."

"Oh yeah? And you know a lot about helping, Prissy Miss I-Can't-Do-My-Job?"

Emily's mouth fell open, the words hitting like a fist to the sternum. Meanwhile, Carlos's eyes darted around the room, looking everywhere but at Emily.

So much she could say, but her breath withered under Sherice's glare. She closed her mouth, her teeth clamping the insides of her cheeks.

Fine. Whatever. A reality check obviously wasn't what Carlos wanted right now.

She pushed off the step and left the room. If Carlos ever answered Sherice, it was not meant for Emily to hear. She would clean herself up and come back later to sleep, after Sherice went out for scout shift. When the lantern would be off and Emily couldn't see how anyone else might be looking at her.

And then tomorrow… Tomorrow, she would do her damnedest to remember she needed to live each day like it could be her last.

3

ARTIFICIAL LIFE

Sleep was a friend who visited less and less. Emily awoke long before the scheduled end of her rest shift. She lay in the dark of the visitors' center theater among her sleeping teammates, absently listening to distant moaning howls and trying, trying to drift off again. She gave up when her mushy brain eventually realized the sounds weren't actually there. Phantom howls.

Shaking the echoes from her mind, she rolled on her sleeping pad to fish her gun from under the wadded towel she used as a pillow. Her bunk was on the top tier of the room's carpeted steps. The mildew stench was bad when they first moved in, then was quickly overtaken by the unwashed body smell of her team, but the human nose adjusted. The completely enclosed space offered a far more comforting place to sleep than their last camp, where wasteland winds rattled duct-taped windowpanes all through the night.

Emily pressed the Glock's cool metal against her cheek and willed away the lingering wisps of her troubled dreams. Usually, she dreamt of better times. Of electricity and running water and smiling old people and puppies and caffeine. Ironically, she preferred such happy thoughts be bitch-slapped away by wakeful reality. But this time, the dreams had been too real. Rosa taking her mission assignment. Rosa pretending to want the vampire's bite, and then—in a terrible twist of dream logic—*liking* it. Swooning into it, giving up the cause, giving up everything. Emily cringed.

Letting her arm fall over the step's edge, she brushed at Rosa's spot below. Empty. Couldn't she sleep either? Emily still didn't know what to say to her. *Why, Rosy? Why did you do it?* No matter the answer, Emily asking would just make them both feel worse.

She pulled on her boots mechanically in the dark and wiggled her holster up her leg, snapped it into place. Toeing down the steps, she avoided tripping over the slumbering lumps of their three newest teammates. What were their names again? Rosa would remember.

A chink of light under the doors guided Emily, and she slipped out silently. As she breathed in the vaguely less-musty hall air, she decided she didn't mind losing precious sleep. No town duty today. That was a good start, at least. And she was exempt from regular drills due to scout shift, so no Daisy either. For a moment, Emily couldn't decide which was better news. But as she recalled the day they cleaned the town's grade school, she decided she would rather do a thousand burpees than town duty any day. She shivered at the memory of toppling the barricades of desks, ripping past the faded construction paper streamers into the classrooms; the milky eyes of those shambling six- to ten-year olds kept her up for long nights after she shut them for good. Thank hell the little town only had one grade school. Emily had joked about regretting not being on duty the day they swept the high school, as if teenagers would be easier to shoot, maybe even satisfying. Her teammates had chuckled. That was back when they liked her.

It would probably be in her best interest to go out for scout shift early. She wasn't due to relieve Sherice until later, but what else could she do with the extra time? Idle in the visitor's center and contemplate the meaning of existence? No, she should look useful, dedicated.

The daylight filtering into the gallery made a haze of the dusty air. Emily pushed through a door marked "Employees Only," and then she was in the dark again. Running a hand along the wall, she made her way to the supply room to hunt down her morning ration bar.

She halted inside what was once the museum staff break room. Rosa sat cross-legged on the floor. She was the only one there, not counting the two inert metal bodies sprawled across its central table.

Rosa chicken-pecked at a keyboard projection emanating from an old-fashioned white pullscreen. It was dimmed low but lit the room enough for Emily to make out the bullet cartons and plastic bins on the counter. Either she didn't hear Emily come in or chose to ignore her.

One way to find out. "Hey…"

"Hey."

Or she was mad. Or something worse. But what could Emily even say? She chewed on her lip, then moved around the table.

The pullscreen's glow cast deep shadows in the mechanical angles of the two android bodies. They were mostly intact, except one's left arm was missing and the second looked like it underwent some kind of sick C-section, with its wiry guts gone from its narrow stomach. Bald and naked, their metal parts had a brushed steel-style finish, but their male-featured silicone faces rested in imitation of human sleep. Like their eyes could snap open at any moment and catch Emily staring. They turned out to be completely drained of power when her team found them abandoned at the Dragon Mart last month. An attempt to charge them from the generators set some LEDs blinking, but neither would wake up. Yet.

A half-laugh escaped Emily as she realized how she squeezed against the counter to keep as much distance from them as possible. She shook her head at herself. "I'll never get used to those things."

"They're just machines." Rosa patted a metal boot-shaped foot dangling off the table by her head.

"Or is that just what they want us to think?" She'd seen robots of all shapes and sizes, but these ones looked *too* human yet not human enough.

Emily tried to think of them as dead bodies. She was used to dead bodies. But they weren't really dead; programs in their brains could still think and remember. Personalities trapped inside their own minds. Not *persons*, per se, just AI thinking itself people, though the

Robot Rights activists made the line blurry in the years before the Ecuador Explosion. Androids as advanced as these rarely interacted with the public sector, but they appeared in the media aplenty. Back when a media still existed.

Emily's only personal experience with anything more sophisticated than the drones crisscrossing her forever-artificially-green suburb was the shop helper at her father's lot. Though she passed it wrenches as it tinkered with the lemons her dad sold as "collectible" vehicles, she never got hands-on with its machinery. She was a software girl, but its limited AI didn't really warrant getting hands-on with either. Her dad named it Bob, so she tried to think of it as a *him*, but it never stuck. Bob wasn't designed to resemble any particular gender, and it—*he*—didn't have much of a personality except for a canned attempt at seriously pathetic jokes repeated from the gullible customers.

She'd named the two bodies on the table Lefty and Yum. Sherice, of all people, called her morbid, but Emily was amused. Either the rest of the team was too, or they didn't care enough to come up with names of their own.

They were military-grade robots, LQ models or something. Despite their over-three-years-old serial dates, the laser gun mounts in their arms were definitely post-Explosion. Ramon hoped to harvest whatever possible off their hard drives. Cocky about her hacking skills, Emily tried every trick in her roster to break through their encryptions for him. But after long hours of failure, she turned the project over to Rosa. She gave up too, over a week ago. So what was she doing now?

"Anything I can help with?" Emily hoped she sounded chill as she busied her hands with securing her hair into a knot on top of her head.

Rosa shook her head and squinted at the black and blue code-carpeted screen.

"Can I turn on a lantern for you?" Snapping her elastic in place, Emily leaned against the counter.

"Nah."

A million things Emily could say, should say. Her insides felt shriveled. Empty. But she still wasn't hungry. "You find something new?"

"Not since I tried detaching the lasers," Rosa answered without looking up. "But nothing I wire can channel enough power to make those work. They need the bodies."

Okay, at least Rosa was talking to her. And she didn't sound mad, exactly.

"That sucks." Emily shrugged as casually as she could manage. "But it's probably not worth it." She'd heard awesome things about lasers against undead flesh, but apparently, even attached to fancy military LQs, the weapons were never good enough. "I mean, androids aren't what LPI assembled to take down the communes, right?" Humans were. Humans with bullet guns.

"You don't know." Rosa finally looked at her. "None of us do. Headquarters could be sending out all kinds of teams."

Emily nodded and glanced away. Her unit concentrated on missions near small towns so they could clean them while waiting for the communes to arrive. It would take a much larger force to clear out an actual city. All other LPI units Emily ever encountered stacked up pretty much the same as hers: fewer than forty humans and no androids. But communication from headquarters remained minimal as a rule, and impossible once they came out into the desert. Some of her teammates grumbled about conspiracies among the LPI heads in Manhattan, about task forces like theirs being puppets for mysterious goals. But they stayed on the team. They must, like Emily, realize it was better than the alternatives.

The alternatives... like joining a commune. A sour tang defied gravity at the back of Emily's throat. "Rosa? I..."

"You're on scout today, right?" Her eyes locked on the screen again.

Emily shook her head even though the answer was yes. "About yesterday..."

"What about it?"

She watched Rosa's fingers move over the virtual keys, catching the blue lines of light. "I just..." Emily couldn't say thank you, could she? That wasn't right. "I don't want that for you any more than for myself."

"Yeah? Who do you want it for then?"

Emily grimaced and rubbed her thumb between her eyes. She couldn't say sorry, either. She wasn't sorry for wanting out, and Rosa made her own choice.

She just thought... Thought what? That Ramon would pick someone else, or decide two spies would be enough? No, she hadn't let her brain go there. None of their previous missions required infiltrators. None were this big before.

Turning off the keyboard projection, Rosa leaned back on her hands. "I never told you this."

Emily met her eyes. "What?"

"I've been bitten before."

"*What?* When?"

"You do what you gotta do." She shrugged.

"Was it before..." Emily swallowed. She couldn't bring herself to mention the two little girls Rosa lost in New York.

"But look at me," Rosa said, unfazed. "I'm fine."

Fine? How could she not be permanently traumatized? Even if she had to do it for her daughters, she'd still been *used.*

God.

The dream image of Rosa swooning into vampire arms rushed back, making Emily's skin crawl. She forced her mouth closed.

"I get you." Rosa sighed and stood, coming around the table. "You have your issues. We all have issues. We work hard; we get over them."

"They're not issues." Emily tried not to sound too defensive. If anyone could understand, it would be Rosa. "They're standards." A reason to live. "It's not something you get over."

"Oh, so you don't think I got standards?"

"It's not— I'm sorry, I didn't mean it like that. It's not like high versus low. It's...people are different, right? Take pride in different things?"

"No." She sighed again. "Emily. *Mi amor.* You got issues. This purity complex of yours or whatever—"

"I don't have a purity complex."

Rosa laughed. Actually laughed. "Your mom, she was Catholic, right?"

What did that have to do with anything? Emily was no virgin; though sex had always meant nothing for her beyond a thing to make her partners happy. She shook her head. "She was Catholic as a kid. But she didn't raise us religious." Her mom stopped going to Mass the day after Grandma Gloria's funeral, a month before Emily was born.

"Yeah, mine too. But that stuff sticks, Emmers."

"No, you don't get it." Emily huffed out a breath. Why was this so hard to explain? Her gaze locked onto Yum's sleeping face. What she would give for the ability to shut herself off and play dead until the hard parts passed. But she could feel Rosa's eyes on her, waiting, expecting. Emily powered on. "I always thought, 'once you're bitten, you're dead,' you know? It's pretty much my motto."

"But vampire bites don't kill you." Rosa's tone fell somewhere between soothing and you're-an-idiot. "Unless they drink you dry, but they're not stupid enough to let people go to waste like that now, and they're definitely not making any more of their kind. And they never will, until there's a cure for zombies. But trust me on this, it's nothing like getting bit by a zombie."

"No, it's worse!" That was the whole, entire, everything point. "When a—a zombie bites you, you're gone. You're just gone. But when a vampire bites you, you're still you. You're still aware. But you're not *all* of you. Once they *take* from you, once you've given yourself to them, you've given in. You've given up your…your…"

"Purity? Who gives a shit."

"I was going to say your, like, sense of self."

"You got a lot more to yourself than that, Em."

"But, no, that's not— If I'm not *all* myself, then I'm not *me*." Emily took a sharp breath. It all felt so simple and right in her heart. Why did trying to put it into words reduce her to an inarticulate mess? "If they use me, I'm not *mine*. I'm not—"

"Says who?"

The backs of Emily's eyes burned. She fought to keep tears from forming with a frustrated snuff. "I'm sorry. I'm trying to explain."

"Issues." Rosa nodded sagely, but then she gave a gentle smile and put a hand on Emily's arm. Her hands were always so soft.

"God." Emily sighed. "You know, you sound like my ex."

"That Travis guy?"

"Ha!" Emily pressed her eye with rough knuckles. "No. I meant Kayla."

"She must have been smart."

She was, but it had been a short romance. Like all in Emily's past. In the end, Kayla was smart enough to cut Emily and her *issues* loose before either of their hearts could break too hard. Emily never imagined old relationship drama would apply to the undead apocalypse. Did nothing ever go away? "Issues."

"So it'll take you a while," Rosa said with a pat. "Not this time, but maybe next."

And there would always be a next time, wouldn't there? The missions would keep getting bigger and bigger. Until the world ended or the LPI saved it. Emily squinched her eyes shut and took a long breath. The threat of tears faded, but now she felt queasy.

Rosa was right; wasn't she always right? The only way to save the world was to work as hard as everyone else. But to let go of the one thing Emily could control? The thing keeping her from dissolving? She didn't even know where to begin. What were the chances she could put it off long enough until the world was saved?

"Do you really think we'll find a cure for zombies?" she asked.

Rosa shrugged. "Who knows, maybe headquarters even figured it out already while we've been out here. That's why LPI gathered all those scientist people in Manhattan, yeah? They're working on it. All they need is time, and we're out here doing our thing to give them that time."

Their thing. Block by block, one by one, shot by shot, bonfire by bonfire. Commune by commune.

"I fucking hate vampires." It came out of Emily like a whimper, which was so opposite her intention that it made her laugh. She wiped at her eyes.

Rosa shook her head, amused. "Welcome to the LPI." Letting her hand slide down, she squeezed Emily's fingers.

Emily squeezed back. She felt lighter and heavier at the same time. "Seriously, though," she said after taking a moment to stew over it, "maybe they're not stupid enough to make any more vampires, but they only look out for themselves while the rest of the world gets the meat eaten off its bones." Did vampires honestly consider their commune system a sustainable plan in a world overrun by zombies? Resources would run out eventually. For supposedly immortal beings, what a ridiculously shortsighted setup. "When you get into the commune, Rosy, you should totally do random petty crap just to mess with them. Like steal all their socks or something."

"You know, you kind of sound like you want to go in after all."

Emily flinched, then shook her head apologetically. But she would work twice as hard in other ways. So many roles to Mission 12. So many other things she could do and do damn well.

She managed an uneven smile for Rosa. "You have a few days before the commune shows up. Maybe a week."

"Never know," Rosa said. "They could make it here tonight if they found, like, three busses."

"Three?" How could the humans recruited from Amargosa be crammed into fewer than ten?

Recruited.

Sure, some people in the world joined communes willingly and needed rescuing from their own idiocy, but not the Amargosa people. Coerced, threatened, blackmailed, scared to death. Intel said the commune in question had over two dozen vampires and five times as many armed human guards. They razed the Amargosa human settlement and herded whoever was too weak or apathetic to resist into their caravan. Hundreds of whoevers.

Rosa gave her an amused look. "You've never seen a New York City bus at rush hour."

This time, no ache laced her chest when Emily laughed. And her stomach finally growled. She turned to the cartons on the counter to stuff protein bars into the snap pockets on the sides of her black canvas pants. She grabbed fresh clips for her Glock along with binoculars and the last radio from the charger.

"Emily, checking in," she said into the radio.

"Too early," Ramon's curt voice replied through the soft crinkle of static.

Rosa cupped a hand over her mouth to hold in a laugh.

Emily shot her a look. "What?"

Shaking her head, she slid around the table to her screen.

Emily imagined what she was refraining from saying, that you could never do anything right by Ramon anymore. That he constantly felt pressure to come down hard to measure up to his new authority. It's what the other guys said, though Rosa never contested his leadership. Even when Daisy challenged him after they lost Michele, when Rosa had ten times more place to be that challenger, she kept her lips zipped.

Ramon had his own style. It worked. And it was time for Emily to show him hers could measure up. Too early, and proud of it, she waved a goodbye to Rosa, slapped Lefty a low-five, and made her way out through the gallery for scout shift.

4

VAMPIRES

The sight beyond the front lobby's glass doors made Emily's breath catch. Ramon and Daisy. Their conversation appeared casual enough, but when he noticed her, Ramon darted a frustrated look at Emily through the glass. She hesitated, her fingers sliding over the inside handle.

As Daisy twirled the end of her yellow ponytail around her fingertip and ran her other hand down Ramon's sleeve, his expression darkened. His eyes flicked to Emily again. Could it be he needed a rescue? What was Daisy up to? If Ramon didn't like it, he wouldn't put up with it, right? But despite how obviously his jaw clenched, he nodded along to whatever she was saying.

Daisy contributed more than almost anyone to their unit's success. Without her, they would have all gone soft ages ago. Except Ramon, maybe. Emily couldn't imagine him ever going soft. But trolling through town picking off shuffling near-corpses didn't exactly make for hard work. Neither did crouching in the bushes on a hillside, watching flies land on the deserted factory, useless for anything other than its tanks of no-expire diesel.

Emily could have been quite comfortable and healthy doing her daily duties without Daisy's sets and reps. She varied them often enough to keep several muscle groups burning through each night. But the team couldn't let getting stationed at a town full of slow zombies make them complacent. If they encountered any of the fast ones, if they couldn't plan their next mission as well as 12, then they would need the stamina. And, of course, if they ran into unexpected *vampires*... She shuddered. None of them would stand a chance against a vampire alone. But as a team, a strong, fit team, trained and determined, they could overpower them.

Unfortunately, they had Daisy to thank for that.

Emily leaned into the door, squinting against the bouncing sunlight as it swung open.

Daisy smiled, her wide princess eyes growing wider. "Someone's up early. You must want to run some drills."

Emily bit the insides of her cheeks. "Couldn't sleep."

"Best time for it. I've got a few minutes before I go into town. Get that tight ass out on the loop. Let me see you work it. What are you wearing under there? That's no sports bra. I love it."

Emily crossed her arms over her black shirt as Daisy's gaze raked her. She shouldn't let it get to her, but Daisy made herself impossible to ignore.

Ramon rolled his eyes and glanced off through the chain-link fence. "What's up, Em?"

"I'm on scout." She showed him the radio before snapping it to her belt clip.

"Sherice's shift isn't up yet."

"I know. Thought she might like to come in, start her sleep shift early?"

Daisy let out a sharp laugh. "Little too late to play teacher's pet, isn't it?"

Emily flinched. Of course, Daisy would have heard about yesterday. Did Ramon tell her himself? How did he phrase it? Knowing him, he kept it wholly professional. But the gleeful light in Daisy's eyes made it clear that no matter how diplomatic, Emily didn't come off looking like anything less than a total asshole.

But no, it wasn't too late. She still had a chance to show them she could be worth her salt.

Ramon eyed Emily, his lips pressing into a thin line. He seemed about to give her some warning before she went out on the hill, some habitual word of caution, but he only nodded. Emily's mind dutifully listed through any sage advice he might offer: stay low, stay hydrated, keep quiet, no sudden movements. She knew the drill. He could probably read it right off her face. He turned to Daisy, who launched back into their previous conversation.

Ramon's shoulders drooped as Emily skirted them to the gate. And, was it her imagination, or did he follow her out of the corners of his eyes even as he nodded along to Daisy?

Despite everything, Emily found herself hiding a little smile. Yes. She would make it up to him. To everyone. And he would let her.

Beyond the gate, she jogged down the path to the cliffs. Precision pops of gunfire floated up from the other side of the hill. Town duty squad was at it already. Emily would see the bonfire smoke rise as her scout shift ended.

She turned her back to the noise, and instead of following the windy drive up to the cliffs and the east road, she cut down the hillside through the brittle shrubs. At the lookout perch, Sherice crouched under a rocky overhang. The spot supplied shade all day, which kept lookouts hidden and offered an ounce or two of relief. Even in November, the days still got into the nineties.

Sherice shot up when Emily approached. "What's wrong?"

"Just felt like getting out. You can break early."

Her lips puckered into a thick cupid's bow. "Why? What's in it for you?"

"I'm—" Emily tensed and shook her head. "I don't want anything."

Sherice studied her dubiously, then moved around her with a half smirk. "Uh huh."

Emily swallowed past the tightness in her throat but kept her expression determined. Monitoring the valley for the commune's arrival was the whole reason her unit chose this spot and the most important thing she could spend her time doing. Even if it would be little more today than watching dust settle on the abandoned factory towers, watching lazy cloud shadows move along the smashed cars in the parking lot, watching buzzards circle for dead things until they gave up and faded into specks on the horizon. Even if she knew that as the hours wore on, she would be less and less able to distract herself from thinking of all she'd lost while the water in her canteen evaporated faster than she could drink it.

She would do it for a thousand hours if that's what it took.

As Sherice crunched her way back up to the road, Emily settled onto the old rag-filled pillowcase. Alternating the three daily scout duty shifts with Sherice was another upside at least. She'd only have to see her when they changed out. Now Emily had a full day of sitting on her butt to look forward to.

She made her rounds with the binoculars, checked every horizon point, and called in the fact that she saw nothing at all to Ramon, which she would do every half hour. She counted the minutes and looked forward to each of his monosyllabic responses. She told herself it was because it broke up the tedium, but whenever Big Joe worked the radio, it never felt as rewarding to hear him say "check."

Even though Ramon was younger than Emily, he reminded her of her dad. Except without the salesman-polished bullshitting skills. Any skills Ramon possessed not directly factoring into keeping their unit from dissolving into a bickering nest of frustrated, impatient twenty- and thirty-somethings, he didn't have interest in sharing. He was that way even before he took charge.

Emily wasn't sure why she equated Ramon with her dad. She never saw her dad as much of a leader, even though he ran a small company. He was more of a wrangler, a man who gathered conspirators into a huddle and whispered instructions with much nudging and winking. The opposite of Ramon's quiet unsmiling gravity. Her dad never took anything too seriously; he had a joke to respond to every problem. It helped him get away with "the racket." People could never stay mad at him.

He and Ramon weren't very much alike at all. Maybe it was just

Emily's feeling of admiration. Or maybe she just missed her dad enough to be desperate to make any connection at all.

A year, seven months, and two days since she'd lost him. The last image burned into her mind: his bushy gray hair matted with dirt, his mouth stretched wide, his teeth coated with the blood from his broken nose, his fingers contorted as if reaching for a rope from the sky. She grimaced and pummeled the picture from her brain.

Go away, go away. Think of him at work or anything else.

Emily filled in at his used car lot in the summers during college. For her graduation, he drove all the way up to Seattle just to watch her cross the stage and collect a fake diploma. She told him not to bother, she wasn't even planning on going through the pageantry. But when he showed up that morning at her dorm, she bought a last-minute cap and gown and walked for him. He just looked so excited. He even dragged her brother Chris with him. A culinary school dropout at the time, Chris would start mime school in the fall, but that May, he had nothing better to do than tag along to Emily's campus and hit on her friends. He said he liked older women, but they snickered at his awkward flirting. The bad puns were great when her dad made them, but on Chris, they dripped desperation.

Emily's mom, on the other hand, did have something better to do than make the ten-hour drive north. She had one of her headaches, plenty of Vicodin to go with it, and big plans to watch reality shows in her damask rose potpourri-scented king-sized bed.

The last image of her mother wormed its way into Emily's mind: the complete lack of shame on her puffy face as she trotted like a limping wildebeest to a commune's entrance. The way the backs of her arms flapped as she scrabbled across the long field. The way she didn't look back.

They had argued about it for days, but her mom wouldn't listen to reason.

"They can help us! That's what they're there for," she'd said. "They'll take anyone. They'll protect us."

"Bullshit," Emily snapped. "That's what they want you to think." *Protect.*

"Susan from work explained it all to me. They're popping up everywhere, and they move around. We just have to find one of them."

"That is the *last* thing we *just have to do*." Her mom hadn't been to work in months. "What the hell does Susan know?"

"More than we do!"

"Mom, Susan's probably dead."

"No, she's not. Shut your mouth. She did it, she joined. That's what we have to do. Think of how many of them there must be by now!"

And so on and on and on as they got more and more lost on the worst roads their stolen car could navigate through the evacuated San Bernardino mountains. That was a month before Emily joined the LPI. Alone.

Emily snorted away the memories and did her rounds through the binoculars, then radioed Ramon. "All clear."

"You sure?"

Emily blinked. He didn't sound like he doubted her; he sounded *conversational*.

Her pulse floated into her throat. He never said more than "check." Did he want to talk? Maybe he was bored back there, manning camp while everyone else worked in town or slept. Lonely?

"Well, actually." She scanned the horizon.

"What? What is it?"

Oops. Now he sounded like he took her seriously.

She smiled to herself, feeling her face grow warm. "There's a big bird by the tall smokestack. A highly suspicious character. We might want to investigate."

Silence stretched for half a minute, and then the tinny voice pierced the fluff of static. "Raven big or vulture big?"

"Like roc big."

"Big."

"Like I said, highly suspicious."

"So, you need back up."

Emily bit her lip to keep back a grin as she stared at the radio's round speckled face. "Well." She cleared her throat. "You know what they say. There's a—" A cloud caught her attention beyond the dent in the far hills. A cloud rising from below. A billowing brown dust cloud. She dropped the radio to her lap and pulled up the binoculars. Something was coming down the highway, definitely more than one vehicle.

The radio crackled on her knees. "Em?"

She held her breath, focused the binoculars past the factory to the road. A truck emerged around the hill. An old Chevy pickup without any solar panels. Puke brown, though the color might be from the dust it plowed through.

The radio's alert blared three short blasts followed by Ramon's voice. "Emily. Report."

She scooped up the radio, holding it to her mouth without pulling her eyes from the lenses. "Trucks." She gulped for air. "Three of them. No wait, five. Coming through the pass. Like they'll go right past Suncrest Hill. Tell everyone to get inside."

"Hostile?"

"Hang on." She dropped the radio to her lap again and adjusted the binoculars' focus. No LPI symbols marked the vehicles, but they could be traveling incognito, though it would have to be one intense undercover job. The caravan had every sign of a small nomadic commune.

It couldn't be the one her team was waiting for; the trucks rumbled along at too high a speed to be leading a herd of hundreds of Amargosans, and no fleet of busses followed. Just three four-door pickups, their loads covered by olive tarps, and two semis with little open windows along the trailers. They looked like farm vehicles, like for transporting cows. But they couldn't have cows, could they?

Emily's entire body compressed like a spring. She gripped the binoculars tighter and pushed to her feet. The radio flew out of her lap and somersaulted down the hill.

"Shit!"

As if he sensed what happened, Ramon's voice came tumbling out of it. "Emily, report."

She shifted to dive after it when the first in the line of trucks veered off the road and slowed, heading straight for the factory. The others followed like a school of fish.

"Shitshitshit." The trucks parked, and a man in a sun-bleached leather jacket far too heavy for the desert heat jumped out and headed through the broken gate. Other men soon followed. One of them whipped up a tarp to reveal two metal crates. Two long, narrow, sealed crates. Just the right size to hold a human body. But the bodies inside would not be human.

Emily froze, hanging half out of the shadows, gripping the rocks above her head.

Three high-pitched blasts blared from the radio somewhere below her.

"Augh, shut up!" she hissed, even though the men at the factory couldn't possibly hear it. But though far out of earshot, it lay in plain sight, and she would be too if she went after it.

She banged the heel of her palm into her forehead. "Idiot."

The radio blasted again, and she could barely hear Ramon's voice. "Emily? I'm coming out there."

No! She took a deep breath and dropped to her stomach. If they didn't face the hill, they wouldn't notice her. She began to elbow through the low brush, wincing as sharp rocks rolled under her.

They were interested in the factory. They wouldn't have reason to look up. Not right away. They wouldn't see her, they wouldn't see what a goddamned moron she was. As she scrabbled down the slope, she cycled through the onslaught of passive aggressive insults on permanent mental record in her mother's memorized voice.

"They can't see you," she hissed to herself. "They won't look up."

But if they did. Oh god. And it would be all her fault.

"Idiot, idiot, idiot." She chanted under her breath with each pull of her elbows. Slow, smooth, like a shadow.

Only one time in her life had she been more furious with herself. She trembled with each inch of progress through the scratchy bushes as the nauseating memories came crashing back.

"Stop! Stop the car!" her mom had yelped.

Emily squashed the brakes. "What? What's wrong?"

"That's it. We found one! There they are, look."

No. Dread coiled into Emily's stomach at the sight of the commune tents in the hilly field off the roadside. She moved her foot back to the gas, ready to peel out, but her mom tumbled through the door.

"Mom!"

"Susan was right."

Was this why she told Emily to take this road? How did she know where to find them? It shocked Emily her mom even possessed the capacity to trick her.

Emily dove after her, catching her elbow. "What the hell are you doing?"

"I'm going where it's safe." She swatted at Emily's fingers. "I can't live like this anymore!"

Anymore? They'd escaped Long Beach less than two weeks ago.

"Mom!" Emily shook her as if trying to wake a sleepwalker. "You still don't get it. What they *do* to people in those places? They're not *human.* How many times have I—" She took a sharp breath. "You can't be serious!"

"Jesus Christ, Emily. What else are we supposed to do?"

"We run! We fight. We keep going. Anything but *them.*"

"You think you can be a little princess forever? Life's not that easy."

What? Emily sputtered. It felt like she was battling some strange dream argument in a reality where logic didn't exist. "Easy? You're the one who's... Going to them is giving up!" She might as well just commit suicide right now! Though Emily didn't dare say that aloud. Her mother would probably threaten to do it until Emily begged her not to and repeated forty times how much she loved and needed her.

She clamped her fingers around her mom's soft wrists, dragged her to the car.

"Stop that." She dug her heels into the ground. "Emily Raye Campbell, let me go. You're hurting me. Stop!"

"No!" Emily's voice came out high and thin. "No, you stop! You've lost it."

"Stop!" Her chipped acrylics clawed at Emily's hands. "Let me go, let me go! I can't! I can't! Not like Alan, no! Let me go!" Her writhing turned the skin of her wrists raw pink under Emily's grasp.

Emily went still as she absorbed the wild look in her mother's eyes, like a terrified animal, all signs of intelligence gone. The sight knocked the wind out of her, and her fingers slipped away.

Her mom fell to the dirt with the sudden release. Emily was too frozen to react, but her mom shrank back, throwing her arms over her head as if afraid her own daughter would attack. "You…" She shuddered and craned away like she lay before a monster. She wobbled to her feet.

Emily took a shaky step back, trembling in disbelief. "Mom…come on."

"Get away from me! You want to end up like Alan? Go follow your idiot father! Leave me alone!"

"If you go in there, Mom, that's it."

"Jesus Christ, I sure as hell hope so." She twisted around and ran off to the camp.

Emily turned her back and got in the car. She wrenched the steering wheel, she put the car in gear, she drove. She got less than a mile before she U-turned.

Her mom would be sitting at the side of the road with her arms crossed. She would spend the next hundred miles berating Emily for all the ways she was a disappointing daughter, and Emily would keep her teeth clenched and tune her out.

But her mom wasn't at the side of the road. The smoke from the campfires at the tents looked warm and inviting. Emily turned off the car and waited, but the sun shrank into the horizon. If she remained near the commune after dark, she might not have a choice about following in her mother's footsteps.

"Come on, come on, come on, come on, come on."

A figure emerged from the tents, and Emily jolted, her thumb on the power button. But it wasn't her mom. A tall, lanky man with long snarled black hair and a leather jacket waved a rifle in the air, flagging her. He began to cross the field.

Emily turned the engine and floored it. She never saw her mother again. She never got to hear about her daughterly disappointments. Not out loud.

Each time her LPI unit took down a commune, Emily sorted

through the bodies. She examined each overweight tan woman with tangled bleached orange hair, searching the torn and withered faces for something her genes would recognize, tuning out the grief-stricken belligerence of the shivering survivors. Her mom was never there. Each time Emily went through it, she thought, *Next time.* And each time she prayed to the universe crumbling around their pathetic broken world that it wouldn't be this time.

Brap! Brap! Brap! from the radio. Muffled somewhere behind her. Emily winced and wiggled herself around. Where the hell was it?

"Come on, come on," she muttered.

Three more ear-grating beeps.

"Yes!" There, next to a small boulder. She refrained from leaping. When she reached it, she flopped onto her back and heaved a breath that shook her whole body.

"Sorry," she rasped into the radio. "I was, um, counting them."

"Em." Ramon's voice mixed frustration and relief.

"Don't come out here! Don't. Tell everyone to stay inside."

"Details."

She took a long breath. She couldn't let him hear her panting. "They've stopped at the factory. Three pickup trucks and two, like, cattle truck things." She rolled onto her side and peered through the binoculars. One of the long semis had a bunch of sparkly Christmas garlands threaded through its grill, and the other's sported an oversized stuffed pink bunny like a figurehead.

"I see eight, no, ten men." No women. And no one looking Emily's way. Not at the moment. "Hang on."

"What?"

She had to get back to the protection of the overhang.

"Nothing." She grunted as she crawled up the hill, doing her best to sound as still as possible. "I mean, not nothing. Ray, they've got boxes."

"Vampire boxes? Coffins?"

She winced at the word. "Yeah, I think so. Two that I saw—can see."

Returning to the overhang seemed to take a tenth the time it did to get down. She threw herself into the shadows and took in the scene at the factory fully. The three pickups sat as close to the entrance gate as they could get, two of their tarps withdrawn. "Make that four boxes. And eleven men."

The cattle trucks were parked farther away, and none of the men showed interest in them. They unloaded the boxes from the pickups one by one, carrying them pallbearer style through the factory doors where she couldn't see beyond the swallowing darkness. The men remaining outside talked amongst themselves with casual gestures. Lip-reading wasn't in Emily's skill set, but if any of them noticed her on the hill, they sure didn't give a damn. She gripped the binoculars tighter to keep her hand still as the adrenaline dissipated.

"Looks like they're setting up camp in the factory," she said into the radio.

"And you're sure there are only four coffins?"

"No. And who knows what's in those cattle trucks."

Probably supplies or, hell, "cattle." Not cows. A commune with four vampires would need more than eleven human men to sustain it. The semis weren't big enough to hold the Amargosa hostages, not unless they crammed in shoulder to shoulder. But they wouldn't. That's why Rosa's NYC bus comparison made her laugh. Communes needed to keep their humans comfortable enough to thrive. Emily estimated there wouldn't be more than forty in the two trucks. But she couldn't see anything through the small windows lining the top of the side facing her.

She cringed as the men whipped back the last tarp. "Six boxes."

After they unloaded the sixth, the last of them disappeared inside and pulled the factory door shut. The echo of its clang reached Emily a moment later.

Several very long hours passed with nothing happening other than Emily radioing Ramon every five minutes that nothing was happening. He told her they were working on a plan up at the compound. The longer the afternoon heat beat into the dirty metal roofs of the cattle trucks, the more Emily doubted any hostages could be in them at all. Vampires were assholes, but like Rosa said, they weren't stupid. They protected their assets and wouldn't leave their human herd to roast and dehydrate. The trucks must only contain supplies or stuff for trade. Both good and bad news. A six-strong commune with a herd of eleven was worse than if they had forty or hundreds.

They would be hungry.

By the time Sherice reappeared to resume the watch an hour before sunset, every muscle in Emily's body felt ready to snap with tension. She passed over the binoculars and radio without a word.

"Don't need these." Sherice offered the binoculars back, but Emily turned away and staggered up to the road.

"Nice to see you too, bitch," Sherice called after her.

Emily didn't have the energy to reply.

5

SCOTT

Two days? Three? Super. Scott had already lost count. The security of the abandoned Curisa complex felt weeks behind him either way, and his destination eons to go. This wonky sleep schedule messed with his brain. Two hours here, four hours there was no way to stay coherent.

He was supposed to be napping—*recharging*. Har har, android humor. But half an hour into the rest stop, he still couldn't sleep.

His legs felt somewhat noodley after climbing eight stories to the apartment building's top floor. He'd followed the rules though, taken it slow. Sore quads tomorrow could get him killed, obviously.

They were in there, beyond the unit doors, puttering around, bonking into things, moaning like they'd eaten bad burritos. But the stairwell was clear and that was what counted. They couldn't get out of the apartments on their own, and Scott was the only living person in the building. Maybe in the whole town. And the top floor was obviously safest from any threats on the street.

The empty apartment boasted one lonely bedroom. The futon sucked, but by the time Scott realized he wouldn't be getting any rest on it, he was on his own and didn't dare try breaking into another unit without help. Not sleeping meant waiting around, though, bored and lonely. He wasn't the only one who needed to recharge.

Time to scrounge.

The narrow kitchen wedged at the front of the unit had no windows. So many roaches scattered when Scott stepped in that he thought it had started to rain.

No point in checking the fridge. He made that mistake at a house yesterday hunting for mustard and almost puked from the stench. Or was that the day before?

"Cupboards are where it's at." Propping his shotgun against the sink and dropping his backpack to the grimy linoleum, he crouched to check the under-counter cabinets in the light angling from the living room. People always stashed the least-perishable stuff down low. Doubtful he'd discover anything more nutritious than his Curisa-issued ration bars, he hoped for packs of ramen or another tasty treat. He was disappointed to find only a few cans of green beans and mushroom soup and other equally gross stuff. They were expired, but not so long ago they wouldn't be edible. He didn't need them, though. His bags bulged, almost too full. He sat back to close the cupboard, leaving the cans for the next guy.

As the door's shadow moved, a hint of red and white in the deep corner caught his eye.

"Yes!" He dove for the cans.

Sweet, sweet, sweetened condensed milk. He fished his multitool out of his backpack's front flap while he shook one as vigorously as his muscles allowed.

"Expiration?" he reminded himself. Squinting at the numbers stamped on the bottom, he made out a rim of rust on the can's edge. The stuff expired even before the Ecuador Explosion. The second can proved no better. *Figures.*

"Welp, here goes." He wiped the can top with his t-shirt and cracked it open. It smelled all right, so he took a cautious test sip, spat, then another.

Thank the gods of preservatives, it was perfect. Like it was canned yesterday. Glorious!

As he drained it, he could hear Jade's voice from years ago in his brain. *You still drink milk? Like a baby? You're a baby man. A man baby.*

Scott told her at the time she didn't know what she was missing. People in their twenties drank milk all the time. What did she think lattes and ice cream were made of? Shakes? She claimed those were different. Milk was weird by itself. Scott never minded being called weird, though. He knew what was up. No helping those who let the mainstream hold them back. The bros and the chads. Where were they now?

"That's right," he answered himself as he wiped his mouth and tossed the can into the kitchen trash. They were behind the doors, in the streets, moaning and groaning while Scott got the good stuff. If part of white privilege included being naturally lactose tolerant, then he would drink it up. What else left in the world was worth enjoying other than the rare find of something ridiculously delicious?

When he reached for the second can, a roach darted over his hand, making him gasp. It came out almost a shriek, and he jerked, falling on his tailbone. His face went hot. No witnesses obviously, but he was embarrassed on his own behalf.

"Real smooth," he muttered.

If he couldn't even handle a roach like a man, what would happen if he ever met a vampire?

Not for the first time, he grudgingly thanked whatever cosmic forces might exist that he wasn't on his journey alone.

6

THE ABYSS

Arguing voices leaked through the visitor's center supply room door. Emily pressed her ear against the thickly painted wood.

"He thinks he's got it all figured out just 'cause he's been in charge while we sat on our asses out here?" Daisy. No surprise there. She had to be talking about Ramon. "He's never led anyone into battle."

"That's not true," Rosa replied, her voice calm and even.

"He's never led *us* into battle."

"This is the best way," Rosa said. "We have to be organized. We have to support him on this."

"He's not Michele."

"And you are?"

"Fuck this."

"Do you have a better plan?" Rosa asked.

"This isn't just knocking out a few humans and torching a few coffins," Daisy said. "This time it's *night*. They'll be awake in there. And knockout gas sure as fuck doesn't work on vampires."

"And like Ramon *said,* we won't use gas. Just bombs."

"And then what? If any get away, they'll spread the word about us. And our cover here is blown. Literally."

"We move up the highway, reestablish position," said Rosa. "We got at least two days, yeah? Target can't take any other road. It's a solid plan." Plastic rustling. Probably the map print. "Look, this ranger station he found. It's as good a stakeout as this place."

Emily pushed away from the door. Ramon obviously wasn't in there. And if the team intended to relocate, that meant packing.

In the theater, the lantern on the floor under the screen blared on full. The LEDs sliced at Emily's eyes as she moved past. If Rosa and Daisy came back up from town early, Emily assumed everyone else would be there too, but Carlos was the only one in the room, and less than half of it was cleared out. He sat hunched on the bottom carpeted step, cleaning his rifle.

"Hey." She jogged up the tiers. "Where is everyone?"

"Early meal, I dunno," he muttered at his gun.

Emily knelt at her bunk area and watched his jerky movements before turning to sort the few things she called her own into her backpack.

She pulled her hair out of its knot and stripped off her shirt, more brown than black now from her stupid adventure through the dust on the hill. She plucked a few burrs from the moisture-wicking material and folded it inside out before stuffing it in the pack. As she pulled on an identical fresh one, she noticed a fist-shaped bruise marring the tan of her left boob. A memento from training two days ago. Thanks, Daisy. Even though the autumn heat baked through the walls, she slipped into her reinforced jacket. It saved room in the backpack, and it sounded like she might be needing it.

Halfway through rolling up her sleeping pad, Emily heard something metal slam into the wall behind her. She turned in time to see Carlos's rifle scope bounce down the steps and land under the screen.

"Piece of shit!" He shoved the rest of the gun off his lap and covered his face, digging his fingers into his poofy hair.

Emily froze, but when a minute passed and he didn't move, she pushed to her feet and climbed down to pick up the scope.

"Here," she said as she sat next to Carlos. He ignored her while she fitted the scope into place. "See? Like that."

She handed it to him, but he pushed it back at her. "I don't even need it."

"Then why were you—?"

He lifted his face, and Emily's words died. His eyes were so bloodshot, hardly any white remained.

"It was an omen," he murmured.

Not this again. Emily sighed.

"My dream, Emily. I told you."

"Carlos."

"I know you think I'm like schizophrenic, but I swear to God, it was an omen." He took a shaky breath. "About tonight."

Tonight? *Tonight.* They never attacked communes after dark; Daisy was right about that part. But Ramon had a plan. A plan with bombs. A bomb plan. A sneak attack surprise plan. Right? Emily was the only one out there, and those guys didn't catch her going down the hill for the radio. They would have done something if they saw. Ramon knew what he was doing.

She shook the "but what if" out of her head and leveled her gaze at Carlos.

"Do you seriously think this mindset is going to help you out there? Help us?"

"There is no help," he whispered.

Ohmygod! She had to laugh, but it came out too high and thin. She forced her voice an octave lower to make up for it. "You've got to snap out of this."

His face had gone chalky in the shadowy green LED glow. When he spoke, an eerie calm infused his words. "Death is coming for me."

Emily ignored the trembling that crept into her hands, told herself it was a result of trying very hard not to roll her eyes.

But what if...

The trickle of bile rising in her throat proved harder to ignore.

She bit it back and put down the gun to take Carlos by the shoulders. "Look," she said as evenly as she could manage. "I overheard the plan. We have the element of surprise. It's just a bomb toss run. It's going to be fine."

He twisted from her and pulled the gun into his lap like a security blanket.

"Fine!" She threw up her hands and pushed to her feet. "You just want..." She huffed out a breath. *Drama for drama's sake.* "Whatever."

Gathering up her things, she stalked to the door. "*Omens* aren't a thing," she said before she left. "You need to grow up, dude. It's either do, or don't. Be, or not be. And you only have yourself to blame if you let your head get in the way. Death doesn't 'come for you.' You're the one with the gun. Tonight, we're the ones bringing death with us."

She waited a minute for him to turn to her, to say something, anything. Even to tell her how cheesy that sounded. But he didn't, so she let the door fall shut behind her.

Omens weren't real. The bomb plan was real.

The element of surprise was real.

Where the hell was Ramon?

After dropping her pack against the gallery wall with the others, straps out, Emily returned to the supply room. The door stood open, and Big Joe and New Guy Number Three packed supplies into crates while joking in soft tones. She didn't feel bad for not remembering this new guy's name. Ever since he implied the Pinay blood in her veins gave a reason he and Emily should hook up, she lost all interest in getting to know him. She made a quick round of the rest of the museum, but Ramon was nowhere to be found.

Outside, she squinted at the sun inching toward the mountains. She made herself take a few long, slow breaths of dry air to steady her racing heart.

"What's the matter with you?" Daisy leaned against the gate at the guard post, cleaning her fingernails with a pocketknife.

Emily jumped. "Huh?"

"You look spooked."

She blinked away the sunspots and tucked her hair behind her ear. She shook her head. "Carlos."

Daisy snorted and mimed shooting herself in the head.

Emily forced a commiserative chuckle. "Seen Ramon?"

"Oooh, and why would you be wanting to know?"

She clenched her teeth. "Thanks." She brushed past Daisy, through the gate.

"Hey cutie," she called after Emily. "I'm locking up as soon as everyone's up from town."

"I'll be right back," she mumbled, not caring if Daisy heard her. "I'm just going to the..." Where was she going? She didn't even know what she'd say to Ramon when she found him. *Carlos has a bad feeling? We should give up the mission and flee into the desert?*

Did Ramon believe in omens?

Or, maybe just you *should stay behind. Call the shots from the hill. Just in case. What do we do if you go down? No one else is smart enough to lead us. Daisy would drive us into the dust. We can't lose you like— I can't lose you like—*

Emily gritted her teeth and focused on the cliff path. Sometimes she found Ramon up on the east road above the ravine, staring out at the desert. She wasn't sure why; it wasn't a good lookout spot. She respected his privacy, though, the lost look in his eyes too much to ever ask.

But when she reached the smashed-through guardrail at the road's hairpin curve, only the deserted cliff greeted her. She shook off a shudder as she leaned against the last jagged inches of railing beside the gap. *Spooked?* Carlos was ridiculous. Self-destructing or something, maybe he needed help. But dreams were just dreams. A shadow with bones? No such thing. Sparkly magic cyborg implant eyes or not, no way did Carlos literally see Death Itself appear when Alaric fell.

Emily stiffened, her fingers clamping onto the railing as she remembered something. Sherice. She had ocular implants too, didn't she? And last night, Sherice said... But no, Sherice was a deluded drama queen. Everyone knew that. Of course she would decide she knew what Carlos meant for the sake of the attention it got her.

And she dared call Emily morbid. She tried to laugh at the thought, but it didn't feel natural. Not natural at all.

She swung her legs over to perch on the railing. The shadow of death was not *a thing*. Everyone with implants would know about it, if so. Though, really, just everyone who witnessed the literal moment of death. And who knew what people were seeing out there now in the cut-off world? Though it was probably just some kind of glitch, if anything, right? The implants making them see phantom shadows?

Emily blinked. Of course!

That thought made so much sense, she relaxed into a slouch and let out a sigh. The high wind whipped her loose hair in a way that quickly got on her nerves, but she didn't have the energy to do anything about it.

She should tell Ramon about dropping the radio. She really should. But the last thing she wanted was another reason for him to be disappointed in her. *That's what happens when you don't get enough sleep, when you go out for your shift too early,* he would say. She got sloppy. *We keep to the schedule for a reason.*

And telling him wouldn't change anything. She hadn't been seen, but he would doubt that, and he didn't need that stress tonight. His bomb plan was solid. Maybe she would tell him afterward. When they holed up at that ranger station. They could laugh about it then.

She watched her long shadow soften into the dusky colors blooming in the craggy abyss below. She liked this place. And not just because Ramon liked it. She picked burrs off the black canvas on her thighs and flicked them over the cliff. The last remnants, she hoped, of her pathetic scramble through the brush. If only she could so easily flick away the tiny voice of paranoia that things hadn't ended so consequence-free as they seemed.

Twining her boot over the bottom bar of the railing, she leaned to stare at the mangled wreck of the car in the pit. It reminded her of her mom's old white Buick. But even as she imagined how this one must have careened off the road, smashed through the guardrail, and plummeted the forty feet below, she could not bring herself to picture her mom at the wheel. Not quite.

She squeezed her eyes shut and tried harder.

Footsteps on the gritty road behind her. Emily's gun was drawn before she finished twisting around.

She froze, then sighed. "Oh, it's you." She sank back onto the railing, a smile blossoming before she could help it.

Ramon frowned back at her. "You were looking for me?"

"I..." She took a deep breath. It was good to see him. The instinct to apologize for yesterday bubbled up irrationally. Her resolve hadn't moved an inch, so why the yearning to say *I'm sorry*? But maybe if she could explain, make him understand where she was coming from, tell him why the way he described her made it all worse. Maybe... "Ray—"

"What are you doing up here?" He hooked his thumb through the strap of the rifle slung across his back and peered past her. "You can't even see the factory from this side of the hill."

"I know." Emily tucked a dancing piece of hair behind her ear. He'd cut her off like he knew exactly what she was about to say and did not want to hear it. Both a relief and disappointment. But now was probably not the time, anyway. Her gaze fell to her holster as she slid the gun into it. "I was just..." *Thinking about you.* "It's safe up here." She shrugged after a minute. Out of sight of the factory, and a steep incline between them and the lingering scraps of the shuffling horde in town. "They always stay on the south side."

"Not always."

Emily held her tongue and studied Ramon's profile in the dimming light. So easy to forget he was two years younger than her. His eyebrow scar wrinkled. Another frown.

"And you know it." He pulled his eyes from the changing colors in the sky and met hers. "Or you wouldn't have jumped when you heard me."

She pressed her lips together in a thin smile and shook her head. "Just a little nervous." Not untrue, and it made about as much sense as any way she could explain herself. "That's all."

"About tonight?" The wrinkle cut his scar deeper. "It's going to be a routine flush."

"I know." Except, part of the routine of routine flushes was that they happened midday. But midday was long gone, and if they didn't attack now, they'd be dead by morning. And sure, let Ramon think tonight was the real thing pricking at her nerves.

"I need you strong, Em. This is the first time for the guys we picked up in La Jolla. They can't see you spooked. Can you do that for me?"

"Yeah, of course." For him. For the team. "Routine flush. Bombs, right? We won't even see any of them."

"And they don't know we're up here."

Right.

"So, when do we move?" Emily's shadow stretched far over the cliff, and all that remained of the fiery glow in the tufty sunset desert below crumbled into grayscale. Emily's pulse quickened as she realized how near night crept.

"We move at ten minutes past full dark."

Her fingers tightened on the edge of the railing. "*Full* dark?" What if vampires came streaming out of the factory as soon as they woke? Maybe Daisy wasn't so off-base after all.

"Dark will give us cover on the hill from their guards. And they always feed first thing when they wake up, yeah? That's our window. It's the best chance we've got."

She didn't like it, but she couldn't think of a better plan. "And Sherice hasn't seen any other humans since she took over watch? No hostages?"

Ramon shook his head. "But either way, our grenades won't hit those farm trucks. They haven't unloaded anything except the boxes you counted. Eleven human guards. We're not even outnumbered."

Numbers wouldn't matter when those boxes opened. Emily pressed her lips tight.

"We'll do our best to take the guards alive," Ramon added as if to reassure her.

Take them? She bit her tongue to keep from wrinkling her nose at the thought of having to deal with containing vampire-loving guards. What would they *do* with them? Her team wouldn't be able to drop them at a turnover station until after the Amargosa mission.

Be merciful, she reprimanded herself.

She started to nod but paused as the explosions to come echoed prematurely in her brain. "What if the noise attracts the swarm from town while we're out in the open down there?" Or even just one. One flesh-eater—one *zombie,* one bite, and the chain reaction could be unstoppable.

"What happened to 'they always stay on the south side'?" Ramon asked.

"Well, not always."

And then he smiled at her. And it felt like a hundred pounds lifted off her chest. She had to return it.

"We'll be down and back too fast for them to get far." He moved closer to her at the railing. "They don't call them the slow ones for nothing."

She gave him a grim smirk and thanked the universe once more that they only had to deal with the slow ones out here. They hadn't encountered any of the fast ones since the day they lost Michele. None of them knew why some zombies were slow and some fast and why the types stuck together. Some people tossed around theories about them naturally getting slower with time, but it was as plausible as guessing the fast ones had high-fiber diets. Most of them were slow, never coming after you faster than a tennis-balled walker-wielding geriatric. But some, maybe ten percent, were fast. Run-you-to-the-end-of-your-life fast with stamina to put perpetual motion to shame.

"You know." Ramon's gaze slipped out over the cliff. "This is where I would do it."

Emily looked from the jutting rocks to meet his eyes. "Do what?"

"If they were coming for me. If there was no escape. If I knew they would get me."

Her gaze dipped back into the abyss, and gooseflesh rose beneath her sleeves. "Here? Why here?"

He blinked into space, his lips tight under his mustache. Then he shrugged. "Maybe it's stupid."

"No." She shook her head. "I get it. Believe me." In the gathering twilight, with the ragged shadows, the cliffs struck her as especially hellish.

"Something about staring Death straight in the face, you know? Come at me, bro." He put a hand on the railing, an inch from her hip, and glowered past the rocks. "And diving into his arms. As the swarm comes over the hill after you, and they just see you go, giving them the finger."

Emily watched the emotions knit his brow. She told herself he was being metaphorical, but after Carlos, the image he described made her nerves spike. "I didn't know you thought about it so much."

He blinked at her. "Don't you?"

As a matter of fact… She gave him a small smile and glanced back to the rocks below. "But what if the fall didn't kill you?"

His dark eyes got darker as he pressed his lips together, and Emily wondered if the same grisly imaginings of lying broken and starving at the bottom of the cliff cycled through his mind. And then they'd find you down there. They always found you.

Ramon shrugged. "Would suck." Releasing the railing, he stepped back. "Shooting yourself doesn't always work either."

As he let out a soft laugh, the sound of it distracted Emily too much to point out it depended how you shot. "Well," she said after a moment, "they're not going to get you. So it doesn't matter." Saying it aloud made it true.

He shook his head and met her eyes. "Not tonight anyhow."

It wasn't her imagination; there was something in the way he studied her. Like she confused him, like he wanted to push her away and bring her closer at the same time. It made an excited flutter swell in her chest.

"Come on," he said, turning from her. "Everyone should be ready by now. Let's do this."

Releasing a breath, Emily slid off the railing to follow him up the road. She watched the rifle bounce gently against his back and couldn't help smiling at how the gravel made half as much noise under his boots than hers even though he was twice her weight. She softened her tread until it matched his.

At the fence, she paused. "Hey, Ray?"

"Yeah?" He looked sideways at her as he undid the lock, his fingers moving on autopilot. "You know, you're the only one who calls me that."

She smiled as she studied his profile, then glanced past him to the compound. She cleared her throat and shook her head. "Nothing." There would be time for talking about themselves later. Right now, she had an entire team to face.

He pulled off the chain and passed through, not bothering to relock it. Emily tucked her hair behind her ears and followed him.

Yes, her nerves thrummed. But together, they could do this. If she couldn't prove herself to him—to everyone—tonight, then she didn't deserve to be there anymore.

7

PLAN B

The stuffy air inside the museum mingled with an essence of burnt beans. Emily followed Ramon to the supply room. Everyone crammed inside lifted their faces up at once, breaking off whispered conversations. Ramon ignored most of them and turned to confer in low tones with Big Joe, who sorted hand bombs into two sacks. After a moment, everyone resumed stuffing packs and prepping weapons. Could Ramon feel all their eyes on his back?

"Hey, Emmers." Rosa's soft voice made Emily pull her own eyes away to glance down at her. Rosa smiled, but the usual dimples in her round cheeks didn't appear. "You missed meal."

"Yeah. I was..." She shook her head.

"I got some almonds. You want?"

Of course Rosa would have snacks. Eternal mom instincts. But Emily was too keyed up for food. Her eyes found Ramon again as he spoke to the three new guys. In their ill-fitting stealth gear inherited from former unlucky recruits, they looked so young and naïve. This would be their first time. Emily steeled what remained of her nerves into determination and returned Rosa's smile. "Thanks though. I'm not hungry."

Daisy snorted from where she slouched against the cabinet on Rosa's other side. "Really?" Her yellow ponytail was tied tight enough to give Emily's scalp sympathy pain. "Imagine that." She nibbled on her thumbnail, her eyes fixed on Ramon's movements across the room.

Other Joe crossed in front of her, and Daisy pushed away from the cabinet to smack his ass. Hard. "Move it, tasty cheeks. You're blocking my view."

Emily bit back the insult her brain retorted and focused on Ramon as he rapped his knife handle against the table. The room stilled.

"All right," he said. "We've got a little over twenty minutes until moonrise. Sherice, anything else we should know?"

Sherice finished punching a fluffy jacket into a too-full backpack. She yanked the zipper closed, then shook her stubbly head. "The trucks are parked on the other side of the big building, but they haven't done anything to try to hide them. So, yeah, they don't know we're up here. Humans with them are definitely guards, not slaves. Real manly-man macho dickhead tough guys."

Ramon nodded and addressed the group. "We don't know why they're here. They could be nobody, or they could be waiting for our target too. This isn't the meticulous stealth rescue mission we've been planning, we never got the backup headquarters promised, and no, LPI didn't send us out here for something like this. But that doesn't mean we can't handle it. We did it last month at that Dragon groceries place, yeah?"

His dark eyes scanned the room, daring any of them to mention Michele and Alaric. Or to mention the lack of vampires at the Dragon Mart. No one said a word. "And, *yes*, it's night this time, but that's not going to matter. A scout is going down, and when the coast is clear, we ninja the factory from two sides before they even know we exist. We take out the guards if we have to, get grenades through the windows, and get out of there. Clean and simple and over in seven seconds. We've only got a few grenades left, but there's a lot of firepower with the tanks on those factory machines. The explosion could be huge, so don't anyone stick around to watch the fireworks. Get behind the parking lot walls, understand?"

"Shit, son," Other Joe muttered from behind Emily. "We're gonna lose our diesel source."

Emily glanced around the room, then back to him. "Why does it matter if we can't stay here?"

Daisy made a kissy face at him. "You're so cute when you're stupid."

His cheeks bloomed red, and he dropped his gaze, scratching his sunburnt nose.

"Lay off," Sherice hissed at Daisy.

"We regroup in the parking lot." Ramon raised his voice over theirs. "And any of them that make it out of the fire, we snipe. Garima, Rosa, you're our sharpshooters. Stay put on the wall no matter what else goes down. If we shoot anything that's going to stand back up again, we get their heads before they move. Daisy, take Phuong, Andre, and Brion. You're our hackers. We've got six targets, but if anyone catches a manly man, try to shoot to wound. They might not be working for the vampires willingly. We can sort them out afterwards."

Emily's fists clenched. *And then what?* Invite these tough guys to join their unit? As if she knew her thoughts, Rosa's hand covered Emily's arm, and she shook her head. Emily let her breath ease out between tight lips.

"Everything's packed," Ramon continued. "After we're done, we grab and go. We take their trucks, we move north, and the mission is still on."

"Damn, if only we had a launcher," Other Joe said. "We could blow the factory from the hill."

"We'll be fine," Ramon said. "We stick with our shift teams on the way down."

Daisy stepped forward. "Andre's not on my team."

"Fuck that." Andre spat on the floor.

Ramon's jaw clenched, but he looked away from them. "Fine, he's with me. Joe, help them out."

"Yup," said Big Joe as he traded his bomb sack for a machete.

Ramon took the two charged radios from the dock on the otherwise empty shelf and stuck one in his belt. "Sherice." He turned to her. "You're on scout."

"No, no. No." Sherice folded her arms and glared. "Oh no, I'm not."

Emily's heartbeat quadrupled. "I'll do it."

Ramon didn't acknowledge her. He stared at Sherice, and then his arm snapped like a rubber band and he slammed the radio onto the table. "Just what do you think this is?"

Emily jumped. Wide eyes filled the room. Ramon never snapped.

"I think this is me not being on scout," Sherice answered.

"*Ramon.*" Rosa's voice was soft, but the emphasis of her accent pointed. "Emily said she'll do it."

Usually, if anyone could change Ramon's mind, Rosa could. The other guys called it Dominican favoritism, but Emily knew Rosa had that effect on anyone.

This time, though, Ramon ignored her as he continued to stare down Sherice. She stared right back. Finally, he gave her a disgusted look and turned away.

When he addressed the group, his voice was even again. "I know it hasn't been the same since we lost Michele, you guys. And I know I'm technically not officially in charge. But if we don't do this together, it's not gonna happen. Someone has to make decisions."

"And I'm making the decision not to be on scout," Sherice said.

"God, shut up," said Daisy.

"Screw you like you screwed Andre."

"Both of you, be quiet." Ramon faced Sherice again. "Tell me, why are you here, then?"

"To save the world," Brion said from across the room, sharpening his machete. Garima elbowed him in the ribs.

Ramon stared at Sherice. "It's not 'cause you're getting paid, I know that." He thrust his knife handle at the group. "No one made us. We're doing this because it's right, and we're the ones who *can*. If we couldn't, we'd be dead. We're good at this. Maybe you didn't know that when you joined LPI, but we haven't had official contact in weeks, lost over half our company, and *we* are still here. Nobody wants out. I know it, and you know it."

Sherice threw down her arms. "And I'm not saying I do! I sat out there for the past hour. Alone. While you all lounged in here eating rice and beans."

Emily took a step forward. "Ramon?"

"No," Ramon said. "I mean it. Think about it. Right now. Why you're here. All of you. Why you signed up. Why it's not you out there who people like us have to save. Why nights like tonight are worth it."

Silence stifled the room. Beyond the shuttered windows, chirping insects harmonized with the distant moaning howls. Ramon might as well have said all this to Emily by the bonfire yesterday. It applied to her assignment ten times more than Sherice right now. Emily tried to catch his eye as his gaze swept the room, tried to show him she understood. Going out for scout now would be a comparably small thing, but it was a start. *Let me do it.*

"We do this, and we do this smart. Emily," Ramon said, tossing her the radio, "you're my man."

She smiled. He almost smiled back.

Clipping the radio into the holster on her belt, she grabbed the binoculars from the table. With them, her eyes would be as good as Sherice's, and her attitude a hundred times better. This was her chance.

Rosa hugged her before she reached the door. "Maybe this one's for your mom?" she whispered.

Emily's momentary high crashed back to Earth, and she clenched her teeth. "No." She glanced back at the team. "Not this one."

"Hey, Em?" Carlos stepped out from behind the others, rifle in hand. Red still rimmed his eyes, but his shoulders were straight. He'd sucked it up. He gave her a tentative, grateful nod. "Remember to watch out for snakes."

Emily rolled her eyes, but she laughed.

Through the dark glass foyer back to the yard, she made her way along the path through the gate and cut down the north side of the hill, where she ducked into the brush.

The radio slid into her palm like it was made to fit as she checked the channel. "Testing."

Ramon's voice came back at her. "Hey."

She smiled and turned the volume down a few clicks. "Going around the bluff now."

Muscle memory guided her in the moonless dark to the jutting ledge on the hillside to the left of the cliff. As she peered through the binoculars at the factory, her hair blew over the lenses. She paused to twist it into a knot and shove it down her jacket collar. When she looked again, it took her a minute before she could distinguish the nature of the shadows lurking about the biggest building. Three moved with seeming-life. A light fixture flared on over a doorway, and Shadows One and Two became man-shaped. A handful of narrow windows along the factory's first floor lit up as well. They had the generators going already. Good sign. Their guard was down.

Emily watched the two men at the door converse. Their gestures appeared human enough. The same guys from earlier. After a minute, one strolled inside. The muffled thud of the door slam reached her a second later. The remaining man slouched against the doorframe and smacked dust from his boots with a rifle.

Emily radioed Ramon to describe the scene, then she moved along the hill's curve to check out the factory's other side. She avoided the dry bushes and made less noise than a gopher. As she slithered down the boulders to the lookout ledge, she thought she saw a lone firefly shoot past a creosote bush out of the corner of her eye. When she turned, it was gone. She studied the bush's bony skyward fingers through the binoculars; its scraggly silhouette couldn't have concealed anything. She waited, just to be sure. Nothing there at all. Carlos and his hallucinations seized her brain, and she shuddered.

Clock's ticking. The team was counting on her. She returned her attention to the factory to pinpoint Man-Shape Number Three. She found him pissing on the parking lot wall. Ha! Vampires didn't piss.

She called Ramon. "It's clear. Two confirmed humans outside down there now. All's quiet at the trucks. Everyone else is inside."

"Perfect," he responded through a low fuzz of static.

"I'm on my way."

"Not yet. Stay there and keep an eye on us until we're down low."

Emily's lips twisted. She didn't volunteer for scout so she could sit out on the action. But she nodded obediently at the radio. "Got it." She fumbled to clip it to her belt but couldn't find the holster and keep her eyes on the binoculars. She shoved it into the back of her pants instead.

She could make out her team's two snakelike shadows splitting off as they crept across the valley's gullet. She checked on the guards at the factory again, then made one last call. "You're good. They haven't moved."

She didn't receive a response but hadn't expected to. When her team disappeared from her field of view, she decided she'd waited long enough and slid off the ledge to follow.

Back on the hill, she scanned the valley one more time. She smiled to herself and lowered the binoculars. Now much closer to the creosote bush, she saw the firefly again, this time near a rock pile a few feet away. *Strange,* she thought. But why?

In a flash, it came to her—fireflies were damp climate creatures.

That was no insect. It was the glowing end of a cigarette.

Emily froze.

8

LEIF

The odor was unfortunate, but it would simply have to be endured. Machine smells, grease and filth. Waste, decay. Leif could hold his breath, of course, as long as required. Some nights he went hours without breathing at all. But those were nights without anyone to talk to. Not that the dull creatures in this commune he'd joined merited much conversation. Their human pets merited even less. Those oh-so-discerning mortal servants who chose a dilapidated factory for camp. They might have found a more suitable, more charming building anywhere else at all, really.

At least the factory had electric light, an improvement over their last stop. Although the great room where the fragrant mortal men arranged the commune's caskets was ugly enough that Leif might have preferred the dark for a change.

The cool satin lining of his deep coat pocket whispered against his knuckles as his fingers wrapped the little igniter chips within. The circuit-crossed things rattled against his palm like so many miniature dice. Last night, he calibrated them to his detonator application. The night before, he laced all the caskets but his own with the odorless spray explosive. Tonight, he would plant the igniters in the caskets. Then come sunrise, all he needed to do was press the boom button.

Of course, it was his jolly luck the caskets now rested in the center of the factory floor in plain view of all within. Someone would be there all night, witness to any of Leif's actions—unless something occurred to send them all out of doors at once. He might wait until tomorrow night, of course. But, oh, he was loathe to spend a minute longer with the commune's dear, dear members and their wretched cargo.

It could be done. Tonight. He would have no repeat of his failed efforts of last month, of yesteryear. A distraction of some sort. That was all he required.

"Where are you going?" The one called Nadia narrowed her pretty, dark eyes as Leif turned to the door.

"Oh, just to poke around. See what we've got for us here."

"Aren't you going to feed?" A lovely young vampire, Nadia, with long sleek black hair Leif's fingers might enjoy slipping through sometime. Perhaps in another life. He liked to imagine how she might look in a well-cut suit instead of the rugged clothing she preferred.

"But of course, my dear." He gave her a smile not far from suggestive. It was difficult to refrain from drifting toward the benches at the far wall where the others fed. The blossoming blood scent already overpowered the factory stench. "Would I miss it? But as you can see, it's hardly my turn."

The two human fellows donating this night to the commune would be swallowed slowly. Each vampire would get his mouthful, a paltry portion indeed, but equal shares for all. They each drank human blood every single night, which was the glorious part of it. Dear Demos, their captain, worked it all out mathematically. Body weight, replenishment time, so on and so forth. Allowing Leif to join the commune earned Demos no small measure of displeasure from his followers in regard to all that, despite how Leif's place in their precious pecking order fell at the bottom.

He might have declined inclusion in the feeding share to ingratiate himself upon joining, offered to subsist on animal blood for the time being, as excruciating as that would be. But such an agreement would have been too convenient of him, wouldn't it? Better to incur the commune's animosity, let them think he needed them, think him desperate to share their human supply. None of them suspected now the fate awaiting them at dawn.

Nadia shook her head, answered Leif's smile with a hard look. "Don't you touch any of the guards."

"I wouldn't dream of it." Leif made her a little bow.

"Demos will evict you as fast as he let you join us."

It took effort to suppress his amusement at the idea of Demos challenging him. Hardly a fair fight.

Although flexing muscle would be counter to his purposes, Leif was the eldest vampire in the commune now. His strength of age was the very thing that caught Demos's interest, after all. But, of course, Demos wouldn't attempt such a thing alone. And there was no sense in letting things get sticky. Not yet.

"I've been with you five nights, my dear. I think I've shown I can follow our darling leader's rules by now, hm?"

Nadia turned her back, and he slipped out of the factory before anyone else might question him. The young man guarding the door jumped when Leif appeared beside him. Gathering himself quickly, he pressed his hand over his heart to await orders. Leif merely gave him a wink and strolled around the corner of the building.

A balmy desert night, to be sure. But what, oh what, could be distracting enough to draw the others out into it all at once?

Leif's gait slowed as his gaze swept over the cargo trucks. Why—yes. That would be rather perfect, wouldn't it?

He chuckled and rubbed his hands together, then shot across the lot to the semitrucks in the twinkling of an eye. A flick of his fingers could break the trailer door locks, but would that be overly obvious? Well, everyone would surely be too distracted to notice for some time. And then it would be too late. This hour tomorrow night, Leif would be celebrating his first success and well on his way to start it all over again with the next commune.

He'd just perched on the tailgate and grasped the latch when Demos's voice cut through the night behind him. "Just what the hell do you think you're doing?"

9

SNAKES

The cigarette glow faded, and a man coughed. "Yeah, I see you," he called to Emily. "And I got a nice fat gun pointed right at you. So you should, um, I dunno, stay still maybe?"

When the cigarette brightened again, the outline of his features warmed into view as he came around the rocks. He looked obnoxiously amused with himself. The orange ember flicked from his fingers and disappeared to the ground like the first.

Emily's hand crept for the holster on her thigh.

"I said don't move." The brush crunched as his shape moved closer. "Give me your gun."

"No." She dropped the binoculars to free her hand.

"Hey. You're a chick."

Emily squinted at him as he came near. She could make out dark bristly hair, a rough beard, and a crooked nose. Either his leather jacket was padded, or his shoulders were just that broad. He stood a couple inches taller than Emily, too, but the arrogant carelessness in the way he moved reassured her of her chances.

He stopped two feet from her and held out his hand.

"I'm not giving you my gun." She kept her voice low.

"Sure you are." He coughed and cleared his throat, then he made a grab for her holster.

Emily jumped back, and he stumbled over the binoculars. Her gun was out in less than a second.

The man swore and kicked the binoculars down the hill. As his jacket flapped open, the sight it revealed stopped Emily in her tracks. He wasn't wearing a shirt, his belly exposed to the night, and from the belt up, he was covered with hair, a double snake tattoo on his stomach, and countless tiny puncture wounds. The holes spread up both sides of his throat into his beard.

Emily almost gagged. *Sick.*

"Drop it." He smacked her hand with the barrel of his gun. "Don't make me have to shoot you."

Her knuckles screamed, and she jerked back, but she couldn't stop gaping at his wounds.

"Hey, are you stupid?" As he grabbed at her again, she snapped to attention and twisted away.

She swung into aim but hesitated to shoot. The noise could raise the alarm at the factory before her team got the chance to attack. Or at least that's what she told herself as the thought flashed through her mind.

Truthfully, she'd never shot a human before. Shooting someone—something—no longer human was easy. Easy when it wanted to devour your flesh or slurp up your blood. But despite how tainted this hairy snake tattoo guy's blood must be from the bites covering him, he was alive. And Emily hesitated.

"You're disgusting," she sputtered in a pathetic attempt to stall for time. Her neck ached as she resisted the urge to glance in her team's direction. Soon the explosions would be distraction enough and she could get away.

"Me?" He snorted. "I'm not bad." He started for her again.

This time Emily kept her feet planted, and she aimed at his pincushion chest. He froze. "You let them feed on you." She swallowed the thickness in her throat. "You're pathetic."

He started to circle her. "Oh yeah. They'll like you. We haven't had a chick with us in a while."

She kicked a rock at his shins. It missed.

He laughed then hacked another cough. "Come on, use your head, baby. Why would I shoot unless you make me? And let all your blood go to waste?" He aimed his gun at her crotch. "But you wouldn't have much fun if I put a bullet in, um, oh, one of your knees?"

Emily drew a discreet breath between clenched teeth, then took a step toward his gun. "I'd rather die from an infected bullet wound than be their whore like you."

He snorted. "Yeah, real nice. They're just gonna love sucking it out of you."

Her mind raced for an idea, any noiseless idea. She took a gamble and lowered her gun to her side. Snakeman's aim remained very much not on her knees, but she could see at once how his entire stance relaxed. She put her free hand on her hip and tapped the tip of her G18 against her thigh in an attempted cocky manner. *Get him to look at the factory.* Away from her and at the factory. If he turned his head even for a second, she could knock him out.

"They won't get the chance," she said with a forced smirk. *Cheesy enough?* "My team is seconds away from torching your camp. Those leeches you sold your soul to are as good as dead." There. The hand on her hip tiptoed toward the radio in the back of her pants.

Snakeman fell silent for a moment, but then he grinned. "Newsflash, baby. I saw your cute little team going down the hill, and I called mine." He lifted a radio of his own and waggled it in the air. "Ready and waiting."

Heat exploded in Emily's face, and a chill shot from her stomach to the back of her throat. *Stay cool!* She kept her eyes on the gun in his hairy knuckles. Fang holes even covered his hand.

Keep him talking, her frozen brain snapped. The more he talked, the more his aim slipped.

"It doesn't matter," she stammered. "We outnumber your guards, and six vampires is no—"

"First of all, babe, it's seven. But you know what? They won't even have to do anything. Yeah, they know your little buddies are coming, probably there already by now. But they're just sitting back and watching the fun. You wanna know why?"

Emily clenched her teeth, battled the adrenaline making a lava lamp of her insides. Just keep him talking. "Why?"

"Yeah! *Hell yeah*, you wanna know why! They don't even have to lift a finger for your friends. Well, maybe one." He laughed, long and raspy, his aim finally sinking to the vicinity of her knees. "Yeah, just one of their lily-white-ass fingers. To unlock the trucks. We got a *special* kind of livestock."

"Oh?" Emily prompted. Let his aim slip two inches more, and then she'd chance it.

"Oh, yeah. Except it's not *live*stock." He laughed, obviously thinking himself hilarious. "Your friends are *dinner*, baby. You hear that?" He cocked an ear to the wind, then grinned as a chorus of howls rose from far too near. "That's it. They just let loose our two glorious truckloads of motherfuckin' zombies."

A bone-hard fist crunched Emily's heart. "No!" Her feet stumbled over nothing, and her hand circled the air for nonexistent support. He was lying. He had to be lying. But the wind swept the moaning up the hill to prove it.

"*Oh* yeah." His laugher pitched up at her flailing. "We've been starving those bitches for a night just like this."

Emily snatched up her radio, but he lunged at her before she could say a word into it. She twisted from his hands, and both her gun and the radio fell. A leather-clad arm caught her waist. She kneed him, but he jammed her in the ribs with an elbow, dropping her to hands and knees. The radio lay in the dust inches from her fingers, but he kicked it before she could grab it.

He shoved the fat round muzzle of his gun between her shoulder blades. "Do you hear it?"

At first, she could hear nothing but his thick breath, clotted with hot moisture against her ear, but then she stiffened. Gunfire in the distance broke through like rainfall. A storm of undead screams rose from the valley.

He squatted over her and ground his gun into her back. "Nothing you can do now, right? Come on. We want the same things, you and me. Shooting you is way down on the list of what I'd like to do with you. We'll treat you nice. You should thank me. I saved you before you went down there. We're always recruiting. Besides, what else can you do?"

She could hyperventilate. She strained to make it stop. The first rays of moonlight squeaking over the hills caught in the eggplant-dyed ends of hair hanging past her face. Oh god, her priorities had been so fucked up. Emily squeezed her eyes shut.

The muzzle trailed down her spine and poked her in the butt. Her eyes snapped open. She twisted to sock Snakeman in the beard, but he caught her fist and shoved her down. The back of her head cracked against something sharp, but she barely registered the pain before she gagged against his gun wedged into her throat. His smoke-stale breath assaulted her face with a fruity afterstench. Mango tobacco? It made her want to puke.

She craned her face away, but then froze at the sound of crunching brush and a whoosh of air as something—someone—rushed past them. Blinking, she made out the flapping of a long dark coat and the flashing of moonlight on polished shoes that ran up the hill too quickly to tell one from the other.

The scraggly face over hers snapped up, his body stiffening against hers. "Hey!" he yelled.

Emily twisted to follow his gaze. At the top of the hill, the blurry runner stilled, solidifying as he surveyed the opposite side. His head of pale hair fluffed in the wind like a wispy second moon suspended over the ridge.

"Hey," Snakeman yelled again. "Where are you going?"

Emily opened her mouth, but her call for help skittered right back down her throat when the man on the ridge whipped around to them. Not a man at all. His face, even whiter than his hair, shone like a mask of wax in the moonlight. A vampire's face. Wide, colorless eyes regarded them for a moment. But, could it be? Even observing half upside-down, Emily could swear she saw fear in his gaze. A second later, the expression melted into a smirk, and one pale eyebrow arched up his forehead.

Snakeman sat back on his heels, his fingers twisting in Emily's jacket. "What the fuck, man?"

The vampire took a step back, cocked his head, sniffed the air. Emily gagged. He took another step, and then he seemed to come to a decision. In a ridiculously exaggerated gesture, he blew them a kiss then disappeared over the ridge.

"Hey!" Snakeman yelled.

Emily didn't waste another instant; she twisted, leaving him holding her empty jacket. She jumped to her feet, but his arms wrapped her knees. She fell hard, but she fought harder. If vampires were running away from the factory with fear in their eyes, then her team must be winning. She had to get down there.

The gunfire and screaming grew louder, louder as she grunted into each punch, but the distant sounds somehow came from all directions. She lost track of left and right, up and down, as she fought in the dust. The moon above the bluff silhouetted the hilltop in the opposite direction from where it should have been.

The sight of a person coming over it distracted her, a person walking slowly, weakly, like they'd been through battle. A person who couldn't possibly be a vampire. Snakeman managed to free his hand from Emily's grip, and she stumbled.

"Hey!" she shouted to the person, but she lost sight of them as Snakeman tackled her.

Emily twisted, kicking at him. When she managed to get on top, she could see the approaching figure again. A short, ruffled dress clung to its frame, and it dragged one of its stilettoed feet. It had only one arm.

Emily gasped, froze. "Wait."

In reply, she received Snakeman's fist to her gut. He pinned her with all his weight, breathing heavily in her face. The mango smoke stench made her retch. With her hand trapped against his hairy stomach, his sweat seeped between her fingers around his tiny raw wounds. Her cheek pressed painfully into the radio on the ground while her gun mocked her from under a bush a few feet away. Too heavy. She couldn't move.

"Yeah," he said between panting breaths. "Done fighting yet? Time to come back down with me. Meet the family. They're *really* gonna like you. They're gonna love that I found you. They—"

He broke into a guttural scream, and his hands shot up.

Emily scrambled to the bush to grab her gun. When she looked back, he was rolling on the ground with the one-armed zombie, its jaws locked on his throat. He bashed it away, but shiny blood gushed down its chin, black in the moonlight.

Emily dove for the radio, and then she bolted. Behind her, the fat gun fired once, twice, and then only anguished groaning and the sound of her own pounding feet remained as she ran for the cliffs.

10

SUICIDE

The burning in Emily's chest forced her to pause for breath on the road. She could see the factory again, half-covered in flames. One, two, three dark figures shot out of the fire faster than shadows in her direction.

She fumbled with the radio. "Ramon? Ramon! Where are you?"

No answer. Three, five, six more shuffling undead appeared over the hill behind her. On the north side of the fence.

"Ramon, what's going on down there? Are we winning? You have to hurry, they're coming over from the town! Where are you?"

She gulped for breath and ran to the ridge above the cliffs. "Ramon!" she sobbed into the radio.

At the place where the railing was torn asunder, she fell against it, choking on her own thundering heartbeat. She could see nothing in the abyss, not even the white car. The wind swirled noises from all directions, bombarded her with a hurricane of distant groans and screams and gunfire. Cramp gnawed at her side as all feeling bled from her legs.

Two cattle trucks full of starving zombies. Her team had no idea. And seven vampires. Seven vampires she could never dream of outrunning. And nowhere to hide. The night had just begun.

And Ramon and Rosa and everyone else... *Oh, god.* It was too late.

Had the guards seen her on the hill today when she dropped the radio? Is that why they posted a lookout there tonight? Was this all her fault? She should have told Ramon. Told everyone not to attack. They should have run in the opposite direction hours ago.

Emily's fingers dug into the twisted metal. She peered into the abyss and clenched her teeth.

All too late.

But the undead would not get her too. Not tonight, not ever.

She would do it.

And this was where she would do it.

She pushed herself upright and stepped through the mangled railing, lined up her toes with the cliff's crumbling edge. She took the deepest breath of her life.

She paused.

The image of lying broken and starving at the bottom flashed through her mind. They would find her down there, and they would eat her alive just the same. She took another breath, squeezed her eyes shut, and lifted her gun to her temple. Her hand shook.

No...no, not there.

She put the barrel in her mouth, where she knew it could not miss.

Let them try to eat dead meat.

Her grip tightened until her hand ached. The tension snaked up her arm into her shuddering shoulders, burned up the back of her neck. She forced herself to tune out the groans echoing in the rocks behind her, closer, closer.

Relax. Relax.

She forced her grip to soften. Focused on the cold metal on her tongue. So that was what forever tasted like.

Long, slow breaths through her nose fluttered up sweet forgotten memories.

The sparkling rainbow lake past the long grass at her grandmother's Midwestern cottage.

Summer bushes full of fireflies like fairy lights.

Her dad stifling laughter while they watched old South African sketch comedy reruns long past her bedtime.

Emily was ready.

Slowly, she opened her eyes.

Death rose from the abyss, arms outstretched to meet her. Swirling out of smoke-like shadows, he looked just like Carlos described—just like she always thought he should look. His skull face was swathed in a deep black hood, his skeleton hand gripped a reaper's scythe.

Emily's smile spread around her gun. *Yes, perfect.* She would die pure.

Death drew near, his tattered black sleeves brushing hers as his arms encircled her. The air temperature dropped, but she did not feel cold. Her finger tensed on the trigger. *Yes.* Everything about this was right.

Her time had come.

She began to squeeze, but the trigger remained stiff under her touch. Or was it her finger that turned stiff? As Emily stared into the pale green glow burning deep in the sockets of Death's skull, she tried to press harder, but her hand felt locked in place, frozen in time. But only for a moment. And then it began to give, and then—

The radio crackled with static.

Emily gasped and pulled barrel from her mouth. The vision of Death disappeared, and shivering instantly overtook her in the frigid night air.

The guardrail clanged as if something knocked into it, but Ramon's voice through the radio distracted Emily from looking. "Emily!"

She fumbled the button with cold sweaty fingers, her heart thundering again. "You made it!" She turned from the ledge to stop the wind from blowing her hair all over her face and shoved her gun into its holster. "Oh, god, you don't even know— I thought—"

"Emily, where are you?" His voice broke the jagged static.

"I'm coming!"

"No! Stay away."

"Ray, what happened?"

"They're down. Everyone down. Get away. For God's sake, get away. They know you're out there, and they're coming for you."

"Who's with you?"

"No one. I'm—" Tiny pops of terrible gunfire replaced Ramon's voice through the radio. "Everyone down. They were ready for us."

"Where are you? I'm coming."

"No! We never had a chance. I've been—" Gunfire again, then a long scream and the static cut off. Out over the valley, the same gunfire echoed a second later as the wind carried it across the distance.

"Ramon?" One breath. Two. Four. "Ray, answer me!"

She stopped breathing. She counted to ten. "Ramon!" she screamed. "Anyone!"

"Hola, hola!" an unfamiliar female voice sang through the radio. "Can't wait to eat you."

Emily recoiled and twisted around to stare at the far-off flashes lighting the underside of the clouds, but she couldn't hear the gunfire over her heartbeat.

The voice came again. "Want to see something cool?"

A second later, something exploded beyond the hill. Undead shrieks replied just beyond the cliff road's bend. Slow shuffling shadows filled the opposite direction.

"No!" The radio hit the ground as Emily clawed her gun back out of its holster.

A sob wracked her body, and she fell against the railing. She wrapped a tight arm around her battered stomach.

Down—everyone down. Ramon, Rosa, Carlos. The scared new guys from La Jolla. Two cattle trucks full of zombies. She didn't know. She gave the all clear.

Emily took a stumbling step backward. Tears burned her lips as she staggered blindly along the cliff's edge. With a shaking hand, she put the gun back into her mouth.

A faint zinging sound rose above the groans, like an arrow set free to fly, and then a heavy body pounced upon her. As it slammed her to the ground, she smelled stale mango smoke. A ravenous moan cloyed at her ear, and the gun flew from her hand.

Struggling with every last shred of energy, Emily pushed to her feet, but the zombie moved too quickly. A fast one? Here? How? Its teeth flashed through the beard on its warped gray face above a throat covered in puncture wounds.

"No!" A deep, echoing voice cried out somewhere behind her. "She's mine!"

The vision of Death reappeared over the path, diving through the air toward her.

Time stopped.

The scythe fell from his hand as if through water and skeletal fingertips stretched from shadow sleeves.

The zombie had her shoulder in its mouth—she saw it the split second before it happened. Fire shot through her skin as its teeth tore her flesh. In the same instant, a sharp cold touch pricked her cheek.

A scream died in Emily's throat. Her boots tangled around each other and she fell, too late knocking the zombie backward off the cliff. It tumbled into darkness, snake tattoos and all, while her own twisted limbs caught the guardrail before the ground knocked her vision black.

It took a minute for the sick realization that she wasn't unconscious to fully register. A sound like bones cracking pierced her woozy hearing. Then a Doppler of static as her radio whizzed past her head over the cliff.

Who?

She forced her eyes open and struggled to lift her face. The night swam, but through the dust clinging to her wet lashes, she could swear a horse's legs, pale as a ghost, moved past her. Icy breath snuffed into her hair.

Her heartbeat should have spiked. But it didn't. It didn't beat at all.

No...

An inhuman groan escaped her throat as Emily fell limp.

11

PLAN F

Well, the night certainly hadn't gone according to plan.

Leif had been running for hours, and he was *thirsty*. The thirstier he grew, the harder to keep up speed, but he could not afford to stop. Although he sensed no one following him, hadn't for dozens of miles, his skin crawled as he imagined the entire commune at his heels. The hard-packed desert earth pounded beneath his shoes, and the wind roaring past him worked through his flesh as if it would siphon the very moisture from his thirsty veins.

More miles. There could never be enough miles behind him. But what lay before him? Demos would send out word, would tell other communes what Leif did tonight. Or tried to do. Tried and failed. Miserably.

It was funny, really. All of existence ought to be laughing at him. He might as well join it. But the sound clotted and died in his parched throat. Every thread of his circulatory system screamed tortuously. Shouldn't he have crossed a road by now? Any road. Anything but this vast expanse of nothing. Signs of civilization refused to emerge as the ugly landscape continued to crag most naturally about him. His usual jolly luck.

How he hated the desert. Wasteland with no beauty, no life. What he would give to stumble over some scavenging night creature. How he wished he could spare the moments to do some scavenging of his own.

But he could not risk it. Surely Demos sent someone from the commune after him. A minute's pause could allow them to draw near enough to catch Leif's scent, hear his borrowed heartbeat on the wind.

Keep going. Push. All too sparse, the hills too low, the rocks too scattered. Find shelter, real shelter.

And then? And then. He would do what? Slink into hiding like a beaten cur? Meld with the shadows, wallow and gnash back the bile of bitter disappointment?

Why yes, that was likely exactly what he would do. Just like the last time. And the time before that. And then, and then try again? If he got far enough fast enough, there might be a chance of it. If he started smaller, if he knocked his ambition down a few pegs. But hadn't he told himself that before? Did any pegs even remain?

He ought to laugh, but his throat would not open for it. Instead, the emotion emerged as enraged moisture in his sand-scored eyes to be wind-lashed into the night. Precious droplets he could not afford to lose. Why must their blood scent linger, making his insides writhe and yearn? Another trick of his abominable fortune? The torturous scent seemed more than he could possibly produce.

More... Yes, that was the aroma of *real* blood. Blood fresh and flowing from something alive. Something not far upwind. Something decidedly not human, but delectable in Leif's desperation. It clamped onto his brain and the world disappeared beyond his thirst.

He changed course and followed his nose over the next jagged hill. When he beheld what the other side revealed, the world came flooding back, and he skidded to a stop.

A solitary vampire fed upon the limp body of one of those wild American desert dogs. Leif was sure he knew what they were called, but its scent distracted him too much to attempt the proper name. The other vampire's head snapped up, beady eyes peering through long straggled hair, bloodied lips peeled to bare uneven fangs. Even as the dog blood on the breeze made Leif's thirst sob, he found the taste to be repulsed by such an unkempt creature.

Lifting his hands, Leif took a step back. "Apologies, my friend." He kept his voice even despite how his veins quavered with longing.

"Friend?" the vampire spat. The dog's body twisted in his hands, bones cracking, canine heartbeat spiking and fading. "This land is claimed."

Commune land. This was no lonely rogue vampire.

Leif could detect no others even at the very edges of his senses, but that could change in an instant. And it would have to be a large commune in order to stake a lookout this far from its core. Large indeed. For a moment, Leif considered the advantages of joining it, hiding in plain sight. But this commune was too close to the one he left, and its size at cross purposes with his diminished ambition.

No, run. He should run.

"Understood." Leif gave a nod and dashed back over the hill. But oh, that scent. His traitorous feet dragged against the rocks.

A warm hand gripped the back of his neck. Leif shuddered and took a long breath to enjoy the contact before throwing it off and turning around. "Can't you see that I'm going?"

The vampire clenched the lapel of Leif's fine coat and drew close to him in the dark. Leif fought gloriously to resist licking the blood from the lips before his face. Black strands of hair stuck to them, the rest of it draggled against the vampire's gaunt cheeks in unattractive clumps. Earth soiled his faded blue jeans, and his hole-pocked t-shirt, two sizes too large, hung off his narrow shoulder. He appeared weeks removed from his last mouthful of good human blood. The dog blood made him warm, but it served poor substitute.

His eyes brightened as they circled Leif's features, and he twisted the coat. "I reckon I know you."

Impossible. Leif flinched and brushed the filthy hand away. He took a step backward down the hill. "Don't let me interrupt your meal. They keep packs, don't they? I'll find my own."

"Yeeeesss." The vampire chuckled. "You're that one they're looking for."

"I am?" Demos had alerted this vampire's commune *already*? Damn it all. Leif gave his most innocent smile as he glanced pointedly at their empty surroundings. "And who might 'they' be?"

The vampire's laugh grated as he wormed his hand into his jeans pocket. Something electronic clicked, making a connection. "You'll rightly see."

Well, then.

Leif fled down the hill, but the other vampire caught him at the bottom, blocking his path. He was young, Leif could tell that much, no more than a hundred years if he was a day. But the fresh blood in his system gave him an energy of speed Leif's parched limbs envied.

"I told you," he snarled. "You're trespassing."

"I could *not* be trespassing. If you would get out of my way."

"I know who you are. Do you think they sent me out here with the coyotes for nothing?"

Coyotes! That's what they were called.

"Traitor." His snarling verged upon hissing. "You dare to cross Lorenzo?"

Lorenzo? The Lorenzo? Mad plague doctor Lorenzo? Leif's Lorenzo? Not possible. No. Word had already reached Lorenzo himself? Perhaps Leif was a bit of an antique, but it boggled him that even after the technological world collapsed, vampires still managed to communicate with satellite speed.

The commune system vampires followed had Lorenzo to thank for its creation. Though vampires freely assembled their own, no commune was as massive or well-armed as Lorenzo's. His absorbed smaller ones regularly to keep it that way, and they all deferred to him. A most dangerous vampire to cross, and a rather valuable one to impress.

And he already knew what Leif did tonight? Tried to do. But trying proved enough to make Leif's face a marked one—far and wide, apparently! So much for his grand elaborate plans. There would be no trying again, no matter how small he started. No commune would be fool enough to invite him in now.

Why, oh why, did Leif go to break open the truck before Demos took his turn to feed? If any of the others caught him, he could have gotten away with denying it. All he needed was the distraction of escaped flesh-eaters to draw everyone out of the factory so he could plant the igniters in the caskets.

Oh, but it would have been no good at any point in the evening. When those humans with their machetes and grenades marched upon the factory, they put the commune on alert and spoiled Leif's lovely plan. Fortune or foolishness, it did not matter. The fact was, he got caught. Now he could feel the black spot on his name spreading like a cancer.

What was the use of running with nowhere left to go?

Except, perhaps... There was always Manhattan, New York. That wonderful little island of paradise surrounded by hell. But that option came with its own set of problems. Problems that made Leif consider the pits of the ocean as an alternative. Besides, he could hardly *run* to New York. Even the seasoned machine of his body was not meant to endure such strain.

No, there had to be another way out of this mess. *Think, you old fool.*

Leif lifted his face to the wind. If this shabby vampire had alerted his commune with whatever lurked in his pocket, no one approached yet.

"I would speak with Lorenzo," Leif said. *Another way.* Lorenzo, Lorenzo, it had been much too long.

"You can try when we send him your head."

"You misunderstand me, friend. I don't know what you've been told—" In fact, Leif wasn't quite sure exactly how much of his plan Demos even figured out. "But it is Lorenzo I mean to please."

"By sabotaging decent vampires working on his orders?"

All right. Perhaps Demos knew everything, then. But Leif could spin it. "They were inefficient. You see, I could fulfill their orders better on my own."

"You simpering faggot."

Leif's mental gears stopped spinning, and his lips pursed into a frown. "Simpering?"

"You think Lorenzo gives one shit about who delivers his cargo?"

"I don't simper."

"What he'll give a shit about is me delivering him you."

Leif sighed and crossed his arms, chafing cold fingertips against the grain of his dark wool sleeves. He was wasting his time, wasn't he? "You insist on being entirely unreasonable, then?"

The vampire clicked the device in his pocket again and grinned at Leif, his teeth slick with coyote blood. Oh, it looked good.

All right, new plan.

"What are you called?" Leif asked.

"You reckon I'd tell you?"

Leif cocked his head. "Pity."

The vampire scoffed, but the sound cut off in a strangled choke as Leif leapt upon him. His cold fingertips dug into the warm throat, popping the skin. A shudder of pleasure coursed up Leif's arm as the blood cascaded over his hand.

Flipping him around, Leif pulled the vampire's back against his chest, and put his lips to his ear. "It's just that I like to know who I eat." His mouth clamped upon the torn throat.

The vampire's blood tasted nothing like human blood. Each thin metallic swallow felt like sucking electricity from copper wire. But that was typical; it was hardly Leif's first time draining a vampire. Although the essence of coyote offered a unique terroir.

Blood was blood was blood, and it flooded Leif's tissues gloriously. As depleted as his thirst rendered him, his brute strength earned over the centuries made the young vampire's thrashing feeble in comparison, and he soon fell limp against Leif's chest.

When he'd drawn as much as he could, Leif dropped the body at his feet. "May I call you Ricky?" he asked.

The vampire twitched and made a garbled sound with what was left of his larynx.

"Wonderful." Leif licked all traces of Ricky's blood from his fingers and then inspected his cuffs. Miraculously clean! "Good habits," he said absently. "They reward you when you need them."

A shudder wracked Ricky's body, and Leif crouched to lift his head by a handful of matted hair. The whites of Ricky's rolled-back eyes glistened in the moonlight with each twitch of his long black lashes. Rather lovely lashes, really. Leif gave the head a twist. Bones crunched, skin and sinew tore, and then he punted the head down the hill.

Sliding a hand along the wiry body, Leif retrieved the clicking thing from Ricky's pocket. About the size of a matchbox with one center button, a red LED blinked at its end.

"Is this a garage door opener?" he asked.

Ricky did not reply.

Leif frowned at him, then stood. He considered crushing the box between his fingers, but then thought better of it and flung it in a westerly direction. It disappeared into the night, and wherever it landed, even his eyes could not make out the red light.

Let whoever tracked its signal go that way. Still no sign of any others, though. Better and better.

Far from satiated, but recharged, Leif picked up running in the opposite direction he threw the box. Straight east.

He made it perhaps thirty miles before the euphoria of escape faded enough to remind him he had no idea where he was going. Ricky's blood diluted far too quickly in his veins, and without living blood, Leif's speed would be nothing compared to any well-fed pursuers. His thirst crested again just thinking about it.

Curse this blasted wasteland, ashen in the nearly horizonless dark.

Nearly horizonless... But what was that, beyond the next hill? A lovely long splash of ink in the sand. And like a mummified hitchhiker at its side, a dirt-encrusted highway sign.

When Leif reached the base of the hill, sharp pebbles pricked through the soles of his poor shoes. Running had worn the fine Italian leather nearly transparent. Leif squeezed his eyes shut, pinched the bridge of his nose. He'd really liked these shoes.

Not a sound but the wind, and the only scent on the air was that which dust brings. Anyone following him remained beyond the reach of his senses, miles from him yet. Yet.

Leif raked his fingers through his feathery hair. Always a yet.

Over the hill he went, and he drew up before the sign. Desert residue caked it so thickly he couldn't make out the writing. He sucked in an almost painful breath and blew. The sign wavered on its stork-like leg, but the dirt did not move a speck. Leif winced; it would have to be wiped away. He would *not* use his coat sleeve. With a sigh, he lifted his bare hand to scratch and scrub as much as it took to read the sign.

Dog Flats – 22 miles.

"Dog Flats?" he asked it, and then gave a sharp laugh. "What a name." But if the place was worth naming, it might very well be worth seeking.

He brushed off his fingers, flicking dirt crumbs from his nails, and then slipped his hands into the roomy pockets of his long, heavy coat. The cool satin swish sent a little thrill along his flesh, plucked a smile from his sorry lips.

His pleasure multiplied as his fingertips brushed a hard, smooth shape nestled deep in the womb of the pocket. Could it be? He was so sure he'd lost it when he fled the commune. He threw back his head, his laughter ringing clear and exultant.

Oh, he was destitute, he was hunted, hated perhaps, outcast most certainly, utterly lacking in existential purpose—but damn it all if he didn't still have his iPod!

Dog Flats, twenty-two miles.

Oh, Leif was exceedingly thirsty, but he could be there in half an hour.

12

DEATH

Dying was nothing like floating. No light, no tunnel. Terrible sensation smashed over Emily's body, turning her to stone, a gargoyle of herself. Space pressed her into a ground that hardened, calcified beneath her. Everything within her skin popped at once.

Warmth oozed from her ears, but through it, she became aware of a scuffing sound.

Who? Could she look?

She worked her anvil eyes open. The night tilted sideways, and she found herself in the midst of a dark fog. It was as if a thundercloud decided to take a nap with her on the dirt.

Several yards away...was that a horse? Pawing at the gravel. At first, Emily took it for translucent, but as her vision prickled into focus, it glowed through the fog with greenish luminosity. The effect made it appear concave, like a hollowed-out mold of itself instead of a solid object.

Its bedraggled tail gave a dull flick, and it snuffed and pawed again. This time, Emily noticed the stick resting before its hooves. The long, black stick. Her gaze grappled along its length to the massive sickle blade at its end.

A shroud of blackness fell over her vision. A moment later, it lifted. Someone had moved past her. Someone wearing a long, black cloak. Emily tried to roll over. Nothing happened. A frantic whine began to pitch up in her ears.

The cloaked figure walked to the horse. The footsteps and the scratch of the trailing fabric on the dirt faded under the shrill buzzing, like a terrified fly swarm, that completely overtook her hearing.

Sudden pain—a jillion needles marathoned over the shell of her body. But it did not hurt enough to distract her from the absolute shock of the sight.

It was Death who passed before her. Death himself. She lay prostrate at Death's feet. But he—he was walking *away* from her. Her vision swam in and out as she watched him move through the thick cloud. She watched him flex skeleton hands at his sides, nothing holding the bones together. She watched him stop short as someone blocked his path.

The someone was an old man with a cropped gray beard. He stood with a soldier's posture. Weathered gray body armor covered his frame, though his blood-colored helmet shone like new. In the foggy dark, he stood out, opaque and impenetrable as he tapped at his boots with something—a riding crop?—in a slow, even rhythm as if he had been there waiting for Death to notice him for a very long while.

And notice him Death did. In his stillness, the night itself settled upon his black-swathed shoulders. The swirling edges of his shadow shape solidified in the fog, everything ephemeral about him collecting into the moment.

Emily could do nothing but lie there and stare as the two beings conversed. Their incomprehensible words beat at her muffled hearing like underwater dream murmurs. Eventually, her eyelids sank. She concentrated on the buzz in her ears, strained at it for answers, pushed it down. She started to count to a hundred but lost her way too soon. It felt like hours passed and no time at all.

When she opened her eyes again, the figures stood there still, all three: man, wraith, and horse. Two of them were arguing; the horse looked on. The horse looked thunderstruck.

The old man held the scythe now. The figure that was Death reached past him, grasping for the horse's gaunt face, but he could not touch it. The old man mounted the horse. It twisted and bucked under him, but a strike of the crop stilled it.

The scampering pain over Emily's skin started to fade along with the buzzing. She could make out the hollow hoofbeats and frantic whinnies as the horse was forced to turn around. She heard the armored man's whistle and the crack of his whip, and then a cavernous cry.

The man, scythe, and horse left Death behind, a solid blot in the mist. They disappeared into the black fog, which followed them like the swirling train of a robe until it, too, evaporated. Alone, Death's robed arms rose in a furious shower of tattered darkness.

Emily closed her eyes again. Too weak to wonder, too dead to care. A sharp metal clang made her wince. A long, grave silence followed.

Alone again.

The air felt sticky, and she turned her face into the dirt. Dirt. Just regular old dirt. Grains stuck to her lips in a way far too annoying to be less than real.

Was she dead or not?

She felt sick, pukey, but the pain was manageable. Was she supposed to get up now? A thick groan worked its way through her throat, and she forced her eyes open. Shades of black. Night. Just regular old night. She sputtered at the grit and groaned again.

"What do you want?" a deep voice snapped above her. Fabric rustled, footsteps retreated.

Who?

Emily's chest burned to cough, but she had no air for it. Could she speak? She had to try.

"Help." It came out little more than a whimper.

The footsteps halted. The grave silence returned.

Emily went still. Was she hearing imaginary voices now? She couldn't be dreaming; everything hurt too much. But her brain felt mushy, disconnected. When nothing happened for another minute, she gritted her teeth and inched to sit up. She felt stiff and battered and queasy, but not dead.

So what, then?

She looked herself over, checked her limbs. Her hand ran up her sleeve. She froze. The high moonlight revealed, clearly enough, a bite-sized chunk of flesh missing beneath a ragged hole on the side of her shoulder.

"No," she moaned.

"Unfortunately."

She jumped to her feet. All blood flushed out of her head, and she wobbled, but she caught herself on the railing. As her swimming vision focused, Death stared back at her. His hooded skull was cocked at a curious angle, his bone hands hanging at his sides.

"You!" Her strangled voice hitched. "You..."

Death himself. No longer swirling ink in water but a cloaked skeleton shape with defined edges. So real and solid she could reach out and touch him. What would he feel like?

Emily shuddered. "Oh... You... Oh, god. That means I'm—"

"No." He cut her off. "Unfortunately." His skeleton mouth did not move when he spoke. His voice, though clear through the clenched teeth, sounded like it rose from a tunnel too cavernous to be concealed even within his imposing frame.

No? Not dead? Death stood there, three feet from her, but she wasn't dead? What about the hole in her shoulder, the zombie that bit her?

She waited, but when he said nothing more, only the support of the railing kept her from crumpling. "Then...I'm one of them."

Pulling her eyes from him, she prodded at her wound. Though it was deep, no blood flowed. It did not even sting as she gingerly brushed the dirt from its sticky edges. What should have been red looked too, too gray in the night.

The impossible presence of a walking, talking, solid, real-life Death before her felt like sweet fantasy compared to the despair that plunked stones one by one to the bottom of her being. *One of them.*

She could feel him studying her in the silence as dark nausea welled in her guts. She wrapped her arms around herself and bent against the railing, but the nausea did no more than simmer. Her eyes focused in and out on the hair hanging past her face. A hysterical laugh struggled to escape, but the breath she drew for it made her choke.

Emily coughed, thick and wet, and she pushed her hair back from her clammy forehead with gnarled, trembling fingers. Her gaze found the cliff's edge. How long had it been? It seemed a lifetime ago she stood there with her teeth against gunmetal.

Her hand shot to her holster. Gone. But no, the gun lay in the dirt, not far from her feet. "I should have done it when I had the chance," she whispered to herself as she picked up her Glock. She almost sobbed.

"Indeed."

She jerked around. He was really still there. He was really still staring. He had no eyes in his skull's black sockets, but she did not like the way the smoldering points of pale green light deep within them fixed on her. She blinked. The light flickered as if he blinked back.

"This can't be happening." She dug the heels of her palms into her eyes. "This isn't real. I don't believe in you. I don't..."

"You don't believe in death?"

"I..." She tried to take a deep breath but choked again. She shook her head and tilted it back up to him, craned her neck. He was taller than anyone she'd ever met. Something like hope kindled in her chest, and she put her gun away. "Where are you going to take me?"

"I? Nowhere. You're not dead."

Hope snuffed to smoke. "Then..." Her gaze fell to her shaking hands. The skin around her knuckles puckered in blotchy lumps. "Why are you here?"

"Why are you talking?"

Her head snapped up. "It hasn't hit me yet."

His gaze raked her over, ending at the bite on her arm. Black now rimmed the wound. "Oh, no, it has."

Emily shoved away from the railing and prodded herself over. "Then why am I still…? I should be a drooling, man-eating monster by now."

"Yes." Death looked to the cliff's edge. "You should be." He lifted his face to the sky. Emily thought his hood would fall back, but it remained in place despite the wind. He sounded as confused as she felt. "I touched you."

She winced at the sudden image of his bone hand on her skin. Icy cold. She shuddered, folding her arms across her chest, glancing away. She failed to clear her throat as her eyes found the moon. It hung high in the midnight sky, and the completeness of the night's silence struck her for the first time. When did the cries in the distance cease? Like a grenade blast, the evening came crashing back.

Ramon. The attack. Everyone down. And she gave the all clear. Emily groaned, the nausea rising again. She couldn't see the factory from this part of the road, only the dying remnants of fire glow against the far sky. The thin blot rising beyond the bluff sharpened into a smoke plume when she squinted. If anything out there had been coming for her, it was gone now. She turned around, and the indistinguishable hills loomed in the distance.

The middle of nowhere.

Alone.

Everyone down.

"All I remember," she said more to herself than anything, "is being jumped by that hairy snake guy. He was one of the fast ones." But how could he be? A slow one bit him. Only slow ones existed in town. Emily shook out her jumbled recollections. "I don't… I remember him biting me."

Death rustled behind her. "It was just as I touched you." His voice was closer than before.

Touched her? He did touch her. Yes. So cold. She kept her eyes averted, refolded her arms in the opposite direction, shifted where she stood. *Touched* her.

"How do you feel?" he asked over her shoulder.

"Creeped the hell out."

"I mean, are you in pain?"

"No." Not anymore. *How did it fade so fast?* She frowned and looked back up at him. And up at him. She brushed her fingers over the hole in her arm. "I'm not, actually."

"Do you feel weak?"

She rocked on her feet, tested her balance. "Not now."

"Stiff?"

She was about to say yes, but the longer she stood, the looser she felt. She flexed her fingers then drew her gun, spinning it into her palm. As she re-holstered it, she shook her head.

"Hungry?"

She almost gagged. "No."

Death stared at her for a minute. Then he shrugged, turned around, and walked away.

"Hey, wait!" Emily lurched after him.

"Yes?"

"You can't just leave me here."

He turned back to look down at her. Something about the way he did it seemed bemused despite his lack of facial features. The light within his eyes was there and not at the same time.

She pushed against the rolling threat of panic. "Is this really happening? Are you really the, the, what are you? The Grim Reaper?"

His eyes flickered before he answered, his voice quieter. "Yes."

She choked down a breath. "Then you have to do something. I can't, I *can't* be a zombie."

"I don't think you can help it." He glanced over her as if to be certain, then gave a decisive nod.

"No," she cried. "Kill me! I'd rather be dead."

His shoulders sagged under his voluminous robe. "You are undead. I have no power over you."

"Chop off my head." She reached for him. "Burn me."

"It doesn't work that way." He took a step back, evading her grasp. "The undead do not die."

"Bullshit! I've killed hundreds of them."

"It's not the same." His voice fell even quieter as he took another step away from her hands.

She stopped. She should be on the verge of hyperventilating, but air proved impossible. "But I'm not *really* a zombie. Right? I can't be. I mean, I don't feel like a zombie. I'm not thinking like a zombie. I'm talking for god's sake." One of *them*.

There had to be a way to end it. *Anything* would be better. For almost two years, she'd clung to that vow like a religion. *Anything* but one of them.

The memory of the first time she saw them assaulted her like a headbutt to the gut. It had been such a pretty day. And there they were, out in the suburban sunlight, on the other side of her house's plate-glass windows. Her mother in the center of the family room, shrieking and shrieking, making everything worse. Such a difference between seeing them on TV versus her own back yard, the glass barrier between them so much more fragile. And even after everything Emily had done, had fought, had killed, now she shuffled with them there on the back porch. Two years for nothing.

She grimaced and wrapped her arms around her waist as if she could squeeze the plague out of her tissues. "This isn't real." She blinked up at Death through her hanging hair. "It isn't. Zombies can't talk."

"I know." His gaze swept her over once more, then he lifted his hands, studied the bones as if they might reveal answers.

"You." She rounded on him. "This is your fault. You're Death." As batshit as it seemed, it made more sense than anything else she could let herself believe. "If you touched me, why aren't I dead? That's how it works, right? You touch people and they die?"

"I was too late." He spoke to his hands rather than to her. "It was at the same moment."

"Too late?" Same moment? She shook her head, swallowing back a tight, raw lump in her throat. Something twisted in her stomach. She watched him for a minute, but nothing else happened. "Then why are you still here?"

"I am at the mercy of time." He dropped his hands and turned to walk along the cliff, away from the visitor's center compound. In the opposite direction of absolutely everything that mattered to Emily only hours ago.

"Wait." She fidgeted, then jogged after him. "Wait, what does that mean?"

"It means everything has changed." His trailing cloak fanned behind him on the desert road. "And the balance is destroyed."

"Oh. Is that all." She ignored the writhing in her stomach, told herself it wasn't there, kept her eyes on the side of his hood. "What am I supposed to do now?"

"I don't know."

She wanted to scream. She was a zombie, or she wasn't. He was the actual physical embodiment of *Death,* or she was insane. But she couldn't be lucky enough to just be insane; it was all too literal and clear. "You have to know!"

He shrugged. "Go to an undead dinner party?"

"God!"

He left the road and crossed the stony plane toward the hills. Emily followed right after him. Just let him even try to object. What else was she supposed to do? Her team was gone. *She* was gone. Their mission lost. The Amargosa hostages would never be rescued. Not by her team.

But... Could it still happen? Someone else could still do it. If she told them they needed to. It could still happen. That was the important thing. Emily had to focus on the important thing. Focus. Mission 12 was still out there, on its way. Coming down that highway. There must be someone she could find, something she could do. But she was getting farther from the highway with every step.

She stared at Death's back as if she would find solutions in the darker impressions of the ancient fabric folds. He was all she had to work with, wasn't he? After another minute, she managed to speak in a calmer tone. "So...what are you doing?"

Death stopped as if her voice startled him, but he only stared into the distance.

Emily waited a minute, then edged in front of him. In the sharp moonlight, his skull face looked bleached, the color of chalk. Bone that never held muscle or sinew. She had seen skulls aplenty during a college-era trip to Paris and its catacombs. At the time, it was a badass way to spend spring break. Now, it felt disrespectfully morbid and like a million years ago, but the human-bone-lined underground labyrinths held favorite memories. All those grinning former-heads had been dirt-brown with age. She'd never seen a *white* skull before. Not a real one.

Within the white sockets, Death's gaze fixed over her head at the night.

"Hey," she said. *What is he staring at?* She glanced over her shoulder, then back to him. "Hey, look. My name's Emily. Emily Campbell."

His head creaked down to meet her eyes.

She gave him a little wave. He waited.

"Okay." The writhing in her stomach calmed bit by bit, and she squared herself where she stood. "So. Right. Here's the thing. I don't understand what the hell happened to me. And you, you're like some kind of god. And you're...here. With me."

"I am not a god."

She shook her head. "But you can help me, right?"

A gust of wind snaked down from the hills. It caught in Death's tattered sleeves, sighed straight through him. His gaze slipped from her, as if the distance beckoned.

No, no. Nope. Never mind. There was no way any of this could be real.

Yes, Emily was definitely insane. She had to be. She bit down hard on her lip and clenched her trembling fists. The flesh sank under her fingernails.

Like a wet sponge.

With a sharp gasp, she shook out her hands. Okay, no such luck. Far too real.

Emily scrubbed at her eyes, then sidestepped to force herself back into Death's line of sight.

"Please. Just, just listen. Please. The point is, you're here. And I'm here. Right? Look. I'm with the Southland ring of the LPI. And, as I guess you probably know, all of my unit are dead or taken. I'm the only one left alive."

"No, you're not."

She stopped. "You mean someone else survived? Who?"

"No." It almost seemed like he meant to laugh, if that were even possible, but his deep tone remained even. "I mean you're not alive."

Emily's heart twisted. Everyone down...

No, shake it off. Focus. "But I'm not dead either."

"Nor are they."

Undead. She grimaced and fought the overwhelming urge to turn away, to pretend he wasn't there. Maybe if she tried hard enough, she could *go* insane.

Focus! Work with it.

Emily forced herself to recall the highway they left behind. "That commune, those vampires, the ones that took down my team. They had human guards, but they didn't have a herd. Any human slaves, you know? That's what we do, right? The LPI." He must know about them. He was the Grim Reaper. He knew everything. "We rescue the slaves and disband the communes. We kill the vampires if we can."

He shifted to interrupt, but she powered on. "But see, we figured out where this big commune was leading these hostages from Amargosa. Innocents. They're going to come through that valley back there and three of us, of my team, were going to pose as survivors, ask to join them, spy it out so the rest of us could break in."

Three of their bravest. Three of their—*no*. Emily couldn't dwell on that now.

"The plan was solid. We've been staking out that valley for weeks. Everything was going to line up perfect. But then today, these assholes show up. But it's not too late. If I could just get the info to another unit..." A chill rushed through her. Yes. It could work! "There *are* other units. Not too far from here. They could pick up where we left off. That's the important thing. I mean, that's what we died for."

"You mean un-died," Death said.

"Whatever. Look, there's this unit at the Nevada border we met on our way out here. If I could just get to them." But would they be able to drop their own mission to finish hers? They had to!

"You wish to seek out mortals?" Death looked from the hole in her arm to her hands to her face. "Do you think they would listen to you?"

Emily's eyes itched as if they were creeping into her skull. She shook off the feeling. "Yes! I don't know what this is. They'd have to know there's something up when they see I can talk."

"If they gave you the chance to open your undead mouth."

Her mouth popped closed. Undead. One of them. *Zombie.* Her tongue grated against her palate like steel wool.

Death started to walk again, down the slope to a dry riverbed path between the high rocks. "Nevada is that way." He pointed straight ahead. "But Emily, you must learn to let go. Your mortal concerns are over now." The way he said it sounded like it must be something he repeated often.

"No, they're not." She followed right behind him. Could he possibly mean to lead her there? Or was his direction coincidence? "There are people out there who still need help."

"The living must help themselves."

"Or what? You'll kill them all?"

Death stopped again. Something about his stillness this time made Emily want to shiver. She waited for a minute and then obeyed her overwhelming urge to edge away. Maybe him pointing the direction helped enough. What else could she even ask *Death* to do for her? She would get to the border somehow. Pass on Mission 12 *somehow*. How far was she? Fifty miles or so? A solid day of good hiking. If they had trucks, they could make it back to Suncrest Hill with plenty of time to spare.

She circumvented Death to start out on her own but froze when he withdrew something from the recesses of his cloak. It was a blocky device, the size of a small book, but with tapered ends that gave it the overall shape of a squashed octagon. As a screen on its flat surface illuminated, Emily couldn't resist moving nearer. It changed pale colors as Death's bone fingertip stroked it, casting an eerie glow up into his hood.

Emily's eyelids blinked like rusty hinges. "What is... that's...touchscreen?"

"Yes." He did not look up as he tapped at it. "And he called me old-fashioned."

"Who did?"

Death was too absorbed in whatever his screen displayed to answer.

Old-fashioned was one way to describe it. It must be half an inch thick. Emily hadn't seen anything that chunky since her kid years. "I'm sorry, but that's just, I don't know. It's weird."

"I have to keep track of everyone's time, do I not?"

"I just didn't expect, you know."

"That I would change with the world?"

Is that what he called it? She shook her head.

"There are so many ways in which Death must continually adapt." He scrolled through an endless spiderweb of tiny words in an alphabet Emily could not identify from what little of it she could see.

"Humans invent new ways to die every day." His hand stilled, and his hood drooped. "Used to invent." The wind picked up from somewhere distant. It took an eternity to gust down the riverbed and roll over them. The device disappeared into Death's cloak. His attention shifted beyond Emily.

"Is that how you knew when I was going to...when I decided to die? That thing told you?"

"Yes."

She hesitated but couldn't help herself. "Who's going to die next?"

"No one."

"What?"

He waved a dismissive hand and started to walk again. Emily was too shaken by his deep, defeated tone to question the convenience of his direction.

"Wait." She half-jogged to keep up with his long stride. "Wait, what do you mean no one? Someone has to be the next person to die." So she didn't technically *die,* neither did her team. But what about everyone else in the world? "What about all the zombies?"

"I told you, it is not the same. Transformation is not death."

"You're saying nobody in the world is ever going to die again, except by zombie?"

"Un-die. And so it seems."

"How?"

"Or become a vampire, I suppose."

"That can't be possible!" For every Michele the flesh-eaters got from behind, an Alaric fell from the roof. It had to be so. Emily would have taken that plunge herself tonight if she knew it would kill her. Why the hell did she hesitate to pull the trigger? *Goddammit! If it hadn't stuck...*

Her fingertips brushed over the G18. Despite what Death said, she had to wonder: was there a way she could fire it now that would end her? Destroy whatever she was? One bullet to the brain never put a zombie down for longer than an hour. But could she keep shooting until her brain disintegrated? She couldn't chop off her own head, but she could build a bonfire.

Not yet. She had to get to the LPI unit at the border first.

Wait—was the border still in the direction Death walked? His somber silence made her hesitate to ask. As their path twisted and climbed, it sank in how completely turned around Emily would get if she struck out on her own. Waiting until sunrise to point the way would waste time she could not afford. She needed a guide. Even if that guide was Death.

But the longer he remained, the more Emily feared he would magically disappear into the inky smoke from which he materialized in the abyss. She did not dare pull her eyes from him, lest it happen the moment she did. She would be so alone. It compressed her with leaden gravity. Alone, and one of *them.*

The space between the rock walls grew narrower for a few hundred yards and then opened into a small, dry lakebed, scattered with the husks of former shrubs. Death set out across it. Every other minute, Emily's fingertips brushed her gun to make sure it was still in the holster on her thigh. Usually, walking with it for long wore on her, but she could barely feel it now.

"I'm sorry," she said, finally convincing herself to shatter Death's silence. Her eyes burned from her efforts against blinking. "But I don't get why you're still here, walking around in the desert with me. Aren't you going to poof away?"

"No."

She blinked, long and slow. It didn't make her eyes feel any better. "Okay." But he could be leading her anywhere at this point. She chewed her lip. "Will you please tell me where we're going?"

"You do not have to come with me," said Death, perhaps for the first time in eternity.

Emily almost laughed. Then she almost cried. "What else can I do?"

A long moment passed. "East."

"What?"

"We are going east."

"Why? I mean that's good. For me." Gratitude caught her in a desperate way she didn't expect. Although, was his unchanged course truly coincidence? How far would he go? "But why are *you* going east?"

"I need some space."

"Space?"

"I must summon my brethren."

The sickled edge to Death's words made any further questions shrivel on Emily's scratchy tongue.

It didn't keep them from running idiot circles around her brain, though. She tried to squash them by piecing together her day's events. Where did she first go wrong? Was it when she dropped the radio? Or before that, when she decided she needed to prove herself? Or before that, when she asked for reassignment? Before that, when she first developed her standards? *God.* But she couldn't help how she felt. Could she? What else could she have done?

Anything else.

"Seventeen months working to overthrow the bloodsuckers," she murmured some time later, "and I get jumped by a flesh-eater. I'd die of shame if I could."

"He was one of the fast ones," Death said, as if repeating her earlier words would make her feel better.

Emily's head snapped up. After such a long silence, the otherworldly quality of his voice unsettled her anew. But the fact that his condescending tone did something as normal as annoy her somehow put her at ease.

"I'd never have let it happen if I was paying attention. I don't drop my guard."

"Only takes once."

"Yeah. Thanks."

"You'd just had very distressing news."

She glowered up at him. Was he watching her then, before she first saw him appear? How long?

Creeped the hell out. It was no excuse. Everyone down. It still didn't even feel real. Too soon, too sudden. But she wasn't going to wake up from this. Ramon, Rosa, Carlos, even Daisy. Her entire team…

Emily's gaze fell to the scuffed toes of her boots. "They're really… really all gone. They were literally everyone I had left in the world. They were…" She shook her head. "If you're right and those assholes didn't kill-kill them, then what Snakeman said was true." Two cattle trucks full of starved zombies. What could any of them have done? Emily swallowed past the sandpaper in her throat. "So, vampires are using zombies to fight for them now. People talked about this kind of thing, but we never thought they could make it work."

How could they control them? Set targets? After releasing the truckloads, how did they round them back up again? How could they keep them from attacking their own guards? If vampires had it figured out, this was a seriously big deal. The LPI needed to know.

The information couldn't help her team now, but others… The world…

Everyone down.

Skin flaked off Emily's chapped lip as her teeth scraped it. "I bet

Ramon shot himself." Did the vampires make him an offer, like Snakeman tried to persuade her? "He would never let them take him. He would never be a blood slave."

"Vampires have a way of making people change their minds."

Her head snapped up. "Are you saying they took him?"

"No."

"But you know he's not alive anymore?"

"Yes."

"Goddammit."

"Perhaps. Theological discernment is beyond me."

Emily's eyes felt dry enough to catch fire. Ramon was one of them too, now. One of...*us*. And Rosa and everyone else. Emily's nausea surged.

"Is he like me?" she asked after a minute. "I mean, could he be? Talking and in his right mind?"

"No."

"God," she whispered. This time, Death remained silent. Her pace slowed, and she let the distance between them grow. He did not seem to notice.

She wanted to blame the vampires. She wanted to put every drop of her boiling, anguished frustration into fueling her hatred for their disgusting, selfish, shortsighted ways. But regardless of when her mistakes truly began, Emily saw Snakeman's cigarette. And she was too stupid to recognize the danger. Too caught up in trying to impress Ramon and the team. *She* gave the all clear. She sent two dozen people, pure and healthy, to a doom so much worse than death.

"God, Ramon," she whispered, her gaze on the black horizon. "I hope you took most of them down with you. If you're one of them now, I hope someone just like you takes you out." And Rosa, would her soul be with her two lost little girls? Would Carlos find Alaric?

The gritty wind tugged at the ends of Emily's hair. It ought to have tickled her cheeks, but for once, her changed skin felt nothing, just as her changed limbs felt no fatigue from the fast pace over rough terrain. Nothing.

"I'm so sorry," Emily whispered, and she named her team of

yesterday to herself one by one, making up names for the new guys she couldn't remember, her changed lips brushing against each other like parchment.

"I won't let it be for nothing." Her changed eyes throbbed, but tears did not, could not, come. "Never let them win."

13

POWER

The pre-dawn called for Schubert. Schubert and solitaire. The *Andante con moto* filled Leif's head, an entire string quartet transported through two tiny plastic earbuds, while each card played out before him, no larger than a child's fingernail on a screen that fit so very nicely in the palm of his hand. He told himself he would only play one game, perhaps two if he lost the first. Five at the most.

That was over two hours ago, and the quartet played for the fourth time on repeat. But this would be the last game. Finally. In fact, he'd already won it. It was merely a matter of dragging every single mini card in the columns to the top of the screen—an obnoxious user-friendliness failure on the game's part. But Leif's victory had been such a long time coming, and his dexterity so quick, that he did not mind the effort. He lounged against thick microsuede cushions, his stark white thumb brushing over the screen while the fingers of his other hand tapped against the side of his mouth in time with the music.

Halfway through depositing his knaves, the quartet cut off mid-note, and the screen went pink.

No battery power remains. Please connect to power.

The black letters stared up at him, and he could do nothing but gape back.

"Power? Where am I supposed to find power?"

His iPod made no reply.

Leif just could not win.

He rubbed his eyes and yanked the headphones from his ears. "All anybody wants these days is power." The screen faded to black. "At least you're polite about it."

He eyed his faint reflection in the dark screen, then gave it a winning smile and rolled off the couch. Broken glass crunched under the handmade leather soles of his fantastic new shoes as he crossed the room to the wall next to the slumbering rhinoceros of an entertainment center. He jammed a fingertip into the eyes of an electrical outlet. The socket crumpled around his hand, but otherwise, he felt nothing.

"Of course." He sighed. Sitting on his heel, he raked back his hair from his forehead, the silky strands caressing the webs of his fingers. "Powerless. Like the rest of us." But weren't all these quaint desert communities supposed to convert to solar systems ages ago? "Tut tut, Dog Flats."

Well, he would simply have to seek power elsewhere. That meant going back outside. But the iPod was worth the risk. Dog Flats wasn't large, and Leif still had a couple hours to fill before sunrise. He wasn't caught yet, which meant anyone chasing him must have lost his trail. Leif did still see the sense in huddling in hiding, of course. But doing so in *silence?* Simply too much to ask.

He hopped up and leapt through the broken bay window, alighting on what was once a suburban front lawn. The lack of automatic sprinklers reduced all manicured grass in the cul-de-sac to a brown anthill utopia.

Smashed-in automobiles here and there along the curb glittered in the starlight. The faint scent of death lingered in the garage doors and former flowerbeds and sculpted pavement, but any corpses once strewn upon the debris-scattered street had long ago been scavenged away.

Leif lifted his face to the breeze. Electricity glimmered in the air; he could taste it. Not that it would do him any good up there. He laughed softly to himself, then he took off toward the cul-de-sac's outlet, his coat flapping around him like woolen wings.

On his way in, he had rushed past a hospital squatting at the edge of town proper. He retraced his steps to seek the hospital's backup generators. If no fuel remained, other buildings with something to use abounded. As wasted as the land could seem, if one knew where to look—and Leif certainly did—power could always be found.

He slowed his pace as he passed through the town's small business district where the buildings stood closer together and the streets narrowed. With all the decay in the air, it took concentration to sniff others out. He listened for any telltale sounds of shuffling footsteps, and the very opposite sounds his own kind could make. The shambling revenants often peppering towns like this were nothing to him. Even the speed of that rarer variety humans called "the fast ones" was negligible compared to the thirstiest of vampires. And though it was not unheard of, it was exceedingly doubtful their snapping jaws would take interest in his cold, lifeless flesh. Like Leif, they preferred the hot pleasure of sinking their razor teeth into mortal meat.

When he first arrived hours earlier, Leif combed the ghost town for prey, but the best he discovered was a lone armadillo. He supposed that much was fortunate if one felt inclined to play loosely with the word. He'd pounced upon the poor creature with desperation he was glad only ghosts witnessed. It provided nourishment of a sort, but now he, once again, felt all the thirstier for it.

Human blood would likely be out of the question for some time, but Leif could not subsist off armadillos. Tomorrow, he would need to find something larger, something with more personality. He'd finished the pathetic thing all too quickly and slunk off into the windy roads of the residential neighborhood. There, he flopped onto the most comfortable couch he could find to wait until dawn, when he'd have to crawl into a dark closet or under a kitchen sink. At least the hospital would have some sealed-off room or other where he could spend the day.

And then what? Manhattan, New York, flickered again across his painfully short mental list of options. As much as the idea knifed his pride, perhaps it would be for the best after all. Why, oh why, did it have to be all the way on the other side of this deliriously wide country? How many communes lay between him and that distant oasis? But even as he considered the option, an old familiar shadow oozed its way into the corners of Leif's consciousness. A desolate effluvium that plucked at strings of his existence he very much preferred remain unplucked.

There had to be a way to avoid giving up his aspirations. Once upon a time, he and Lorenzo were on intimate terms. Surely those days were not entirely forgotten? After all, Leif hadn't technically *done* anything. Could he spin Lorenzo a more convincing version of the story he tried on Ricky? Make him believe he merely meant to secure his own future? Was it unheard of to wish to exist on one's own in a nice place with nice things? What was immortality for, if not that?

Lorenzo was ruthless, but he was reasonable. If he wanted something Leif alone could provide? Well, that would help.

But what did Lorenzo want? The resources to demolish New York. To triumph over the great Apollonia and the vampires who pushed the buttons and pulled the levers in Manhattan. The strength to fortify his communes against the world. Which would be easier with no world left to rally against him. And that was his angle, wasn't it?

Apollonia, the oh-so-mighty Apollonia. That's what Lorenzo wanted. To take her down, to take her place.

Power, like everyone else. Leif laughed and folded his hand around the iPod in his pocket. Music first. Then blood. Then he might be able to manage the mental prowess to concoct a plan.

Keeping to the shadows out of habit, he cut across a school parking lot, then dashed around a convenience store and down the back alley of a strip mall until he reached the high fence at its end. He hopped over without touching it, then paused to survey the parched field between him and the hospital. Beyond the wafting overgrown grass, the highway that brought him to town stretched like a tether to every vainglorious risk taken for failed ideals. The hospital's tattered flag danced at half-mast like an undead marionette in the wind while the electricity in the air positively crackled.

A light blinked off to the left in Leif's periphery. He spun around, and his eyes made out an antenna several hundred feet down the fence in the darkness. It perched atop a small, lonely building. Some sort of utility shed or control console. Two patient, deliberate breaths, and the antenna's light blinked again.

Leif reached the building before the light had the chance to blink a third time. The door hung ajar, its latch broken with a force no human could manage unaided. He paused to sniff the air but picked up nothing more than a faint human scent, too weak and too old to be anything more than a tease.

Inside the shack's first room, darkness cloaked the machines, but Leif heard the humming of electricity in the walls, felt its microscopic titillations. He rubbed his hands together and grinned. Mechanical things filled most of the space, but Leif didn't give them much attention. He could tell at once no one was there to give *him* attention, and that was all that mattered. Whoever broke the latch and activated the generator, living or undead, remained nothing but a fragrant memory. He moved through the interior door to the smaller back room before scanning the walls for an outlet.

In the far corner, the steady blinking of a tiny orange light caught his eye. He paused to stare at it, hypnotized for a moment. It emanated from the breast of a slumped figure that looked like a woman covered with metal. As he drew closer, he decided it was more like metal covered with woman. Pure machine of pure feminine build. Two cords extended from an open panel in her tapered waist to a torn-out wall socket.

She was nearly as tall as Leif, or rather, would be if she stood straight. Like the android soldiers who once dominated military advertisements, she had no artificial hair or skin. But unlike those marching drones, her figure must have been sculpted by some engineer with the eye of a classical artist. So elegantly-proportioned, yet there was no mistaking her solidity. Despite her lithe shape, he wagered she could withstand an explosion or two. Leif had never heard of an android that so mixed fetishistic aesthetics and battle-readiness. What could her purpose possibly be?

Her silver-gray body was delightfully nude save for a long, thin blue scarf looped once around her slender throat. Metallic threads in its polyester weave twinkled as her breast light blinked. Against her feet rested a bulging duffel bag, greasy stains marring its pale blue canvas. Leif nudged it with one of his new shoes, and it clunked with hard, metal sounds.

The mechanical woman's face did not appear as solid as the rest of her. Her eyelids folded delicately, half-closed above fine cheekbones, and the sockets around the matte eye bulb covers looked made to move. To *express.* And other places abounded—the crooks of her elbows, the webs of her fingers—the same brushed color as the armored parts but made of softer stuff. Leif's fingers itched to discover how soft.

He found he liked the way she smelled, the way all the scents about her blended. Plastic and steel and silicone and copper and carbon fuel and human. He plucked up the end of the blue scarf and brushed its slippery fringe against his nose. Yes... Faint, a tease, but human. Recent human. Where was that human now?

A sudden whirring and the entire mechanical body straightened. "Powering up," said a pleasantly-intoned female voice.

The head lifted, and two indigo eyes flared alight in the silver face, accompanied by the sound of a laser weapon activating.

"Step off," said the voice much less pleasantly.

Leif leapt across the room. His back hit the wall with force to make the entire building shudder.

The metal woman frowned, the soft corners of her mouth wrinkling in a perfect imitation of human disdain. In fact, her whole face was so very human, except for the eyes. Why ever would anyone design such a human face with such inhuman eyes? No visible pupils in the round glowing centers behind the lenses. Leif would have shivered in delight if he weren't preoccupied by the rather intricate gun protruding from her right forearm.

"Go away," she said.

"Oh, no." A quiet laugh escaped Leif. "Just like that? But you're my first android."

The orange spot on her breast blinked to amber. "I will fry you."

And why hadn't she already? Leif slid his hands deep into the pockets of his coat.

She took a quick step but stopped when the cords connecting her to the wall jerked taut. The gun did not waiver in its aim on his eyes.

"Easy!" Leif pulled his hands from his pockets. One held the iPod, headphones wrapped neatly around it, and the other presented the charger. "I'm not going to hurt you." He bit back a chuckle. Could she even feel pain?

"No," she said. "Leave."

"I'm harmless."

"Get out."

"Hmmm." He eyed her gun, then the door, then focused back on her. Androids always on edge, like they used to say in the news when they mocked those adorable Robot Rights activists. "I can see you've got trust issues."

"I can see you've got fangs. The only reason I haven't shot you yet is to avoid attracting your friends."

Friends? Now that was really worth a laugh, but Leif refrained. Perhaps it would be a fitting end to the night, but he didn't particularly want to be shot.

"Come now," he said. "There's an outlet right over by that cabinet behind you. Allow me to plug this in. Then while it's charging, you can tell me all about your tormented childhood and how your robot daddy didn't love you."

He stepped toward her, and her gun went off four times, lighting up the room with sapphire fireworks. With each blast Leif avoided, he gained a few steps, and then he sprang upon her. Snatching her forearm, he shoved the weapon back into it.

She swung at him with her other arm, but Leif ducked, and her fist made an impressive dent in the metal cabinet. The blinking light on her breast turned back to orange as his fingers flashed out to grab the cords connecting her to the wall. He twisted them around his palm, and the android stilled immediately.

"You don't want me to rip these out of you, do you?"

Her electric eyes smoldered furiously, and her silver lips clamped tight.

"I didn't think so." He forced his fingers to remain steady, but the effort of evading her gunfire reduced his veins to quivering again. The human smell about her became ten times more of a tease.

"What do you want?" she snapped.

"To charge my iPod."

"That's not an iPod."

Wasn't it? Leif did his best to keep up with these things, but centuries of information tended to have a way of blurring in his brain. So many names for so many things. He knew how to program the little contraption; that was all that mattered.

"Whatever it is, I want to charge it." He took a soft breath as he studied her pliant face. "That's all, really."

She looked to the door, and her eye bulbs flickered, changing color to pistachio, then emerald, then back to indigo. Leif could hear the faint whirs of the components inside her marvelous head. A smart cookie, this one. He supposed she deduced by now he had no friends.

The not-flesh around her eyes narrowed as she focused on him. "Why here?"

His hand tightened on her arm, but the metal did not give in the slightest even under his grip's considerable pressure. He gave her a gentle smile. "The same reason you're here, it appears. Where else?"

His gaze dipped to the light on her left breast. She moved her hand to cover it. Carefully, he released her forearm. The gun popped right out again at first but then folded back in with a muffled click.

"You're smoother than I thought you would be," he said. "And warmer."

"The air temperature is warm." Her eyes fixed on his hand on her cords.

"In the films, you things always looked hard and cold all over. And shinier. You're not very shiny."

The soft ridges that served as her brow knitted, and her eyes glowed darker.

Her face begged to be touched, but her hand snapped up and caught Leif's the moment it moved. The force in her grip might have cracked human bones.

"What do you have against vampires?" he asked as he sniffed her discreetly. So good. Too good. The recent human must have been quite recent indeed. "It's not as if I'm going to bite you. I don't drink lubricant, or whatever runs through your artificial veins."

She threw his hand back at him. "You're all power-thirsty parasites with no respect for humans."

Oh-ho. There it was. He gave her a slow nod. "Hm. I see. And all robots are war machines."

"I'm not a government android."

He smiled. "And I'm not a commune vampire."

"I don't believe you."

"Very well, but it's true."

"How could I possibly know you're not lying?"

"What difference does it make?" Leif's smile faded, but he gently released her cords and backed off. "The only power I'm thirsty for is enough to bring my little music box back to life. Really."

She twisted to inspect the nest of wires, but he noticed how she positioned the duffel bag between her feet.

"Watch." Leif took out his iPod—or whatever it was *technically* called—and charger again. "See?" He plugged the adapter into the wall outlet by the cabinet and nestled his iPod against the nearest ledge below. He had no idea if proximity helped the wireless charge speed, but it seemed a safe assumption. He patted it with his fingertips. "There you go, little one."

The android frowned. Her orange light blinked back to amber.

Leif glanced at her through the flaxen tendrils of hair that fell over his eyes, then they dropped to the dark message on the small screen.

Please wait. Very low battery.

"Do I have a choice?" he asked it with a glum sigh.

"Do you regularly talk to your music box?" the android asked, watching him closely.

Leif lifted his face. "No. Of course not. It's just a machine. That would be unheard of." He offered her another smile.

She frowned back at him. Again.

He crossed the room to retrieve a folding chair from the wall. The four freshly-singed holes in the corrugated metal above it practically winked at him. He winked back, then dragged the chair over to her. Flipping it open, he perched on the back of it, his feet planted in the seat. Resting his elbows on his knees and clasping his hands, he commenced to look her over, making no effort to be discreet about noting every curve and bend. His gaze came to rest on the blinking amber light on her breast.

She moved one of the hanging ends of her scarf to cover it.

"Does it become green when you're all done?" he asked.

"That is none of your business."

He pursed his lips. "I'm cranky if I get interrupted while I'm feeding, too."

"Not amusing." She turned away.

He cupped his chin in one hand. "Oh, come now. Blood is the electricity of life, wouldn't you say? What goes around comes around, the circle of creation, et cetera, et cetera. You're sucking energy out of that wall, just like I might out of a human."

"Humans aren't walls."

"Some of them are."

She made a grating sound, not unlike a scoff, and faced him again. He let his smile spread slowly for her.

"What do they call you?" he asked. "Let me guess. May I? Is it Galatia XZQ789? Gynoidatrix? Antivampireattackbotomatic?"

"Carol."

Leif laughed. "Carol? Oh, how charming! Carol! What a pleasure to meet you, Carol." He slid off the chair and offered his hand. She ignored it.

"I'm not being sarcastic," he said. "It is a lovely name."

When she continued to ignore him, he circled to take in her back side. Symmetry slithered about her curves with a perfection the human form it imitated rarely attained.

"Well, Carol, you may call me Leif. I am not a commune vampire, and I'm not going to hurt you."

Carol turned her back against the wall. Could it be? A self-conscious android?

Her eyes locked on his, her hand tightening around the end of her scarf. "You could be as dangerous as they are without being a part of the commune system."

"Yes, I could."

"I've known enough vampires."

"And they were all bad, were they?"

Her lips remained clamped for a moment. "I am aware that there are vampires who are 'good' individuals—"

"But I couldn't possibly be one of them, could I?" Leif took a step back. Who could she mean? Not Apollonia and hers, could she? Leif didn't know of any others, but wasn't Carol a rather long way from New York to have such an association? "Carol, Carol. Really, what do I have to gain from deceiving you? We've only just met, after all."

What indeed? Exactly what sort of information did she have stored in her mechanical brain?

She stared at his not-Pod for a quiet moment, then back to him. "Why aren't you with a commune?"

Leif's face twisted, and he returned to his chair. "Oh, because they treat humans—*people*—like cattle. And it never used to be that way with our kind. It gets old so quickly. They think that simply because now they can do it, they have a right to it."

"And you don't think so?"

"It's not very sporting, and frankly, it puts me off my appetite."

Carol shook her perfectly symmetrical head, but her brow puckered. "You are telling me what you think I want to hear."

"Am I?"

"If it all gets so old, why do an estimated ninety-six percent of vampires still do it?"

Because Lorenzo sees to it. Because they're *thirsty*. Leif's veins rippled, but he hid the tremor beneath a shrug. "That's the thing, you see? Most of them out there, they're all so very young. Younger than I am, anyway."

"And you have achieved enlightenment in your old age?"

He laughed and ran his fingers through his hair. "Oh, Carol." He focused on twisting and untwisting his headphone cords. Four and a half centuries was an age an increasingly small percentage of his kind endured to achieve, but Leif was no Apollonia. Would that he ever lasted as long as she, he might begin to approach something like enlightenment. On the other hand, Lorenzo had a couple centuries on Leif, which proved "goodness" was no aged trait. The other commune masters and the vast multitude of young ones Lorenzo influenced simply preferred the easy road, really. Sheep herding cattle.

Carol looked down at her bag.

"It's not so complicated as all that," Leif said after a moment. "Some choose that way of life, and some don't. I don't. I have my reasons, and they're enough for me."

"There are some vampires who are trying to change things," Carol said as if playing a trump card.

Leif bit his tongue to hold back the bitter laugh threatening to bring all the oozing blackness to the front of his brain. Trying? And trying and trying. And failing and failing and *failing*.

He shrugged and got up to check on his iPod. "I suppose there are."

She must know of Apollonia and her council of fasting hero-saints in New York. Who else could she mean? Easy enough for them to hole up on their fortress island and play the long game. At their age, the thirst was so much easier to manage. Or so they claimed.

"You know," Carol said. "You're no better than the communes if you do nothing to try to stop them."

This time Leif couldn't keep his clipped laugh from escaping. "You know, you're the most judgmental android I've ever met."

"I thought I was your first."

"Quite." He twisted to look at her. "Spokesbot for your species as far as I'm concerned."

"You can't form an opinion of all androids based on me."

"Can't I? Then tell me, how can you form an opinion of me based on all vampires?"

"You—" She stared at him for a moment, then at the door, then at her bag again. "Caution is not equitable to prejudice."

"Hm, no. Just robot trust issues."

"How can anyone trust a stranger? Tell me that."

"Carol." Leif sighed. "Carol, Carol. You have nothing I want. Really. I'm no scientist. You tickle my curiosity as a novelty, and you seem like a simply fascinating person, but I wouldn't begin to know what to do with whatever mind-boggling technology zigzags inside your microchips in order to make you such a brilliant conversationalist." Though he could think of a few things he might do with her well-crafted body.

But what might someone like Lorenzo do with her? Even though she was Leif's first, he knew enough to realize her *uniqueness*. Her value.

Especially if she knew details about the vampires in New York.

Lorenzo would love her.

Leif let his next words slide out as if that thought never occurred. "Nor am I working for any evil overlord who might want to defragment you to harvest the secrets of whoever it is you're working for. I didn't even know you were in here when I came. I'm merely a well-dressed vampire, all alone, who might go a little mad if he were too long deprived of good music."

The color of Carol's eyes flickered in a way that would have been imperceptible to a human as her silence stretched. When she did speak again, her voice was gentler, almost sad. "I'm not working for anyone."

"Good." Leif made sure his countenance reflected her gentleness as he returned to his chair. "I'm sure I wouldn't like you so well if you were a government android."

Her glowing eyes followed him, softened in color subtly, and then she smiled, just a little. The sweetness of the expression struck Leif as altogether un-machine, and it sent a thrill across his skin.

“What brings you to Dog Flats?” he asked. “Or have you always been here?”

“Passing through.”

Could that explain the recent human scent about her? Would she be near one again soon? Perhaps even possibly, more than one?

No antenna light had blinked when Leif entered town hours ago. If she arrived since then, had humans as well?

“Where are you heading?” he asked.

“Nowhere.”

“I don’t believe you.” He gave her another smile.

“Where are you heading?” she asked.

“Nowhere,” he said. “But that’s the truth. I’m not heading, I’m leaving.”

“Leaving.”

“Oh, vampire politics. You can be as disinterested as you please, but the larger a party gets, the more persuasive they can be.” Especially when they had two semitrucks full of flesh-eaters.

“So you *were* involved with them.”

“Not that way. But a vampire has to abide to some extent, or he wakes up to a sunroof in his resting place. Either abide or disappear.”

“And you’ve disappeared.”

“I try.”

She nodded. What a lovely, thoughtful expression. Then she checked on her cords. The scarf slid over her breast to reveal the light again. It glowed a steady violet.

“That’s a charming scarf,” Leif said. “I like how it sparkles. Brings out the magpie in me. I suppose you don’t wear it to keep your neck warm?”

She glanced at him from the wires. “A friend gave it to me.”

“Another robot?”

She made no response other than a soft pinging sound and disconnected the cords from the wires in the wall. She tucked them into the panel at her waist, then closed it with a muffled flap.

Leif’s gaze lingered on the soft parts of the back of her knees until she faced him again. "Don't leave yet." He gestured to the iPod with a tilt of his head.

Carol picked up her bag and pulled the strap over her shoulder. Metallic objects within clunked against each other.

"What have you got there?" Leif asked.

A faint smile, a sweet brightening of her features.

He brushed his fingertips against his silken lips. "I can't imagine at all what an android might need to carry around with her."

"You certainly are curious."

"Is it spare parts?" He slid off the chair and stepped to her. His hand moved as if it would touch her face through will of its own. He repressed the impulse.

She looked to his hovering fingers, then back up to his eyes, but only shook her head in response.

"Is it portable fuel for generators like the one in this shed?"

Another pleasant little quirk of her lips. The color of her eyes lightened to same shade as the spot on her breast.

Leif put his hand on the bag, as if he might guess its contents by feel, but his gaze remained on hers. He leaned closer. Oh, that delicious scent… It clamped onto his brain in a way he did not want to resist.

"I can't help it," he murmured. "I'm fascinated."

Her perfectly-shaped lips parted, but she did not reply.

The tip of his nose lingered an inch from her cheek. "You know," he all but breathed, unable to help himself, "you smell so like a human."

Carol's eyes flashed dark, and she jerked back. A click and the laser gun aimed at Leif's face again.

He barely had time to lift his hands before she shoved past him and ran through the room and out of the building.

Leif blinked. Oh-ho. It was like that, was it? He ran a hand through his hair and closed his eyes. Not breathing, he listened to her fleeing footsteps as long as they echoed, and then he pressed his palm to his face, drawing in the scent of the bag. A human had touched that bag.

Only one, but it had touched it tonight. He exhaled luxuriously and returned to his iPod.

Some minutes later, the flashing green battery on the screen stilled and the lightning bolt turned into a plug. Leif took his time to snap together the charger pieces, fit in his headphones, and choose a playlist before he left the building.

The wind had changed direction. Not much, but enough. Carol's scent lingered in his nostrils. Tease, tease, tease. Leif stood completely still, feeling the coming of the dawn, listening through the music, breathing, making no move to seek cover. Eventually, as the eastern sky neared gray, his collection of senses targeted a point beyond the field's wall.

"A human for me, and an android for you," he whispered.

Lorenzo would love her indeed.

Leif grinned and took off after her.

14

FLIGHT

A cold inhuman hand jolted Scott awake. He sat up with a gasp and fumbled to free his shotgun from the blankets.

"Hush, it's me." Carol's voice penetrated the hammering heartbeat in his ears. He rubbed his eyes, and she came into focus, silhouetted against the dim bedroom window blinds.

"I knew that," he said between panting breaths. "Your hand is just… really cold." His shirt had bunched around his chest from his flailing. He dropped the gun to tug it down, then immediately felt stupid. Carol didn't care about his pasty white abs. Yawning, he shook out his hair like a wet dog. "What time is it?"

"Time to go."

Past her dark shape, gloomy morning light sneaked through the broken blinds. Scott groaned and flopped face down on the bed. Mistake. A cloud of dust ballooned around him, and he coughed for a minute straight.

"Hush," Carol said at whisper volume. When he didn't stop, she gave him two sharp whacks on the back.

"Stop that." He batted at her hand and covered his mouth. "That doesn't work."

"It should." She stopped anyway. "You are making too much noise."

"For what? Am I disturbing the termites?" They were totally alone in the abandoned house. Scott blew a circle of dust from the ratty bedspread, making a nice clean spot. He burrowed his face into it, tucked the shotgun under his arm, and pulled one of the lumpy shammed pillows over his head. "You woke me up too soon. I've only had like three hours of sleep. It's not healthy. We humans have something called REM cycles. This should matter to you." The bedspread smelled like old shoes. He could already feel himself drifting off. "Give me four more hours at least."

The pillow was wrenched away, and cruel demon light assaulted his face.

"You can sleep in the car." Carol dropped the pillow on the floor.

He twisted over. "What is your problem?" He could never sleep right in the car. She knew that.

"We are not alone here."

Scott's heart leapt to attention. He sat up straight and flipped the shotgun around. "What?" he whispered. "What is it?"

"A vampire."

Scott blinked. "A vampire?"

"Yes."

Scott blinked at her again. He looked past her to the brightening window, then met her eyes once more. "Carol, you do realize that when that star we call the sun comes up into the visible part of the sky, that means it's daylight, don't you?"

Her purple eyes narrowed, and she bent to grasp him by the bicep. "We are going. Now." She yanked him to his feet like he weighed nothing.

Ow! "Okay, okay, calm down." He pushed her hand away and massaged his arm. Finger-shaped bruises would be emerging later. He was twenty-three. Why did she have to treat him like an irrational toddler? After months of her pushing him around, he was reaching his limit. She was supposed to be protecting him, but the last time he searched the definition of that word, "bullying" wasn't part of it. Sure, he couldn't even remember the last time he bothered looking up any words. But the point was, she was freaking out over a vampire in broad daylight. How did her "superior intelligence" rationalize that?

"We have like nine hours before it could even try to follow us." He used slow, simple words in case she needed them. "*If* it even knows we're here." He scanned the floor for his hiking boots.

"He knows."

"What?" Scott's head snapped up. "Carol, what happened?" Did she let the vampire *see* her? *Superior intelligence.* Right.

"I'll tell you about it in the car. Hurry up."

Scott fought another yawn and plopped onto the bed to lace his boots. "Where's my backpack? Oh, there it is. How do you know there's only one?"

"I don't. But he led me to believe he is alone here."

The laces fell from Scott's fingers. "Hold on. You talked to him?"

Carol spread the blinds with two fingers to peek out the window. "But he would want me to believe that."

"Obviously. But Carol, you *talked* to him?" Were her circuits damaged or something?

"But probability dictates it's likely he told the truth."

"A vampire alone?" Wasn't that supposed to be unheard of? Finishing his shoes, Scott grabbed the backpack and went to the bedroom door. Carol followed, almost stepping on his heels.

At the bottom of the creaking staircase, Scott glanced around the boarded-up living room. Tacky knickknacks and dead digital photoframes abounded. Old people must have lived there. Sighing, he rubbed at his eyes. "I was going to check out the kitchen for stuff."

He also hoped to find a pair of scissors this time to snip off some of his hair. In the dusty mirror over the mantle, it looked like a straw mop. But he was so tired when they rolled into town, he'd put it all off, and now he wouldn't get the chance. He'd be tempted to take his electric razor to his entire head if he didn't know painfully well how dumb he looked with a buzz cut.

Carol jabbed him in the center of his back. "You can forage when we stop in Colorado."

Scott flinched and hoisted on his backpack. *Super.* Another day of hair itching his neck and eating the dense foil-wrapped bars he suspected consisted of more cardboard than protein. "Did you even get to charge?" He shuffled to the back-porch door they broke through earlier. "Or do I need to monitor the car while it drives?"

She jabbed him in the side where the backpack didn't protect. "I told you, you can sleep."

Scott grunted and jogged around the house to the curb where the silver hybrid sedan they found yesterday sat halfway onto the dead lawn at a careless angle.

He eyed the cracked panels on the roof and hood. "It's barely even started charging."

Carol's arm drew back, but he jumped aside before she could jab him again. "Get in." Her eyes changed colors as she scanned the street in all directions.

Scott was too tired to argue. He poured himself into the car, but he doubted sleep would come again anytime soon.

15

THE BORDER

Emily found it too easy to keep pace with Death; she walked at his side for miles and hours without ever beginning to feel tired. She asked him why her body didn't wear out after all that happened to her. He told her this was the longest single distance he'd ever traversed on foot. She waited for an actual answer, but that was all she got.

Just get to the Nevada border unit, her mental loop repeated with each hill they rounded. *Pass on the mission, and it won't have been for nothing.*

As the gloomy wee hours wore into crispy morning, Death led her along no discernible road through the low mountains, consistently east. The longer they walked, the less Emily worried he would reach his destination before hers. In a way too convenient to be coincidence, the terrain never obstructed their path, and they met nothing and no one along the way. If anything alive at all existed around them, it did not want to be noticed.

Yeah, Emily wouldn't want to be noticed by the likes of her new self either.

In his silent, preoccupied way, Death did not object to her trailing after him like a string of stuck toilet paper. Emily objected to the silence though, so she talked to him. At him. Her life story seemed appropriate. She rambled about her childhood and about joining the LPI, the missions she completed, the people she lost. The less he reacted, the more she talked. It kept her mind from dwelling on her body's changes, kept the horror of it squashed deep.

Her working theory was that this hike could be some kind of test, some kind of purgatory. She was walking through a literal valley with Death himself, after all. Maybe everyone did this? He said she couldn't die, that she was a zombie, undead, but maybe he wasn't being completely honest? Her mind prevailed, intact. Maybe she was a *dead* zombie? And her soul—or whatever zombies lost with their reason—had returned to her? So her entire life's decisions weighed heavy on her, and she combed through every last one to ensure no overlooked detail remained to damn her in the afterlife. If Death existed, there had to be an afterlife, right?

For hours, she funneled her nervous energy into indulging the desperate need to simply remember her life aloud, every bit of it she could, and Death let her. In fact, every once in a while, right when she felt convinced he was tuning her out completely, he would make some quiet response. He offered little more than a "Hm" or "Ah" or "Indeed," but it did the trick, and she rambled on to the end of her story.

When she got to the part about dropping the radio, about mistaking the tossed cigarette for a firefly, she forced herself to admit her worst fears. Was it her fault the commune sent Snakeman to hide behind the boulders? Not knowing for sure made her brain want to break, but her eyes remained stupidly dry. She pushed past those parts, on to the bite. He wouldn't have come after her if she stayed to shoot his zombie head instead of running for her life.

Her *life*. She could almost laugh.

"And I saw you then, I think," she went on. "After it happened. When I fell. That was you, wasn't it? You were talking to someone. He had a horse."

"My horse."

She halted mid-step and looked up at Death. A *two*-word reply? With actual content? "What?"

He did not stop. "He took my horse."

"Who did?"

"Time."

"What?"

"Time took my horse."

"Wait." Emily shook out her head and caught up to him. "Time is a person?"

"Am I a person?"

"That was Time I saw? I saw Time?"

"Yes."

"Like Father Time?"

Death waved a hand as if to brush the question away, and his eyes remained ahead.

It occurred to Emily they might not be as alone as she assumed. They existed *in* time after all. She glanced behind her and then back to the side of Death's hood. In the daylight, its blackness looked unreal. She couldn't see any texture to the fabric, as if it were made of a seamless sheet of sculpted plastic or metal but with the soft flow and give of satin while somehow maintaining the weight of heavy wool. If she stared at it too long, she grew dizzy.

"Did you know I could see you guys?" she asked.

"I wasn't paying attention to you."

"But wasn't I—? Right after you just killed me?"

"Failed to," he corrected. His hand bones flexed at his side. "I had no more business with you."

So, that was it? Emily's chest tightened. "You were just going to leave me?"

"Yes." He sounded unaffected by her tone. "But Time was in my way."

"And he stopped you from leaving me?" *Thank God.* Or thank Time? She couldn't imagine what she might have done if she got up last night and found herself truly alone.

Death's pace quickened as if he realized he could walk faster. "He stopped me absolutely."

"What?" Emily half-jogged to keep up.

"He took my horse."

"What does that mean?" Was this about Emily or not?

"It means I don't have a horse."

She clenched her teeth. "I mean, why does that matter?"

"Wouldn't it matter to you if someone took your horse?"

"I don't have a horse."

"Neither do I."

She groaned. A second later, the sound repeated in the hills. Emily's instincts locked in, and she stopped, bracing for an attack before she realized. It was her own echo.

God...

She had to stand with her eyes closed for a few moments to work her brain back into the conversation. Was Death this frustrating with everyone he walked through purgatory? "Where did he take it?"

Death paused and looked back at her. "What?" He stood only a few yards ahead on the not-path.

Emily lifted her face to meet his gaze. In the daylight, the glowy centers of his eyes were almost invisible. It felt more like she was talking to a giant Halloween prop than anything supernatural. "Your horse."

"Ah." He turned and continued walking. "East."

Emily caught up but remained a step behind him. "That's vague."

"Yes. It is."

She sighed. It made her chest hurt. Was he even capable of a straight answer? She told herself his attitude must be all part of the purgatory test and took her time to choose her next words carefully. "So what did killing me have to do with Time stopping you and taking your horse?" Could it be about her mission? Time took his horse in the same direction *she* needed to go to do her last important task before the afterlife.

"I did not kill you."

"Whatever! You know what I mean."

"Yes."

"What?"

"I failed."

"What?"

"I touched you."

"Right, but that zombie..." She shook away the chilly memory of Death's touch crashing against the fire of the zombie's jaws, of the sound like an arrow flying.

"Yes."

"Look." She exhaled. "I don't get what me not dying has to do with Time."

"On this day, three years ago," said Death, "two hundred fifty-one thousand six hundred twenty-six humans fell under my touch."

"'Kay..." Emily let a long step stretch between them. The way he said it sounded not *proud* so much as *hungry*.

"Yesterday, before Time stopped me, I touched three hundred forty-six."

"Three hundred forty-six?" Emily moved back to his side. "Wait, in the whole world, three hundred forty-six?"

"Not you too." Death shook his head and glanced away.

"What?"

"He kept repeating it."

"Who, Time?"

"Yes."

"Well, it's a big difference!"

"I know."

"Okay, so, I get it. You failed. You failed a lot. What was I, like the last straw or something?"

"Something."

Emily clenched her teeth and pushed some stringy bits of hair behind her ear as she worked to sort out everything he didn't say. "Why does Time care?"

Death glanced at her, then looked ahead again. "I'm not sure. He usually just passes by."

Was that supposed to be a joke? Maybe he would give her clearer answers if she pretended to be amused. But if it wasn't a joke, she probably shouldn't risk laughing at him.

"Okay, so," she tried again after taking a moment to focus, "when you say Time stopped you absolutely, that's why you said no one else anywhere in the world is going to die."

"Yes." Death's voice lowered, something sorrowful in his tone.

"And this is possible how?"

"It's possible if I can't get to the where and when someone is meant to die."

Right. Okay. "And you can't get there without your horse."

"Not exactly."

"Then what?"

"Time and Space have bound me."

"Space is a person too?"

Death sighed. But Emily didn't care if she exasperated him as long as she could put it together. *Bound.* Not entirely metaphorically, either. Death was bound by Space and Time—just like everything else in the world. And stuck in the middle of nowhere—just like Emily. But that answered only the *how*. She still didn't get the *why*.

"So, wait," she said. "Then why does the horse matter?"

Death's entire frame went rigid, his hands clamping into fists. He twisted around, and his eyes flashed down at her. "Have you ever had a horse?"

"No," she answered on the edge of her breath, frozen.

"Then you wouldn't understand."

Emily made the decision then to give the questions a rest for a while.

There went her purgatory theory. She wasn't in Death's realm; he was in hers. Test for the afterlife? She could smack herself. Death might be traipsing through the desert because of her, but he wasn't there *for* her at all. The entire morning blabbing out her life story felt so stupid now.

The sun clawed its way over the hills, and their generous shadows burned into nothing. Emily finally did the thing she least wanted to: she examined bits of herself in the raw daylight. The skin on her hands was the characteristic cement color, her veins dark, gnarled ropes. She pulled back her sleeve to follow the pucey lines cobwebbing her arm. Her fingertips felt swollen like tiny water balloons, and the deep blue of pooled bruise blood unable to circulate showed through her well-chewed nails. She almost asked Death about it but suspected she wouldn't like his answer. Thank the universe she didn't have a mirror. She wasn't ready to confirm her face was as bad off as her hands. Probably worse.

Maybe approaching the Nevada border unit wasn't such a good idea after all. But no. She had to try. She'd start talking even before they saw her. She'd come at them quoting Shakespeare or something. They'd have to hesitate long enough for her to explain. She wasn't a zombie, not really. At least, not yet. Would she get worse? Death said the transformation was complete, but could she believe that? She could be getting worse with every step she took. She didn't know how it worked. She didn't want to think about it. Instead, she pondered how to explain the mission.

Goddammit, why couldn't she remember any Shakespeare?

It might have been her silence or occasional uncertain footing, but as the day wore on, Death began to pause every so often to peer back at her. Each time he did it, Emily met his stare, but she couldn't keep it up and would look down. Then he would start walking again. It was like he was waiting for something. Just what did he think was going on with her? That she'd start drooling and gnawing on her own arm at any moment? He knew something she didn't, she was sure of it. Finally, she couldn't take it anymore.

"Stop it!"

Death stiffened and paused on the road. "What?"

"You're giving me the creeps."

"I am?" He sounded incredulous, as if it should be the other way around.

"Just…please stop looking at me like that."

He cocked his head to the side like he had no idea what she meant. But then his eyes flickered, and he gave a small nod. "Ah."

He resumed walking and did not look at her again. She should have been glad.

She didn't let herself think about the vague, queasy disappointment that surfaced instead.

In the early afternoon, Emily spied a camp huddled between low hills. The equipment was generic, but the setup had LPI style all over it.

"That's it!"

Death stopped to follow her gaze.

"That's them! It's got to be." The arrangement appeared temporary, a row of quiet dust-brown tents hugging the base of the hill and a squared stack of supply cartons. Weird that everyone would be resting in the middle of the day. Or maybe not. Maybe it was safer? Though the lack of lookout was weirder. And no truck? No way they carried all those supplies on foot.

Someone's using the truck. Scouting while everyone naps. Of course.

"Hey!" Emily called down the hill. "Hello! Hi!" She turned up the perky and put as much Iamnotazombiepleasedon'tshootme into her voice as possible.

Come on, AP English. Bring on the Shakespeare.

Four score and seven years ago. No—shit.

Whatever. "Helloooo!" She started down the rocky slope but paused when Death continued to walk east along the crest of the hill.

What? So that was that?

Should she thank him? He didn't even say goodbye.

Fine. Whatever. *Focus.*

She turned her back and jogged down to the tents.

"Hey! I'm LPI, and I'm alone." Emily forced her tense cheeks into a smile she hoped didn't look freakish. "I'm from the Southland unit." *Forsooth, good morrow?* Better not.

Unzipping the flap of the nearest tent, she angled herself behind it before pulling it back. "Okay, let me explain. I know I look—" A gasp strangled her words.

Two zombies lay entangled on the sleeping mats. Or more like one and a quarter zombies. The second consisted of more holes and tattered clothing than flesh, drippy bones protruding from all its bendy places. God, how long was the dude being eaten alive by the other one before the change finally took over? It had to be dead now.

Both twitched.

Or not.

It rolled its head to look at her. It had no bottom jaw, but that didn't keep it from screaming.

Emily yanked the zipper closed. Stumbling, she collided with another tent. Sudden fingertips raked her back through the poly.

"Holy—!" She jumped and bolted to the supply pile. From the other side of it, she gaped at the tents. All but two of them sprang riotously alive, rocking and roaring, their spikes straining at the ground.

Emily's knees gave out, and she slumped against the supplies.

God fucking dammit.

Gone. Just like her team. Just like *her.*

Mission 12 would never happen. She knew that now.

Emily's chest heaved, and she gagged, but as sick as she should feel, nothing came of it.

Nothing. Because she wasn't alive. She was just as undead as what howled in those tents.

How did this happen? Some random attack? Did any of them get away? But why take their truck and leave the supplies? Emily didn't know, and she could never find them now.

The screams, the groaning. What did they want? Couldn't they tell she wasn't edible anymore? Were they that far gone? *Nothing.*

There was one thing Emily did know. What they were, that was not—was *never* going to be her.

She slid into a crouch and unsheathed her gun. *Before it's too late.* To conserve bullets, she rarely used the G18 on full automatic, but if there ever was a time, this was it. A flip of the switch, a strong squeeze, a good twist of the wrist, and it would make a mess of her head before she collapsed. There would be no brain left. Slamming her eyes shut, she bit down on the barrel.

A hard hand covered hers and tore the gun away. "Don't do that."

Emily gasped and fell against the cartons. Death stood over her, blotting out the sky. Shocked, she stared at him, cradling her hand. It felt like he zapped her with a tiny taser. "Why—why not?"

"It won't work."

"What the hell do you care?"

"Do you genuinely want another hole in your head?"

She pushed herself to her feet. "Seriously, what do you care?"

He fell silent for a moment as if he might actually give her an answer. But then he sighed and handed back the gun.

She snatched it from him. "I can't be a zombie."

"On the contrary. You can't not."

"You—"

"You *cannot* die, Emily."

"I won't be like them!" She flung a hand toward the tents.

"Then don't put holes in your head."

The gun suddenly felt too heavy. Is that how it worked? Their bodies were ravaged, their minds broken. Without her brain, would the shrieking monster emerge? "Will that do it?" Her voice shook. "You're sure?"

"No." He sighed. "I'm not. These are matters of undeath."

She didn't believe him. Why else would he stop her? The screaming behind them was hoarsening into low groans. Emily clenched her teeth, but the determined moment abandoned her. She couldn't shoot herself now, and she knew it. She smushed her gun into its holster.

"When did this happen?" she whispered as she watched the tents settle back into their slumbering row. Days ago? Weeks?

Death gave her no answer but a slight shrug.

Bullshit! "Aren't you supposed to know everything?"

"I know everything of death, but this—"

"Undeath. Right. Fine! I get it." What was she supposed to do now? The mission couldn't all be for nothing. "I don't even know where to look for other units."

"Why does that matter?" Death asked her quietly. "You tried to kill yourself, after all. You were done."

She wasn't sure if he meant just now or last night. Was it seriously only last night? "Maybe I wasn't really going to do it." It seemed unthinkable now. She'd been alive and pure. She wanted to tear her new undead body apart, but could she truly have shot herself last night?

"Oh, no," Death said with a decisive nod. "You were going to do it."

Emily rubbed at her eyes but stopped when she felt them sinking beneath her fists. "I…"

"You were scheduled."

She forced a thick swallow and pulled her gaze from the silent camp.

"Tell me." Death gestured for her to follow him around the supply pile. "Why do these affairs matter to you still? You were done with your life."

She let herself think on it as they hiked up the hill. Was she just supposed to say what's the point of making the world a better place to live if she couldn't live in it? Let the living help themselves, as Death said?

She *was* done, last night when she squeezed the trigger. If it hadn't stuck, she would be dead now. Actually really dead. She would have left the living to fight without her. Because dying pure was more important than finishing what she started.

How selfish.

"I don't know." She sighed. "I guess I just… There's got to be some reason I *didn't* die. Maybe I really was going to kill myself, but it would have been wrong."

"Death is never wrong if the time is right."

She shook her head. If the undead shouldn't care for the living, then she shouldn't be undead. She needed to be alive. She wasn't a zombie, not truly, not like any other zombie. But whatever undead thing she was couldn't be permanent. One way or another, she would *not* stay like this. If she couldn't die, then living again was the obvious other option. And there would be a way, wouldn't there? Like Rosa said, maybe it even already existed? Emily felt a surge of excitement and moved up to Death's side. "They always said they could find a cure for—for this." She gestured to her stupid whatever body. "They were still working on it, last I heard. The Island Initiative."

"East Potomac Park and Martha's Vineyard fell months ago."

"But Manhattan made it." A cure. Was it too much to hope for? A second chance. "Manhattan is where they spent all the effort, stockpiled all the weapons. They blew up the bridges and caved in the tunnels. Cleared out the zombies and fortified against the vampires. That's where my organization headquarters."

"I know."

"All those skyscrapers, all that storage, enough resources to last tens of thousands of people for years on end."

"There aren't tens of thousands of people there anymore."

"But the ones who are there are safe. We met someone just a few weeks ago when we came back through Nevada who relayed orders from headquarters. They said the safe zone was thriving."

"Did you believe that?"

Emily narrowed her eyes at the side of his hood. What was with that tone? Did he know better, or was he just a skeptic? If he knew, he'd say it, right? If all he knew about were Matters of Death, then maybe he didn't know *because* they thrived.

"I have to believe something. If there's any place that has a chance, it's Manhattan." Every assignment she took, every instruction she followed for the past year and a half came from LPI headquarters. It might be thousands of miles away, but it was all she had. "They're working on a cure. They found a way to stay safe. Keeping the vampires off the island was the reason they started our task forces. Our work to disband the communes is only a means to that end. I mean, I know a perfect solution's not just going to happen, but I can't believe this is the end of the world." The cure would see to that. "I just can't."

"Do you mean the apocalypse?"

Emily stumbled and caught herself against a boulder. She stared at Death, but he said nothing as he passed her by and led the way into a narrow ravine.

"Is this the apocalypse? Is that really a thing? The End Times?"

"It could be."

"You don't even know *that*? You didn't like, plan it?"

"I?" It almost sounded like a scoff. "This is not how I would plan it."

She wanted to ask. But then she really, really didn't.

"Is that why Time and Space bound you?" she asked instead.

He stopped so abruptly that Emily got a couple paces ahead. When she turned back to him, he had his electronic device thing out and tapped at it intently. Why did he keep checking it? Was he counting all the people scheduled to die who now weren't? Kind of masochistic, wasn't it?

"Look," she said after an impatient minute. "You can't do your, um, thing anymore. That's a pretty big deal, right?"

"I certainly think so." Tap. Tap.

"Because the...balance will be destroyed?"

"That is what I said."

She rolled her eyes at his tone but considered his predicament. No death might seem like a good thing, but Emily was not naïve enough to think the world would be better off without it. Was that what he meant by balance? Of course, Death needed to get back to business.

A ridiculous idea came to her then.

Help him.

This was a whole lot bigger than rescuing a commune's hostages. This was the whole world they were talking about.

And then, if he recovered his omnipresence, then he could go back to poofing around wherever he wanted. He could poof right to Manhattan. To the cure. Could she seriously hope? And headquarters —if they didn't know vampires had figured out how to use zombies as weapons, someone needed to tell them. If Emily helped Death, could he repay her by poofing her there, too? It was his fault she was like this, after all.

His *failure*. If she was scheduled, then what went wrong? Something *he* did?

"Is that why you stopped me just now? From shooting myself?"

Death's fingers stilled, and he lifted his face. He stared at her as if waiting for her to explain the random question, but then he spoke softly. "No."

It was funny. The way his bony hand felt on hers a few minutes ago. So different from his touch last night. That pierced her flesh like an icicle, but this time, a jolt ignited it. Like he shuffled over some serious carpet before he touched her. *Touched her*… She shuddered.

"I don't even know if it would have worked." She looked down at her G18. "Last night, the trigger. It stuck." Or did her *hand* stick? She hadn't tried firing the gun since then.

Death pocketed his device and started walking again. Emily followed right after him.

"But I guess last night it would have worked; otherwise you wouldn't have shown up, right?"

"Right."

"It's weird that it stuck, though." Super weird. "It's never done that before." How was it even possible?

"Indeed."

Emily looked up at him, and he turned his head with a jerk to avoid her gaze. Okay, he was definitely keeping something from her. Did he know why her trigger stuck? He quickened his pace, and she had to jog again to keep up.

Just *how* had he failed? And how could she help him? What did Time want? The apocalypse or not? To keep people out of the afterlife? Why would he want that? What even was it? She needed more information before she could attempt to Criminal Intent a cosmic force of nature.

"So what happens after we die?" she asked after giving the awkwardness a few minutes to dissipate.

"We do not die."

"I mean humans. What happens after?"

"After I reap their life?"

"Yes."

"I turn it over to the beyond and then move on."

"No, not *you*. What happens to them?"

"Their bodies?"

Was he being deliberately obtuse just to mess with her? Instead of taking the bait and snapping, she drew out her words. "What happens to the life that you turn over?"

"It goes beyond."

"Beyond what?"

"Itself. Beyond life."

"What *is* beyond?"

He sighed. "You want to know if there is an afterlife such as humans have imagined beyond life." He spoke as if he heard the question too many times to be tired of it anymore.

"No. I want to know what *is* beyond. I don't care about speculations matching ideals. I want a clear answer."

"I'm sure you do." He sounded amused.

She bit the insides of her cheeks. "And you're not going to give it to me."

"There is no *it* to give, Emily. There is no is."

"So you're saying there's nothing beyond. The life just ends."

"No. That's not what I'm saying at all."

"Then what happens to it?"

"It goes beyond."

"I swear to god!"

Death stopped walking and blocked her path. She folded her arms and looked up at him, waited. He leaned over and poked the tip of her nose with one of his bone fingers. "There is only one way to find out, Emily."

She jerked back. That jolt again. Her face seriously tingled. In the dry air, was his cloak full of static electricity?

He stared down at her. Too close. "And you'll never know now, will you?"

Her body itched to back away, but she fought it. "I will if you tell me."

He remained still for a moment, but then slipped from her and started walking again.

"But you don't know that either." She stared after him. Did Time know? And want to stop it? "So you've never been there."

"Am I beyond?" Death flicked a rhetorical hand to the horizon.

Emily's feet moved to catch up. "You're beyond life. You're Death."

"I am the *transition* between life and the beyond."

"Well, not anymore you're not." She kicked a rock. This plan was going nowhere.

Death stopped. All humor in his tone expired. "I am." His hand snapped up as if reaching for something out of habit, but clenched thin air. "I am still the transition. If a human scheduled to die at this moment stood before me, reap her I would."

"Right…" The where and when were the problem.

"The balance is already greatly skewed."

"So what do we do about it?" Emphasis on the "we." She lifted a hopeful eyebrow, but his gaze remained on the clear sky.

"I must summon my brethren."

"Right."

"They will not stand for my binding." He started walking again. "Together we will right this."

Right. Okay. This might be something she could work with. "And then what?"

"The balance will be restored."

And poofing. Poofing would be restored. She chewed at the edge of a fingernail as she built a mental flowchart out of his words. "And to summon them, you need space, right? Or did you mean Space?"

"A wasted place." He eyed the tall walls of the ravine. "I can make them come to me if enough emptiness surrounds me."

The Great Basin surrounded them. How much more wasted could you get? She followed his gaze to the piled rocks. "Why not go up to the top of one of the hills?"

"Not high enough." He flicked a pebble off a boulder they passed. "There is too much life here."

"What, like bugs and plants?" So he was seeking someplace completely flat and dead. Or at least less-alive than here. Emily pulled her fingernail out of her mouth with a gasp. "I know a place!"

Death stopped and looked at her.

"Little Salt Basin."

"I have never been there."

A place so wasted no one had ever even died there? "Sounds good, right?" Shit, where was it? "I think we're pretty close, actually." A few hours at most. Her team had passed it on their way back into California. Its vastness below the cliffs they traversed had struck her, and she giggled over its ironic name at the time. "If I had a map, I could show you."

"But you don't."

She scratched her head and scraped her brain. "It was… It was…" Yes! She remembered the name of the road that ran above it. And the highway it crossed not much farther on. People definitely died at that intersection; he would know where that was. "If I tell you, will you do something for me?"

"For you?" Somehow his eye sockets looked wider than before. "Do what?"

"Get me to Manhattan?"

Death pressed his hands together and studied her for a quiet minute. "How do you expect me to do that?"

She bit her tongue to keep the word "poof" from escaping. "Are you saying you can't?" *Shit.* Even when he wasn't bound by Space and Time, she would still be.

"No." He tapped his fingertips and tilted his face to the sky. Clear and blue in every direction. "There is one way."

"Yes! Okay! Come on, then. Deal?" She started to extend her hand for a shake, but then stopped herself. She didn't need any more shocks today. Maneuvering the gesture, she instead tucked a piece of hair behind her ear. "You'll summon your bros, they'll fix you, and you'll be back in business before you know it."

"Yes…"

"Yes?"

"Yes."

Perfect! Everyone would win.

16

JADE

"Why are you turning around?" Scott flipped back the pink washcloth keeping the sun out of his eyes. A crick seized his neck, and he grimaced.

"We're going back to 95," Carol said.

"What?" Scott pushed up his seat. "Are you scrambled?"

"Look behind the car."

He twisted to peer through the back windshield. A long-dead traffic jam clotted the highway, but the desert on either side of it stretched flat and open.

"Carol, stop. Just go around it."

"No. I am rerouting our map."

The sedan wasn't exactly made for off-roading, but better to get it a little beat up on the shoulder than lose an entire half day's driving.

"I'm telling you, it's fine. Look!" Scott stuck his arm out the window and waved it in circles. "Wiiiiiide open spaces! We can drii-iive arouuuund it."

"It is not safe."

"Carol, stop the car."

"No, Scott."

"I am ordering you to stop the car."

"My mission objective does not require me to obey your orders."

Well, there was one way he could get her to obey. "Carol: Ro—"

She released the wheel and slapped a hand across his mouth. "Look at the fuel gauge, Scott."

"Mmff!" He shoved her hand away. "That hurt."

"Look at it."

He did. It was low. Too low.

"Aren't the panels working?" He tilted his head back as if he could see through the roof to them.

"Not enough."

"And you're driving *away* from the cars? We could siphon—"

"The probability that those vehicles are empty of occupants is zero. The probability that their occupants are not also lurking between the cars is zero. As my radar and infrared are both nonoperational, I cannot detect them nor determine how many miles the stalled vehicles persist. You wish to drive past them, but if our fuel runs out before we are well beyond their end, your safety will be compromised."

Scott rubbed at his bruised lips. So she was right, but… "You're talking hours of backtracking."

"This is the safest course."

"And then we go north? Cause going Vegaswards is kind of the opposite of a safe course."

"We will test the vehicles we passed earlier for fuel."

Did they pass vehicles? Scott tried and failed to sleep through most of the morning. Their five-gallon fuel can was full when they left that janky town at dawn, but now it slid around in the back seat. Their plan to avoid the often-clogged interstates by sticking to side roads got a lot more difficult when suburbia turned into desert.

Though their journey began in Pasadena days ago, getting out of the city itself and onto an open road took a lot longer than expected. So far, they'd barely even poked into Nevada. It would be weeks before they made it to New York at this rate. Carol had originally estimated a five-day drive but prepared for possible delays. Before they left the Curisa complex, she packed water bottles, purifying tablets, and ration bars to last Scott a month. He'd go crazy from having to eat the mealy things long before he starved.

One thing he missed more than anything since the world ended was sushi. Cold, moist, succulent sushi. And he wouldn't be finding any of that in abandoned kitchen cupboards. The first thing he would do when they got into the New York fortress was scrounge up a huge pile of sushi. They must still have sushi. Rice existed everywhere, and the city was coastal. They lived the high life out there. *Someone* must know how to sushi slice a fish.

The second thing he would do was find his sister, of course. She'd want Carol back, and surely somewhere inside her twisted heart she'd be happy to know Scott was still alive.

The third thing... The third thing would be to find Jade. Oh, Jade was definitely going to get found. Yes, Jade would not be able to avoid the...find-getting of Scott.

He still didn't know what he'd do when he found her; he'd been turning it over in his mind for months and months since he last saw her at Curisa. Almost a year now. When he imagined their reunion, sometimes he walked right up to her and slapped her in the face. But he knew he wouldn't really do that. In other versions of the fantasy, he just stared at her, his eyes dark and full of meaning, and she would break down into tears of shame and remorse. Other times it played out like one of those slow-motion romance movie montages where the music soars and they run across a field into each other's arms. Scott didn't know where to find a field in lower Manhattan, but it was just the end embrace that mattered. And then he'd pull away from her and his gaze would go cold, and he'd tell her it was over. Jade would beg him to change his mind and then...well, he might. Maybe. Maybe not. He would see how it went.

They spent their last months together at Curisa Robotics, the plant where his sister worked. It was the safest place he could think to go with Jade when emergency evacuation hit their neighborhood. The Curisa guys let them in along with a few dozen other employees' families before the complex went on lockdown. Curisa kept them all safe and fed while the engineers did their work. Zombie-killing robots were on top order. Scott was one of the lucky ones.

Reconnecting with Nick had been…interesting. She, Scott, and their brother were all close in age, but any emotional closeness disappeared before their teenage years. She was into numbers and machines, and Scott was into culture and history, and Eli was into humanitarian charity stuff, and that was that.

At Curisa, Nick spent all her time working. Scott wasn't sure she even slept. He never saw her unless he hovered in her lab while she tinkered with circuit boards and robot limbs.

The first time he saw Carol, Nick was wrists deep into her chassis. She bent over, working on something with the tiniest wrench he'd ever seen.

"Making yourself a friend?" he asked.

"I didn't make her," Nick said. "She's an LS model." She gestured to another deactivated humanoid robot slumped against the wall. "I am improving her. Vastly, vastly improving her. She's going to be like nothing you've seen before."

"Obviously." Scott found a toolbox to sit on. "Considering I don't exactly spend my time mingling with robots. Oh, excuse me, *androids*."

"Gynoid." Nick gave Carol's forehead a loving stroke, then glanced at Scott. "What? What is that face?"

"Pedantic much?"

Nick grinned as if it were a compliment and adjusted the claw clip thing holding the sloppy pile of hair on top of her head. It was the same sandy color as Scott's, but much longer. She never let it out of that clip, though, so he had no idea why she didn't go ahead and cut it short. She'd look better if she did and wore it loose. When they were young, people thought they were twins, but Scott got the better end of that deal. Nick was too boyish to be pretty.

"Was afraid you had a problem with 'gynoid,'" she said.

Scott made another face. "Well, it does sound kind of dirty. Gynoid, vagina. You know."

Nick spun around and thrust her tiny wrench at him. "Vaginas are not dirty!" She said it so fast, it was as if she were waiting for the chance. "You've made them dirty in your mind by sexualizing nature."

Scott jerked back. "Me?"

"You, the Patriarchy."

Scott rolled his eyes. He learned long ago not to take on Nick in an activism argument. He watched her close Carol's stomach panel and then heave her up by the shoulders.

"Need help?" he asked.

"You," Nick grunted, "do not get to touch her."

Fine. Scott stayed on his toolbox while Nick shimmied Carol onto her side. The svelte silver arm fell over the amply built chest, and with her human-replica face, she looked pretty much like a picture off an AI kink website. Nick's exterior modifications were obvious when Scott compared Carol to the other LS in the room.

"If you hate the Patriarchy so much," he said, "why'd you make your gynoid so sssexay?"

"I make what I want. For me." Smiling, she brushed her knuckles along Carol's cheek.

Scott's brain retorted, *Didn't know you were into that sort of thing,* but honestly, wasn't she? Not in a pervy website way, of course, but her robots came before human relationships any day.

Gynoid. Scott didn't care about Nick's political agenda, but it bugged him when she was pedantic purposefully to seem smarter than him. "Android" wasn't like saying "man" instead of "woman." It was like saying "human." Right? He was pretty sure.

"Besides," he thought aloud, "it depends on the vagina."

"What are you even talking about?" Nick muttered without looking up from her work on Carol's back.

"Some are dirty," he said.

"You would know." She returned Carol to her back and yelled over her shoulder. "Midori!"

"No thanks." Scott smirked. "I'm more of an amaretto man."

A door at the lab's rear swung on its hinges, and some chick popped her head through. "What's this about dirty vaginas?" Her soft, perky voice held a hopeful note.

"Are my batteries charged yet?" Nick asked without lifting her eyes from Carol.

The Midori chick had one of those choppy haircuts, longer in the front and bowled in the back with a line of bangs cutting across her forehead. Blue-black, but an inch of pale roots showed. Scott stopped slouching on the toolbox as he took her in. Her heart-shaped face would be kind of cute if she washed off all the thick black eyeliner. Though it did make her blue eyes really vibrant.

"Almost?" Midori shuffled on her feet. "I mean, I'll check." Her gaze lingered on the back of Nick's head as if she would ask her something. She didn't seem to notice Scott there at all. After a minute, she smiled to herself and ducked back into the doorway. Cute smile.

"And give me back my wire nuts," Nick yelled after her. "The little ones. I know you took them."

"Sorry," Midori called from the other room.

Nick flipped down her goggles and leaned into Carol with what Scott guessed was a soldering iron or something. He scratched the back of his head. "Your assistant seems…" Awkward, nervous, weird, kind of pretty, mysterious? "Nice."

"Midori's in weapons R&D."

Hot. "Oh, cool."

"She's not my assistant."

"Okay."

"I'm not her boss. I'm not anyone's boss."

"Funny, could never tell from how you act." He smirked and rocked on his seat, but then felt something crack under him. He jumped up and inspected the toolbox. The plastic was bent, and Nick was glowering at him.

"You know," she said, "there are like a hundred other places you could go be annoying. Where's your little girlfriend?"

"She's not that little."

"I could put her in my pocket."

Scott pushed on the plastic, tried to pop it back into shape. He didn't know where Jade was. Making friends, drinking beer with the guys, avoiding him.

"I dunno." He gave up on the box. At least the drawer still worked. "Things are weird."

"Ohhhh."

"What ohhhh?"

"What do you want?"

He wandered over to her work area. "Can't I just hang out with my sister who I haven't seen in years?"

She snorted. "What do you want?"

Scott sighed and leaned against Carol's table. "I don't know what to do with her."

"*Do* with her?"

"Ever since we got here, she's been weird, touchy."

"Maybe because you're avoiding her."

Jade was avoiding *him*. Definitely more than he avoided her, anyway. He shrugged and fiddled with some tiny screws on the edge of the table. "She's been drinking a lot." He didn't like her when she drank. She got sloppy and inconsiderate. She left the top off the toothpaste and wet towels on the floor. Her hair got greasy. Zombies swarming over half the world didn't mean she got a free pass to abandon basic hygiene. Curisa still had running water and everything.

"She didn't want to come here," he said when Nick didn't reply. "She wanted me to take her to her mom's in San Diego." They never would have made it. It was a war zone out there. But she treated Scott like it was his fault. Like he was the only thing keeping her from going.

"You're too old for her."

"I'm only twenty-two."

"And she's what? Twelve?"

"Almost twenty."

"You're a whole college education older than her."

"She's graduating early." *Was.*

Scott met Jade on campus during her second year. While he was still in undergrad, dating an underclassman felt perfectly acceptable. But once he started his master's, their domestic situation deteriorated. Maybe they cohabited too soon, but living together made more financial sense than Jade keeping her dorm. Their studio apartment wasn't much bigger than a dorm, though, and tension compiled in the small space. Tension that only got worse at Curisa.

He shook his head. "I don't know what to do with her."

"Do you even realize how much of an asshole you sound like right now?"

"Now you're on her side?"

"I don't get how anyone would want to date you."

"Thanks."

Nick pushed up her goggles and looked at him finally. "Sorry, not sorry, but it runs in the family. Look at Dad." She gave him a sympathetic grimace. "I'm just as bad. We aren't good mates."

Scott wasn't going to argue with that. He flipped the teeny screws onto their ends, lined them against the table's rim. "But I can't break up with her." He sighed. "I brought her all the way here." And now neither of them could leave until New York sent out the airships.

"Sure you can."

"I don't want to."

Nick pointed her soldering iron at him. "You're doing that coward guy thing."

"No, I'm not."

None of his past girlfriends were this serious. He let himself be *vulnerable* with Jade, and that was a huge deal. To him, anyway. Most people were about using and losing; that was a fact. Shouldn't Nick know that? Even their mom had taken Eli with her when she left a decade ago, but he and Nick didn't warrant the effort. Scott took a leap with Jade, let her in on parts of himself he never shared with anyone. Jade wasn't allowed to push him away now.

He *loved* her.

Well, he loved the Jade he knew she could be. "I just...don't want to."

"So then don't." Nick's attention returned to Carol.

"Thanks."

"Anytime."

Scott pushed away from the table. He shouldn't have said anything.

Nick and her wall of robots wasn't going to get it. Her last serious relationship was with her AI software designer who was as obsessed with machines as Nick. Scott was pretty sure it involved more geeking out together than any actual romance. The only way Scott even heard about her was when Nick gushed over the AI. He wondered if she even knew how to mourn.

He made his way out the lab door but almost walked into some guy coming in.

The guy stepped back. "Sorry, bro. Didn't see you there." He had shoulders like two soccer balls and a head like Mr. Clean's, a few shades darker.

Scott nodded and moved to go around him, but the guy held out a hand. "Colin."

Well, isn't that just super. Scott shook it as firmly as he could, but Colin's grip still hurt.

"Call me Nick's brother," Scott said. "Everyone else does."

Colin glanced into the room, but Nick ignored them both.

"Scott," Scott acquiesced.

Colin grinned. Good teeth too. Of course. "Any bro of Nick's is a bro of mine."

Joy.

"Sup, Nicki?" he called into the lab.

"At least three more hours," she said. How did she allow this guy to live calling her Nicki?

"Right." Colin shot her finger guns. "I will...come back later then."

Scott made it into the hall, but Colin caught up before he could escape.

"Want a beer?" he asked. "We still have real beer. Only the best at Curisa."

"No thanks." What Scott wanted was to find a book with dragons on the cover and a quiet corner, or anything to get his mind off real people. But Colin waved him into a left turn leading to a break room. He got himself a beer from the fridge, glancing at Scott over his shoulder. "You sure? Soda?"

"Mountain Dew?" Scott asked.

Colin laughed and tossed him a bottle of Cherry Coke.

How long would Scott have to stand there making inane small talk before he could leave? "What do you do here?" he asked to fill the space. "Security?"

Slurping a mouthful of beer, Colin shook his shiny, bald head. "I transferred from Frisco to work with Midori. Calibration and stuff. But since lockdown, been focusing on keeping the systems operational. And keeping the hackers off our servers, of course. Call me Jack of all trades."

Of course. Scott took a sip of Coke to avoid having to answer.

"Couldn't help overhearing," Colin said between swigs. "About your girlfriend. That Jade chick, right? Sorry, man. Bitches."

"She's not a bitch."

"Course not." He grinned at Scott again with his perfect teeth.

"She's not."

"Got it. Sorry, bro." Colin shook his head all sympathetic-like. "My girl took off the second everything went down. I know how you feel."

"I doubt that." Scott kept his eyes on his bottle.

"What about your sister? She with anyone?"

His head shot up, and he almost choked on Coke. "*My* sister? Have you even met her?"

"She's a pretty cool chick."

"You're, uh, not her type."

Colin chuckled. "I get it. Gotta be the protective brother."

This time Scott did choke. Sticky cherry fizz burned up the back of his nose. He coughed and shook his head. "You can try." In fact, he kind of hoped he would. "Call her Nicki more. She loves that." Seeing Colin get squished under Nick's disinterest would be pretty amusing. The last thing Nick wanted were muscly bros who used the word "Frisco."

In the weeks after that day, once Carol became operational and the combat testing resumed, Scott saw even less of his sister. And Jade... Things with Jade got worse and worse.

Scott set his brain against thinking any more about Jade, pulled himself back to the present, and scowled at the desert beyond the car's window. He'd spent almost a year plotting what he would say when he caught up to Jade in New York, and if he hadn't figured it out yet, he wasn't going to know until he saw her. It would come to him. And it would be brilliant and heartbreaking, and then he would eat more sushi and…

Yeah.

Bitches.

17

BRETHREN

Over the course of the afternoon, Emily and Death came across several open spaces, and she worried one would suit his needs enough to negate their deal. But he kept on leading her through the winding rock alleys toward the destination she suggested.

When he halted abruptly at the summit of an inclined path, she walked right into his back. It felt like walking into a tree. She stumbled, but he ignored her.

"Oof. What is it?" The echo of the texture of his cloak's fabric lingered against her face. It was softer than she expected.

"What I need."

She rubbed her cheek and leaned to look around him over the cliff. "Oh, yup. That's it." Little Salt Basin. Even vaster than she remembered.

"It will do," said Death.

Together, they surveyed the sun-swept plain. Tumbleweeds far outnumbered the few low boulders scattered across its brown flatness. Holes pockmarked the ground, but they were ancient. Half a mile from where they stood, the craggy hills extended in a crescent up to the plain's north end. To the south, the horizon flatlined. The late afternoon sun at their backs stretched their shadows far over the valley. Emily noticed Death's settled more than a shade darker than her own.

He pointed a skeletal finger into the middle distance. "I must go farther." He glanced aside at her, hesitated. "You should stay here."

She looked up at him and nodded, but for the first time wondered what kind of "brethren" Death could possibly have. "Are they like other versions of death?"

"Other…?" He shook his head. "No."

"Oh. So…"

"You should stay here."

She nodded again, and he moved to the edge.

"Wait." She squinted at the northern cliff. "The road runs along up there."

"It doesn't matter."

"What if someone comes?"

"I imagine they will be extremely confused."

She rolled her eyes and looked to the opposite direction. "Wait—"

"Just vultures," said Death with a sigh. He was right. Four of them circled something out over the clear horizon.

Emily rushed to the edge. "Is someone dying out there?"

"I'm not there, am I?"

She frowned up at him. It couldn't be an animal, could it? The whole point of coming to the Basin was nothing lived there.

"It's fine," he said. "Stay here."

"Okay, okay." She pointed to the vultures. "But what are they circling?"

"I don't care." He jabbed a finger at the ground under her feet, and then he turned away. Without another word, he glided like a shadow down the rocks and proceeded out across the plain.

Emily waited where she stood. For about a minute. They had a deal, but now that her part was up, she wasn't going to let him get far from her. Even though she kept as quiet as possible when she climbed after him, she was sure he would turn around and tell her to stop. But he made no sign he noticed.

She didn't have to follow him far. A couple hundred yards past the hill shadows, the open space gaped stark and lifeless on all sides. Two more vultures joined the sky circle in the distance. Emily crouched behind a boulder as she watched Death move to a spot beyond a clump of snaggly tumbleweeds. He faced the south.

Emily stayed low and crept into the dead bushes. Linked like the arms of terrified survivors, their twigs hid her while offering a clear view of Death's every action through the tangles.

He stared at the birds, and then he took out his screen thing and tapped at it. After another minute or so, he drooped and put it away. She could hear the air rustle through him as if the cloak itself sighed. Super black, super soft cloak. Emily rubbed at her cheek again.

Death lifted his arms to the south. For the first time, she could see the complete fullness of his sleeves, hanging almost to his sides, but with so many folds of fabric, his arms remained concealed. The cloth fluttered, and a moment later, a breeze caressed Emily as a roll of thunder broke the lifeless silence. She waited for it to stop, but instead, it crescendoed, drumlike, heralding dark clouds. They boiled up too fast for her to see where they came from, piling into a bulbous tower before spilling across the sky toward Death in crashing waves. Lightning-speckled their crests, like phosphorescence in the foam. In all directions from where Death stood, the day became a dark one, blotting the vultures from view. The wind sharpened, shrieked up the Basin, and the tumbleweeds around Emily chattered and groaned.

Out of the flashing clouds, three figures emerged. At first, they subsisted of mere colors, one white, one black, one red, distorted blurs galloping over the air, their ephemeral forms only hinting at shapes. The shapes of horses and riders. The sounds of world's end clamored about them, hooves beating an iron sky, but as they descended through the storm, their bodies solidified. When they landed upon the barren waste before Death, their swirling shapes took on distinct proportions and definition, settling into the time and space of the moment.

Death lowered his arms and folded them across his chest. He

looked between the three of them. The wind carried his voice to where Emily hid. He said, "Hi."

"Greetings."

"Hello, hello!"

"Brother."

Emily's dismayed hands pressed her face so tightly she was hurting herself. But she couldn't look away.

Horsemen.

Horsewomen? The first two looked and sounded like women. None of their voices were as deep as Death's, but they resonated with that same cavernous quality, like they belonged to much larger beings.

Is the apocalypse really a thing? Emily could kick herself. Who else would *Death's* brethren be?

The three riders all wore comfortable smiles even as their horses pawed the ground and sniffed the air as if unsure what to do with their newfound solidness. The leftmost one on the white horse was swathed in a gown the color of cobwebs. She held a silver crossbow aloft, aimed at nothing. The middle rider was sausage-stuffed into a black leather bodysuit, and her black horse's gnarled knees quivered under her weight. Her empty hands stroked the creature's sparse mane. The man on the third horse contemplated the length of an upraised sword. Its surface, laser-like and liquid at once, glistened red and reflected the robotic body armor covering him and his sorrel stallion.

If Emily hadn't been so close, had seen them in any other circumstance, she might have mistaken them for human, or maybe vampires with their white skin and creepily fluid movements. But their eyes gave them away. No whites or pupils, just shadowy globes and light within burning the same color as their horses.

The wind calmed, and the cataclysmic noise stilled, but the dark cover remained above. Death took a step forward.

"Where is your horse?" the red rider asked. Armor, sword, what did that make him? War? Emily needled her brain. Who were the other two Horsemen supposed to be? War leaned to the side in his silicone saddle to look Death over, as if he expected to spot his horse hidden behind his robes.

"I require your aid," said Death.

"Ah, now I understand," the woman in white said with a sniff of her high, beaky nose. She gave her own horse an affectionate rub between its gnarled ears. "That's how he did it."

The woman in the middle jiggled with laughter and pressed her dimpled hands together in delight. "Oh no."

"Oh. Yes." Death unfolded his arms.

"What are you doing without it?" War asked.

"Walking."

The three of them glanced at one another and then shook their heads in obvious sympathy.

As Emily watched the figures before her, she better understood the glare Death gave her that morning when she asked why his horse mattered. They moved with ease, at-one with their steeds. Death looked stiff and adrift, as if the wind might claw him by the cloak and drag him away.

Could that actually happen? Apparently anything was possible.

Emily tried to tell herself that if she walked through the desert with Death himself for almost twenty-four hours, what she beheld now had to be real. The four of them, really real. She bit down on her hand to keep from laughing. Her eyes burned, but no tears came. The creaking tumbleweeds muffled her dry sob.

"You must help me reach Time," said Death. "My work is behind schedule, and I must restore life's balance. Before it's too late for the world."

The three riders glanced to one another again and then shook their heads, this time with no sympathy at all.

"Brother." The white rider moved her seriously sick-looking horse forward. "This is for the best." She put a hand against her waspy waist and regarded the other two with a regal air. They nodded. She looked back down at Death. "The world has changed."

Death snatched the reins of her pearly bridle. "What are you saying?"

Her horse's bloodshot eyes rolled, and it made a soft groaning sound.

"I know it's difficult to accept," she said. "No one foresaw this."

A rivulet of drool spilled from the horse's scaly lips. Death stepped back to evade it. His gaze followed its progress to the cracked earth below, then he pressed the horse's mouth closed with a bony fingertip.

Everyone stared at him.

"I see the boils are gone," he said as he studied the horse's scabby neck.

Emily couldn't tell if that was a good thing. Death sounded uneasy. As far as she could see, the horse looked too diseased to be alive. Hell, it looked undead. Plagued. *Pestilence!* That's who the lady in white was.

She smiled. "The fever and leprosy too." Her protuberant eyes glowed brighter with pride. "But it appears similar enough, doesn't it? I used to carry around thousands of arrows, but now I need only a few."

Death's gaze lifted to the quiver on her back and the two arrows lounging within. She twitched her crossbow with a smirk on her flaking lips, then laid it to rest in the lap of her gauzy gown.

Death took an abrupt step back, turning to the others. "You cannot mean you are on Time's side in this."

"We're not," said the woman in black. Process of elimination made her starvation or something. *Famine.* She looked the opposite of hungry on her emaciated horse. "He's on ours."

War ran a thick finger down his sword. "Whoever thought it all needed to end with Death in the first place had the wrong idea." He rubbed his fingers together and sniffed them.

"But that is our way!" Death pointed at them one after the next. "You lead them to each other in turn and then lead them to me."

Famine's glossy black hair rippled over her bare shoulders when she shook her head. "Not anymore."

"And why should we?" Pestilence asked. "Undeath has proven itself superior."

Death stood before the black horse. "Even you?" he asked Famine. "The undead don't produce food any more than the dead do. This can't be any better for you than it is for me. You must help me."

She pressed her hands against the cleavage spilling over her leather bustier. "I? Are you blind?"

Her horse trembled and wheezed on Death.

"Behold, brother." Her smirk was nothing short of sumptuous. "The new, modern me. My new hearty helping of starvation. Surely you see it? It *is* what afflicts them. Food surrounds them, but they cannot eat it. Once changed, they only crave to devour mortals. The more they fall victim to our sister's plague, the fewer and fewer of them there are to eat. But they don't die. They're still mine. They still hunger. Oh, how they hunger! The *undead* keep going and going. Craving and craving. I never have to give them to you, and I don't want to. Sustainability, at last. It's my turn to keep my victims."

"But I never keep my victims."

"Well things are different now," Pestilence interrupted. "Improved."

War did not even look up as he spoke. "You're just sore because you can't go on without life, but we can."

Death turned to him. "How will you be satisfied with the mindless battles of the droning undead? What of your glory? All humans do now is hide and desperately cower to stay alive. Peace is precious to them. There are no more grand strategies or fantastic weapons."

"Oh, I wouldn't say that." War pulled his eyes from his dripping sword to look down at Death. "I am wherever strife and destruction dwell." His lips twisted in satisfaction. "And I like this new cycle, this control I keep over it. The undead have their skirmishes. With humans and among their own ranks. And when the humans lose those battles, they become soldiers for the opposite side. I like it quite a lot."

"And my double plague," said Pestilence, her pointy chin tilted high, "has achieved perfection."

Death shook his head. His hands lifted, then fell again.

"My children," she continued, "they spread it faster than fire, cleaner than any of the old carriers. The humans themselves have become the vermin, and it never fails to catch."

"Do you not see the significance in that?" Death twisted to her. "Viruses, bacteria, they are natural. This is not."

"You are being simple," Famine practically chirped. "None of this is new. I love this backward hunger. There have always been undead, and they have always been favorites of mine."

"And it has always failed you in the past," snapped Death.

"Not anymore," she sing-songed. Batting her luscious eyelashes, she ran voluptuous fingers over her horse's raised vertebrae. "Before, it was a small, secluded experiment. But now since the plagues have combined and claimed the industrial world, the balance has tipped so far in my favor that even my scales broke." She threw up her empty hands, wiggling her fingers in the air.

Death's hood turned, and Emily followed his gaze to two chrome units hanging from a clip on the black saddle. They reminded her of her grandmother's old round, flat kitchen scales. Connected to each other by a coiled wire, their LCD displays flashed and cycled through gibberish symbols faster than Emily's eye could follow.

War brought his horse forward, its armor chinking as he moved around Death. "Accept it, brother. When we told Time our projected tolls for the near future, he more than understood what we could accomplish—"

"*You* told Time?" Death took a step back.

"With you out of the way, that is," Famine added.

"It didn't take much convincing," said Pestilence.

"What tolls?" Death demanded. "What did you tell Time you would do without me?"

A thin smile twitched Pestilence's hollow cheeks. "Only he can tell what is best."

"What does he want? Where is he headed? What is he after?"

She shook her head. "Accept it, brother."

Death turned to the side. Emily could see his skull within the hood again, but he seemed to see nothing at all.

"We do not need you." Famine flashed a robust smile.

"Our victims are ours to keep," continued her sister. "You turn yours over to what is beyond if you like, but we will no longer turn ours over to you."

"Meanwhile, we're amassing legions," War said. "You ought to try it."

"How can I?" Death's voice rang hollow. He looked at none of them. "Bound by the fabric, without my horse."

They allowed him a moment of silence. A brief moment. Then their expressions hardened.

"He took your scythe, too," Famine noticed.

"At least it's not broken." Death shot a look at her scales.

"I keep them as souvenirs." She gave them a pat. They flashed, making an injured beeping sound as they spewed nonsense symbols.

"I will get mine back." Death lifted his head. The pale green fire in his eyes blazed at the three of them. "This will not last for you."

She laughed, and the black clouds above churned, rumbled in applause. Death threw up a hand as if to silence them, and they ignited. A jagged streak of lightning tore free to dagger the ground.

Emily jumped. The tumbleweeds around her jerked in the wind. One broke loose and fled.

"What's that?" Pestilence twisted to look over. Famine stopped giggling.

Emily flattened herself into the bushes, pressed her hands over her head. She could see nothing but brambles.

Hoof steps moved near, but War's voice sounded no closer when he spoke. "What did you honestly want for our house, brother? True apocalypse would mean the end of us all."

A horse wheezed less than a foot from Emily.

"You have let our sisters convince you," Death murmured. "This isn't your battle. This is their starvation plague."

An excited squeal from one of the women drowned any retort, and Emily found herself discovered.

"Ooh," Pestilence cooed from the edge of the bushes. "It's one of my children. Oh, hello, my darling. Oh, come to me."

Famine's giggles sounded just as close.

What were the chances of them going away if Emily just didn't move? But something compelling in their resonant voices tugged at her. Her hands disobeyed her rationality, sliding down to push herself from the sand. Her head poked up through the bushes. The two women smiled down upon her. This close, they almost looked beautiful. And big. Not as big as Death, but they made her feel tiny.

Emily peeked at Death from the corner of her eye. He avoided her gaze.

Pestilence extended her hands to Emily. "Come to me, dear one," she crooned. "What a pretty little one. Oh, you're fresh, aren't you? Come to me."

Dreading to disobey, Emily shuffled through the bushes to the horse's side, her eyes fixed on the white glow in the woman's dark orbs. She stopped when her forehead brushed against the outstretched fingers. They felt weirdly nice.

They combed back her hair, stroked through it. "There you are, dearie, that's a good child. Oh, how sweet. You are a good, good girl."

"Um, thanks?" Emily's voice felt even tinier than the rest of her.

The hand jerked away. "What!"

Emily gulped and looked to Death. He shook his head, his hands clenching at his sides. The three horsemen looked at him as well.

"What is this?" Pestilence took up her reins and steered around to examine Emily.

"She talked," Famine yelped. "That's not one of yours."

"Yes, it is." She leaned down to peer into Emily's eyes.

"Um." Emily tried to swallow.

"One of my arrows hit you. I am sure of it. Last night. You are undead, and yet not."

"Is she un-undead?" Famine asked.

"Does a double negative make a positive?" War rode closer.

Emily shook her head and took a step back. Desperate, she looked to Death again.

He remained still for a moment, like a graveyard statue, but then his shoulders sagged. He stepped forward and gestured to her. She jumped up and ran to his side, sliding around so he stood between her and the horses.

Pestilence gasped. "Oh-ho!"

Famine giggled, and War joined in with a low chuckle.

"So I see." She gave a sniff. "We got her at the same time. Is that it?"

Death sighed, but he nodded.

"Fantastic blunder." War laughed, deep and rich.

Emily peeked around Death.

"Then we made her together?" Pestilence put a hand to her thin lips. "Oh, she's like our baby. Oh, this is so dear." Her raspy laughter weaved with the others'. "She's our child, brother, yours and mine."

The light of Death's eyes narrowed. "She ought to have been mine alone."

"It's a blessed event." She stroked her silvery crossbow as she laughed. "I'm her mother, and you're her father." She turned to the other two. "Oh, congratulate us, won't you!"

Famine threw up her hands to applaud giddily.

"She was scheduled for me," Death shouted. Lightning struck the tumbleweeds, and they burst into a pyre.

Pestilence stopped laughing. "Well." She sniffed, but then she smirked again. "Well then, you can have her. I do feel so bad for you, no longer having any victims. I bequeath this one to you. I give you sole custody of our child."

"Soul!" Famine shrieked. Her emaciated horse sagged as she bent double in a fit of hysterics.

"You have a legion now, brother." War's armor rattled with his laughter.

"A legion of one," said Famine between gasps.

"Just for you, O Death," Pestilence continued. "So that you know there are no hard feelings." She looked at her companions, then back down to Death and Emily before backing up her horse.

"Enjoy your spoils." War saluted Death with his bloody sword and then spurred his horse into the sky. His solidity melted as he split the darkness and disappeared in a streak of wound red.

"Make sure she gets plenty to eat." Famine cackled, slapping her horse's rump. It staggered and took off as well. Her disappearance, black on black, left a puff of emptiness that grumbled among the clouds.

"Goodbye, my beauty." Pestilence blew Emily a kiss. She took up her bow and waved it at Death as her horse followed the others into the night. They popped in a white burst and then smeared into nothing.

The sounds of the world's end thundered through the valley. Lighting stabbed the earth again and again, and wind tore from the mountains. It snuffed out the fire and scattered the weeds in every direction. The clouds churned, rose, tipped, then toppled into a final echoing crash that rolled out in an exhausted haze.

Silence.

Gloom clung to the evening, too early fallen upon an irrecoverable day. The parched air sizzled in a way that made Emily's hair lift from her shoulders. "Holy hell," she whispered.

"No." For the first time, Death's voice matched his clenched teeth. "No."

18

UNION

"I'm thirsty."

On a high rock, stretched out on his stomach, Scott adjusted his binoculars. The land appeared deserted, but he stayed low, confident the dusty lump of his backpack blended with the boulder shadows.

"Hey, is that you down there?" he called in a low voice over his shoulder. "Or is someone else in metal shoes sneaking up on me? Did you have any luck?"

"It doesn't make sense," Carol said from the other side of the ridge, closer to the road.

"Hey, did you hear me?" he said a little louder.

"Yes, I heard you."

"It got dark way too fast." Scott squinted harder through the binoculars for any definite shapes in the valley below. The wild flipflops in the air pressure over the last few minutes left him with a headache. The dust in the high wind also scratched in the back of his throat, and his body creaked, stiff and sore from spending all day in the car. He felt overheated, his back itched, and he'd scraped the center of his palm while climbing the rocks to get a look at the freak heat storm that apparently took place in only one small section of the sky.

And he was thirsty.

"I have no record of weather like this." Carol kept her volume on low, but Scott could still hear every nuance of her wariness through the rocks. "Of lightning flashing in such a pattern."

Scott sighed and cleared his parched throat. "Well, there's no one out there. And whatever fire that smoke came from is gone now. I can't find it. I think we're fine to keep going."

"This is bad," she said. Her feet crunched the gravel around the boulders below his perch. "We are now on foot after dark. Your safety is compromised."

If he heard the word "compromised" one more time, Scott was going to throw something. They'd had no luck with fuel on the highway and then took to side roads to continue their search. He adjusted himself on the rocks, mindful of his shotgun by his arm. They were in the middle of nowhere, no buildings, no places from which anyone, living or undead, could jump out and surprise them. He was on guard, obviously, but an attack ranked low on his list of concerns. "There's no one on the road, right?"

"No," she said. "But no stranded vehicles either."

He scanned to the south. "You don't— Whoa! What's that?" His binoculars slipped from his fingers.

"What?" The fuel can made a hollow ring as Carol plunked it below Scott's rock.

He tucked the gun under his elbow so he could use both hands to focus the binoculars. "There's something out there."

Carol scaled the boulders to crouch beside him. He pointed into the valley. "Do you see it?" he whispered. "I thought it was a big shadow, but then it moved. And look, there's where the smoke came from, those bushes are all black."

He put his face back to the binoculars and held his breath. As the shadow turned, Scott better saw the outline of a man-shaped figure in a hooded cloak. A white hand at its side stood out against the dark like a dim star.

“Human?” Scott slid backward on the rocks. Carol’s eyes flicked to the green glow of her night vision.

“What do you think?” His voice quavered. He cleared his throat again.

“I’m not sure,” she said softly, her eyes adjusting to high focus. She glanced at Scott’s fingers, trembling around his binoculars. “What’s the matter with you?”

He gnawed his lip and shook his head. “Nothing. I don’t know.” Sitting up, he arm-pitted the shotgun. "What? Nothing."

She stared at him.

"Carol, just tell me what it is."

“It might be a vampire.” She edged around the side of the higher boulder. “Get back down.”

“Out here all alone?” Vampires always traveled in packs, caravans.

“You’re right,” she said. “It might be human.”

“No.” He shook his head. Somehow, he was convinced it was absolutely not human.

She looked at him for a moment, her silver-blue brow furrowed in uncertainty. The light of her eyes changed to paler green as she leaned to examine the valley. “I can see him better than you can.”

“I don’t know,” he said. “But it’s not— Hey, did it get colder out?”

“No.” She frowned as she faced him. “Get a hold of yourself, Scott. He is looking the other way.”

He shook his head again and shifted his grip on the shotgun. He lowered his face to the binoculars, but then dropped them. “Shit!”

Carol caught them and shoved Scott down. He slid off the back of the rock with a thump, and she jumped after him.

“He was staring right at me!” Scott batted her away from him. “I looked, and he was looking right back at me. And he didn’t have a face — Carol, did you see? He didn’t have a face. And the eyes. The eyes, they... Did you see?”

“Quiet,” she hissed at him. “Yes, I saw.”

“The eyes, the... What the heck is it?” His hands shook almost too much to loop the binocular strap around his neck.

“What’s the matter with you?” Carol reached for him, but he

pressed against the rock and shook his head. Catch his breath, that's what he needed to do. He needed to catch—catch his breath.

After a moment, he edged around to peek through a crack between boulders. "Shit." He staggered back right onto Carol's foot. "He's coming."

"We can take him," she said. "He's alone. I'm seventy-eight percent charged, your shotgun is loaded, and we have a forty-three-foot elevation advantage."

"No, I—You don't understand. I—You—I can't explain. Do..." He took a shaky breath. "Carol, you don't feel that?"

"No. Scott. What do you feel?"

His throat tightened to nothing. "He's coming."

She stared at him then shook her head with an artificial sigh and stepped back. She grabbed the fuel can in one hand and Scott's arm in the other. Together, they ran to the road.

"Across!" She dragged him past a tower of boulders and through a weedy area sheltered by slopes.

"The car's the other way," Scott gasped as he sprinted to keep up.

"It is useless to us without fuel." She led him through more rocks and around another hill. Carol jumped from a sloped ledge to crouch beneath a rocky ridge. Scott slid down with less grace, rolling into the shadows at her side. He put a hand over his mouth to muffle his ragged breathing.

After a minute of silence, she sat back. "I detect nothing."

"We lost him," Scott said between shallow breaths. He lowered his hand. It no longer shook.

"Maybe." Carol took his arm, and though her grip wasn't tight, he got the feeling it would be if he tried to get up. "But without my radar, my senses are limited."

Scott shook off a shudder and eyed the roomlike space they'd dropped into. Rock walls taller than his head surrounded them on all sides, but one wider fissure on the far end looked like it led out. He couldn't tell its direction, but Carol could also help him climb back out the way they came. His palm throbbed where he scraped it earlier and was bleeding again. He wiped it on his jeans.

"How far are we from the car?" He tilted his head back to analyze the haze-covered sky, but all stars remained blotted out.

"Not far." Carol turned where she crouched to face him. "One-point-three miles. The road follows the shape of the rocks." She took one of the straps of Scott's backpack and tightened it for him. He hadn't even noticed it was uneven.

"And you didn't see anything we could pull fuel from?" Scott's thirst grated his raw throat now. He slipped off the backpack and dug out a dented water bottle. He took a swig, then another, then stuffed it back inside.

"No."

"Great." He hoisted the backpack on again. "Just great. We should have gone the other way. Where the road forked. Let's go back there. I could put the car in neutral and you could push." He winced as Carol's eyes changed to that dark color they turned when she got pissed. "Well, this is your fault!" he snapped. "The plan was to take the straightest line to New York. We're going completely the wrong direction."

"Not completely."

"And now we're sitting here hiding from that thing that looks like some freaking Nazgûl."

She shook her head. "There's no direct route up to the road from that valley. Although that would not stop a vampire."

"I thought you said it wasn't a vampire."

"I don't think it is."

"Then what was it?"

"Inconclusive."

Scott sighed and rubbed at the moisture on his upper lip. "You don't hear anything now?" He shivered.

"No."

"I don't know how it's hot and cold out at the same time."

"You're chilled." Carol studied him. "But the air temperature is sixty-eight degrees."

His adrenaline did somersaults. *Ignore it.* "If we're going to be walking anyway, I say we go back to the car and push it until we find something that's got fuel."

Carol's eyes darkened again, but Scott lifted a hand. "What? I'll help."

She stood. "I do not need your help to push a car."

"You're the one who dragged us out here at turbo speed." He got up as well, shook out his knees. "We should've siphoned more before we left that dog town this morning. Found some extra fuel cans."

"We needed to leave," she said. "That vampire could have followed me."

"It was daylight!"

"Where there is one, there are always more."

"Stop talking like a fortune cookie! What happened to your probabilities, huh? Now you agree with me? We don't *have* to follow the safest possible course. We'll never get to New York if we keep zigzagging away from every potential threat."

"You'll never get there at all if you die."

"You said the vampire didn't even know I was with you. Why would he follow you? And how? Vampires can't drive in the day." Scott smacked his gun against his hand. "We should have taken the other highway. There would've been fuel. It's over two and a half thousand miles to New York, you know. That's over a hundred gallons of fuel, or how many hours of charging we can't afford to wait? Why would he follow you anyway? You're just a robot, what would he want with you?"

"Well," said a voice behind them, "perhaps she got to know me better than I thought."

Scott spun around and aimed his shotgun. Carol did the same with her laser.

A vampire stood in the center of the rock room. It had to be a vampire. Scott knew they were pale, but he never realized how pale. Its face seemed made of soft clay, like if Scott punched it, his fist would sink right in. And so weirdly smooth. It looked about Scott's age, but even Scott had smile lines. And its hair was too light, that platinum non-color Scott's hadn't been since he was a little kid. The heavy calf-length coat it wore despite the desert heat provided another dead giveaway. It made Scott think of those military Navy coats with shoulder straps and two rows of buttons. Underneath, a collared shirt tucked into pleated pants, like it was ready for a business meeting or something. Who the heck bothered dressing that way anymore? Not any human.

The vampire tilted its head and lifted its eyebrows. It pulled its gaze from the weapons and smiled. "Hello, Carol. And hel-lo Carol's human." As its eyes settled on Scott, its smile grew fangier.

Scott clenched his teeth. *Ew.* It studied him as if it could see straight through his clothes.

"Leave." Carol's volume was low but her tone firm.

"You didn't tell me you had one." The vampire's eyes roved over every inch of Scott. "Though I thought you smelled too good to be true. And isn't he a beauty?"

That's it. Scott pumped his shotgun.

"Be judicious with your ammunition," Carol said. "He's fast."

"All vampires are fast." The training videos Scott watched at Curisa flashed through his brain. He kept his aim steady through the gun's sight.

The vampire smiled. "What's your name, beautiful? Did Carol tell you about me?"

"Don't answer him," Carol said.

"Oh, let him talk, Carol. Perhaps he wants to." The vampire folded his arms so his hands settled in plain view on his coat sleeves. He pursed his lips at Carol, then looked back to Scott. "You can call me Leif."

"I'll call you dead," Scott said.

Leif blinked twice, then laughed. "Come now. You're too pretty for cliché one-liners. Perhaps I can help you."

"We don't want your help."

"What happened to your hand?" Leif's face tilted, and he sniffed the air. His pale eyes glinted as they fixed on the bloody streak Scott had just wiped on his jeans.

"Carol," Scott said. *Do something.*

"What was that you were saying about New York?" Leif asked. "Is that where you're heading, Carol? Got a way into Manhattan, do you?"

"Carol." *Get me the hell out of here.*

Leif dropped his hands and took a step.

Carol leapt in front of Scott and shoved him against the rock wall. He jerked up his shotgun to keep it from hitting her, and her laser blasted. The blue flash dazzled him, but he blinked the spots away. Over Carol's shoulder, he saw the scorch mark in the rocks. The vampire stood two feet to the left of his previous spot.

"Carol," Leif said, his tone a perfect imitation of Scott's.

Scott pushed from the wall and aimed again.

"I'm not going to let you get to him," Carol told Leif.

He shook his head and actually pouted. "Really. And I thought we were friends."

"Friends?" Scott gaped at Carol.

The vampire's freaky ice eyes fixed on Scott's, and the lineless smile crept back across his features. "He might like me too if he got to know me."

"No," Carol said.

"Wait, you *like* him?"

"No," Carol said, and Leif laughed again.

"What are you going to do in Manhattan?" He tapped his fingertips against his white lips as he looked back and forth between them. "Oh, what was that you were saying last night?"

Carol shot at the ground right in front of his feet. As Leif took a nimble step back, she elbowed Scott's gun so it tipped up. He started to protest, to tell her to blow Leif's face off already, but then he saw what she intended. A thin slab supporting a pile of boulders jutted from the rock wall over Leif's head. *Yes! Bury him!* She fired at the ground again, and Scott refocused his aim on the slab.

Leif looked from Carol to Scott, then tilted his head back. His lip curled when he saw the rocks, and he put his hands up. "Really?" He retreated a foot more as her blast splattered dust over his stupid shiny shoes. "This is hardly necessary."

She crossed to him, her gun aimed between his eyes. *Yeah!* Scott stepped up behind her.

Leif kept his lips pressed, but then his gaze swept Scott's face as if admiring a work of art. "It's a long way to New York. You must be the only human around for miles."

"The last one you're going to see," Scott snapped.

Leif rolled his eyes again and looked up the length of Carol's arm at her. "Does he always talk like—" He froze. His eyes widened, fixed on a point above the wall behind her.

A chill shot down Scott's spine and coagulated deep in his guts. He tried to hold the shotgun steady, but clamminess erupted over his hands worse than before.

Carol scowled. "Do you think I'm going to fall for that?" Her eyes darkened, and she pushed her gun against the vampire's forehead, her hand almost on his nose.

He blew at her fingers and tilted his head to the side to see around her. His lips parted, and his pupils dilated.

Carol's eyes flashed. After a moment, she said, "Scott, is there something behind me?"

Scott stumbled. He tried to swallow, but his throat refused to work. As his boots slid over the ground, the sand under his heels rattled into his brain. The muscles in his neck locked, changed to steel, but he forced them to turn so he could look over his shoulder.

"Yes," he answered Carol in a ragged whisper.

"Shoot it?"

Scott's slippery fingers would not move. Atop the rocks stood the robed figure from the valley. And it was still staring at him. Now Scott could see the white hands at its sides were made of nothing but bone, and the facelessness inside its hood took the shape of a skull. Points of cold, glow-in-the-dark-colored fire pierced from the eye sockets. In a moment that lasted a lifetime, Scott understood that, across the smallest of distances, he was staring into the face of Death. His gun dropped to his side.

Carol spun around and fired. The blasts disappeared into the black cloak like puffs of air. Carol grabbed Scott and shoved him behind her.

Scott gasped as he bumped sides with the vampire. So cold! Carol's grip on him tightened, and she started to yank him out again, but then the space next to him emptied. He caught a blur in the corner of his eye as the vampire disappeared through the fissure in the rock walls.

Carol released Scott and shielded him with her body, her gun aimed at the figure on the ledge.

She waited, but when nothing happened, she whispered over her shoulder to Scott, "What is he?"

Scott's voice departed. He shook his head, clenched his jaw. He pushed at the tension in his stomach and willed his fingers to cooperate enough to get his grip back on his gun.

"Do you think you can make it through those rocks?" Carol asked.

The way the vampire ran? He shook his head. He could not look away from the dark figure. The clouds parted in the sky behind it, and moonlight broke through to cast its shadow—*Death's* shadow—over the space below. Although the rock room sheltered Scott and Carol from the wind, up there it tossed the black cloak in amorphous billows.

Carol fired again, but the figure did not seem to notice. It did nothing at all until she shifted where she stood in front of Scott. Then, it moved a step to the side so that it could keep Scott in its line of sight.

"What does he want?" Carol adjusted her aim to the sandy rocks right below it.

"I don't know," Scott croaked between breaths as his heart pounded in his brain. "My soul?"

Death spoke. "You are going to Manhattan."

Scott gasped. Carol clicked and pressed against him. His backpack ground into the wall, and the binoculars gouged his stomach, but he did not protest.

After a moment of silence, Death shifted his fire eyes to Carol and spoke again. "Is that not so?"

"Who are you?" she demanded.

Scott put his hands on the back of her shoulders, his gun caught between them. He started to answer her question, but the word died on his lips.

Death met his eyes again. "Yes."

Carol glanced over her shoulder, then back up. She shook her head. "What do you want?"

"Tell me your purpose in Manhattan."

Scott bit hard into his lip, but then sucked in his breath and squeezed out from behind Carol. He gripped his shotgun in both hands but didn't bother aiming it.

He wasn't dead yet. Maybe he could bargain. "Why do you want to know?" His voice came out creaky.

Death's fiery eyes fixed on him again, and Scott lost all of his breath. A moment passed, Death's fingers tapping against his side. "Is it a good purpose?"

"Yes!" Scott gasped. Carol put her hand on his arm, but he stayed put. "People I care about are there. I only want to be with them. I swear. Everything about it is goodness and innocence and love."

Carol shot him a bemused look.

"It's judgment day," he whispered to her.

"Not yet," said Death. His voice resounded like something from the deepest pits of the ocean.

Carol squeezed Scott's arm, and he let out a hiss of pain.

"What is about to happen in Manhattan?" Death asked.

Happen? What was that supposed to mean? Scott started to shake his head, but he froze when something scuttled over the rocks at Death's side.

"Zombie!" Scott shouted.

Carol released him and fired at it. Scott's shots exploded a moment after hers.

Death sidestepped in front of the zombie so fast none of their fire hit it, but Scott sure as hell wasn't going to stop shooting. He reloaded as Carol blasted again and again. He was about to fire when a voice cried from behind Death, "Stop!"

Scott paused, and Carol moved to the side to get a better angle.

"Wait," the voice called again. A *lady* voice.

"Hold on," Scott said to Carol. She nodded but kept her aim.

"I know it looks bad," said the voice, "but it's not what you think."

"You're not a zombie?" Scott asked. Because from what he saw, she sure looked like a zombie. He pretended to ignore Death's soul-piercing stare and craned to see around him.

Carol hesitated. "She doesn't sound like a zombie."

"She speaks," said Death.

"Yeah," said the voice. "I speak. All I want to do is speak. Just listen to me a minute, please? My name is Emily."

Carol shook her head, but Scott frowned and lifted his face from the shotgun's sight. "Step out where I can see you."

"Do you think I'm stupid?"

Death turned his head to speak over his shoulder. His faint voice echoed like a peaceful nightmare. "I will not let them shoot you."

After a moment of shuffling, the so-called Emily edged into the murky moonlight, her hands in the air. Despite the telltale lank hair and gray skin with its look of one giant faded bruise, her movements were fluid. Dark shadows ringed her sunken eyes, but they focused with intellect, with personality.

Zombie? Not zombie? It was too disgusting and real to be any sort of disguise. Was she sick? Was it contagious?

She held a handgun, but she kept it to the side, pointed at the sky.

Carol aimed at her. "Put it down."

Emily glanced up at Death as if asking his opinion. If he responded to her, Scott couldn't tell how, but a moment later, she set the gun on the edge of the rocks. She started to speak as she straightened, but a low blast from Carol's laser cut her off. The gun tumbled into the shadows.

"Hey!"

Carol shook her head, but she retracted her own weapon and waved at Scott to lower his. "All right," she said. "Speak."

Emily's clenched fists trembled at her sides, and her face twisted in anger. She definitely looked like a zombie now. Scott lifted his shotgun again.

The voice of Death broke the silence. "They are going to Manhattan."

"Maybe," Scott said with a thick swallow. "Maybe not." Could Death tell he was lying? Would it be worse if he lied? If Death wasn't there to kill him, would he change his mind if Scott didn't give him and his maybe-zombie pet what they wanted?

Emily nodded, and her hands relaxed. She focused on Scott, started to speak, but then addressed Carol instead. "Is Manhattan still secure?"

Carol did not answer.

"Are they still working on a cure there? Does headquarters remain uncompromised? LPI headquarters, I mean."

"What do you know about the LPI?" Carol asked.

"I'm with them," said Emily. "You too? If you're going to Manhattan, let me come with you."

"What!" Scott's shock crushed his fear.

"No, I need to get there." Emily took a step forward. "Look, I know I look like a zombie, but I'm not. This just happened to me last night, and you're the first person I've seen since then. I have to get to headquarters." She looked to Death, then back down at them. "My name is Emily Campbell, and I'm with the Southland LPI unit. You can have them look me up. Records were pretty thorough back when I joined. I still have ID." She started unflapping various pockets in her tight cargo pants to root through them.

Scott shot Carol a wary glance. "Did a zombie bite you?"

Emily looked up. "Yes, but—"

"Then you are a zombie."

She shook her head and lifted her hands. "Look, how are you getting there? Do you have a truck? Do they still send the airships out for pickups?"

"You are not coming with us."

"I have to get there. Just let me— My unit—" She paused and pressed her hands together. "Look, this is Death. Hi, yes. You probably noticed that already. But he's not supposed to be like this. Here, I mean. With us. Weird, right? Some serious shit is going down that you can't...well, I can explain if you'll listen. But the point is that everyone —*everyone* is in danger."

Carol moved back to Scott's side. "That's not our concern." She picked up the fuel can, and her gun surfaced again. She pointed it at Emily as she nudged Scott's arm. "Let's go."

Emily shot to the edge of the rocks. Scott pumped his shotgun and aimed at her. "Don't." He backed up with Carol to the gap in the walls.

Emily's expression twisted, but Death blocked Scott's view of her once more.

He could hear her scuffling, and he felt Carol pull him out of the rock room, but the sight of Death consumed him. His eyes bored into Scott as if they could taste his soul. The skeletal hands drew something from the cloak. It reminded Scott of his granddad's old handheld gamer he used to sneak off with during holiday dinners. The memory evaporated when the red glow from its screen lit up the inside of Death's hood, set ablaze every contour and crevice of the grinning skull. Scott's blood rushed past his knees.

Carol jerked him around the rocks, and his vision blurred. They were running then. Faster than he could have ever managed on his own. The binoculars pounded against his stomach as they ran and climbed and ducked and turned all the way back to the car.

19

MANHATTAN?

Every way Emily twisted, Death blocked her path. He didn't move in any obvious way, but no direction she attempted allowed her to reach the edge of the rocks. The wind whipped her hair all over her face and made his cloak envelop her repeatedly.

After her third mouthful of fabric, she smacked at the cloth, took a step back, and pushed her snarled hair out of her eyes.

"Ohmygodstop!"

"Hmm?" He didn't look up from his device, but the wind calmed.

Emily curled her fingers into her scalp, then dropped her hands. Death turned away to walk along the rocks, and she jumped to the brink, straining her ears. But all sounds of the fleeing boy and his robot ceased to be.

Emily kicked a stone into the pit and rounded on Death. "You just —" Something slid under her boot. She glanced down. Shotgun pellets littered the ground.

Why did Death shield her? She wasn't complaining, of course, but she didn't get it. She didn't think she hurt his attempt to get help from his brethren, but her presence definitely hadn't made anything better.

His fury literally thundered when they abandoned him, and now he was playing with his little toy as if none of that mattered.

"What the hell are you doing with that thing?"

He tapped at the screen and the glow changed from red to yellow.

I swear to god. She squinted over the ledge. Her Glock hid down somewhere among the shadows. She kicked at the shot, watched it shower with the dust. Okay, she was glad he shielded her. Even if she didn't get why he did it. His reasoning shouldn't matter to her anyway. Getting to New York mattered. "I can't believe you just let them go."

"Why?"

"*Why?* Are you serious?"

Death flipped his device vertical and scrolled.

"That guy's going to Manhattan." Emily flung a hand in the direction he ran. "He could get me in! Why did you stop me?"

"They would shoot you." The glow became blue.

"Not if he listened to me. I didn't get the chance to explain. We just *happen* to bump into some dude who's going exactly where I need to go, and you just let him get away!"

"I do not need him." The glow went white.

"Well, I do. God! *You* can't help me; you're more bound by Space and Time than ever now. If it weren't for you creeping him out, he would've listened to me."

Death looked up from the screen and fixed Emily with a stare.

She stared back. She lasted almost ten seconds before she had to avert her gaze. Okay, so maybe she was a bit creepy too. But nothing like him. She quietly picked at the edge of a jagged broken fingernail. The skin around the nailbed felt loose, itchy. When she peeked back up to Death, he was still staring. "All right, fine," she muttered.

His attention returned to the screen.

What was so engrossing on that thing? And why was he being so chill all of a sudden? Emily let out a slow breath. It made her chest hurt, but it felt necessary. "If you don't need them, why did you chase them over here in the first place?"

"Scott Sullivan is a living human."

"Is that his name? How do you know? Does that thing tell you?"

She leaned in to read the screen, but he turned away from her.

"What about his android? Does it tell you her name too?"

"Her name doesn't matter to you."

"Yes, it does." Emily tilted her face to the sky as she strategized. The flowing cloud wisps made the moon a slow-motion strobe light. "Maybe if I can catch up to them and I know their names or other stuff about them, they'll listen to me. What else does it say?" Silvery illumination spilled over the pit, and she caught a glimpse of her G18 in the dirt before shadows scampered back across it. It did not look good. "Ugh, robot bitch."

"It tells me nothing about her."

Emily crouched and eyed the incline. "I have to get to New York." The wind in her tangled hair required both hands to keep it out of her eyes. She opened her mouth to speak but had to grit her teeth against a sudden clenching in her guts. She eased onto her knees and it faded, but the back of her throat burned. Was this a zombie thing? She didn't want to think about it. *Get to headquarters.* "If there's any place that can save the world, it's New York."

Death's head snapped up. "What?" The wind tugged at his long, tattered sleeves, and impossible volume ebbed and flowed in his robe, but his hood remained in perfect place. How the hell? Wasn't his hood subject to space and time and wind too? He stared at her expectantly.

Emily blinked back at him as she caught up her hair to braid it into submission. "Um. You asked them about New York before I did."

Death turned his head and contemplated the horizon. His screen went black, and he tucked it away.

"You did," she insisted. "What does that Scott guy being a living human have to do with that?"

He turned back to meet her eyes. His burned like pilot lights. "Manhattan," he said after a moment, "has the most valuable collection of life left. Potential. You're right. Manhattan..." He lifted a finger as if he would touch it to his unmoving mouth, but it did no more than hover. "The power to reverse the plague is brewing in Manhattan."

Emily gave up on her braid and returned to him. "Exactly—"

"Manhattan is—"

"The cure—"

"—East." Death looked again to the horizon. "And so Time is ripe for it. Is it where he is running? It must be."

"You mean with your horse?" She tugged a strand of hair from her broken fingernail then gnawed at the jagged edge.

"Yes. And it is where I may be able to intercept him myself." Death's hands clicked as he brought them together. "Terminate my brethren's plan for the future of humanity."

Was there an actual plan? From what they said, it sounded like they meant to passively let the world deteriorate. Was their plan more sinister than that?

"They have led Time astray," Death said before Emily could stop biting her nail to ask. "If I can catch up to him..." He paused and shook his head. "How can he not realize the gravity of their intentions? He must listen to reason. The balance..."

Emily made herself drop her hand. "So now you want to go to Manhattan too?"

"I must stop Time."

"Then why did you stop me? Scott and his—"

Death brushed at the air. "You do not need Scott. We can get there without him." Emily felt a surge of relief at the "we," but it didn't do much for her frustration. He retreated from the edge of the rocks.

She did not follow. "How? Do you plan to *walk* all the way to New York?" Her nail found its way between her teeth again.

He paused. She pulled her finger from her mouth and shoved her hands into her back pockets and waited. Waited.

"They will hurt you, Emily."

"Oh, please. You were ready to kill me last night."

"Reap you."

"Whatever."

Death turned and walked back to her. As close as he came, she had to tilt her head far back to meet his eyes. She kept her feet planted and forced herself not to chew on her lip. It wasn't that he made her anxious. She was fine. He was just so... The greenish centers in his eyes flickered like they were taking a thousand snapshots of her upturned face. What did he even see when he looked at her?

"They can't kill you," Death said. "What they would do would only cause you pain and suffering."

"You think that scares me?" It didn't. It couldn't. She couldn't let it. "It would be worth it if it worked."

"I'm not trying to scare you."

Emily tore her hands from her pockets. "You—" Her words choked as her broken nail snagged and the whole thing tore off. She slammed her other hand around the finger for a wincing moment. When she dared to examine it, the jagged flesh where the nail hung from its roots looked too gray and bloodless to match the bright raw pain. She shuddered and clenched her hand into a fist.

"I'm a fucking zombie now," she whispered. She set her jaw and lifted her face to Death's unchanged expression above her. "Nothing scares me. Why should it? The worst has already happened. Nothing except *not* getting a cure and *not* stopping this from happening to other people."

He remained motionless for a long moment before giving a slight tilt of his head. "Vampires scare you."

Emily blinked. "What?"

"Don't they?"

"No." She took a long chest-hurty breath. "I mean..." Vampires? Why the hell would he even mention vampires? She looked down and picked her hanging nail loose, flicking it to the ground with a shudder.

"You need no pretense with me, Emily."

"It's not like that." No way he could understand how important autonomy was to her. Had been. Used to be. And it wasn't a fear thing. It wasn't. It was a pride thing. But if he hadn't worked that out from her story this morning, it wasn't going to get through his skull. Why waste breath she didn't even have? She cleared her throat and busied herself with attempting to contain her hair again.

"A vampire was here with them when I arrived. You did not see him."

"I don't care." She contemplated the waning moon as she concentrated on braiding the snarls over her shoulder. The moon reflected sunlight. Totally not fair that it did nothing against vampires. "Seriously. So what? Why are you trying to change the subject? What could a vampire even do to me now?" That was one thing she never had to worry about again. At least until she got cured.

"Not to you..." Death trailed off.

Emily glanced his way. Was he going to finish that thought? "You..." Her hands stilled on her hair at the sight of him. With his head cocked at an angle, the light in his sockets faded, almost too dim to distinguish. His fingers tangled in the sides of his robe. What? She peered over her shoulder, but the night air hung empty behind her. She blinked and turned back to him. "Why are you looking at me like that?"

His eyes flickered. Then his gaze drifted, and his hands fell at his sides.

"What is it?"

He shook his head. She opened her mouth to insist on an answer, but then he finally spoke. "You reminded me of someone."

"I did?"

He gestured to the hills beyond the pit. "We do not need Scott and his unliving companion to get to Manhattan."

For a moment, the change of subject annoyed her, but that "we" proved too distracting, too promising to let go. "Okay. But even if we got there without them, how would I get in?" She knotted the end of her braid. "Like you said before, I'll get blown to pieces by their guard squad before I open my undead mouth."

"Hm."

That's right, *hm*. She waited to see if he'd offer anything more, then she stepped to his side. "Think about it. If Scott can get in, he can get me in. If I can get him to listen to me." Another step. Two could play the proximity game. "If you're worried about them hurting me, come with me." She lifted a hand, almost touched his sleeve, but hovered above it. "Help me."

He ignored her gesture and tapped his fingertips together as he gazed east. "If only I had my horse."

Emily blinked and dropped her hand.

Okay. Fine. Whatever. She strode to the ledge. "Well, I'm going after him." She turned her back on Death and crouched. "Have fun hitchhiking across the country."

As she slid down the incline, gravel scattered and rocks broke loose to fall with her, but she landed without injury. She tried to ignore the tender pain where her nail used to be as she searched for her gun, but that made it throb worse. At least she wasn't full of holes. Without Death, how could she get close enough to talk to Scott Sullivan? She considered terrain shield options, but when she found her G18 among the shadows, the thoughts dissolved, and she groaned. The polymer was scorched and melted by the laser blast, and the trigger would not even fit her finger. "Robot bitch," she grumbled. "I could kill her."

"No, you couldn't." Death's voice came from directly behind her.

She jerked up and put a hand to her chest. But nothing raced underneath it. A shudder wracked her frame, and she forced an exhale just to feel it move. "You know what I mean."

"Unlife is as resistant to my power as undeath."

His power? His touch killed people, of course, but even when he just stood there, he had an obvious effect on the living. Could she work with that? "Scott trembled like a scared puppy at the sight of you," she mused. "But his robot was fine the whole time. So, unlife? That's a thing?"

"I mean nothing to machines like her." He brushed past Emily across the space. "The living who are not ready for me, like Scott Sullivan, hate and fear me." He paused at the gap in the walls and gestured for Emily to follow.

"Some people aren't afraid of death, of you." She made herself sound as chill as possible as she accepted the invitation. "Or at least they say they aren't." She tried to wiggle her slagged gun into its holster, but it refused to fit.

"Do you fear me?"

"No." No? No. That was actually the truth. Instead, she felt... Well, she had a lot on her mind. They emerged into an open area where the wind settled into a soft breeze. "I've gotten used to you. And I'm not alive."

Death stopped, turned around, studied her. "Your fear ended while you yet lived. You invited me. Your time had come. You were ready to embrace me."

Emily blinked. Why did he have to keep using that word, *embrace*? His hands lifted as if he meant to demonstrate. *Oh my god no.* It was too similar to her first vision of him rising from the abyss. She could taste the cold gun again, hear the explosions, the screaming.

She took a quick step back. "I...well..." She glanced away, cleared her throat, and took a moment to note the different paths leading through the rocks around them. "I was out of options."

"Indeed."

Indeed, indeed. Ugh. *Get a grip.*

She forced another unnatural deep breath and attempted to clear her throat again, but a fit of coughing seized her. Her stomach clenched, gripping tighter than before. The gun fell from her fingers as the pain bent her double. Between ragged inhales, she spat sticky green onto the ground. It left the taste of mildewy towels coating her tongue.

"What the hell?" she gasped. She could feel Death standing there watching her. She turned her back to wipe her mouth. "I thought you said my transformation was complete. What's happening now?"

No answer.

So he didn't know that either.

"Am I rotting? Is that it?" She rubbed at her face, shuddering as the pain faded. "Am I just going to rot apart and disappear until I finally die?"

"You will not be dead."

"Ugh, whatever!" She turned back to him. "Why not just call it that? I'll be all gone. I don't get it. If that happens, won't you take my soul then?"

"Your existence and what you call your soul no longer have anything to do with me no matter what becomes of your body."

"Are souls not even real? What is it then? What do you call it?"

"Words do not matter."

"But you reap souls, right?"

"I reap life."

"But is there a difference? I mean plants don't have souls. Do animals?"

"I reap human life."

"Zombies and vampires used to be human." She snatched up her gun. "But you say you don't have power over them. Does that mean they don't have souls anymore? Does that mean I don't have a soul anymore?"

Death sighed and started walking.

She darted after him. "What about Scott's robot friend? She doesn't have a soul, right? I mean some human built her. They couldn't build a soul into her. No one has that power. I have to have more soul than she does."

Silence. Walking.

"What's going to happen to me, then?" She stepped ahead so she could see his face as she matched his pace. "If I rot completely away. There's just, what, nothing?"

"Why do you think you'll rot completely away? Undeath is immortality." He said the last word with particular disdain.

"So I won't just keep rotting?"

"It depends if you keep ripping off your own fingernails."

"What?"

He waved a hand over her. "Your flesh has the look of rot. Your blood is sludge in your veins. Your body cannot heal like a human's, but your wounds also won't spread or rot further than their surface appearance."

So he did know *some* things about undeath.

Emily picked at her sleeve over the bite on her arm. "So this...?"

"Is just a hole. And so it will remain." He stopped at a line of boulders. "There is a road beyond these rocks."

"Hang on." She moved around him. "Zombies fall apart. They're animate, constantly decaying corpses."

"No."

Yes. She shoved the gun into the back of her pants. "I've seen them walk their own feet off."

"Have you?" Death paused in his progress along the rocks to regard her. "You've seen the ones you meant to destroy. Have you ever observed them for lengths of time when left to their own devices without threat or the temptation of human flesh to drive them to distraction?"

"What? How could I?"

He shook his head. "Emily, if you are careful not to further damage your undead flesh, you could last indefinitely. You feel stiffness in your muscles and bones, but you can still bend your joints."

Emily flexed her hands. What stiffness? "I..."

"Perhaps you are less quick than you were."

Was that supposed to be a pun? She doubted it; he probably just meant slow. She sure didn't feel slow. "Is that why the fast ones are fast?" she asked. "They're not as damaged yet? They get slower after they take hits?" Was she going to get as slow as the slow ones if she got shot?

"No."

"What's the difference then? Why are some zombies fast and manic, and the rest like the walking dead?" Would her speed make a difference for the cure?

"You are quite certain you've never been bitten by a vampire?"

She blinked. "Quite." Maybe he wasn't listening to her story that morning after all.

"Hm." He lifted his hands, turned them over as if he expected to see something new about them. "Your speed must be due to my part in your creation."

"What do vampires—? Wait. I'm like this because of you. Doesn't that make me less undead?"

"No." He dropped his hands and drifted through a shadowy space in the tall rocks.

"Wait." She jogged after him. On the other side of the boulders, she stopped short. After so many hours of uneven wilderness, the desolate stretch of a paved highway snaking into the desert looked out of place in the night.

"Yes?" Death examined both directions.

Emily followed his gaze. Neither went east, but they would cross other roads eventually. One way appeared endless and empty as far as the horizon, nothing but mile markers glittering in the moonlight. If Scott had gone that way, he'd still be in sight. The other way bent around the hill. That's the way he must have gone. "That's the way I'm going." Emily brushed off her hands and faced Death. He stared in the other direction.

"If you're not coming with me, then I have one more question for you." She'd hesitated to ask about his brethren; she didn't want to poke a sore spot. But he was calm now, and she had to know. "What did that hag lady on the zombie horse mean when she said she was my mother?" Pestilence? It felt too weird to say the name aloud.

Death's head moved left and right as he considered the road. "Just as I bring death to humanity, she brings the plague of the undead."

"So she's Undeath?" That name wasn't much better.

He sighed. "She may as well be."

"And you two made me this way together."

"It was not intentional."

Yeah, she knew his intention. She fought back an irrational scowl. "Why doesn't she want people to die anymore?"

"I am Death. Not the state of being dead. I am the transition. But she, she is a condition."

"So the state of being undead?"

"Her power is that of all affliction."

"So when people are...afflicted...with undeadness, she's getting off on it?"

"Or any physical malady. It is what she is."

"So when people die, they stop being afflicted, and she loses the power or whatever energy she draws from them?"

"The undead do not die."

Emily rolled her eyes. "I mean when they die from being afflicted with literally any other maladies or whatever."

"The dead are useless to her, yes."

"But they're useless to you too, right?"

"You do understand how that is beside the point, don't you?"

Did she? Yes, okay, it made sense. "And the other two? Also conditions?"

"The condition of yearning, hunger, need of sustenance. And the condition of conflict with others."

Conditions the undead would eternally suffer. Until humans wiped out every last one. But how did Death being out of the way make that less of a possibility? Trying to follow the "logic" of cosmic beings made Emily's brain ache. She watched Death's back and forth focus until it settled on the bend in the road, and he set off toward the hill.

Together, then!

Emily followed along the dusty shoulder, trying to wrangle her simmering excitement. "What did she mean when she said she gave me to you? Am I really your legion or whatever? Is that a thing? Are you stuck with me now?"

He shrugged. "I could leave you."

'Kay… "So why don't you?"

"I don't like to travel alone."

Emily missed a step. Dust puffed around her ankles. That couldn't be all there was to it. Could it? He just wanted company? She could be anybody? "Wait, is that who I remind you of? Your horse?"

"No."

She caught back up to him. "So who then?" Why did he look at her like that while she braided her hair?

"I feel responsible for your situation. I took part in creating you."

Oh. Guilt, then. Fine. At least he had feelings at all. She massaged her sore fingertip as she thought of how his sister mocked him. "Yeah, *Father*."

He sighed, and she smirked, but her expression soon dissolved, and she let a pace fall between them. So what if it was just guilt? Why should she care? "My real father died two years ago." An image of him alive blossomed in her mind. The way his eyes would twinkle like Santa Claus's when he closed a sale, the warmth of his big, strong hugs. She sighed and pushed the memories away, focused instead on the silky brown dust her boots kicked up with each step. Like little grenade blasts. Death's cloak trailed over the ground without even leaving a groove. Despite its tatters, it remained perfectly clean.

"None of your immediate family are dead," he said.

Emily rolled her eyes. "Seriously, whatever. He got zombied. So did my brother. For all I know, they're chopped to pieces and burned to ash and scattered to the winds, but you're telling me they're still not dead. Fine, they're undead. Forever." Just like her entire team last night. And there was no release from undeath. Ever. She knew the universe was messed up, but the abysmal horror of it was more than she could digest. *God...* "I've lost everyone I ever cared about, and there's not even any kind of afterlife or magical-religious crap to delude me into some kind of consolation."

"Your mother is not undead."

Emily's despair immediately flushed into bristling hostility. "Yeah, she's worse."

Death wisely remained silent.

They walked for several minutes until marks in the dust caught Emily's eye and her rigidity evaporated. "Footprints! Hey, look." She dropped to a crouch. "Treads and shoes. Running's too sloppy to be a vampire."

Death watched her. "He wasn't truly with them." His voice softened. "The vampire I saw. It appeared they meant to destroy him."

"Good." Emily straightened and squinted at the bend. "Too bad it got away."

"Hm."

"Scott can't be that far ahead." She turned to Death. "We can still catch up."

He took a small step backward, then seemed to think of something and took out his screen again.

"They have a gas jug," she reminded him. "They must have a truck.

Time is of the essence, right? Another chance like this might not come along."

"Indeed." Death looked to the hill, his hands clicking against the screen. "But they will not listen to you."

Emily shook her head and caught the tattered edge of his sleeve.

She had a plan.

Time for some epic bullshit.

"Just tell me exactly what that gizmo of yours says about our pal Scott."

20

LEVERAGE

One of the most deplorable consequences of society's downfall had to be the deterioration of the roads. Leif clenched his sharp teeth as another pothole bounced his head against the truck's torn ceiling and one of his earbuds went flying. He snatched it midair and wedged it back into place. He refused to miss a moment of the music. The old battery in the ancient little machine managed to hold a charge for but a few hours, and the November nights lingered long. Half the music saved on it by whoever used to own it wasted Leif's time. But the other half was quite nice indeed. As he hummed along to a satisfactory toccata, his fingers played the steering wheel with each pothole-avoiding swerve.

The speedometer quivered at sixty-six, and the truck groaned against every mile. The fuel gauge read half when he found the hulking thing cowering off the roadside a few hours ago, but now it edged toward E. Leif doubted the rickety contraption would make it many miles more. Diesel fumes swirled through his open window, the spicy odor waltzing with the cloying scent of rotting hay.

Leif estimated he had the better part of three hours until dawn. He would give himself an hour more on the road and then seek shelter. If nothing could be found, he could theoretically burrow between the rectangular hay bales in the back of the truck. But it was a risk; God forbid a hungry horse should wander by.

A horse... Leif could drain a whole team right about now. The proximity of Carol's human had been torturous. His body's fleeting warmth against Leif's side still prickled through him, teased at his nostrils. Exquisite agony.

Why didn't he simply grab the boy and run? Oh, regrets, regrets. But before tonight, Leif had never seen Death in one place for so long. And Leif's sense of self-preservation always was his strongest trait. And so he fled, left the life behind for He Who Could Not Be Escaped.

"And did he claim you, beautiful boy?" Leif murmured to the music. "And will your Carol be lonely now? Such a shame. Such a waste."

It was perhaps a touch delusional, but he fancied Death a bit of an acquaintance. With every life Leif took, the old fellow joined him, right at the end. He rarely stayed longer than a split second, but it was always one of Leif's favorite split seconds. *We are in this together,* he would think. And it was a pleasant thing, to not be alone with a corpse in his arms. If only for a moment.

After more than four hundred years of it, one couldn't help but feel a touch of attachment.

And so what would Carol do now? Would she bury the body? How sentimental could artificial intelligence be?

A wistful sigh sang past Leif's lips. Could he ever find her again? Without a human to protect, he imagined she would be much less trigger-happy. They were going to New York. Would she continue her journey without her charge? What information did she possess?

Leif couldn't help but think again how much indeed Lorenzo would value a machine with connections to Manhattan. How much he would value whomsoever delivered her to him.

But best not to mourn what never was. It had been a pretty idea, playing Lorenzo's game one last time, long enough to finally take him down, like a vengeful god. To be the One Vampire to end his reign and to topple the Accursed System sure to Doom Them All. For the credit to be Leif's alone.

But it was time to let go of his foolish fantasies. Time to turn himself over to the great Apollonia in Manhattan. Tell his pathetic desperado story, confess his failures, and become a lowly cog in her wheel.

Leif squeezed his eyes shut, and the hard plastic of the steering wheel crumpled under his hands.

Another teeth-gnashing bump. Oh dear.

His eyes snapped open. Road kill this time, the smell of it distinctly human. Leif's trembling thirst spiked, his shoe slamming the brake of its own accord. But as he slid out the door, he could already tell how less-than-fresh the corpse must be. He covered his nose and walked around the truck to have a look.

What remained of a twisted woman sprawled over the pavement. A swarm of ants writhed upon her carcass, gleaming black in the starlight. Those on the upper body feasted, unsympathetic to their twitching compatriots squashed by the tire's tread at the corpse's other end.

"And so you were here not long ago," Leif said to the night as he imagined Death meeting this woman. Did he strike her down in wrathful fury? Or embrace her tenderly like a lover? The way Leif might have?

He sighed with longing as he used his foot to nudge the thing over. The ants streamed in every direction like black lava.

"Flee, little scavengers. Run home to mother."

The body's back side glistened white with maggots. There was nothing for Leif here, and his veins sobbed.

As he walked back up the truck's side, he ran a hand along the wooden slats and plucked out a piece of hay. He was twining it between his fingers and reaching for the cab's door when his body stiffened on instinct.

A small sleek shape zoomed through the air a few hundred yards ahead. This time of night, it wouldn't be a bird. And if Leif doubted his ornithological deductions, the blinking lights gave the drone away.

Leif dropped beside the truck out of sight. But it was too late. A minute later, he caught the guttural rumbling of vehicles on the wind.

Two of them, big ones with loud engines. Only a couple miles off and coming his way.

He eased up and scrutinized the black sky through his truck's windows. The little drone was coming right for him.

Leif jumped atop the truck and launched himself into the air. He caught the drone and somersaulted into a landing. As he ran back to the truck, he punched at the thing's switches until the lights blinked off.

Its two big lenses gave the impression of bubble eyes above a round knob of a nose. It was kind of cute. Leif wondered if he could get away with keeping it.

"Who do you belong to?" he murmured.

He didn't expect an answer, but its lights blinked back on again. The damned thing was on a remote.

So much for that. Leif squashed it between his hands like a giant spider and punted it into the bushes off the side of the road.

The engine sounds picked up speed, coming from the northwest. Leif supposed it was too much to hope they would turn left at the crossroad ahead and drive away from him. He doubted his quaint hay truck could outrun such engines, but if he backtracked, perhaps he could lose them in the town he passed a few miles ago.

He reached for the cab door, but then froze again. This time because a hand like iron gripped his shoulder. The touch seeped warmly through his coat, but not warm enough.

Again?

Naturally, a vampire could catch up to him faster if they simply left their truck. Whoever the hand belonged to, the recent human scent wafting from them was oh too good. Leif shrugged off the hand and turned, preparing for Ricky v. 2.0. But when he saw who stood there, his brows shot up and an incredulous laugh escaped him.

"Nadia!" And who was that, coming up behind her? "Hector." Of all the vampires in all the deserts, it had to be two from the very commune he abandoned last night. Damnable coincidence? Impossible they tracked him so far and so fast. His foot trail ended in Dog Flats, after all.

Nadia took a step back as Hector joined her, his great hammy hands flexing in the air, ready for a fight. They looked even less happy to see Leif than he was to see them. And Leif was very, very unhappy to see them.

"I'm so glad to see you!" He gave his most convincing smile. "But I knew you would fare well." Last night, he fled the factory as soon as the attacking humans and their grenades distracted everyone. "Tell me, were there any casualties?"

"Not yet." Nadia signaled Hector to have at him.

Leif jumped, alighting on the truck's roof. He put a flabbergasted hand to his breast. "What is this animosity?"

"You ran away."

"Coward."

"Traitor." They jumped onto the hay, triangulating on him.

Leif evaluated his chances. They both looked good, empowered, as it were. Nadia's long black hair glistened, especially luxurious. Human blood flowed fresh in their veins. She was a sharp one, and Hector was a glorious giant of a vampire. Leif was too depleted to take on both at once.

It wasn't going to be another Ricky situation. Leif would have to work for this one.

"Traitor? You offend me! I left to seek help."

They laughed at him. Both of them. Leif hadn't even known Hector *could* laugh.

"Demos told us how he found you." Nadia's pretty lip curled. "Trying to release our horde."

"We were under attack." Leif smiled. "It seemed the logical thing to do."

"He caught you *before* you received the alarm."

Leif let his jaw drop, and then he nodded as if in understanding. "Oh, so that's why you think…" He shook his head and laid on a musical chuckle. "My dear, I sensed them coming."

Nadia was not in the least charmed. Her lips pulled back in full snarl. "He caught you with the igniters."

Oh, yes. Those.

But Demos did not know Leif calibrated them to his detonator or that he sprayed the caskets with explosive. There was no way he could know. All he knew was Leif had a pocketful of igniters and his hand on the latch of the cattle truck. Of course, the brat assumed the worst. True, he was correct, but he had no proof, no idea what Leif was really up to. For all he knew, Leif thought he could turn the flesh-eaters into bombs by shoving igniters down their throats.

Leif sighed as if all this wasted their time, and he shook his head.

"Saboteur," Hector growled and started for him over the hay.

"Whoa there!" Leif lifted his hands. "That's not it at all. I merely took initiative. Or tried to."

"I knew we couldn't trust you," Nadia said. "I told him so when you came out of nowhere and offered to join us like you're God's gift to commune. I don't care how old you are or how long you spent with Lorenzo. Demos calls the shots. The only vampire he answers to is Lorenzo himself."

"Obviously I was wrong. I see that now." Leif hesitated as if ashamed, lowered his eyes for added effect. "I panicked."

"And you will pay with your head." Hector lunged.

Leif jumped, landing on the road. He put his hands on the truck's hot hood. "Oh no," he said up to Hector. "Lorenzo prefers it attached. I assure you of that."

"I don't trust you as far as I could throw you."

"To be fair, you could probably throw me rather far."

Hector's features wrinkled into a dark conglomeration.

"Listen." Leif patted the hood, gestured for them to join him. "Call me coward; it is true I ran. But I can prove my loyalty, how about that? While I searched the desert for help, I made the most amazing discovery."

Hector landed behind him with a ground-trembling thud, but he held off at a sign from Nadia. She stepped down onto the hood and eyed Leif.

He lifted a hand before she could speak. "I've found an android with intimate ties to our enemies in Manhattan. It's out here alone, but heavily weaponized. Between the three of us, though, we could capture it. Oh, we could. Think of it. This thing could provide Lorenzo the information and power he needs to finally break down Apollonia's initiative and take Manhattan."

Nadia was still for a long moment, and then she crouched, her eyes drawing level with Leif's, her tight blue jeans stretching over her shapely knees. "Where is it?"

"I will show you."

"No. You tell us where it is."

"Southwest, about a hundred-twenty miles as the crow flies."

"What makes you think it's still there?"

"It is." Leif nodded, very sure. "I trapped it in a rock cave."

Hector grunted. "If it's heavily weaponized, it can get out of the cave."

Had he just used his brain twice in as many minutes? Leif should perhaps start to give Hector more credit.

Nadia straightened and looked down the road toward the approaching sound of the two big trucks. "We can't make that before sunrise. What are you trying to pull?"

Leif laughed. "There is nothing being pulled."

She landed at his side. "Tonight we go to this cave together, and if it's not there, I take your head to Lorenzo myself."

Oh-ho! She knew Lorenzo's location? Well now, how could Leif get her to share that?

The squealing of brakes distracted him as the trucks pulled up. One was a four-door pickup with Nadia and Hector's caskets in the back. Offensively ugly brown color. The guard driving it though, Karem, was a lovely shade of brown and looked beyond scrumptious through the windshield. The other was one of the semitrucks complete with livestock trailer. Undeadstock trailer. And it was full and groaning. Leif hadn't expected that. The stench of the cargo might have killed his appetite if its driver, Muk, didn't smell so combatively delectable.

Now what in the world were Hector and Nadia doing with Demos's cargo?

And only two humans. Pity.

"Where is everyone else?" Leif asked.

"That's not your privilege to know."

Karem hopped out of the pickup truck. "Yo, what happened to my drone?"

"Sorry, old sport." Leif offered him a smile. "I didn't realize it was yours."

"You!" Karem started. "Ooooh, Demos is gonna piss himself."

Leif blinked. "That would be a sight to see."

Nadia turned her back to Leif, and he felt rather sandwiched between her and Hector. "Did the drone find anything else?" she asked Karem.

"Yeah, man. There's a factory or machine plant or something outside a town a couple miles that way." He waved an arm the direction Leif had been driving.

Another factory. How fitting.

"Of course, I'll follow you there." Leif slid from between them, but Hector's hand slammed onto his shoulder before he could reach the hay truck.

"You ride with us."

"Should we bring this truck?" Karem gave it an appraising eye.

"It's garbage," Nadia said as she strode to the passenger door of the brown pickup. "Leave it."

Hector's grip tightened. "You ride with me and Muk." He strong-armed Leif rather marvelously into the middle seat of the semitruck's cab. Entirely unnecessary, but Leif thought better of telling him so. The human Muk's aureole of warmth rendered him speechless anyway. Muk smelled downright acidic with weeks' layers of sweat and grime. Too delectable.

What could Hector really do to Leif if he ripped out Muk's throat right there? It would be worth it, wouldn't it? Though whatever Hector did would presumably leave Leif with little time to enjoy it. He sighed and shivered as the engine vibrated the seat beneath him in response to Muk's wide U-turn.

Leif focused his nostrils instead upon the stench of the flesh-eaters in the trailer, revolting enough to keep him in control and make him dearly miss the hay.

Last night, Demos's commune possessed two of these cattle trucks. Did they lose half the horde in the battle? Perhaps his little mind-control trick wasn't as effective as he boasted. If one could even call what lurked between flesh-eater ears a "mind."

"Is this all that survived?" Leif asked.

"Shit, you kidding me?" Muk laughed. "We got more than we can handle. These are going to Lorenzo. We cleaned up good and new recruits need their training."

To Lorenzo! Their little carpool suddenly became a lot more interesting. "Where's he set up these days?" Leif asked without sounding too interested.

"Shut up," said Hector.

"I guess I'll find out when we get there."

"Not so sure I wanna take you with us. How 'bout I take him the android and your head and get double points?"

Leif frowned and let his much-desired head fall back on the seat top. "That would be something you could do, yes."

Think, you old fool! A reason, any reason they should need him whole. Something only he could know about this Carol. An access code, perhaps? Yes, he would tell them he knew how to bypass some security. Surely plausible enough. Surely androids had such systems? If he didn't know, Nadia and Hector certainly wouldn't.

Leif shivered again. The heat on either side of him was almost too much to bear. Hector's warmth undoubtedly was also Muk's. Leif's head rolled against the seat to eye Muk's throat. The freshest bite marks in his lovely flesh were only hours old.

Hector clamped Leif's arm in a meaty grip. "None for you."

Was Leif being that obvious? He batted his thirsty eyelashes at Hector. "Perhaps when he's done driving?"

"No."

"Have a heart."

"Demos gave him to *me*. He lasts me until Lorenzo's camp. You don't get any."

Muk's knuckles paled around the steering wheel. "Shit, guys, I'm right here."

Leif ran a hand down his hot human thigh. "Oh, I know." He could feel each of Muk's muscles clench through the rough denim.

"Hector, make him stop!"

Too late, Leif felt Hector clamp a fistful of his hair and then a brain-rattling crack as his head hit the back windshield.

"Stop distracting the driver."

Leif sighed. He would have to avoid inhaling for the rest of the ride.

Thankfully it was short. They followed the ugly pickup around a bend where dark structures loomed into view. A building compound squatted between the hills beyond a fork in the highway. Smokestack shadows spilled through chain-link fences and stretched like hungry fingers across an empty parking lot.

As they parked the trucks out of sight behind the main building, the factory showed all signs of abandonment. A side door hung off its hinges. Hector's touch toppled it to the ground with a crash.

"Just tell the world we're here," Nadia muttered.

"There's no one here," Leif said. "Except perhaps some rats."

"You don't know that."

"As a matter of fact, I do." He might be starving, but his senses remained keen enough to tell that much. If any human skulked here, he would be draining it already. Leif reminded himself that she was young; sometimes he forgot how weak his nose was at that age.

"Pardon me if I don't trust you," she said.

Leif shrugged and stepped over the threshold. He lifted his face to the cavernous warehouse. "Halloa," he called. "I come in peace."

He waited. Not a sound.

"Halloa! I come to eat you."

Nothing stirred.

He glanced back to them in the doorway. "You see? Not even a mouse."

"You said there were rats." Hector glowered at him.

"It's a figure of speech. It... You know what, never mind." Leif hopped over debris and followed his nose farther into the building. If Muk and Karem must be off-limits, rats would be better than nothing. He'd been teased too much tonight to go to sleep on empty.

The scent of carbon fuel led Leif across a machine-filled room into a labyrinth of pipes and ducts. As if it were waiting for him, the generator proved too easy to find. He smiled and rubbed his hands together. "Bravo." He checked the tank and found it far from empty.

He spoke over his shoulder at the others. "I hope you don't mind if we get things a little turned on?"

He reached for a lever, but Nadia shook her head. "Don't waste the fuel."

"Sure." Karem shot an anxious glance to Muk. "It's not like we'd want it while we're hanging around here all day or anything."

"Quiet," said Nadia. "Get our coffins. Put them in a windowless room." She turned back to Leif. "And you. Stay where I can see you."

"I don't have a coffin." He gestured to the shadowy passage behind him. "I need to find a place to sleep."

She stared at him as if considering whether that was a reasonable request, and then a small smile parted her lips. "Actually, boys, take a break. Blondie's going to do the heavy lifting for you."

Leif blinked. Was this an attempt at degradation? He could offer her some tips. But he only returned the smile and made her a little bow. "My pleasure, my dear."

Outside, he hopped into the back of the pickup truck and told himself to focus on the task to keep his poor senses from tracking the humans' every move as they sought rest in the building. Nadia and Hector's caskets nestled against the flatbed's side, braced by tool boxes, a suitcase, and…oh. *Oh dear*. Could it be? Had all of Leif's stars aligned? He fought not to laugh.

Those were the igniters in that weapons bin.

He crouched and flipped open the case. The very same igniters Demos snatched from him. The little mechanical buttons radiated warmth from the night's heat. Leif's fingers curled around them. Could it possibly be so easy? He could secure one igniter under each of the caskets right now. They were still calibrated to his detonator, the caskets still laced with the explosive spray. He could take the cargo of flesh-eaters for himself. He could use them to capture the Carol android. He could deliver her to Lorenzo, and he could begin his plans anew. He could—

Arms locked around him, and Nadia's weight barreled him to the ground. Her hands tore at his like talons, then she leapt from him just as quickly. Leif sighed and rolled onto his back to look up at her.

Or he could get caught thinking instead of acting, like the damned fool he was. "Excuse me?" he said as incredulously as any innocent vampire could manage.

Nadia stood over him, the igniters in her hand. "What do you want with these?"

Leif got to his feet and brushed himself off. If his coat were stained, he was going to be very angry. "Protection," he snapped, as if offended. "Hector's going to take off my head the second I show you the android."

Nadia tilted her head thoughtfully. "Not a bad idea." She rattled the little button chips in her palm. "You know, they don't do anything if they're not in spark range of an explosive, right?"

Leif blinked and let his mouth fall open. Not too much; he didn't want to give the game away. "They don't?"

Nadia laughed, tossing her hair over her shoulders. "Go back to the thirteenth century, sweetie."

This time Leif's expression of disdain took no talent. He wasn't *that* old.

"What's funny?" Hector came to Nadia's side. "What's that?" He reached for her handful of buttons.

She let him take some, then slid the rest into her pocket. "Snowflake here thought he was going to make a bomb without any explosive."

Hector glowered at the igniters as if blaming them for looking so tiny in his immense palm, and then he pocketed them.

"You keep threatening my neck and I'll do worse than that," Leif said. "But let us work together as comrades, and I promise you shan't regret it."

Nadia let out another snort of laughter, and Hector shook his slow head. After all, how threatening could Leif be if he didn't even know how igniters worked?

The sky above them eked toward gray. "Get the coffins inside," Nadia ordered.

Leif stacked them and carried them over his head into the factory. He made his way through the main machine room and out into a loading yard. One end opened to a driveway that led back to the parking lots, and an elevated loading dock filled the other end. A forklift lay on its side a few yards from the dock.

"Naptime already?" he asked it as he passed by toward a promising door on the opposite wall. Leif broke the lock with his free hand and found himself in a garage the size of a jet hanger. Whatever vehicles it once held were long gone, but it was windowless, and it would do. He set the caskets in the center of the room, side by side.

"You sleep in here," Nadia said behind him. She opened a broom closet in the back wall. Fresh life scent tumbled out of it, assaulting Leif's senses. He was hanging half into the door in less than a second.

"You have a roommate." Nadia snickered.

A scraggly raccoon reared in the corner, eyes wide and needle teeth bared as it hissed and hissed at them.

"Awww," Leif crooned. "Isn't she pretty? I shall call her Dinner."

He couldn't see them, but four tiny heartbeats gave away the pups she hoped to protect. How adorable. He would call them Dessert.

Once he put an end to all the screeching, he left his coat on a hook behind the door to keep it free of cobwebs and then huddled into a duct vent in the back of the closet. He didn't think Karem and Muk would be suicidal enough to open the main door and disturb his slumber, but Leif was never one to regret taking extra precautions.

The scarce animal blood slugged through his veins, but it was warm and better than nothing. He felt rather raccoon-like altogether curled in the confined space.

As he listened to Nadia and Hector secure themselves in their caskets, he slipped the iPod from his pocket and opened the remote detonator application.

Now, how many igniters did they each pocket? They were tiny things, but they were fierce. Could they spark the spray explosive lining the caskets even through their blue jeans?

Let's find out.

The stiffness of imminent sunrise crept upon Leif, muffling the world, reducing all his senses to the true undead state that daily rejuvenated his eternal night. In the garage, Nadia and Hector were falling into similar mindlessness.

All in all, the night could have gone worse.

Leif's lips pulled into a rigid smile as the blood slowed in his veins and the last of his self-awareness seeped from his fibers. And then, just as it left him completely, his thumb brushed over the boom button.

21

REUNION

"That's the third roadcycle." Scott rubbed at the headache gnawing the brainspace behind his temples. "None of these are going to have any fuel left."

Carol's eyes flashed at him through the murky dawn light as she straightened beside the bike. "There are eight here." She gestured to the scattered mechanical bodies. Covered with an inch of dust and floating on a sea of brown, they looked more like prehistoric fossils than abandoned vehicles on the highway. "Do you mean to suggest I not check the other five?"

"I'm just saying. If three are out of fuel, they all are."

"We are going to test them all," she said in that voice she always used when he challenged her logic.

Their car managed less than ten miles on fumes before it died. They had abandoned it and hid for hours. When nothing emerged from the darkness to suck Scott's blood or steal his soul, they set out on foot. After a while, he legitimately started to doubt what he'd seen. He didn't bring it up, and Carol focused on their search for fuel. If they never mentioned it again, who was to say it happened at all? He definitely didn't intend to ask Carol for confirmation.

The farther they walked, the more his own focus dwelled on his diminishing enthusiasm for filling their fuel can and hiking all the way back to where they left the car in the center of the highway on the other side of the pile of hills.

Scott sighed and followed Carol to the fourth roadcycle. She slipped the plastic hose through the serpentine tubes into the tank and pushed its other end at him. “Suck.”

He licked his teeth and put his mouth around the tube. A quick slurp, then he turned away with a grimace. A childhood memory of his mom forcing him to clean the family fish tank while his brother and sister got to watch TV mocked him out of nowhere. The permanently soaked-in fuel tang of this hose tasted somehow even worse than the fish-crap flavor of the one from his past.

If any of the bikes did have juice, Scott would much rather get on one and ride until they found another car. As long as it provided enough legroom for naps, he couldn’t care less what they drove. He smacked down the inner voice jumping to remind him he’d never driven a roadcycle in his life and would probably fall and get his foot chopped off. Instead, he stewed over the opinion that all of Carol’s going backward to go forward was the worst of ideas. Especially in the middle of the desert.

“There, you see?” he said after the tiniest of dribbles tinkled into their can. “Nothing.”

Carol tapped around the tank valve with the hose then pulled it out to examine the moistened end, her headlight brightening to compensate for the gray morning.

“Don’t tell me I’m not sucking it right,” Scott said. “It’s totally dry.”

“Not totally.”

“Give up. They’re empty.”

She turned to him, her LEDs hitting him smack in the eyes. “Give up?”

Scott’s hand shot up to block the light. “Ugh, I can taste the fumes.” He scraped his tongue with his teeth.

“And then what, Scott? What do you propose?” Her headlamp clicked off. “Probability dictates at least a seventy-six percent chance one of these four remaining bikes holds some fuel.”

He rubbed at his mouth. What he would give to be twelve again, hating his mother for making him clean that fish tank. "No. Carol. It doesn't. Where do you even get these statistics? Practicality dictates that someone else—probably someone just like us—came along and saw all these roadcycles lying here and drained off every last one into a glorious spacious can that somehow held all those gallons. Or *maybe* they had more than one can. Or *maybe* these tanks were already mostly empty considering they had to get out here in the middle of nowhere in the first place. Did you factor that into your probabilities?" He wiped his forehead with the back of his wrist. The sun hadn't even emerged yet, and he was already sweating.

"Scott."

"Huh? Did you?" His mom had served a fish dinner that night too. To rub in his suffering. It was his most disgustingly vivid memory of his last year with her. He strove to ignore the hollowness pummeling the bottom of his stomach. "Huh?"

"Shut up, Scott."

"You shut up!"

"Is that an order?"

"Ugh!" He wiped his mouth again and turned from her to his things on the highway's shoulder. He kicked the duffel bag off his backpack and pulled out a water bottle. He swigged, gargled, and spat into the dust.

"I cannot make the vacuum for the hose myself," Carol said. "I am not designed with a respiratory system. You know that."

Scott shoved the bottle back into the pack and yanked the zipper closed. "Blah blah blah. I'm so miserable because I'm not a real boy. If only I could breathe and have babies."

Carol whirred and her voice dropped. "You are making irrational presumptions."

In one of the backpack's side flaps, Scott found a square of mouth cleaning gum. He slipped it into his jeans pocket. "Yeah, I'm just a stupid human without trilobites of memory. And I couldn't pick up one of these bikes over my head and throw it across the street."

"Trilobites?" She paused. "Why would I throw a bike?"

He turned back to her. "I don't know. Stress? Frustration? You do have emotions. You're frustrated right now, aren't you? I know you are because I'm making you. You have *feelings*. Don't try to act like you don't and like it doesn't matter to you that you can't suck on a stupid hose and you need me to do it for you."

"Why do you even bring this up? I wouldn't need to get fuel at all if not for you."

"Oh, it's *my* fault we ran out of gas? It's *my* fault you raced out of that flat dog town because you thought that vampire was following us?"

"Why do you think he followed us? It's not my blood he wants to drink."

Scott twitched at the memory of the way the vampire ogled him, at how its frigidness seeped through their layers of clothing for the second it pressed against him by the rocks. If it had managed to put those icy hands on him, or its slimy lips on his neck... Scott shuddered from head to foot. He shook out his hands and focused on Carol. "He said you were friends."

"We're not."

"Then why didn't you shoot his face off?"

She stared at him, like she was trying to decide how to reply. The hesitation appeared almost human, but Scott knew better. She was probably analyzing all possible responses she could give to get Scott to react in the best possible way for her desired goals. He *hated* that. Hated feeling like he was being *handled.*

"Why would you believe a vampire?" she asked, her tone exasperated, tired.

But she didn't get tired.

"How did he even catch up to us? Huh? Have you worked out an answer for that one yet? How did he know which way we drove? Oh, I know. You must have told him something."

Carol bent to drape the hose over the red fuel can. "You don't believe that." She straightened and stared at Scott. "You are trying to manipulate my emotions by implying you doubt my intentions."

"*I'm* trying to manipulate?"

"And you're doing it poorly because you are under-rested and chemically imbalanced. It's been seventeen hours since you last ate."

"I felt carsick." And then all that *thing* on the rocks did to his guts... *No, not going to think about it.*

"A moment ago, you criticized me for leaving town in haste to escape the vampire for your safety, and now you accuse me of betraying you to him? You know my mission objective."

"And I also know you have total free will! How do I know you didn't randomly change your mind?"

"Because I'm your friend, Scott. And I care about you. Is that so hard to believe?"

He rolled his eyes and kicked a roadcycle tire. Of course, she would say that.

When he didn't answer, Carol turned from him and crossed the highway. Scott looked up. She stopped on the opposite shoulder, her back to him, and just stood there.

How the heck was Scott supposed to tell if these represented her real true feelings and not more manipulation? *Women.*

So what if he was hungry? His points remained valid. Food bars stuffed his backpack, and he had no good reason not to eat one. But even as his stomach grumbled, he made a face as he imagined their sandy roughness and twangy flavor on his tongue. What he would give now for that resentful fish dinner of eleven years ago. He never told his mom sushi later became one of his favorites. Thinking of it made the insides of his cheeks hurt.

First thing, he reminded himself. *First thing.*

He watched Carol's back for a minute. She didn't move, and for all he could tell, she had powered down. He hated when she did that. Who was she to decide when an argument ended? Just because she possessed infallible rationality didn't mean she was always right. The rationality also remained open for debate as far as Scott was concerned. Too often, he found her as annoying and stubborn as any human girl he ever attempted to understand. And she definitely didn't have any of their other assets to make up for it. Besides, it wasn't like he meant what he said.

When his stomach growled too loud to ignore, he kicked the tire again and sighed. "Hey, forget it. Sorry. You're right, I'm hangry or whatever." He waited another moment. "I'll eat a bar."

"As if I would not sacrifice everything for your sake."

He winced. "Yeah, I know." It wouldn't be the first time.

He stepped around the bikes to her. "Carol, you just, you know. I can't ever be a hundred percent sure. That has to make sense to you, right?"

"You think I'll change my mind on a whim because I'm not human and I don't have real feelings. I know."

When he reached her side, he wiped some dust off her shoulder. The back of her metal head framed his face's blurry outline. "No." He sighed. "I know you wouldn't do that."

"That's not true. You think I'd do it unintentionally. You trust me, but you don't trust what makes me."

"Well, can you really blame me?" Scott let his hand fall. "You're just, you know..."

"Yes. I know."

"Carol, come on. I know Nick made you the best. There's no other AI like you. Nick put her all into you. You practically *are* her. I guess I...I don't know. Sometimes it feels like I'm with her again? And then it hits me that you're not her. That we don't actually have all that history. That you're, you know."

"Yes. I know."

"Carol." He sighed.

"No, it's fine. I understand. How could I not understand? I am not Nick. I do not want to be Nick. I am Carol. It is logical that you miss her. You miss your life with humans. My companionship cannot be more than a pale substitute. I understand." She left him to return to the fuel can and picked up the hose. "Don't you worry, Scott. I'll get you back to her. I promise you. You will be among your own kind again." Using the end of her blue scarf, she wiped the mouth of the hose.

"Carol, you're not being fair."

She offered the cleaned hose end to him. "Probability calculates this is the fairest of courses."

"Stop that." He pushed the hose away.

"Stop what?"

"Pretending to be all like a pre-personality computer. You can make choices based on how you feel."

"Don't you think I have been?"

He met her purple gaze. As morning light spilled over the hill at his back, her silicone features stood out with sharper definition. The usual irritated twist to her expression often negated her pretty LS face, but as she stared at him with wide eyes, he was struck by the gentleness there. She looked almost lost.

"Carol..." He shook his head. "I just—"

A cry interrupted him.

"Huh?" He gasped. It sounded like...

"Scott!" It came again, a voice from beyond the rocks.

He whipped around and squinted at the hill. "Did you hear?"

Carol dropped the hose, and her laser sprang out.

"Scott!" The voice sounded familiar. A moment later, Scott placed it. He shuddered.

The talking zombie chick.

He ran to where his shotgun lay by his backpack.

"Scott Sullivan! Wait! Please."

He glanced to Carol as she planted herself at his side, her laser aimed at the rocks. "Easy," he whispered.

A silhouette emerged from the boulders and made its way down the hill. With the light at her back, Scott could almost mistake her for human.

"Please wait!" She had her hands up, empty. "I just want to talk to you."

"You..." Scott trailed off. He scanned the hill behind her as the sun crept over its ridge. She was alone. Or so it seemed. "How do you know my name?"

"I didn't recognize you before." The words tumbled from her as if she were out of breath. But zombies didn't get out of breath? Her cautious footing appeared only as uncertain as any human's on the downhill slope. "But as soon as you ran away, it hit me."

Scott squinted at her sunken face. "You know me?" He was pretty sure he'd remember a talking zombie.

"No, not exactly. But I knew your sister. Nicole? We went to school together."

Scott heard Carol make a whirring sound. "Wait." He lifted a hand to keep Carol down. "You know Nick?"

The girl paused a dozen feet above the road. "I mean, we weren't really good friends or anything, but we had classes together."

"You did? Wait..."

"And Elias." She carefully lowered her hands. "I heard about what happened to him. I'm so sorry."

His brother's name punched him in the gut. Scott exhaled against it. He refused to think about Eli. Perfect Eli, the martyr, the hero. *Stop.* He peered at the zombie. What was that other thing she said? "Wait. You're from Pasadena?" He took a step forward. Carol snatched his elbow, but he shook her off.

"Well, Long Beach, originally, but we, um, moved halfway through high school. You were three years behind us, right?"

Only because Nick skipped a grade and Scott's birthday came after the cutoff date. But he never mingled with Nick's friends. This chick was out of luck if she hoped he'd remember her.

"Scott," Carol said on low volume with a shake of her head.

"Wait," he whispered.

The girl picked her way down the slope. Before Scott could speak, Carol knocked the wind out of him with a backward shove.

She placed herself in front of him, her heels almost on his toes. "Stop." She aimed her laser at the zombie girl. "Go back the way you came."

"Please." Her hands shot into the air.

Scott grabbed Carol's shoulder and pulled. "Carol, come on." It was like trying to move a statue. "Wait a minute."

"No," Carol snapped at him, then focused on the girl again. "Go. Now. Or I will shoot."

The girl glanced over her zombie shoulder, then back to them. "Just hear me out. I'm harmless, I swear."

Would Nick believe her? Probably. Nick would be all fascinated and stuff.

"No." Carol shot at the ground in front of her zombie feet.

"Carol!" Scott dropped his gun to grab her laser arm in both hands.

She shook him off and fired again. Zombie girl scrambled away from the blasted dirt.

Scott jumped in front of Carol and threw his arms around her. He heaved his weight to push her back. "I said stop! She knows Nick."

"You are being foolish, Scott." She reached around him to fire again.

"Stop! I order you to stop!"

"I'm nullifying your orders for your safety." Carol grabbed his arm and twisted. *Ow!*

Then she caught him by the shirt and shoved. The next thing he felt was his cheekbone hitting the ground. *OW*!

Before she could fire the laser again, Scott rolled over and shouted, "Carol: Robot slave mode!"

Carol froze. The light in her eyes dimmed and changed to yellow. She drooped, her weapon retracted, and her arm fell. Three long seconds passed, then she stiffened to attention.

Scott exhaled a half-sigh half-groan and rubbed at his face. *Owwww.*

"Why the heck are you always so damn pushy?" he muttered from the dirt.

A glance at the hill showed him zombie girl frozen mid-step in climbing the rocks. She peeked over her shoulder. He lifted a hand to halt her, then grabbed his gun and pushed to his feet, facing Carol. Her face was arranged in neutral, and her eye lights focused on the middle distance past his head.

He wanted to sock her in the chest, but it would only bruise his knuckles and she wouldn't feel it. Instead, he smacked his gun against his non-sore hand, squared his shoulders, and used his authority voice. "Carol: Report."

"Mode change successful." The emotionlessness of the mode's tone unnerved him as always. As much as he used to roll his eyes at the Robot Rightsers, RSM felt sleazy even to him.

"Mission objective:" Carol continued, "Protect Scott Sullivan. Design prerogative: Perf—"

"Yeah, yeah, okay," he cut her off. "So, protect me." He gestured to the hill. "Attack if this zombie makes any sudden moves. Cover my back. But shut up and let me hear what she has to say. Get it?"

"Yes."

"Good." He gave a curt nod and turned his back to Carol. He heard her weapon extend to aim over his shoulder.

"So," he lifted his voice to zombie chick, "what are the chances? Small desert after all?"

She was staring at him. Or at least he thought so. It was kind of hard to tell exactly with the milky film coating her eyes and the light behind her.

"Right?" she said. "Though it's been a while since I've seen Nick. I mean since way before the Ecuador Explosion."

"What did you say your name was again?"

"Emily Campbell." She started down the hill. "Is she still building things?"

"Well, she..."

"She's in Manhattan now, right?"

"How do you know that?"

"Like I told you before, I'm with the LPI. I've got people there. Please Scott, there's so much I have to report. And you can help me get there. Like, look what's happened to me. I was bitten by a zombie, right? But I still feel and act human."

"You don't look human."

"Exactly. This is new. Something's going on."

"Hold on." Scott lifted a hand to stop her, and she paused a few feet away on the road. He'd almost forgotten the most important part, and it felt like ice crystals crackled over his flesh as it rushed back to him. She was alone now. Good. But he had questions. "What about...Death?"

"No, no, I'm not dead. I'm undead. Which means I'm *not* not alive. So I'm still living, see? I've got to let them know about this. Scott, you know they need to see me. And there's all this other—"

"No, I mean *Death*. That, that thing with you earlier. Where is it? It's gone, right?"

"Oh, him." She glanced up the hill, then back to Scott. "Yeah, he needs to get to Manhattan too. We figured—we were hoping—maybe we could hitch with you?"

Scott almost dropped his gun. "What!"

"You've got a gas can." She pointed at it on the roadside. "You have a truck, right?"

"He's not gone?" He's *real*. "You mean you want *Death* to hitch with me? Are you crazy? I don't want to die!"

"Nononononono, don't worry! He won't reap you. He's not like that. He's like, retired now."

"Death is retired?"

"Kind of, basically."

"Where did he go?" Real and retired and real. "He's not coming back, right? He is *not* riding in my truck. I mean, I don't even have a truck. But that's beside the point. I'm not taking *Death* for a ride."

"No truck?" Emily took a step closer, speaking in a quieter voice. "Do you have anything? What about these bikes? Look, all I'm really asking from you is to explain things to the LPI in Manhattan for me when we get there. If I go by myself, they'll shoot me on sight. Like you did. All I need is to get into the city to see my coordinator. Let me just ride along behind you."

Scott's grip on his gun tightened, his eyes following her movements. "None of these have any fuel."

"But we'll find fuel, right?" Giving him and Carol a wide berth, Emily crouched next to one of the roadcycles. "These are good bikes. They don't need charging at all. Look, how about we roll along one each until we find fuel, and then fill up and all ride together? Then you don't have to have me in your car or anything."

Scott shook his head. "What about Death?"

Emily glanced up the hill again.

Wait, was he up there? Oh, shit.

"Um, well, he can follow us if he wants to?"

"I don't want Death following me!" Scott backed against Carol.

Emily let go of the bike to turn to him. "You don't— Ah!" She yelped as her foot caught the tire. Her arms flailed for balance, and she came stumbling toward him.

Carol whirred. Before Scott could speak, her blast fired.

In the same instant, ice picks shot down his spine and a dark blur obscured his vision. Emily disappeared, and *Death* stood before him.

Scott choked and jerked back. He lost hold of the shotgun as his head clanged into Carol. She fired over his shoulder again and again.

His hands clawing his slippery face, Scott's fought the seizing in his chest. He felt Carol separate from him. Between his fingers, he watched her run circles around Death, firing from every angle to try to hit Emily. But Death stayed between each of her blasts and Emily's body, moving too quickly for Scott to comprehend. The whole morbid kaleidoscope picture made his brain want to fragment. But the longer it went on, the less paralyzed he felt, and the more he grew queasy from trying to follow the circles.

"Carol, stop!" Breathe. He needed to breathe.

She froze in place on the far side of Death.

Scott clenched his hands into tight fists against his eyes and choked the nausea down. When he lifted his face to look, his brain fought the reality, but his body could not deny it. This was the realest thing to ever happen to him.

Death grinned, his bone hands clasped before his skull mouth, his index fingers tapping against each other. The clicking sound made frigid vines entangle Scott's heart. He clutched it and staggered backward. "Carol," he rasped. "Come here."

She jogged to him, and Scott jumped behind her before he dared to look at Death again. Carol's hard shoulders slipped under his sweaty, clutching fingers as he leaned into her. *Come back, balance, come back.*

Two thin gray hands appeared against Death's robe to pull it aside. Emily emerged. "He's not going to do anything to you, Scott." She glanced up at Death. "Right?"

Death's head tilted to the side as if considering her question. *Click, click, click* went his fingertips.

"Stop that!" Emily smacked his hands and then, after a stiff pause, gave Scott an apologetic half-smile. "He's just messing with you."

Death sighed and dropped his arms, turning from them to the bikes.

"What?" Scott gasped. "Why?" Inch by inch, as Death moved away, warmth returned to Scott's limbs, and his heartbeat re-sane-ified in his chest.

Emily shook her head and smiled at Scott. With the tension in the air and her shrunken skin, the expression came off forced. Strained, stretched. And really, really gross.

Scott edged around Carol to keep her body between him and Death at all moments.

"She's not going to do that again?" Emily eyed her up and down.

It took a few swallows for Scott to croak out a reply. "Yeah, she… I mean you looked like you were…" He flapped a hand in the air. Over Carol's shoulder, he watched Death drift past the roadcycle graveyard. "Death is just…here? I mean, he's…"

"He's helping me stay in one piece." Emily waved after him, but when her eye followed the gesture, her hand fell. Death was heading for the highway's curve in the direction of the climbing sun at a pace that would make him disappear around the hills in a few minutes.

"Hey," Emily shouted. "Where are you going?"

Death's voice floated back to them without a break in stride. "East."

His voice… Scott wanted to call it awful, terrifying. But the first word that came to his mind was *musical*. Was it supposed to be alluring or something? That was even worse. Scott shuddered.

Emily met his eyes. "We should follow him."

"We should?"

She sighed as if she knew exactly how Scott felt but was resigned to it. "We should."

Turning Carol to face him, Scott gave her unfocused eyes an

expression he hoped she would record, access when he switched her mode back, and understand as honestly, deeply apologetic.

She would not like this.

He picked up his gun and turned to Emily, who struggled to right one of the roadcycles. "Those are no good," he said.

Her dark eyebrows rose, but she did not argue. She dropped the bike and wiped her dusty hands on her black pants. "So…?"

"So…all right. Okay." If she could do this, then so could he. He slung the gun over his shoulder. "Come on, Carol."

Waiting only long enough for Carol to grab the fuel can, hose, and bags, the three of them set out to follow Death, *Death himself,* down the highway.

To hell, Scott thought. He almost repeated the joke aloud, but the reference would probably be lost on Zombie Emily.

Zombiemily… Zombily…

Well, shit.

He made Carol walk in the middle, and they stayed far enough behind Death that the chill of his presence remained only a loose tingle in Scott's deepest parts. Though the pace Emily set ranked brisker than his cranky legs liked, the sun in his eyes won the obnoxiousness prize. He wanted to ask Carol to dig his shades out of the backpack, but it felt wrong to have her do something so menial in slave state. A nagging feeling told him he should switch her mode back, but the same nagging feeling also dreaded how pissed she would be the second she returned.

He cleared his throat and talked across her to Zombily. "So, you're a…whatever you are. You don't, uh, have the urge to eat me or anything, do you?"

"What? No! No. I mean…" She leaned to see him past Carol. "Honestly? I feel like crap. Sort of shaky sometimes. I haven't eaten or slept in almost two days, but I'm not tired, and the thought of eating at all makes me feel like puking."

"I think I know what you mean." Scott's empty stomach grumbled in disagreement.

"You seriously are the first human I've seen since this happened to me. But it hasn't been very long."

"Two days? Sometimes it takes less than an hour after you get bitten to zombify while your body dies."

"You mean un-dies."

"And even less for the fast ones." And she was fast. Maybe not as fast as some of the fast ones, but as fast as any able-bodied human. "Did you let vampires drink on you?"

"What? Vampires?"

"That's why they're fast. The fang bites, the tainted blood. You had a hook up with a vampire?"

"No! Never."

"Even if it happened a long time ago, it doesn't matter. Once you're bitten—"

"Seriously, no." The dark bruises around her eyes cragged into a scowl and a green vein bulged from her forehead. "Jesus fuck, no."

Scott did nothing to suppress his grimace. "Okay, sorry I asked."

Did she used to be pretty when she was alive? She looked as fit as a ninja, good chest, and in silhouette, he supposed her face was all right. A nicely small nose, kind of flat. And her eyes had that exotic slant thing going on. Scott wondered if she was part Mexican or something. Or maybe Hawaiian? That would have been sweet. Except Scott couldn't exactly get past the now-gray chalky cheeks and flaking bits of skin on her lips. Her dirty black clothes didn't help the aesthetic either.

"I'm completely pure," she continued. "I mean, I was before this. But still, it's been like thirty-six hours since the bite? If I was going to get all brainless, I would be already."

But everything else about her looked zombie. The unevenness to her walk, the jerky way she moved her head when she talked. Except something was off about the image. Something missing.

"What happened to you? Why are you different?"

"I don't know. I mean, I don't exactly know how to explain." As if pulled by a string, her gaze fixed on Death's back.

"Something to do with him?"

She wasn't covered in blood. That's what was missing. Her face was clean. Scott gagged a little.

"I think so. I mean, definitely yes. Something about dying and undying at the same time."

Scott made himself follow her gaze. Just peeking at Death caused the icy tendrils to swirl the pits of his stomach. He walked a step closer to Carol's side. "Why is he with you? Is he waiting for you to finish dying?"

"No. I'm not really sure. He's kind of a vague guy. But look at it this way, wouldn't you rather he be on your side than the other way around?"

"He's on my side?"

"He wants to get to Manhattan as much as I do. And if you're going to help me, then yes. Think about it. He can stop bullets, right? And lasers. If we get into any trouble on the way, he'll shield us."

"How do I know he won't just let me die?"

"Because I need you, and he is going to help me."

Death did scare off that vampire last night. The one Carol hesitated to shoot for some reason. That's what Scott had to keep reminding himself.

Emily looked across Carol at him. "And don't you think the LPI would want to know about him? This is huge."

"He one hundred percent gives me the willies. So do you."

"Wouldn't Nick want to know?"

Death and Emily weren't robots, but sometimes Nick did, in fact, care about other things. Inexplicable-by-science things especially. "She would flip."

The nagging feeling tugged Scott again. He glanced sideways at Carol. He sighed and stopped walking. "Just a sec," he said to Zombily.

Carol stopped as well, and Scott took the dirt-colored backpack from her, hoisting it over his shoulder. He cleared his throat twice, then used his authority voice once more. "Carol: Nick mode."

Carol whirred. Her eyes brightened, the yellow turning to purple. Then they narrowed into a glare.

Scott could only hold her gaze for a moment before dropping his eyes. He pretended to do it on purpose and rooted through the backpack for his sunglasses. He cleared his throat again. "Did you, uh, process that information?"

"How do you know she speaks the truth?" Carol's laser popped out of her arm, then retracted.

"Instinct?" He slipped on his shades before daring to look up at her and took a swig from a water bottle. "You'd know it if you had a gut."

"Your probability of danger is exponentially greater in relation to your proximity to this zombie."

From the corner of his eye, he saw Emily's fists clench, and he gave her a warning shake of his head. The last thing he needed was to be caught in the middle of some freaky monster bitch fight.

"No, Carol. Come on. Executive decision here. Let's keep going."

To his relief, she obeyed. Good. Let her superior logic deduce he would RSM her again if she didn't. A minute later, though, she snatched the backpack from Scott's shoulder and put it over her own.

They walked in silence long enough for Scott to notice the sun shift in the sky. It chased a tower of clouds hovering inkblot-style in the center of the blue yonder. Scott watched Carol's focus tick between Emily and Death like a clock display. Her vigilance did not falter even as she took a ration bar from the backpack and thrust it at Scott. By the time the sun disappeared behind the clouds, his t-shirt felt permanently stuck to the center of his back. He assumed Carol would object to how fast they walked, give him some lecture on dehydration and water rationing, but she did not speak a word until Death turned off the highway to take a dirt road.

Scott glanced to Emily. She shrugged.

"Explain to me," Carol said to him as they followed Death like sheep, "why are you frightened of that person?"

"He's not a person."

Emily spoke up. "He kind of is."

Carol fixed her focus on Death's back. "What is he?"

Scott watched her eyelights change from purple to green to red. "He's Death."

Carol clicked. Her eyes became that deep-between-blue-and-purple color.

"You know, like the Grim Reaper? Yeah, look that up in your encyclobrain." Scott strove to remember another name for him but gave up. "It's an old myth, I guess. That when people die, there's a thing, a guy, who comes and takes you. I mean, us."

"He transfers them from life to death," Emily added.

Scott nodded. "He's an angel."

"No, he's not."

"He isn't?"

"I don't think so."

Carol shook her head. "I know what angels are."

"Okay," Scott said. "Right, so think of him like that. He's the Angel of Death."

"But angels are myths."

"Well, apparently he's not a myth because he's right there." Scott looked to Emily. "Because he's retired?"

She shrugged. "Someone stole his horse."

"Huh?"

"Look, he knows where he's going, okay? He's got like mental GPS—"

"My satellite maps," Carol interrupted, "are accurate to a—"

"And," Zombily interrupted louder, "he has all these shortcuts. And he knows where *things* are. Trust me, we should just follow him, at least until we find a car. Then you can lead the way."

"What makes you think we'll find anything at all?"

"You will." Death's voice made all three of them halt in their tracks. He faced them in the middle of the path ahead. Slowly, his arm extended, and one of his freaky fingers unfurled toward the distance. "There is a ranch not far from here. You will find what you seek there." When he lowered his arm, it was as if his fingertip meant to tear a slit through the air. And then he started walking again.

Scott stood frozen, inside and out. "Is he..." He swallowed. "He's listening to everything we say?"

Emily shook her head, which Scott took to mean probably. Before he could ask her what Death assumed they *sought* exactly, she broke into a jog. Scott watched her half-purple braid smack against her shoulders as she caught up to Death. She was much less painful to observe from the back. Those pockety pants didn't do her butt any favors, but Scott had seen worse. She spoke to Death, but he couldn't hear any of it. He could ask Carol to tell him what they said. Though if it mattered, she would inform him automatically. He hesitated.

"Are you mad at me?" he asked her instead.

"Yes."

"I'm sorry about the RSM."

"No, you're not."

He sighed and rubbed the back of his sticky neck. "How's your power level?"

"Low."

"Don't use the laser any more. We've got the other guns."

Carol unzipped the duffel bag to withdraw two handguns. She slid them into the silicone holsters on her hips, then she unzipped the backpack. "Your power level's low, too. Here, eat another bar."

Scott regretted asking at all. He gnawed on the cardboardy thing and took what felt like hours to choke it down bit by bit. It must have been at least a couple hours because when the sun reemerged from the clouds, it sat at the top of the sky.

He shoved the wrapper into his pocket. The world had ended, but he still couldn't bring himself to litter. "He said not far from here. It's been what? Ten miles already?"

"Six point two."

"Ugh."

"This is unwise, Scott."

"Okay, fine. Fine, fine. Fine. If this supposed ranch doesn't materialize in ten minutes, we can go back to the highway. Okay?"

"Yes."

Nine minutes later, *of course,* they crested a shrubby hill and he saw it. A vandalized, haunted-looking place, but there it stood.

Figures.

Bodies littered the grounds, humans and some dogs. Scott tried to ignore how Death drifted down among the corpses, and instead, he focused with Carol and Zombily to find what they sought.

22

THE RANCH

"You see," said Death. "It is as I told you."

"I didn't...doubt you." The truth of the words sank in as Emily spoke them. As much bullshit as she slathered onto Scott to put him at ease, she actually trusted Death implicitly when he said he would lead them to a ranch.

As Scott and his robo-friend caught up, Death drifted away into the compound. He was keeping his distance from Scott. Ideal, as far as Emily was concerned. But was that more for Scott's benefit now, or Death's own? Last night, he took off after Scott, the "living human," like a zombie after flesh.

Death said he only *reaped* at a person's time to die. But was that a law of nature or more of a moral code? Maybe it was too agonizing for him to be around something he wanted but couldn't have?

Emily glanced at Scott. If she were the kind of zombie who ate people, she could possibly see what his appeal might be. He did look... supple. And...hearty. Young, strong. Full of...vitality.

Warm, soft, oozing vitality. Yeah, oozing was definitely the right word. Humans seriously were squishy creatures.

Yeah, she could see it.

Good thing she wasn't that kind of zombie.

"I'm checking out those trucks." Scott's voice snapped Emily back to the moment.

A trio of pickup trucks lounged in front of the long ranch house. She jogged down the hill after him but could tell right away the first two were a bust. They had no tires.

"And this one doesn't have an engine." Scott groaned and dropped the hood of the third.

"We could take the engine out of that one and put it in this one?" Emily put in a lot of hours at her father's lot, but that kind of mechanical skill was beyond her. Just a bit. But maybe between them, they could figure it out?

"No." Carol lifted a bullet-hole-riddled hood to inspect one of the existing engines. "I will take the tires from that one and put them on this one."

Right. Or that. Duh.

"How can I help?" Emily asked.

"You can't."

"Come on." Scott gestured to the buildings. "She works better alone."

"Scott." Carol's face snapped up. "You should stay with me."

"I'll be fine! Fix the truck."

Emily hesitated at the driveway's edge, hoping they didn't start fighting again. "I'll stay six feet away from him at all times, I swear."

"She's not even a real zombie."

Carol's head rotated in Emily's direction, her uncanny-valley robot eyes narrowing into glowing slits.

"Come on." Scott waved Emily toward the stables and sheds. "Supplies and fuel."

"Right."

Walking backward as she followed him, she watched Carol lean into the driver's side and pull out the panel below the steering column.

"Is she going to bypass its system?" she asked.

"Unless she miraculously finds the fob just lying there, then probably, yeah."

"What if it doesn't work?"

"Well, she has two chances, and if it's an engine problem, she can fix it."

"She knows auto-mechanics?"

Scott snorted. "She knows lots of things. Her memory is huge."

"Does she know kung fu?"

He gave her a confused look. "Probably? Though she's not exactly light on her feet."

Emily shook her head. "Never mind."

Carol didn't seem about to shoot her in the back, so Emily allowed herself to relax. Just a bit.

"Okay," Scott said as they walked around the fence. "First thing we do is scrounge up some fuel for the truck and check the house for food, batteries, bullets, shells, the usuals. Second thing is drive to the nearest place we can find with power so Carol can charge for a few hours. Third—"

"Wait, how many hours is a few?" Emily tried to calculate the time until nightfall. She didn't like the idea of being anywhere after dark in the company of Scott the Live Bait other than speeding down the road.

He waved an unconcerned hand. "Technically, she only needs to be at twenty-five percent to function at full capacity. If she can get to forty, she'll be really good for a while as long as she doesn't use her particle weapon. That drains her like a bitch."

"How low is she? What if we don't make it somewhere with power before she runs out?"

"She has enough backup to keep going in low-power state for days. I mean, even if she gets completely drained, obviously I would power her down for a while. But she's so heavy, I couldn't get her out of the car on my own. We make sure she always has enough left to walk. She just gets really…"

"Bitchy?"

"No, she's always like that. I was going to say slow."

A rust-colored stable filled most of the compound's center. The wide double doors at the end of the long building creaked back and forth in the wind. A thick, rotting odor made Emily want to pinch her nose as they approached. "Ugh."

"Worst case scenario," Scott said, strolling in as if his nose were made of steel, "I'll have to deal with her in power-save mode for a while." He pushed his sunglasses into his hair, making the ends of his long bangs stick up like fan palms. "Check those shelves over there. But, yeah, she can jump on emergency juice if she absolutely has to, though full energy only lasts for a few minutes. While she's in low-power state, she's little more than big bulky computer."

God, how could he keep talking through the stench in the air? Emily could barely open her mouth. Was this a zombie thing? She made herself ignore it as she moved on from the shelves to search the stalls on the left while Scott glanced through those on the right. Dark unrecognizable rotted chunks of meat and bone lay scattered throughout the slimy hay. *Uggghhhh*. Caving, Emily's fingers clamped her nose.

"She can keep her personality," Scott continued. "The bitchy one. Though she lasts even longer in Robot Slave Mode."

A snort of laughter blew past Emily's fingers. "I can't believe you call it that."

"Not *my* name. Nick always said if you're going to take away a sentient being's free will, you should call it what it is. A 'Compliance State' command won't work on her." He knocked his gun against one of the stall doors. "But, anyway, don't ask her to run too many programs at once, calculate anything crazy, or use any of her communication servers, and she can hang on to that extra juice for a while."

"Wait, can she contact New York?"

It was Scott's turn to laugh. "There aren't any servers left she has access to, so no."

"What about radio?"

"Nothing that long-range."

"But isn't she an army robot?"

"They wish. She's an LS model, yeah, but Carol is a one-of-a-kind Nick Sullivan original. I mean, her local network's all right. A few miles reach." He juggled his shotgun to his other arm so he could pull something out of the bulging pocket of his too-loose jeans. "She can reach me on this."

Emily had to break into the six-foot radius just a little to see what he held, but Scott didn't object. The touchscreen wafer in his palm reminded her of a watch phone without the band.

"Like a walkie-talkie?" If she unpinched her nose, she'd sound less like a chipmunk, but it was so not worth it.

"It's more like an extension of her." He flipped it over to wipe the smudged screen on his shirt. "She's in this as much as she's in her own head. I can't use it to access her hard drive, though. Not even any shared files. Nick made it that way to 'respect her privacy.' It's more like a glorified baby monitor. For her to use on me."

Emily peered at it over her knuckles. "She's listening to us right now?"

"It's off." Scott slipped the ancillary wafer back into his pocket and gave her a mischievous smirk. "Got to save power, right?"

"Right." She smirked back, then realized too late he couldn't see it past her hand. But they reached the end of the stable, and she forgot the awkward moment as she broke into the open air beyond the doors.

Oh, god, *so* much better! She kicked the door closed to lock in the stench. *Uggghhhh.* And they hadn't even found anything inside. She took deep breaths of the hot dry air, extra relieved when they didn't make her choke like before.

She was getting the hang of this zombie breathing thing!

Fuck.

"Okay, so, we drive until we find a place with power," she recapped to distract herself. "Then wait there an hour or two until your android's at forty percent, and then we can get moving?"

"If we can hold out longer, it would be better. That way she'd get her laser back."

"But she's got those other guns."

"Her aim's better with the laser. And it works great on vampires." Scott's suntanned expression brightened as he went on. "If she gets a square hit, sometimes they burst into flames. It's really cool. When she gets a zombie in the face, its chomping days are over. Doesn't beat a shotgun for blowing their heads off, obviously. Though it *can* get strong enough to slice through flesh and bone. But if she turns it up that high, a few blasts, and she needs to charge again."

"Uh huh..." If chattering to Emily about his robot and guns was what put the guy at ease, let him go. She followed him, six feet behind, into the largest of the sheds. Bins and tanks lined its shelves. Jackpot! They took opposite walls to go through them one by one. The stuffy air simmered at least ten degrees hotter in the closed room, but after the stable, Emily wasn't about to complain.

"They tried to get it to work on a solid stream like a laser knife," Scott continued as they searched. "So she could slice off vampire and zombie heads left and right, but battery life was a joke. She can rip into them with her bare hands faster. Just as long as there aren't too many. She was overwhelmed in a room of them once. They *buried* her. I don't know if they thought they could eat her or if it's more like self-preservation. Know what I'm talking about? When they'll like bite your gun because you're whacking them with it. Like a hive mind thing going on? But I guess you would know about that."

It took Emily a moment to realize what he meant. *Seriously?* She looked up from the plastic bins to glower at him. "Actually, I wouldn't." She definitely didn't feel any kind of special zombie connection to the ones she encountered at the border camp.

Scott ignored the comment and shoved aside a tub to reach another behind it. "But anyway. She was no match for a big pile of them. And they never could get the androids strong enough to be worth the cost, even with the military contract."

"Who's they?"

"Curisa Robotics. Nick's people?"

"Oh, right." She mentally whacked herself. She supposedly knew Nick, after all. The information Death's screen gave her about Scott all had to do with the lives and deaths and locations, past and present, of his relatives. Either his device didn't include employer names, or he chose not to share. But Emily needed to fake it better before Scott noticed.

"Before Nick got her hands on her," he rambled on, "Carol was an experimental LS for the zombie studies. Except she didn't have her personality then, so I guess it wasn't really *her*. But she still remembers it all, so kind of? But they threw too much at her, and she got messed up pretty good, so the battle test guys left her behind when they abandoned the facility.

"Nick and her crew didn't fly out with the first evacuation. I moved in right around then. We really should've gone, but you know how engineers are. When Nick found Carol, she rebuilt most of her body. She was super hardcore into Robot Rights stuff. That was the main reason she wouldn't take that first airship to New York. She refused to leave all those androids behind. It was a total waste though. Like six months later, they all got destroyed anyway."

"Except for Carol?"

"Obviously. Nick installed this illegal AI her, uh, friend, Kim made before she died. Like seriously illegal. The *LPI* even banned Kim's software. Nick said they—the government or whatever—were especially afraid people would use it with LS's. Which is exactly what she did. I guess it lets them make any choices they want? And they can have a full range of human personalities, from good to evil. Nick was all about that."

She couldn't recall when it happened, but Emily had stopped searching and just watched him now. The thick heat made her brain feel mushy. And when Scott's eyes lit up while he spoke about his sister, it brightened the whole room.

"Nick said it was the same as genetically selecting baby traits, you know?"

"Uh huh." God, the shed smelled so much better than the stable. Anything would have smelled amazing after that, but there was something about this room in particular.

"To her, robots were people and deserved to be treated with as much human rights as us."

"Sure." Like the best anything had smelled since Emily could remember.

"But also not like Nick wasn't totally narcissistic about it. The program still needs to start with a base personality type, right? She put her own in Carol. Or at least what she thought was her own. To Nick, Carol had every trait of the 'perfect female.' To me, she's just annoying. Shows you how subjective it all is."

What was it? So fresh and...*pure* smelling. Definitely pure. Maybe one of the bins held scented candles or something?

Oh, he'd stopped talking. Emily should say something. He was looking at her now.

"Why..." Um... *His sister.* Right. "Why do you keep talking about Nick in the past tense?"

"She..." His gaze fell, and then he turned back to his shelf. "I don't know. I mean, I try to believe she made it safe. It's just, she was supposed to come back, or send someone back for me, and she never did."

"But she made it. I mean, I know she made it." Death's device knew absolutely Scott's sister lived in Manhattan, but Emily didn't want to admit her source. "How would I know she's at headquarters if she didn't make it?"

"But who knows what's happened since? That was months ago. What if she's like you or something?"

"She's still alive. One hundred percent absolutely still alive."

He shrugged and shoved aside another bin. Emily wondered if he was one of those people who liked to dwell on the worst possible outcome to avoid being surprised by tragedy. He didn't strike her as generally pessimistic, but did it provide a coping strategy where his sister was concerned?

Though she didn't see how anyone could be negative in a room that smelled so nice. But maybe, like in the stable, he couldn't smell it like she could?

Or maybe he just couldn't smell himself?

Emily's entire frame went rigid. It *was him* she smelled. And the longer they stayed in the closed room, the more it magnified, filling every corner.

"Blegh." Scott leaned against the shelf and wiped at his glistening forehead with the back of his wrist. "Can't you prop that door open or something?"

"Sure." But she didn't move. A bead of sweat slipped along his hairline, twinkling like a diamond in the dusty sunlight streaking through the high windows.

She blinked and strained to look away, but more droplets gathered at his temple, caught under the arm of his sunglasses. They shimmered like a string of crystalline pearls. She could smell them too. Each little drop. They smelled... It sure wasn't sweaty guy smell. No, it was crisp. Fresh. Like he oozed purified mountain spring water.

What?

Emily's brain did a little recoil.

Gross.

...Right?

But it emphasized how cottony her mouth felt. Her chapped lips burned, tight like they would crack in a hundred places if she smiled. Some clear, fresh, clean, *pure* water would be so good right now.

Could she ask Scott for a sip from his bottle? Would that squick him?

He left his shelf to move around the work table in the center of the room. Where did he keep his bottle? In his backpack? As she moved to the table, she realized he was talking again. Crap. She should be listening, pretending to care, but the thirst plugged up her ears, the smell of it all putting her to sleep.

Wake up. She licked her lips and shook out her head.

Scott was staring at her. He wasn't talking anymore. Was she getting too close? The radius was more like four feet now.

Should she back off? She should back off.

Emily lifted her hands, about to apologize, but Scott cleared his throat and moved to the end of the table.

Ask him a question.

Right.

"So, um," she started in what she hoped came off as a conversational tone. "You never said. How did Carol get out from the zombie dogpile?"

"Oh, the Curisa guys opened up the room and lured them out." He took the edge of the stained drop cloth covering the table. "As soon as they noticed a human, they left her alone."

Flipping the cloth aside, he craned sideways to peer under the table. The muscles in his neck stretched, and the shaggy ends of his hair fell away from his collar. Emily's foot slid forward.

No...

This was the opposite of backing off.

But she didn't have to get close enough to make him uncomfortable. Just a little closer, to see under the table too. There had to be something interesting down there. The way the tendon rose from his hairline surely meant there was something to be seen.

Scott's head snapped up, and Emily froze. He peered at her, then pointed across the room. "Check out that cupboard."

She nodded and turned to go, but something in her gut twisted at the effort it took. She told herself it was because his story was just so, so interesting. "Did..." A hazy curtain rose behind her eyes, like a fog machine in her brain. *It's the heat,* she reminded herself. *Be cool. You're fine.*

She squeezed her eyes shut and shook her head to clear it. "Did they ever..." What was she going to ask?

Whatever it was, going all the way across the room to examine a cupboard and possibly not hearing his answer felt like the worst thing she could do at the moment. Her voice sounded too loud to her own ears as she forced the question out. "Did they put her in there again?"

"They were going to." A hollow metallic clatter came from under the table as he rooted around. "Never got the chance."

Maybe he wouldn't mind if she asked for some water after all. She'd pour it from above, not let the nozzle touch her lips. He'd just have to hand it to her. She'd try not to touch him when he did, she really would.

Although, would it be so bad if his fingertips brushed her skin? Maybe he'd feel that her flesh wasn't so different from his. She might even feel soft to his dude hands. And his fingertips might feel like snake scales rubbed the wrong way. A tingle ran up her arm as she imagined it.

No. Gross.

She made herself go to the cupboard, but the fragrant, fragrant brain fog worked its way through her sinuses, filled her throat. She smacked her lips, forced it down as she looked over the racks inside.

"Nothing useful in here," she called over her shoulder, the words sounding a mile away. As she closed the doors, a tucked-away corner of her brain registered that she couldn't have told him a single thing in the cupboard if he asked.

But he didn't ask. He pulled his sunglasses out of his hair and wiped the sweat from his forehead. He set them by his butter-brown boot to sort big round metal canisters from under the table one by one.

"Who the hell would keep so many used propane tanks?" As he leaned sideways to reach deeper, Scott kept his head up, his gaze flicking in Emily's direction every few seconds.

"Yeah." Her feet were sliding over the gritty floor again as if they hoped the rest of her wouldn't notice. Did the six-foot radius really matter anyway? It's not like the robot could see her. And for the moment, Scott didn't seem to notice. When he bent down, the tan line on the back of his neck crept out of his over-washed t-shirt. His skin below it was so creamy. Like pudding. So pure and puddingy.

Emily blinked and shook out her head again. "I mean, um, recyclers?"

"Yeah, right." His voice rang against the empty cans. "The environmentally conscious."

His shoulder blades moved under his shirt like wing tips. Above them, the tag stuck up out of his collar. Emily was still a few feet away, but even through the heat of the room, she could feel the warmth radiating off his back. Actually feel it. Was warm pudding a thing?

So warm... She ran her dry tongue over her parched lips once more. She reached out. Her fingertips stretched, yearning to just...just fix his tag for him. That was all. Just...tuck it back in.

The radius became two feet... One...

Scott jerked around and smacked the air in front of her hand. "Hey!"

"Sorry!" she gasped. The room's hot air shot down her throat and dissolved into a fluttering in her chest that felt more like a trapped swarm of defrosting flies than any heartbeat she ever knew in life.

Scott flailed backward, cans flying in every direction.

"Sorry," Emily repeated, making herself slide away from him. The grit under her boot soles scraped, so loud. "You had a…" She swirled a hand in the air above the back of her own neck.

"What?" Scott jumped to his feet. "A bug? A spider?" He swatted at his collar without looking away from her.

She shook her head and labored to gulp up some moisture into her aching mouth. Where had her words gone? She tried to focus on his eyes, to meet them levelly.

You are in perfect control of your senses. Let him see it in your calm, collected, completely and totally and absolutely focused gaze.

Bloodshot webs laced Scott's eye whites like spidery hands holding the dark green crystal balls in their center. If Emily had dexterity enough to pluck out each of those full veiny vessels and squeeze them of their fluid, turn his gaze back to clear, to blank, pure white, drained of color, his color, his warmth, his moisture, she could help him with that. He had too much, clearly. Squishy. Oozing. He couldn't possibly be comfortable with all that excess, all those juices.

Scott's eyes narrowed, and he took a step back, lifting his gun. "What? What is it?"

Emily pushed her hands to her face and rattled a breath into her hollow lungs. "Sorry, I'm just…" What was that word? That word… "I'm zoning out? It's so hot in here. But you're fine. No spider. It's gone." She forced her cheesiest grin.

"Augh! Don't do that."

"What, smile?"

He nodded.

She was just smiling. Just…

She must look like a nightmare.

She was supposed to be putting him at ease.

God...

"If you're not going to help, then go back out to the yard."

And leave him? But— Ringing in her ears underscored the twist in her stomach. Somehow, she tore her feet from the floor step by step. "I'll just…I'm going to check out that other shed."

"Yeah, you do that."

"Right."

Right...

God.

23

SPECTER

Outside, Emily managed to make it around the shed's corner before she had to stop. Slumping against the fiberglass siding, she dug the heels of her palms into her eyes until they felt about to pop out the back of her head. She should return to the stable. The rot smell and buzzing flies would flip her stomach and squash out any particles of sweetness lingering in her nostrils. Snap her out of it.

But that would also mean she'd have to go back into the stable. And things were already coming back into focus. She was fine. She dropped her hands and bonked her head back against the wall, looked out at the clear sky. She was fine.

So different from only a moment ago in the close air of the shed. What the hell? *Don't think about it.* Where was Death?

He won't know anything.

But somehow just imagining him made her head feel clearer. She pushed away from the shed. And as she staggered around the next corner, she almost walked right into him.

He caught her by the shoulders, but she jerked back, steadying herself against the wall.

"You're still here," she whispered without meaning to. She shivered a little. His grip hadn't been hard, but she could still feel distinctly where each of his bone fingertips pressed her scapulae.

His head tilted as he gazed down at her. "Where would you have me go?"

She shook her head and tucked a loose piece of hair behind her ear. "Where were you?" Should she tell him about the smell? The weird…thirstiness?

He swept a hand in the direction of the decaying bodies in the yard. "I've been here before."

"Yeah, I noticed."

If she told him about it, she wouldn't like his reaction. She was sure of it. If she kept it quiet, then she could forget it happened at all. Besides, she felt a hundred percent better now. Completely fine.

He put one of his long fingers in front of his mouth as if to shush her. The gesture didn't really work without lips. "Come this way."

"What?"

With a curl of his finger, he beckoned her across the yellow-brown yard toward the long, low house. The wind swirled cute little tornadoes in the dust of the expansive corral off to their right. What happened to all the horses? The chunks of dead things in the stable had been too small to be equine. Did they all escape? It was a nice thought.

She assumed Death would lead her inside the house, but he went around it. She could tell the back yard used to have a lawn and a garden border, but now it was all the same cracked dead straw color as the rest of the land. No trees, but a tire swing hung from a pine frame. *Kids used to play on that swing.* A cloud of tiny insects filled the tire's center, lording over fetid water caught between its drooping edges. The last rain couldn't have been that long ago.

"Here." Death held open the door to a tool shed in the corner of the yard.

Two five-gallon canisters sat side by side within.

"You found fuel!"

Why didn't he bring them out to the trucks? Why show it to her like this?

"*You* found fuel," he said before drifting away again.

And that was just what Emily told Scott five minutes later. If Death didn't show them to her, she would have found them on her own eventually, right? And Scott was so excited, he forgot all the weirdness from before. Or maybe it hadn't been so weird, after all? The memory of their conversation fuzzed in Emily's brain, and she let it fade.

Even Carol begrudgingly thanked her when the truck she'd repaired guzzled both jugs.

"You ride in the back," Scott told Emily once they were ready to go.

"Right." This drive was going to suck, wasn't it?

"And you ride over there." Carol pointed Scott to the passenger seat. "You need to sleep."

Emily climbed into the truck's big bed and squinted over its roof into the sunny yard to search for Death among the buildings. Should she call for him? Surely he heard the engine starting. Yelling out his name would be awkward. She couldn't bring herself to do it.

"We're leaving now!" she yelled instead.

"I'm aware."

Holy hell, he was right behind her again.

She turned and glared at him. He sat in the opposite corner of the wide flatbed by the tailgate. The truck lurched, and Emily almost fell over the side. She dropped to her butt, bracing against the cab. Death stared at her.

"You don't have to look so amused," she muttered.

He tilted his head as if considering that possibility.

With a sigh, Emily twisted her fingers around the strap running the length of the truck's side. At least two of its six tires must be flat. Yup, this ride was going to suck.

"If she stays on this road," said Death a few minutes later, "we'll come across a structure with electricity before nightfall. A factory."

"How do you know?"

"I was there not long ago."

"How not long ago?" Just because the place had electricity once didn't mean anything now.

"It was deserted by the time I left it." He drew his device thing from the depths of his robe and swiped the screen a few times. "It is deserted now."

Emily leaned up to tap on the cab's rear window. Through the grimy glass, she saw Scott twist around. He slid the pane open a crack. She realized she was bracing herself. For what? The smell?

But nothing emerged.

She put her face to the hole. "He says there's a factory on this road up ahead."

"He? Oh."

"It has working power and everything."

Scott smiled and yawned. "Okay, cool."

Emily gave him a thumb's up. "A few hours. Keep going straight."

"That far? Well. Sound good, Carol?" She didn't reply, and Scott nodded to Emily then slid the window shut. "Night."

Yeah, things were definitely fine. All she could smell was truck exhaust. It must have been the stuffy heat in the tiny shed room that made her head go all wobbly before. She was so totally fine. And Scott was fine being around her, and the robot wasn't trying to kill her, and Death was being useful, and everything was just downright spiffy.

Scott had the right idea. It was time for a long overdue nap.

Sleep refused to come for Emily. No way she folded herself into the truck's corner lent itself to relaxation. The gun in her waistband dug into her back, but removing it didn't make her any more comfortable. More than forty-eight hours since she woke from her last sleep shift, she should have been exhausted. She wanted to blame it on the truck's uneven bouncing, but that wasn't the truth. The LPI trained her to sleep in the roughest of conditions.

No, she knew the truth, she just didn't like it—Emily could no more sleep now than she could die.

She glanced to Death in his corner. His legs were folded under the black tent he wore, his fingers steepled in his lap, and his gaze fixed on the road they left behind. At least she assumed so. She couldn't see beyond his hood, but without eyelids, she didn't think he had much of a choice.

Turning her G18 over, she ran a finger along the distorted polymer. It would not be firing again. She might as well be carrying around a rock. She sighed and threw it against the opposite side of the truck by the three empty gas jugs. It clanged a lot louder than she anticipated. Flinching, she glanced to Death again, but he didn't move.

The dry wind scratched and scored at her eyes. It should have made her want to sneeze, but sneezy sensations seemed as distant as sleep. She drew her legs to her chest and pressed her face against her knees.

Zombies don't sleep.

"He's finally fallen to sleep," Death murmured into the wind.

Emily lifted her head. "What?"

"The human."

Lucky bitch. Through the dirt-streaked window, sunshine glinted off the robot's metal scalp, but Scott slouched too low for Emily to see.

"How do you know?" she asked.

Death's face remained hidden by his hood.

Nothing.

Emily wrapped her arms around her shins. After a minute, she offered a suggestion. "Is it a knowing-everything-of-death thing?"

"Hardly."

Fine. She didn't need to conversate. She could sit back and enjoy the scenery. The gritty, brown, seriously boring scenery. Disheveled civilization couldn't be far off, but for the time being, nature's own wasteland stretched far and wide. Brown, brown, brown. Everything they passed looked the same.

"Everything looks the same," said Death.

Emily stiffened. Had he just...? "What did you say?"

His head rotated, and he met her eyes. The sight of his face took her by surprise. He looked different somehow. Was it the direct sunlight making the bones appear flaky and gray? More like old newsprint papier-mâché than the bleached white they gleamed in the moonlight. The light reflected off whatever invisible marbles filled his black sockets, and she couldn't see the little green flames deep in his eyes at all. As if his off button had been pushed.

But it didn't affect his ability to stare at her. After a long moment, he finally replied. "Were you thinking the same thing?"

A dry laugh escaped her.

Death's hand flicked at the road. "I am not used to this."

"What? Driving?"

He turned away. Emily stared at the back of his hood, waited, then bit her lip and burrowed into her knees. Although the sun throbbed at her hair and simmered the tips of her ears, she did not mind it the way she would have a couple days ago. Long past when she should have broken a sweat, she still felt even and dry. The rhythm of the truck's flat tires reminded her of a racing heart. She counted the beats.

"You are bored."

Emily jerked and turned to Death. "How do you—"

"So am I." He withdrew a pack of cards from his cloak. "Here." He tossed it to the center of the space between them.

Emily stretched to retrieve it. No box, but a black elastic bound the cards. Their frayed edges and soft surfaces caressed her gnarled fingers more like fabric than paper or plastic. Vintagey. She tugged off the band and let it slide around her wrist as she fanned through the deck. Vibrantly painted skeletons in big hats and flouncy clothes decorated the backs, danced across the face cards. Emily smirked.

"La Calavera Catrina," Death said.

"Cute." They reminded her of a long-ago trip to Mexico. "Where'd you get them?"

"I won them."

"Who from?"

"He's dead now."

"Oh." Emily smoothed the edges and shuffled with care.

"He lost the game, after all."

"Right." She cleared her throat but paused mid-shuffle. "So, that's a thing? If I challenged you to a game when you came for me, would I have had a chance?"

"Don't be ridiculous."

Excuse me.

He spoke again before she could say anything. "Why would a suicide challenge me?"

"A..." Emily frowned, her gaze falling to the happy little skeletons. She tried to recall her frame of mind at the moment she tried to squeeze the trigger. She'd *invited* him. What she wanted— She pushed the thoughts away and shuffled. "So, do you want to play something?" She could remember the rules to about three games, but he probably knew them all.

Death sighed and presented the back of his hood to her again. "What would be the point?"

Emily blinked, then rolled her eyes. So he only liked playing with lives on the line? She restrained a patronizing reply about alleviating boredom and dealt herself a game of good old-fashioned Klondike. A few minutes later, it occurred to her she should thank him for the cards, but she let him rest in silence.

A groan escaped her when she lost the game. The creaking undead sound oozed past her lips before she registered it. *Oh gross!* Emily cleared her throat violently.

Death twisted toward her, his hands clattering against the floor. The intensity of his stare made Emily flinch, and the cards kerfluffled out of her hands. One of them caught the wind and took off into the air. Before it could get far, Death's hand shot up to catch it. He did it without even looking. Slowly, he twirled the card between his fingers. "You've lost your game."

She'd lost her—*no!* Shoving the rest of the deck off her lap, she rubbed at her eyes.

Death leaned over to scoop up the cards. He lingered for a moment, hovering like a black umbrella as his gaze raked her over, then he settled back into his corner.

"You just..." Emily dropped her hands, huffed out a breath, and scooted to his end of the truck bed. "Please. Do not look at me like that."

He shook his head and shuffled, the cards buzzing flawlessly under his long fingers. "How do you feel?"

Not this again.

"Frustrated. What do you think?"

"Tired?"

"No."

"Hungry?"

"No!"

"Hm."

Calm. Control. Goddammit. She hated the way he stared at her. Like she was some kind of specimen. Or a boil ready to pop. She dug her fingers into the black canvas over her thighs. "Why? What is it?"

Death shrugged and turned his attention to the cards, fanning out the entire deck between his hands.

Oh no you don't.

Leaning in, she put a hand over his spread, pressing the cards down. "You keep asking me these same questions. You're waiting for me to start craving human flesh and stuff, aren't you?"

"It's only rational." The way he looked at her then was a little less awful. She couldn't say how, but something sympathetic filled it.

"Well, we've already gone over this. I'm not." Her hand slid off the cards, and she slumped against the side of the truck, facing him. She had her weird moments, but never once had *I vant to bite your flesh* entered her brain. That much was for sure.

"Hm."

"What?"

"It's unprecedented."

"Yeah. We've established that."

Death took a quiet moment to sort through the cards, then shuffled again. "Your behavior is less like that of the undead, and more akin to that of a specter."

What? "What? Like a ghost?"

"If you like."

"Oh, so now ghosts are real." Death was real. Flying horsepeople of the zombie/vampire apocalypse were real. Father Time was real, and apparently an asshole. But something about ghosts sent Emily up to eleven in uncomfortable. Ghosts implied an afterlife. Implied a lot of seriously Big Questions even Death didn't have answers to.

"Not in the sense that you consider them." He cut the deck and set one half aside.

"How do you know how I consider them?" She folded her arms across her chest and ground her shoulder blades into the truck's metal.

Death shook his head and laid out a row of cards face down in the space between his knees and her boots.

"Okay." Except, not really. "Then is that what I am? A specter?"

"No. You are undead."

"Uh huh, okay. So then why don't I want to bash through that window and devour Scott's brains?"

"Are you sure you don't?"

"Yes!"

He shrugged. "Your lack of appetite is rather specter-like."

"And what does that mean?"

Instead of answering her, he flipped one of the cards and held it close to his face to study it.

"Come on, I'm tired of this! You have to tell me."

Death lowered the card enough for his eyes to meet hers. "I do not know."

"But—"

"Listen to me, Emily. I know *everything* of death."

Calm. She forced a slow breath. "But you don't know about me."

He nodded.

"Because I am undeath."

"You are...unprecedented." His gaze fell to the cards, and he flipped two more.

It seemed impossible. "There are millions of zombies."

"Not like you. Not created like you."

"This can't be the first—"

"It can. It is." His fingers hesitated before he flipped the last three cards. "Undeath is... She and I have never..." He sighed.

"Am I seriously the only person in the world like this right now?"

"More than that. You're unlike anything I have ever known."

A good thing. If she kept repeating it, she'd accept it. It beat the alternatives. And it kept him interested in her.

So why did she feel so shitty?

Specter. She'd been thinking of herself as part human, part zombie, but that would make her half life and half undeath. And that wasn't right. More like half undead and half just plain *dead*.

What if...?

God.

Stop thinking about yourself.

She had a new mission. An important mission.

Death sat as still as a tombstone, staring at his cards. Abruptly, he swept them up and laid out another row.

Emily shivered in the warmth of the sun as she watched his hands. They definitely seemed dustier than before. Thicker somehow, as if he dipped them in wet clay and let it dry and crack.

"What are you doing?" she asked. It looked like tarot. She'd never believed in tarot.

Death shook his head again. His voice sounded muffled within him. "I don't know what to make of it."

Emily closed her eyes and leaned her head against the edge of the truck. *Bounce, bounce, bounce.* "An unknown future. How exciting."

She should just try to relax, starting with putting her head elsewhere, and strategize how she would approach her LPI superiors when she got to Manhattan.

Death's response floated to her, almost inaudible. "Not really."

She had a good idea what she would say about her team and the vampires, but how would she explain Death? Would he even stick with her until then? What exactly did he have to *do* in order to catch up with Time? The more she thought about it, the less she understood his vague-ass plan. Did *he* even understand it? Was he so desperate he was flailing at the unknown? What did he see in his tarot?

"Are you afraid?" she asked.

"I'm…hungry."

Her eyes blinked open. He bent over the cards, his hood obscuring his face, his hands pressed against the floor.

"Like—"

"Yes."

Did he know she almost asked *like a zombie*? She felt no hunger, but what must it feel like for him? Did reaping serve the same purpose as eating? Sustenance? It made up what he was. He *existed* for it. The same as the energy his brethren drew from their conditions.

"Are you…okay?"

He shook his head and pushed back, gathering up the cards. "For now."

"How long is now?" What would happen to Death if dying ceased to exist?

"I suppose we'll find out." The forward presence of his voice returned, but the grim humor to his tone troubled Emily. He knew everything of death. This was definitely a death thing. But he didn't know? Or was he evading the question?

He met her eyes and lifted a hand to her, palm up.

Um? She blinked at it, her lips parting. What did he…? Oh! She slid the elastic off her wrist and dropped it into his metacarpals. "Sorry."

He bound the cards and tucked them away.

"Is there anything I can do?" she asked.

"You could kill Scott."

Emily laughed. He was joking. Right? He had to be joking.

He shook his head in a dismissive gesture. Okay, yeah. Just joking.

"Actually, I probably couldn't." It came out a bit strained despite her attempt at sounding bantery. Even if she wanted to do something so heinous, Scott was well-protected, and she was weaponless.

"You're probably right." He sighed.

She scowled at him. Like Scott was so much mightier?

He looked up at her. "What?"

"You're not supposed to agree with me."

"Aren't I? All right." He paused as if giving it some thought. "You could snap his neck if you managed the proper leverage. Or mix a tincture from desert flora to poison him. Or even now break the window behind his head and slit his throat. Or—"

"Dude, stop!"

Death sighed heavily. But despite the dramatics, he seemed amused.

"You are seriously awful." Emily couldn't help it, she was a little amused too. Poor Scott.

Mostly, it shocked her Carol hadn't stopped the truck and evicted them both. Maybe to conserve power for driving, she didn't have her robot ears turned up high enough to hear them?

Either way, Death needed to stop. No one was killing Scott. Scott would die an old man in his bed, gaming on his favorite channel or whatever he was into. No one was killing *anyone* as long as Emily could help it. So Death was hungry. People went hungry all the time. His turn for a while.

"Is there anything *else* I can do?" she asked.

"Distract me?"

What, how? He refused to play cards with her. What else?

"Talk to me," he replied to her puzzled expression. "I like listening to you talk."

She almost laughed. She was tempted to quiz him on the life story she unfolded during their walk yesterday. But why would he lie? She was a decently interesting person. Maybe he had some kind of life-envy? Hmmm…

"Did I tell you I won the lottery?"

"No."

"That's a funny story."

His posture lost some of its stiffness as he shifted against the tailgate. "I'm all ears."

"You don't have ears."

"Not now."

Emily blinked. "Did you used to have ears?"

"Tell me your lottery story."

She nodded and took a moment to dredge up the details. It felt like so long ago. "So, I was crossing the street, right? It was raining, but you know, SoCal rain, so I didn't have an umbrella. And I saw this fifty-dollar bill stuck to a parked car's tire. It was a gold car, a Lexus or something. Lots of mica in the paint. I called it the money car. Anyway, I was like 'sweet, free coffee!' but when I picked up the fifty, it was clipped to a bank deposit slip with some business checks. The slip had some company's name on it. So I was like fiiiiine and looked up the company. I emailed them, and they asked me to drone the deposit back to them. They said I could keep the fifty as a thank you. I gave it back with the checks anyway, 'cause, you know. But then they sent me fifty dollars' worth of lottery tickets. I won six-point-three million."

"That is a lot?"

"It's more than fifty!"

"You don't say."

"I mean, not enough to quit my job and pack off to New Zealand or anything, but I could have finally moved out of my parents' house. I'd been living there since I graduated, working seventeen-hour days out of my she-cave to chip away at my student loans."

"Yes, I know."

"Right. So, yeah, six-point-three million. Enough to get me out of debt and still have a little capital for the startup my friends and I were brainstorming for years. And then like three days later? Zombies."

Death stared at her as if waiting for more. But there was no more. Zombies killed everything.

"I never even turned in the ticket."

He nodded contemplatively. "That is a funny story."

Neither of them laughed.

Emily wrapped her arms around her legs and rested her chin on her knees. "Though I guess the Ecuador Explosion was like winning the lottery to anyone with student loans." None of the skills she learned in college helped her survive in the wild after the world fell apart. She should have majored in medicine or people management or something. Information systems? What a joke.

But still not laughing.

"Tell me about your ears." Her turn to be distracted.

"I don't have ears."

"Not now." She stared at him.

He waved a hand in the air as if he could brush the conversation away. Emily stared harder.

He stared back.

She wasn't going to stop this time.

"Very well," he said finally. "Why do you think I look like this?"

"Because it's what dead people look like? Eventually."

He plucked at the cloak over his lap and then studied his crusty skeleton hand. "This is a rather Western interpretation of me."

"So 'Westerners' had it right?" Emily frowned. Now that he mentioned it, that sounded seriously wrong.

"I look like this often. Most often. But not always."

"Like shape-shifting?"

"If you like. But I was with you when Time stopped me."

"Right…" And he looked exactly how she thought he should.

"It was your time. I was there for you."

"So…you looked like what I wanted?"

"Yes."

"So I basically willed you into existence?"

"No."

Basically, yes. Emily smirked at him. "Is that why you're so attached to me?"

"I could leave you."

"Sure you could."

He shrugged. His expression could not change, but he seemed even more amused than before. "Who else am I going to travel with?"

"Literally anyone else? Or alone?"

"Besides, you're mine."

"Uh huh, sure. Cause horselady 'gave' me to you, right? And I was totally hers to give."

It seemed like he might laugh. He could laugh, right? He was close.

"I've lost everything else," he said. "I might as well keep you."

"Yes. You need me to be your 'legion.'"

"Legion..." He went still, then drew his touchscreen thing out of his cloak.

What, did she say something wrong? "That's what the horsepeople said." Emily was just kidding, though. Why was he poking his screen so severely?

He shook his head with an effect as pointed as saying *shut up* aloud.

She blinked and sank against the truck's side. Well, he was distracted. Mission accomplished?

Bounce, bounce, *ouch.*

What was going on in his brain? Did he even have a brain inside that skull? Would she be able to see it if she peeked through the holes of his not-ears?

Stop thinking about brains, you creep.

Was Death's personality also an aspect of him she willed into existence? Or did it remain the same regardless of how he looked? Probably that. What about his voice? His eyes? Did he have many friends before? Or any ever? Other than his brethren, but fuck those guys.

Though when would he ever have the time to socialize? Every moment he wasn't reaping became a moment the world went wonky. Did natural moments on Earth when someone wasn't dying ever exist? There had to be some once in a while, right? When he wasn't bound by Time, he could presumably stretch those moments as long as he wanted. But who could he hang out with in a frozen moment?

No wonder he missed his horse so much.

Unprecedented.

Emily folded her arms and smiled to herself.

24

THE AIRSHIP

An especially evil bump in the road jolted Scott awake. "The airship!" He gasped for breath.

"There is no airship, Scott," Carol said from the driver's seat, her tone more mechanical than usual.

Scott groaned and dragged his sandpapery fingers down his face. His tongue impersonated a block of driftwood in his mouth. He swallowed twice, three times, and shook out his head.

"Watch the potholes," he muttered.

"I am."

"Not very well."

"As well as I'm capable."

His dried-out husk of a brain couldn't decide between snapping a retort about her needing an upgrade or accusing her of doing it on purpose. And then too much time had passed for anything he said to be considered snappy.

Cracking his neck, he sighed and rolled his face to the window. There never was an airship. Well, there were lots of airships, but never for Scott. The first ship he missed, though, was not his fault. That one was all on Jade.

The day she left Curisa, he wanted to believe it was some kind of mistake. The battery in the alarm went bad or something. She couldn't have intentionally reset it. She didn't possess that kind of deviousness. She lacked the creativity. But reset, it had been. The battery ticked on in perfect working order.

She must have gotten the idea from Colin. Mr. Frisco. Or maybe Colin even did it himself. Fuck Colin. If not for him, Scott would have been in New York almost a year ago. Fuck Colin and his fucking bald-headed, girlfriend-stealing, ship-seat-stealing, bald-headed baldness.

Scott ran his hands through his own shaggy hair and glanced to Carol. Bald, bald Carol.

The day Jade left, Carol lay in Nick's lab, but he didn't know if she witnessed his breakdown. Nick was working on her when Scott stormed in, but he never knew how much Carol recorded when she appeared to be off.

Scott hadn't been crying. Angry rage tears weren't crying. Not the same thing at all.

"Busy here," Nick said without looking up.

Scott kicked a table, and a tray of circuit boards took flight, clattering to the floor.

Nick jerked up. "What the heck?"

"Fuck Colin."

"What is *wrong* with you?"

He gripped the edge of the table and glared at it. Wrong? He wasn't Colin. Apparently that's what was wrong. "She left."

Nick's gaze darted around the floor, tracking the scattered circuit boards, but she didn't pull her hands out of Carol. "Midori!" she called over her shoulder.

Scott looked to the door in the back of the room, but Midori didn't appear. He was relieved. He did not need to see another girl right now.

"Where the heck is she?" Nick shot Scott an accusatory scowl. "Pick them up. But be careful."

"She left," he repeated.

"Midori?"

"Jade!"

Nick would forget Scott existed if he didn't force himself on her. Why did he even bother?

"Good. That's what you wanted, right?"

Scott gaped. Didn't Nick know he was supposed to be on that ship too? Would she have even noticed he left?

"No! This is most definitely not what I wanted." He wanted to be *out* of Curisa. He wanted to be in New York where there would be real food and normal people and Jade could finally relax and go back to treating him like she actually liked him.

Nick stared at the circuit boards like they might combust. "Midori!"

"I'll get them," Scott snapped.

Nick gave him another glare but turned her attention back to Carol as Scott stooped to gather them up.

"You two were awful together," she said as if decreeing the final word on the longest romantic relationship of Scott's life.

Wrong. She was just wrong. Things had been bad for a while, but they were going to get better again. How could Jade just *go* without him? Just...go. No. Not even just go. Actively rob him of his escape. Scott won the right to that ship seat along with hers in the last lottery. Colin didn't win shit. And now Colin was floating off to the promised land and Scott was stuck in Curisa purgatory, and all Nick cared about were her precious circuit boards. He should snap them in half.

"I never should have let her start hanging out with him," he said to the boards he collected in the tray on his lap.

Nick made a *pbtbtbt* sound. "Oh yeah, can't imagine why she ever would want to leave you."

Scott's anger had him shaking. Literally shaking. He tried to fold one of the boards between his hands, but it didn't so much as bow. The knobby parts bit into his fingers, and he dropped it in pain.

He looked up at Nick from the floor. She hadn't so much as noticed. Fuck her too. She didn't give a shit.

He hiccupped. "What is wrong with me?" He wasn't going to cry. No.

This was where Nick was supposed to say, *Do you want the whole list or just the highlights?* or some other sisterly insult, but she didn't answer. She apparently didn't even hear him.

Is this what Scott deserved because he stopped sending her birthday messages? Well, she stopped too. She moved out when she turned eighteen and never came back. Two years later, Scott did the same. They grew up. Life moved on. Who even cared about birthdays anymore? No one. No one cared. Scott's birthday had been two days ago. Jade spent it drunk. Nick spent it working. It didn't matter. Twenty-three wasn't an important year.

He pushed the tray off his lap, but Nick caught it before it scraped to the floor. Setting it aside, she knelt and pressed his shoulder. She looked kind of pissed, but she was there, really studying him, which was enough to surprise Scott. He didn't know what to do with it. He felt more awkward than comforted.

Get over yourself. You're better off without her. Told you so.

But Nick didn't say any of those things. She just looked at him, her hand on his shoulder, warm and light. As the quiet minutes ticked by, Scott's breathing evened out, the waves of fury and misery receded.

"Sorry," he mumbled.

Nick gave him a little squeeze before letting her hand fall to the lap of her green coveralls. He didn't know how long they sat there like that, staring at the red-brown stains in the grout between the floor tiles, not saying anything. But by the time they finally got to their feet, Scott's knees felt numb. Numb knees, but his soft insides hurt less.

"Just keep it together, Scoscar," she said. He couldn't remember the last time she'd used that nickname. Years. It almost made him want to cry for real. "We've got the next ship, right?"

He nodded and put the tray on the table for her. Gently. "Yeah."

Yeah. Missing the first ship? Not his fault.

Missing that next ship, though? The last ship... Scott's throat tightened as Carol jerked the truck around another pothole. He clenched his teeth, shaking the memories out of his head, and he focused on the road through the windshield. Silver mirages shimmered in each dip of the unending pavement stretching before the bumper. He should probably drink some water.

"Carol." He shifted in his seat to face her. "How many days since we left Curisa?"

"One hundred and sixteen."

"No, not the first time, this time."

"Four-point-four-one."

How many hours did that work out to? Point-four-one times twenty-four… Wait, what was he was doing? He shook out his focus. So far, he'd only finished three of his water bottles, and all his purification tablets remained. He could definitely spare a bottle now. Digging one out of his backpack, he chugged.

He braced for Carol to chastise his indulgence, but to his surprise, she kept her mouth shut. He found himself strangely disappointed.

Reaching over, he flipped up the soft pad under her arm to check her power meter. On reserve already? Shit. No wonder she was being so weird. "You're low."

"Go back to sleep. I'll alert you if I reach emergency levels."

No way. He needed to think up a backup plan in case this factory ahead didn't have juice and Carol couldn't charge. The last thing he needed was to be stuck with a brainless junkbot and *Death* following him around.

Scott shivered just thinking about him. When he'd joined them in the truck and the distance between them shrank to the closest since early morning, Scott braced himself to be hit with the chill. But though he felt something like it slither under his skin, the sensation hadn't staggered him like before. A sort of hollowness swirled in the center of his being, but it grumbled more like hunger than the terror of his own mortality. Maybe he was too exhausted to be afraid of Death at the time? Though now that he'd napped, he didn't feel any of it at all, even though Death was still back there. But Emily would keep him in check. He obeyed her for whatever reason. And the fact that Death answered to some random zombie chick made Scott find him much less intimidating.

"What do you think of her?" he asked Carol.

"Are you referring to Emily Campbell?"

He nodded and wiped his mouth, capping the bottle even though it was empty.

"You know what I think." Her eyes never left the road. "Why do you ask if you will only dismiss my conclusions? She presents danger to you, and you should get away from her."

"No, I mean, what's her deal? How does she exist?"

Carol's bluish-gray lips pursed in a silicone frown. After a silent minute, she shook her head. "I can't answer that."

Scott should know better than to ask a robot to theorize. He wondered if Nick would have speculated with him. She wasn't That Kind of Scientist, but Emily would pique her curiosity for sure. And then Death…

It was going to be one interesting reunion when they all got to New York.

25

MANHATTAN!

Death made a noise that jolted Emily upright. Not quite a gasp, it sounded like a sudden shower of sand.

His fingers blurred over his screen like frenetic spider legs, while the hand gripping it contorted in a way she feared might crack its bones.

"What is it?" She leaned forward. "What does it say?"

He ignored her. A few seconds later, he stilled. The device dropped into his lap. When Emily scooted over to look, Death spread a hand to cover the screen. He shook his head, staring into the distance.

"What?" she whispered.

Death's mouth opened. Emily didn't know what she expected, but the expression confused her. Then his jaw closed again with a soft click. He stood, and Emily fell back on her heels. He wouldn't jump out of the truck, would he? She almost grabbed a handful of his cloak to hold him back, but he sat on the tailgate and focused on his screen again.

Before she could ask a third time, he spoke. "Time and my brethren intend to destroy Manhattan."

"What?" *What!* "What? Why? How do you know?"

"It's complicated."

Oh no he didn't. "So am I. What do you know?"

Death pressed the device against his lap, his hands shrouding the screen. He stared over Emily's head. She glanced over her shoulder. Too much dust coated the truck's window to see through from so far, but something made her imagine Carol staring back at him in the rearview mirror.

"What do I know? I know that..." He paused, then started again. "Many lives in Manhattan are scheduled to end soon."

Emily whipped back to Death. "How soon?"

He lifted his face to the sun for a moment, then returned to his screen. "Twelve days from now."

"But they won't, right? Because you can't get there?"

"I can get there in twelve days. That's not it." He tucked the device away and tapped his fingers together. Then he pulled it back out again. "All around the world, there are concentrations of life whose scheduled terminations are being put off due to my absence. Murderers are showing unexpected mercy, suicides change their minds, executions encounter delays, accidents are narrowly escaped, and the ill and wounded linger with unheard of tenacity."

"Whoa. Seriously?"

"But in these dark times, with the population so dwindled, and so many falling to undeath, there's been little true dying left in the world."

"Ha. Yeah." Compared to before the Ecuador Explosion, of course. She recalled what he told her the night they met of how few people died that day. "Three hundred forty-si—"

"*So* little," he cut her off with a perturbed look, "that all the people not dying today can still meet their proper end when I return."

Proper end? Emily could only hope them not dying today meant they'd get an extra sixty years. Maybe not the mortally ill, but the people escaping all the violent situations for sure.

"I *must* return. Time must unbind me."

"Right. But you have to catch him first?"

Death's fingertips drummed the screen with sharp clicks. "The temporary delay of the deaths scheduled in the next eleven days won't alter the balance too radically."

He didn't sound so sure. "Are you going to explain this balance thing?" she asked.

"On the twelfth day, however…in Manhattan…"

That was a no, then.

He sighed wistfully. "It is the largest concentration of end of life and potential life on schedule for, well, quite some time."

Click, click, click. That couldn't be good for his screen. Emily resisted the impulse to reach up and still his hand. "So you're saying Time doesn't want all those people to die?"

Death shook his head. "He must mean to destroy the balance by stopping me so near to when I should take so many."

"Wait, wait. He has to know you can get there in twelve days, right? That doesn't make sense. He should have stranded you in Fiji or locked you up or something if that's what he wanted."

"Bound by Space, I can only go one place at a time. He does not know Manhattan is where I choose to go."

"Isn't he like omnipotent? He's Time. Can't he like see and hear us right now?"

"I have not sensed his observation."

"Sure. Okay. But even so, he has to know you'd choose to go to Manhattan."

"Why?"

"It's obvious, isn't it? Manhattan is where the *Life Preservation Initiative* is. And as far as I know, it's the only place working to cure the plague. Cure undeath." Wasn't that what he meant by *potential life*? "What else is more important?"

"*You* say it's obvious. It is important to you."

"Don't you want undeath cured?" Didn't everybody?

"I want to protect the integrity of the balance."

Whatever the hell that even was. Emily bit the insides of her cheeks as an uneasy feeling burbled up from her stomach. "Are you saying Time wants the plague cured, and that's why he wants to keep you from going there and killing them all?"

"Reaping. And no. My absence would make it worse."

What? "Can we back up, please? You're saying he's stopped you from being able to *easily* get anywhere you need to be to *reap* all the people you're scheduled to reap. So now, you have to be more selective about where you go."

"Correct."

"And *why* wouldn't he assume you'd go straight to the big one?"

Death sighed, but Emily didn't care if her questions exasperated him. She dug her fingers into her knees and waited.

Despite how much the truck jostled and bounced on its floopy tires over the uneven road, Death remained completely steady perched on the tailgate. "Life follows the order of Time," he said after some consideration. "He'd expect me to continue to reap chronologically. If he expected me to continue at all. He said…never mind what he said. I follow the order of life."

"You have to?"

"If I don't respect the balance, apparently no one will."

"So, if not for *me* telling you Manhattan's more important, it's not where you would have chosen to go? You would've gone after everyone on your schedule in order? Even if the first was in Alaska and the second in Timbuktu and the third back in Alaska again?"

"I don't know."

"But you just said—"

"Emily, I cannot say what would have occurred if our paths unfolded in different directions. Or what choices I would have made. It didn't happen that way, so *I don't know*. There are many places nearer in space where I am required sooner in time."

"You mean like if there was one forty miles south of here scheduled for tomorrow?"

He nodded. "With what's become of the world, I may *forever* lose the deaths I pass over while I travel to Manhattan. Because those humans will not die according to schedule, they may instead un-die, and the plague will grow more than it would have. Considerably more. Irreversibly more."

"So if you don't kill the guy forty miles south of here tomorrow, he's going to become a zombie instead?" No extra sixty years, no life at all.

"There is no guy forty miles south of here."

"You know what I mean."

"And I don't kill."

"You *know* what I mean!"

"Very well, yes. In your hypothetical situation, that is what I am saying." His shoulders sagged as he looked at his screen. "Unless I make Time unbind me when I catch him at New York, I cannot touch the thousands of dying people there all at once. I don't even have my scythe. My attempt would be desperate and ineffectual. If not for my interaction with you, yes, I may not have scrolled so far ahead and afield in the schedule. For me, it's..." He sighed. "I may have felt driven to pursue the nearer lives instead. It would certainly be less demoralizing."

Emily blinked. "Did you just say thousands?"

"Why would he not want me to take them?" Death murmured to his screen, stroking a fingertip over the list of words—names?—as if it were a kitten's spine.

"Thousands! Why would you *want* to take them?" Emily got to her knees and gripped the tailgate. "Hello? This is a good thing! If so many people there—*there* of all places—were going to die all at once, and now they're not, maybe the world can be saved."

"Not when they un-die instead."

When? No... He knew for sure? If she weren't holding the tailgate, she would have fallen.

"Do not misunderstand me, Emily. For a life to linger and escape me, I feel no prolonged malice. It is exceedingly rare, but if something naturally occurs to change someone's course, it is possible their scheduled time can change." He paused, his hand curling into a fist against his thigh. "There are those who have cheated me, but they always came to me in the end. If these lives in Manhattan were to be spared so that I might claim them later, I could be satisfied."

He didn't sound satisfied. He sounded just shy of disgusted. But she got what he was saying.

"But they will be stolen from me for *undeath* to claim them instead. That is a robbery I cannot abide."

She was really getting what he was saying now. She was feeling sick. "*That's* why you want to get to Manhattan? To kill all those people? The same people I told you were so damn important?"

"Reap. And better that than they un-die."

In theory, Emily should agree. But, no. No, this was all wrong. There had to be more to it. Some other option.

"But you just said your attempt would be pathetic anyway!"

"I didn't say 'pathetic.' And only as long as I'm bound by Space and Time. But if Manhattan is where Time and my brethren concentrate themselves when this event occurs, I will intercept them and regain my power."

"And then you'll just kill all those people?"

"Reap."

"I swear to god—"

"They will be mine."

Emily gritted her teeth, biting back the urge to scream. She twisted her fingers into her hair, but the lack of resistance from the loose roots in her spongy scalp made her freeze. For a moment, she'd forgotten what she was.

If breathing still came naturally, she couldn't have managed it as she scrabbled to absorb everything. If the scientists in Manhattan died or got zombied, the cure would be lost. But maybe...maybe when Death said they'd un-die instead, he meant turned into vampires? They could still do their work then. Vampires needed to stop the zombies and keep humans alive, too, right?

But the politics would be all thrown off. The LPI would be finished, anyone left alive would fall to the slave camps, and human rights would become ancient history. No, it was bad. Every option was bad. This couldn't happen.

She stared at her purple-green-gray hands, but it did nothing to stop their shaking. Easing to sit between her heels, she eyed the pool of Death's robe. The urge to lift it and see if he had any feet under there caught her off guard. She slapped a hand over her mouth to stifle a giggle.

Oh god, she was losing it.

Above her, Death sighed once more.

"So." Her voice squirmed out, too high-pitched. "You're telling me the world is doomed either way? There's no way the humans in Manhattan can live?"

"Yes."

No.

"It is scheduled."

"How can you be so calm about this!"

"I am not calm. Time and my brethren mean to cheat me on the grandest scale imaginable. I will not allow it."

All those people. *Thousands* didn't constitute a grand scale by standards of mass-deaths in humanity's history, but by current standards, it encompassed a significant chunk of the population. The most *important* chunk. Not only would they be lost, but so would all the people they had potential to save with the cure and the LPI's initiatives. The *future* would be lost.

"You—you just want them to die rather than let your brethren get them."

"Very much."

"But you don't even want to…to consider…" What? What else could even be done? She felt like she was choking.

"I do not want to do anything, Emily, other than ensure that they die in twelve days. All of them."

How could he be so heartless?

How… Oh, god…

How could she have ever thought he would be *otherwise*? What had she seriously expected?

And yet he responded to her stricken look with a defensive edge. "You asked if I was okay. Twelve days from now, I will *not* be okay."

Was she supposed to pity him because he was *hungry*? "Then go get the guy forty miles south of here! And then the guy in Alaska, and then—follow your stupid schedule!"

"No."

No? No. He would rather starve himself to the point of what? Crazed ravenousness? And hold out so that he could smorgasbord on Manhattan? And this was a choice he made because of her?

He didn't want to stop the apocalypse. He just wanted it to happen his way instead of theirs.

"Then why—why are you even with us? If you can get there in twelve days, why don't you just go?"

Death's gaze drifted past her to the window again.

She twisted to follow it. What? Scott? What about him? Oh god, was he scheduled to die soon? Did Death expect him to be like a road trip snack? "No…no."

Death nodded. If he had lips, Emily was sure he'd be smiling.

"When?"

He lifted a languid finger to his mouth to shush her.

She was on the edge of a scream. How long had he known? Did he see it on his screen when he looked up all that stuff about Scott for her? Or had it appeared because she pursued him, because of her bull-shit plan, because she dragged Death along? She messed with Scott's future, meddled with his schedule. Scott wouldn't have found the ranch without her. He wouldn't be in this truck. *She* set him on this literal and figurative path. His life was going somewhere now it wouldn't have otherwise.

And evidently not for much longer.

The shaking in Emily's hands overtook her body. Why, why did she talk Death into following Scott? Soft, squishy, mortal, killable Scott. She wanted a way to the cure. She thought she could help Death out for the greater good. Well, she was helping him out all right.

Idiot, idiot, idiot.

Scott was doing them a favor; didn't that mean anything to Death? God, an hour ago she was thinking about what *friends* they were. Death didn't give a shit about camaraderie or loyalty or saving her world. How stupid could she be? This was *Death*. He wasn't a *person;* he was a force of nature. Cold, unfeeling. He existed to consume, destroy. His precious schedule and rules didn't make him *moral*. He was just another asshole opportunist. Why go after the guy forty miles south when one snoozed right here? Why leave her and get to Manhattan on his own when he could get a free ride and a snack if he hung around? Of course, *Death* didn't play fair.

Idiot!

Digging her palms into her eyes, Emily slumped into the corner of the tailgate. Let her eyeballs pop out the back of her head. Go on, pop. She was a *zombie*. A completely useless zombie who made stupid decisions. She would bust herself to pieces, or she would get all weird with Scott the next time they entered an airless shed and he would blow her face off, or she would get nuked on sight at the Manhattan gates. And Death would waltz on in and devour everyone there. Or not. It didn't matter. Either way, the LPI was done for and the communes would flourish, and no one would ever get cured, and undeath would inherit the earth, and that was it.

It was already over.

26

THE FACTORY

The air felt degrees cooler when the truck slowed. Emily lifted her face for the first time in hours. She almost gasped. Remnants of civilization! The sight of approaching factory buildings mixed an excitement and dread cocktail somewhere beneath the place her heart used to beat.

Her mind was made up. She would tell Scott everything, and they were going to get away from Death. As soon as she figured out how to phrase it without making Scott want to get away from her too. Considering how she talked him into letting Death tag along, she needed to approach it carefully.

But if they could beat Death to New York, then they could…do something. Maybe Scott would know what to do? They'd think of something. They had to.

As the truck rolled up a serpentine drive, Emily pointedly ignored Death and crawled to the window. She pressed her face against it but couldn't see through the late-afternoon dimness. She knocked on the glass.

When Scott opened it, she almost recoiled. The sudden smell smacked her like a pie to the face. So rich and deep—not altogether unlike pie, if pie were freakin' perfect—that she forgot entirely what she planned to say. It didn't smell like the shed at the ranch, that sparkling clear water scent. No, this was warm and thick. Did Scott have food in there? Something cooked? Was that even possible? How could it be so potent?

"Yeah?" he asked.

"What *is* that?"

His eyes narrowed. "What's with you?"

Emily shook out her head. *Focus!* "Um, I mean, are we stopping here?"

"Uh, yeah, that was the idea."

Scott eyeballed her through the crack. She leaned closer. Those bloodshot eyes of his... She gave her head another shake. "No, I mean, that's good."

"Uh, yeah." Scott looked her up and down again, then he moved to close the window.

"Wait!" Her hand shot out to stop it.

"What?"

The scent was so...so *familiar,* but what was it? She couldn't name it. It didn't literally smell like pie, maybe more like fresh baked bread or deep red wine. Yeasty. She didn't see any food in there. What did he have? Would he share it? "After we stop, we're gonna keep going, right? To Manhattan?"

"Uh, yeah."

She nodded, nodded. An ache bloomed across the insides of her cheeks like a blood spill as her mind wandered toward a floating place. "'Kay... Great."

Scott's eye roved her again. She leaned in to peer at it. The moist red-veined white surrounded a green so deep she could imagine swimming away in it. Curling into it like a liquid blanket, happily hibernating in its cocoon. And then by the time she woke, it would all be over. All this...all over...

A tug at the back of her shirt snapped Emily's attention away. She turned and scowled. Death hovered over her, and the window popped shut. For some reason, the sound made her want to cry. She clenched her teeth against the impulse, her eyes narrowing. "*What?*"

"You're drooling." Death leaned closer, as if he would poke her face.

"What?" She smacked his hand away. *Ah!* She'd forgotten about the creepy jolt thing that happened when he touched her skin. She shook the sharp tingles out of her hand.

The clicking his bones made as he clenched his fist sounded oddly melodic, distracting. What had she just been thinking? Goddammit, he made her lose it. It had been such a peaceful thought, whatever it was. He needed to back off. *Drooling?* Emily wiped at her mouth.

Her hand came away perfectly dry.

Ugh. She covered her eyes. Maybe he would be gone when she opened them. All she could smell now were road dust and truck fumes. She forced a breath out then dropped her hand.

Not gone. "*What?*"

Death remained still for a moment as if waiting for something, but then he shook his head and slid from her.

"Wait."

He turned back to her. What was that look? Hopeful? Expectant? Confused?

Doesn't matter.

Emily's eyes narrowed, and her jaw clenched. "Are you sure there's no one at this factory?"

He sighed without sound. "Yes." And then with a heavy ruffle of fabric, he rose and leapt from the truck.

Had they pulled to a stop? When did that happen?

Chain-link fence loomed over their parking spot, a dingy compound of squat factory buildings filling the lot on the other side. She climbed from the truck and tried to stretch her limbs, crack her back. The effort did absolutely nothing. So zombies couldn't stretch either? What other good news awaited her?

Once she stood upright, though, the cramped stiffness she should have felt never manifested. Okay, that was something, at least.

She jogged around the truck and found Scott outside the driver side. Emily tensed in anticipation, but when he opened the door, the smell of cloth mildew greeted her and nothing more. It was gone. The *scent*. Whatever it was…just gone.

Scott pulled one of Carol's silver arms over his shoulder and hoisted her from the seat.

"What happened?" Emily asked. Carol's sluggish movements reminded her of a sleepy drunk.

"Critical power." Scott grunted as he eased his robot friend to the ground. "Maneuvering mechanics not so good."

"Do you need a hand?"

"No, I got it."

Carol's eye lights were so dim, Emily could barely make out the violet color. Were they even on at all? As she leaned in to see better, they flashed to brightness and focused on her. Emily jumped back.

"You are in danger, Scott," Carol said. "I should activate emergency power."

"Nah, I'm fine." He shot Emily a *be cool* look as he put an arm around Carol's waist and nudged the door closed. "Save it. Wait until we're at least sure you can charge." Scott heaved her toward the factory, his scuttling footwork cartoonish alongside her slow mechanical steps. She could clearly walk on her own. What was he trying to prove?

"No." She started to whir, and her eyes grew brighter.

"Carol, stop."

She paused. "This is dangerous."

"Everything is dangerous! You'll be more useful if you save it." Scott glanced to Emily as if he needed her agreement. She clasped her hands behind her back and nodded with as much authority as she could muster.

"Now, shut all the extras off," he ordered. "If it takes longer than ten minutes to find anything, I'll hit your alert."

Carol studied him for a quiet minute, and then her eyes dimmed. She walked like blind clockwork up the ramped driveway to the factory gate, which stood wide open in welcome, Scott pushing and tugging at her as if that would do any good. Emily waited until they got out of sight into the building, and then she wrenched open the truck door and stuck her head through. She sniffed.

Nothing.

What the hell?

Sucking air in through her mouth only made her cough. The scent was completely gone. Had it even been there at all? She'd smelled nothing on either of them outside of the truck. She wiped her lips and closed the door.

Whatever. Right? Whatever. She needed to talk to Scott. With Carol powered down and Death out of sight, now would be great.

Inside the factory, Emily's gaze swept the murky room of looming machines. Long, barred windows along the top of the high walls admitted a few inches of the sinking sunlight in a way that made everything below appear underwater. Death said there was no one here, but Emily didn't want to stay any longer than they had to. Where did he go anyway? *Forget him. Talk to Scott.* A sudden rumble made her tense, and then the dim space came alight with blinking LEDs. Cold cathode ceiling lamps flicked to life one after the next.

"Found the generators?" she called. Wherever he was, Scott didn't answer. She surveyed the room again. Nope, definitely didn't look any less creepy with the lights on. Brown dust layered the machines, every nook and cranny clotted with cobwebs. It looked thirty-years abandoned, not two.

Emily heard the bang of a door falling shut somewhere off to her left. She followed the sound through the maze of machines until she reached a wall with only one door. The plaque beside it read, "Charging Station."

She pressed the handle, stepped inside, and stopped short. She caught a flash of the giant apparatus filled with mechanical forms before the door fell shut behind her. In the dark of the windowless room, a dozen glowing yellow eyes stared from the pinlight-speckled machinery looming to the ceiling. She reached for her gun that wasn't there.

She waited a moment for her vision to adjust to the dark, but nothing changed. Blinking, she squinted at the yellow eyes. She lifted a hand and waved. Nothing happened. Her hand swiped across the wall for a light switch, but when she found one, it didn't work. Stepping back to the door, she nudged it open. When the light fell on the machines this time, she made out the faces holding the eyes and the clunky ochre bodies attached. Six identical strange robots stood in the charging station slots along with Carol. Unlike Carol's slumped posture, the oval bubbles that made up their bodies and limbs stood at rigid attention in their harnesses. Their needlelike faces pointed at right angles. Three empty charging docks remained between them and Carol at the far end. Her eye lights were off, but the others all had enough charge to be staring at Emily.

She backed out of the room, letting the door slam again.

"What are you doing?" Scott's voice came from much closer than she expected, and Emily spun around to see him in the aisle between machines. He held the blue duffel bag in one hand and a red gas jug in his other. His backpack dangled over the opposite shoulder from his gun.

"What are those?" She waved a hand at the door.

"Those," he said, "are old school."

"They look like they're on."

Scott shrugged. "I flipped their stations off, so they're not drawing power. I didn't bother shutting them down. Did you try giving them any commands?"

"What? Why would I?"

"What are you so nervous about? They aren't going to hurt you." He set the jug on the floor and adjusted his grip on the bag. "Did Carol really freak you out that much? They're just worker bees."

Carol didn't freak Emily out. She was fine. She shook her head. "Of course not. It's just he said there was no one else here."

"Who? Oh. *Pfft*. Death knows where everyone is at all times? Sees you when you're sleeping, naughty and nice? Ew."

"Actually, it's that thing of his. His retro tablet thingy? He doesn't just know. It tells him where people are. And about that..." She hesitated.

"Hate to break it to you, but as much as my sister will swear Robots Are People Too, I'm pretty sure your buddy would disagree."

Of course. Though if Death knew enough to tell them the place had power, he likely knew about the robots. Would have been nice if he had warned them. Asshole. But the machines seemed harmless enough for the moment. Emily needed to get down to business. Death was *not* her buddy.

"I'm going to fill this up." Scott retrieved the gas jug. "After Carol's charged, we can take whatever's left from the tanks in the other two cans. You scrounge for tires."

"Actually—"

"What?"

Actually, she had no idea how to begin. Should she tell him his death was imminent? That might freak him out, and it wouldn't matter once they got far away from Death.

Get him away first. Yeah, that was better.

She shook her head. She needed to strategize before diving in. "Right. Tires. On it."

Working her way around the perimeter of the room, she discovered an actual exit. Through the door, she emerged into the rusty twilight of a loading yard. The only vehicle in it was a tipped-over forklift. Directly across the yard from her, a door with a broken handle hung open a few inches. On the wall to her left, behind the forklift, a ladder led to a double-high recessed dock. A closed rolling door at its back end reflected crimson stripes as the sun sank toward the hills at the open end of the yard to her right.

She wondered what might be behind the rolling door as she approached the ladder. The edge of the platform jutted a few feet above her head, and a red light blinked on a control panel up by the door. She put a hand on a ladder rung, but then paused. She was procrastinating. *Strategize.*

Okay. Think. She should tell Scott about the horsepeople first. Let him know how big this all was. And then explain about Manhattan? But that would be a lot to take in. She should buffer it with something positive. Like finding tires. Impress him like she did with the fuel at the ranch.

The forklift's tires obviously wouldn't work, but Emily recalled how the parking lot wrapped the main building. No vehicles stood on the side where they parked, but she would check around the back. There had to be something out there.

There was something all right.

One vehicle, and only one. A semi. Its cab pointed directly at Emily as she came around the wall separating the back parking lot from the central factory building. She stopped short, throwing up her arms. After a second, she lowered them, realizing the truck wasn't running or about to plow straight into her. But as she stared at it, stared at the lumpy stuffed bunny strapped to its grill, all her strength drained from her limbs.

Emily knew this truck.

How long had it been? Without sleep, the days and nights blurred into a slippery miasma. Was it seriously only two days since she last saw this cattle truck through her binoculars parked outside an entirely different factory?

She'd spent hours staring at it and the second one like it, making up stupid names and backstories for the dirty pink bunny while worrying for the people she feared might be inside. Parked under the desert sun while the drivers chilled in the factory. But no commune's human herd inhabited those trucks. No. What did hairy Snakeman say?

Two glorious truckloads of motherfuckin' zombies.

But how was it here now? Off and quiet and deserted? Emily forced her legs to move until she could put a hand on the grill next to the bunny. However long ago it arrived, it was cool under her touch now. Where did the driver go? Emily's hand swiped at her empty holster, and she spun around, her eyes scanning the lot.

"You said there was no one here," she whispered, even though Death was wherever and wouldn't hear her.

Nothing. No other trucks, no sign of the commune. Had they stopped here just like they did at the factory at Suncrest Hill, then left this truck behind when they moved on? They released all their zombies when her team attacked, but wouldn't they keep the truck? Especially after bringing it this far?

What did Snakeman say? She scraped her memory. Something about starving the zombies. The commune *used them as weapons.* Something supposedly no one ever managed to do before. They let them all loose on her team. But if they'd wrangled them once…

Slowly Emily turned and looked down the length of the truck. Everything was so quiet. They wouldn't leave the truck here unless something was wrong with it, right? It was empty, broken, useless? It had to be.

But something…something made her not so sure. Her palms itched. Her nose, her lips were tingling. Something…

Step by step, she crept to the back of the truck. The windows along its side were too high for her to see into, but as she passed under them, the smell became impossible to deny. A dry, musky smell. A lifeless smell that wasn't dead.

Pulling herself up on the lip above the bumper, she gripped the handles of the back doors and stood on her toes, lifting her face to the window. Countless faces stared back up at her.

Emily bit the insides of her cheeks to keep from screaming. So many of them! They stood packed shoulder to shoulder, slouching against each other, squished to the sides. Frozen, she could not turn away. But after a few moments, they did, their faces drooping noiselessly. Most of them stood still, though some sighed. And were those two nuzzling each other? Most appeared asleep on their feet, their eyes half-lidded. But the eyes Emily could see were contemplative, thoughtful. Intelligent?

And so, so miserable.

God, these were just people! Gray, sunken, shriveled, people. Many of them missing obvious pieces, but look at them!

You said there was no one here!

So zombies were no one.

Emily's hand twisted the door handle before she realized what she was doing, but it clicked against the lock.

Maybe Death's screen didn't tell him zombie locations? They weren't living; they'd never died. He didn't have power over the undead, so neither would his screen.

Or was he just lying? Was this part of his plan to get Scott killed?

Zombies couldn't kill Scott. They would do the opposite of what Death wanted. But whoever left this truck here, would they be coming back for it?

Emily's gaze shot to the blazing horizon. "Fucker!" How much longer until sunset?

Soft groans rose from inside the truck. Emily clamped her mouth shut and put her face back to the window. They all stared at her again. Big eyes, small eyes, milky mud-colored eyes—eyes she recognized? Emily gasped. One head rose above the rest, the tallest zombie in the crowd. Its dark skin had turned a deep purple color, but she knew that big stubble-covered head.

Big Joe! From her LPI team.

And he was focusing on her. He nudged against the bodies in front of him, worked his hand out of the press. He knew her! She could tell he knew her.

Lying son of a bitch. Why had she ever trusted Death? No other intelligent zombies like her? Bullshit! Look at how Big Joe studied her. And there, that poofy hair. Carlos! And there, the Flip boy whose name she couldn't remember. And— "Rosa! Rosa!"

The creaky groans erupted into guttural screaming, and the truck lurched as they all pressed to the door. Rosa's short, round frame was swallowed by thrashing limbs that beat the walls below the windows.

"No!" Emily wrenched at the handle, battled the lock. "Rosy! Get off her! Let her out!" Her ankle twisted, and she fell off the tailgate but clawed her way right back up. Bracing herself against the truck's corner, she bashed at the handle with her boot.

She'd seen it! Focus, attention. Rosa had to still be there, behind those clouded eyes. Never as a human had Emily seen a zombie look at her like that. But she couldn't find Rosa in the crowd, and all signs of intelligence abandoned the faces she could see. They pushed each other to the floor, climbing over themselves. Teeth caked in black blood snapped through the window bars.

But they couldn't eat Emily. The damage was already done. She had to get her team out of there. She jumped down and scanned the lot for something to use. They could be like her! She could reach them! She'd given the all clear, she sent them to their doom, but this was her chance. She could still save them.

Grabbing a chunk of concrete from a shattered parking bumper, she climbed back up and smashed at the lock.

One—two—the handle bent, and the door casing around it cracked. Emily yanked at it, but the lock held. Three—four—

A shotgun blast exploded beyond the factory wall.

Emily jerked back, lost her footing, and fell hard on the asphalt. The concrete flew from her fingers.

Silence.

Ohgodno.

Scott!

27

ZOMBIES

Getting around the parking lot wall and back into the loading yard felt like a bad dream, like running through high water. When Emily finally made it, Scott stood next to the door with the broken handle, his gun aimed at the sky.

"What—" She gaped at him. "What happened?"

"Oh, there you are." He made a face like he wasn't exactly pleased to see her again.

"What?" He was fine. No one else was there. He was fine. "Why did you shoot?"

"I was calling. You didn't answer." He stepped around his bags, which flopped against the wall, and he pushed open the door. "You have to see this."

She shook her head. "I thought—"

"What?"

"You were being…attacked or…" Emily felt like she ought to be shaking. But as she stood completely still, her actions at the semi came rushing back to her.

Holy hell.

Had she completely lost it? Did she seriously try to open that truck? What the hell was wrong with her? If not for the gunshot…

She pushed her hands against her face, rubbing hard at her squelchy eyes. "You scared the shit out of me."

"Pfft. Come look at this, then talk to me about scary shit."

They had to go. They had to get out of there. Carol could charge somewhere else.

"Scott—" But if she told him about the truck, he would want to set it on fire. The thought of her team going up in smoke with the rest of them froze her tongue. She followed him speechlessly through the broken door into a huge garage.

The first thing to hit her was the smell. She knew that smell. The smell of Town Duty, of completed missions, of the end of undead. The bonfire smell. "Devil's barbecue," Rosa used to call it.

In the center of the room amid a ring of blackness, lay two charred and twisted metal boxes. Boxes just the right size to each hold a body. Vampire boxes.

"What—" Emily tilted her head back. Scorched black rimmed the garage ceiling, but no residue of burnt wood or kindling lay near the boxes. How had metal caught fire? It looked like they'd combusted from within.

Scott poked at one with the tip of his shotgun. The brittle side cracked open, spilling dark ashes to the floor.

"We have to scatter them," she said. "Now. Before dark." Not like vampire ashes could reform immediately, or even in a week, much less a night. Supposedly. But Emily had never taken that risk, and she wasn't about to start now.

"Obviously." Scott glanced around the garage. "Who did this?"

She shook her head. Whoever did it was long gone, but they finished what her team started. That explained the abandoned zombie truck. At Suncrest Hill, the commune consisted of seven vampires, but hadn't she seen one running away that night? Maybe her team destroyed the rest? Only these two survived, and now they were extra crispy toast. What about their human guards? Abducted by whoever did this? Or maybe they did it themselves and took off. Good for them.

"Here." Scott handed Emily a push broom.

"Where'd you get this?"

He gestured to an open closet at the back of the garage. "Don't go in there. It stinks."

"Worse than this?" She cursed her zombie nose, gagging as she splintered the metal with the broom's corner to push through the ashes. Worst superpower ever.

"Dead raccoon." With a broom of his own, Scott helped her scoot the mess to the huge garage door. They found the controls to open it and swept everything out to be scattered by the winds of the driveway as the sun disappeared beyond the horizon.

Emily took a deep, long breath of relief. Too late she realized what she'd done, and the coughing seized her. She dropped the broom and braced herself against the parking lot wall.

"Are you okay?" Scott asked.

She nodded, wiping her mouth. Zombie problems.

He turned to the wall. "Did you find tires?"

The reminder of the semi made Emily jerk up. It hulked so close on the other side of the wall, but she couldn't hear a thing. Without her there to rile them up, the zombies had gone silent again. But how long before they sensed Scott?

"Oh, um, no actually." She couldn't let him go around to that side of the parking lot. Stepping over the broom, she waved him back into the garage toward the broken door. "There's nothing here except that forklift. But maybe those would work?" Its tires were way too big for their pickup truck, but she had to get him away from the wall.

He looked doubtful but shouldered his shotgun and followed her through to the loading yard. Once the forklift came into sight, the stupidity of her suggestion became obvious.

"We should just go," she said. "We'll find something in town up the road."

Scratching the back of his head, Scott surveyed the yard. "Yeah. As soon as Carol's done."

This would be a good time to tell him she planned to leave Death behind. She tried not to let herself wonder at his whereabouts; his habit of appearing just when she did was the last thing she wanted.

She told herself it didn't matter if he overheard. What was he going to do about it? Plead his case?

She tried to ignore the absurd sinking feeling that accompanied the thought of going on without him.

"Did you fill up the fuel can?" she asked Scott instead.

"Yeah, I left it by Carol."

As the last of the purple evening light faded into nightfall, Scott passed under the forklift's mast, jutting sideways like an arm that would never grasp what it reached for. "What do you think's behind that rolling door?"

Emily glanced up. Scott pointed his gun at the elevated loading dock in the back of the yard.

"I was wondering the exact same thing earlier."

He crossed to it and grabbed a rung of the ladder built into the wall under the dock. "It's worth a look."

Emily waited until he reached the top before following. She'd pretty much given up on the six-foot rule, but keeping him comfortable still mattered.

Just tell him. Death wasn't who she wanted him to be. Asshole. He wasn't even a *who* at all. And Scott needed to know.

Why was this so damn hard?

Scott eyed the control panel on the wall to the right of the door. "This would be where they received their supplies. There might be all kinds of stuff back there."

Stuff. Sure. Useful stuff. Tires, even. It could make or break their drive to New York. "Depends if someone else already got to it," she mused. But it looked in good shape, not tampered with in any way. And the generators had clearly not been activated in ages, so whoever came to the factory earlier, valiantly exterminating vampires, didn't use the control panel to access the door.

"This isn't like the garage," Scott said, poking at the panel. "I can't get it open."

Emily pulled her eyes from the rolling door. The teal glow of the panel's screen cut a crisp shadow in the furrow between Scott's brows. He sighed loudly and hitched up his loose jeans as he stepped back. "It needs a print or a PIN."

"Let me see." She moved beside him. "Wow, it's a pullscreen. Who was even still installing these?" And outdoors at that. She lifted the shield to pinch at the command, clearing the display, then she scrolled through the menu and twisted to the settings page.

Scott moved along the wall. From the corner of her eye, Emily saw him open a switchboard.

She tugged through options on the screen. "I think it's—"

A deep-voiced alarm blared overhead, and she jerked back. A rotating light above the door illuminated the dock in a jarring blast of carnival orange.

Scott flipped his gun around and put his back to the wall. "What-didyoudo?"

"Nothing!" Emily's eyes darted over the dark places in the yard below.

A few seconds later, the alarm silenced mid-wail, though the orange light continued to spin. It flashed into the yard's corners and made the shadows in the forklift's crannies swell and fade like breathing inkblots. Emily glanced to the door behind them, hoping it would roll up, but nothing happened.

"You must have done something." Scott lowered his gun and pushed sweaty bangs from his forehead. "That scared the shit out of me."

Your turn. But Emily couldn't take the credit. She turned back to the screen. "I wasn't even out of the menu yet."

"Are you sure?" He joined her at the panel and reached past her to the screen, but his hand froze above it. It hovered inches from her face. In the teal glow, punctuated by rotating orange, his ragged cuticles wavered like tiny stalks of seaweed. Little curling flakes of skin rimming short stubby nails. Dark, raw. He must chew on them. Chew on them with his teeth. His... So raw... Tangy. They would taste like copper.

"Do you hear that?" Scott whispered.

Emily's attention snapped to the yard, over to the door with the broken handle.

No.

Oh no.

"I hear it."

Low groaning seeped from the space beyond. Unmistakable groaning. And not just one groan. The sound festered into a brain-winching chorus of groans.

"Well, shit." Scott's gun popped into position, and he backed to the far corner, crouching to take aim.

No.

Nononono.

Emily staggered to the front of the dock and gaped at the door. How could this be happening? That truck was *locked*.

The door moved, pushing outward in staccato pops as if stiff on its hinges. As the orange light circled over, she could see thick gray fingers clenching its edge.

Locked!

She smashed it, but it didn't work. It didn't. The lock held when she left.

Another bump, and the door flew back, clanging against the wall.

Oh, god, no.

What the fuck had she done?

Zombies filled the doorframe, clawing and snapping at each other. For a minute, the sheer number of bodies kept them back as they wrestled to get through. Then, all at once, they spilled into the yard. Emily jumped against the side wall as the first blast from Scott's shotgun exploded past her.

"Wait!"

"What?"

"I mean…" Fuck, no, he was right. This was bad. There must have been over a hundred in that truck. And for the moment, she didn't see anyone she recognized. They had to shoot. Her stupid hand swiped her empty holster.

Shit.

"Do you have another gun?"

Scott focused his aim and shot again from the dock's corner. Then he dug into his pocket, but all he pulled out was Carol's ancillary.

Emily attempted to count them as they trundled through the yard, but the spinning light multiplied them impossibly. Slow ones, most of them, but six or ten zagged through, getting ahead of the crowd. Shuddering, Emily shook out her hands and slid along the back wall to Scott's side. "A gun?"

"Get back." He straightened in his corner, pumped another cartridge, and took aim.

Emily pressed her hands over her ears as the blast went off. One of the zombies dropped, but the rest surged past the forklift to the base of the dock, the nearest ones disappearing from sight below its edge.

"They can't get up here." Scott's gun drooped, and he fished cartridges out of his sagging jeans pockets. "And Carol's—"

A blood-caked hand appeared at the top of the ladder. A snarling white-eyed face rose after it.

Scott's handful of cartridges clattered to the floor.

Emily grabbed his arm. "Give me a gun!"

He wrenched away, his eyes darting between her and the zombie clawing onto the dock. "They're in the bag." His shaking hands took three tries to thumb cartridges into the shotgun before he could snap it closed. He fired at the zombie—too fast. His shot went wide.

"Where's the bag?" She'd just seen it, hadn't she?

"Scott!" Carol's voice rang over the groaning howls. Emily turned to see her run into the yard from the factory door, gas jug in hand. She plowed through the crowd shoulder first, bodies falling to the ground in her wake.

Scott moved around Emily and worked to load again, shielding himself behind her as the zombie at the top of the ladder pushed to its feet. It had once been a man, no more than forty. Ribbons of flesh hung from his throat over the broad shoulders of dark blue coveralls like epaulets. Dried blood and old grease streaked his sunken cheeks. His black hair clung to his head in sticky clumps on one side and was entirely gone on the other. The raw exposed scalp oozed green, almost black, in the orange light that circled round and round.

He didn't look like *just a person* now. None of them did. He looked feral and ravenous and like everything Emily ever fought to destroy. How did she ever see intelligence in eyes like that? Only one thing filled his brain: the desperate, starving, miserable, anguished desire to eat Scott. The insides of Emily's cheeks flinched in pain. She clenched her teeth and swallowed thickly.

He had several inches on her, but he wobbled on his feet. A well-balanced kick would send him back over the edge. She put one foot behind her and coiled for it. "Stay back," she called over her shoulder to Scott.

But before she could launch into the kick, the zombie's arms shot into the air as his feet flew out from under him. Emily spotted the silver hand around his ankle as Carol flung him into the yard.

She hoisted herself up the ladder, swung the jug onto the ledge, and kicked out behind her. The bodies *smack-smack-smacked* the ground.

Scott fell to his knees to gather his scattered cartridges, and he pushed past Emily to Carol. "How much charge do you have?"

She twisted to sit at the top of the ladder. "Not enough." Pulling two handguns from holsters on her hips, she fired at the zombies grappling at her legs. Her bullets hit precisely in their snarling faces, blasting their features clean off. They fell into a writhing, screaming heap at the base of the ladder, but others immediately replaced them. All too quickly, her guns began to click. "Scott, where is the bag?"

He looked up from where he knelt, and his gaze traveled across the yard to the broken door. The crowd obscured them from sight, but Emily could picture perfectly the dusty backpack and lumpy blue duffel bag resting against the wall.

Carol glanced over her shoulder. When she saw his devastated expression, her eyes narrowed. She started to say something but stopped herself and shook her head. "How much ammunition do you have?"

Scott swallowed, and his dazed gaze drifted from her to the sea of zombies. They filled the yard from wall to wall. "I'm…"

Carol's attention snapped away as undead hands scrabbled over her lap, tugged at her thighs, grabbed her scarf. She shoved the snarling creature down into the pile and kicked ruthlessly at the next two who took its place, her heels cracking ribs. Flicking her scarf over her shoulder, she bent and snatched one below them. She tore off its jaw then hurled the whole body at the three behind it, knocking them to the ground.

For the moment.

Emily turned back to Scott. He was sitting on his heels and staring at his handful of cartridges as if they would do him as much good as a handful of walnuts. All blood had completely drained from his face. Emily winced. With his shaggy bangs hanging over his eyes, he looked like a thin, pale version of her brother on that last night in Long Beach. She shuddered as the memory clenched her with icy fingers. Too many of them, scraping at the sliding glass doors of her family's nice suburban house with its perfect yard. Windows breaking. Dad yelling from the family room. Too many of them and not enough bullets. Not even close to enough bullets.

There was nothing she could do then. Nothing any of them could do.

But Emily damn well would do something now. This was happening because of her. The semi drove here because of her. Her entire team was undead because of her.

Scott would *not* die because of her.

Emily strode to him and pushed at his shoulder. "Hey."

He recoiled, clambered to his feet. "Don't!" He shoved the cartridges into his pocket, then pointed his gun over the edge. He aimed here and there but seemed afraid to fire.

Emily's hand tingled. He'd felt so warm through his shirt, like he had a fever. She clenched her teeth. "Look, I'm going to get the bags, okay?"

Scott stilled. He looked from her, to the crowd, then back again. His eyes widened. "They can't hurt you."

Emily wasn't so sure about that, but she nodded. "Just don't shoot me, okay?"

He hesitated, his eyes flicking to Carol, who stomped on the face of each zombie mounting the ladder.

"No," said Emily. "Don't let her move." The pile under her grew body by body. Soon they wouldn't need the ladder. But for now, her butt on top of it was the only thing keeping Scott safe.

He hesitated another moment, then finally nodded and lowered his gun.

Emily retreated to the opposite end of the dock and crouched at the lip. With the bulk of the crowd's attention on the ladder, fewer scalps milled below, leaving enough space for her to slip between them.

Could they hurt her? *Doesn't matter.*

She slid off the edge, twisting to hang by her hands, then dropped the last couple feet to the ground. The zombie she landed beside snarled and shuffled around to face her as she eased up to stand.

Carlos.

Emily remained absolutely still as his milky eyes lifted. She tried to hold her breath before she remembered she didn't breathe at all. Her lips parted, but she bit her tongue. No recognition in his gaze, nothing. Like he couldn't see her at all. His head flopped to the side, and a red film burbled from the corner of his mouth.

It's me, she pleaded with her eyes. Were they as cloudy as his?

Emily waited one moment more, then took a slow step to the side. "I'm just gonna…"

The change was instantaneous; his mouth twisted, a screech exploding from it. It sounded like every screech that ever shattered her nightmares. Emily punched Carlos square in the solar plexus, cutting off the sound, then she shoved past and plowed into the crowd.

She kept her head tucked and led with her shoulder. The web of limbs blurred past in the swirling orange light. She struck out at each in her way, but after the first few toppled, the rest took notice.

The howling pressed in on her, raked her ears. Ragged, sticky fingers snatched at her clothes, clawed at her hair. The snapping jaws became a barrage of castanets as she danced and twisted through the writhing nest. She couldn't see the bags, or the wall, or the door, but she was getting close. She had to be.

A heavy body slammed into her. Pain shot through her skin as razor teeth grazed her cheek. She shoved the biting face away but felt another mouth clamp onto her shoulder. Big hands gripped her waist, and her feet flew out from under her. Her scalp screamed as her hair tore in the opposite direction.

No!

She kicked and shoved and snapped her own jaws right back, but too many of them piled on. Their weight pressed her to the ground. Her limbs contorted at excruciating angles as teeth snagged her pants and jagged nails dug against her throat. So many of them. Shoving her back and forth, and then she was flattened under dead weight.

Undead weight.

When she screamed, it sounded just like their howls.

Oh, god. Her chest was going to cave in.

What had she done?

She shouldn't have fought them. She wasn't a solid metal android. Her talking set them off. She should have snuck through, went around the perimeter. Too late. She should have known better. What had everything since Long Beach been for now? What had he died for? He should have known better. He was shooting them neatly in the hearts. He was such a good shot. But you can't shoot neatly. Neatly does nothing. They got right back up and piled onto him, dragged him down, tore him apart. And Emily could do nothing but fight her stupid hysterical mother, shove her into the car, speed away from her own father's howling.

All too late.

28

SHOTGUN

Don't shoot her. Don't shoot her.

How the heck could Scott shoot *anything* when she blended right in with all of them? He tried to track her half-purple hair through the bodies, but it was too dark, and the spinning orange light only made it worse. His eyes couldn't keep up, couldn't adjust, and everything looked black when it circled away. Was that her? She was going the wrong way! No—there she went. What the heck was she doing? Drawing them away from Carol? The entire back half of the crowd zeroed in on Emily like a school of piranhas.

Oh. Well, shit.

Scott aimed at the pile of bodies that swallowed Emily's. Did he have enough cartridges to unbury her? He already used his last slug, only buckshot left.

His chest was jerking, his shoulders heaving. Impossible to aim straight. This was a stupid plan. His breath came in gasps. "Stupid, stupid zombie girl."

His hands worked without his brain. Shoot, shoot, load. Shoot, shoot, load. It didn't matter if his aim was shit. The crowd crushed so thick, he hit something every time. Some went down. Some didn't even notice.

Again. Again. Orange, black, orange, black, orange, black.

His fingertips scraped the bottom of one pocket, then the other. Tucked under the slippery shape of Carol's ancillary, he found his very last cartridge.

Oh.

Scott didn't remember sitting down. Someone was calling his name. The cartridge rocked in his palm like a gold-capped Vienna sausage. He should load it, shouldn't he? But the gun felt so heavy across his knees.

"Scott! Get back!"

He blinked at Carol. She was waving frantically. His gaze shifted to the edge of the dock.

Hands. That was a lot of hands.

"They're climbing on each other!"

Scott staggered to his feet and backed to the rolling door. "Carol." He swallowed past the thick clot in his throat.

We can do it, he'd said. *Let's just go. We'll drive to New York.* He had a super zombie-killing robot, after all. He'd be fine. For months, he waited alone with Carol at the deserted Curisa. One hundred sixteen days. The airship never came back. He wanted to believe Nick made it to Manhattan. With Carol, he could make it too. They had weapons, they had food, they had everything they needed.

They didn't even make it through Utah.

What a waste Scott's life had been. Not even a waste. What could he have done with it? What was he supposed to do? What was anyone ever supposed to do? Survive, live. What did that even mean? Try to make a difference? Like his hero brother? Look what happened to him. If you don't try, you can't fail. If you don't care, you can't get hurt. How could he have regrets when it all meant nothing?

Scott's fingers moved, steady and cold as he slid the cartridge into the gun and pressed it closed.

"Carol."

Her head owl-turned to him while her hands and feet worked on the zombies on the ladder. Her eye lights shone green, night vision. Nick had taken the 360 camera out of the back of her LS head. To make her "more human." Nick loved her so much.

"Keep going." His hoarse voice creaked. "Finish charging. Fill up the other cans, take the truck."

"Scott, what are you doing?"

He sank to his knees, braced the end of the gun against the metal floor between them, lifted his chin over the barrel.

"Scott!"

He swallowed again. "She's waiting for you, Carol." Without him, she would have no trouble driving across the country. She and Nick would be together again.

"Scott, put down the shotgun."

And then what? Count the minutes until they climbed up and ate him alive? When he looked at her, the expression on her silicone face confused him. So visceral, so distraught.

"Scott, please!"

Couldn't she see the probability of him living through this was zero? He had to do it before his numb fingers started shaking too much to manage the trigger.

"Please!"

Carol cared because Nick cared, because he was Nick's brother. Because Nick would prefer him alive. And she loved Nick more than anything. That's why she stayed with him. Why she programed her own mission objective to protect him. For Nick. All for Nick.

Scott had never loved anyone like that. Not his parents, not Nick, not Jade. He never let himself. His vision misted over as he stared across at Carol.

Orange, black, orange.

Orange streaked the sky that evening one hundred sixteen days ago when he chased the second airship down the runway, the swarm snapping at his heels. Late again, and he had no one to blame but himself that time. Everyone else was already aboard. He leapt for the speeding ship's open door but lost his grip on the edge as the wheels left the ground. When his body slammed to the tarmac, it was Carol who jumped down after him. Scott saw Nick lean out as the ship climbed the murky sky, heard her scream his name. Or was it Carol's? Impossible to tell over the roar of the engines and the snarling closing in around him. And then small hands pulled Nick inside, and he could see nothing else but silver limbs crouched over him. Tortured howls drowned out the fading engine as Carol mowed the zombies down. She fought them off, gathered him up, and ran him back to the safety of the abandoned facility.

"Scott." Her voice snapped him back to the present. His name came out of her mouth like her heart was breaking. And she didn't even have a heart.

"Sorry," he rasped. Not for what he was about to do, but for everything before. She did care, she did. Because she chose to care. Was that all that really mattered? It had just been easier to assume it couldn't be authentic. Easier. But Nick made her with that capacity. Carol drove so he could sleep, pushed him so he could thrive, annoyed him so he could feel real. She chose to be his friend when he had no one else in the world.

If Carol were made capable of crying, she looked like she would be. How could he leave her now? It felt like two hands of bone crushed Scott's heart. His artificial sister. She tried so hard.

"Thanks," he whispered.

Closing his eyes, he nestled his chin onto the shotgun's barrel. His numb fingers moved like twigs to find the trigger. Snowman hands. Even the air around him felt arctic. When did that happen? Well, it fit. Death was near. But unlike the icicles of terror Scott felt the night before, this cold was welcoming, soothing.

It was his time.

His heart drumrolled in his ears. Carol was saying something, but he couldn't hear her over it. It didn't matter. They were words for another life. Scott's time had come. He was ready.

Take me.

So cold. So right.

He took a long, deep breath. His last.

His finger tucked against the trigger.

And then, just like that, an inhuman grip wrenched the gun from his hands. Scott gasped and fell against the door. When his eyes flew open, blackness consumed him.

29

GAMBIT

How long since the muffled shotgun explosions ceased to make their way through the pile of bodies pressing Emily to the ground? How long would the groans and undead screaming be the only sounds she heard?

Undeath is immortality.

Forever, then.

They weren't trying to eat her. She figured that out as her panic petered into despair. They knew she wasn't food. But they also knew she presented a threat, and they planned to keep her down. That intention thrummed clear. How?

Zombie hive mind thing.

God…

Anything, anything to get up again. But only live bait would distract them. And Scott was out of bullets up there. What had she done?

Fucking idiot.

Cringing back what would have been tears if she could shed them anymore, Emily worked her hands over her head and curled tight under the pummeling mass. Each time the weight shifted and stupid hope teased a chance to break through, pressure from another angle replaced it.

She managed to twist onto her side, but when she opened her eyes, a zombie's face hovered inches from hers, its jaw working, teeth clicking.

Not an it. A her.

"Rosa," Emily breathed.

Too dark to see details, but the soft profile proved too familiar to be anyone else.

"I'm so sorry. Please..."

Could she see Emily?

Another shift in the weight, bodies rolling over them. Emily groaned. Who else joined their pile? Where was Ramon? She didn't see him in the truck or in the crowd. He was destroyed, wasn't he? And the rest of her team... Gone... But she already knew that. The face before her wasn't Rosa anymore. It was Emily's fault. Her fault, Snakeman's fault, the commune's fault, the universe's fault.

"Rosy."

Nothing.

"What do I do?"

If their places switched, would Rosa be lying there feeling guilty? Shame wouldn't help Emily or anyone. If she ever got out of this, Emily couldn't let shame, pride, *standards*—stupid ideals that meant nothing—get in her way ever again.

"Rosy," she whispered. "I wish I could do everything over."

A gunshot boomed overhead.

The groaning swelled, and the pile shifted. Rosa's face disappeared behind a tumble of shoulders and limbs. Emily pushed up but jerked as a hand gripped her arm. A hand too hard to be one of theirs. Painfully tight, she felt the jolt even through her sleeve. Before she could react, it pulled her through a sudden hole in the pile with bewildering strength.

Air! She didn't need it, but god, she'd missed it. She gasped a choking lungful as her feet gained purchase on solid ground. The hand on her arm was joined by another around her waist, and she found herself tight against Death's statuey side.

"You—"

The crowd pressed in on them, but before her reeling mind had a chance to catch up, the savage faces melted into an incomprehensible blur. When her vision stilled again, she stood once more above them all on the safety of the loading dock.

Death released her before she was ready for it, and she fell to her knees. Pins and needles popped over her entire body, and buzzing erupted in her ears. Too, too much like the night she un-died.

For a long minute, she could do nothing but stare at her blotchy fingers knotted against the dusty diamond plate floor. It shuddered with each thud of the pounding mass below. Emily squeezed her eyes shut and pushed to sit on her heels, rubbing at the stinging scratches on her cheek and neck. New holes shredded her pants, but it didn't feel like she was missing any pieces. Nothing important anyway. She looked for Scott, and her eyes found him crumpled in the dock's corner behind Carol, his skin clammy, almost green. He was turning his shotgun over and over in his hands and staring at where his bags lay invisible beyond the swarm.

And Death...

Emily's neck creaked as she looked over her shoulder. His back was to her, but the blue glow of his device's screen haloed his cloak, clashing with the spinning orange light. Her throat felt full of sand. She turned back to Scott. Scared puppy, Scott.

"You're empty, aren't you?" she asked.

Scott jerked as if waking from a trance. His eyes narrowed into offended slits, his chin jutting like she'd insulted his manhood. Instead of answering, he glowered down at his gun, his hand running along its length. His lips set in a grim line as if coming to a decision, then he got up and faced the swarm.

What was he...?

He took a deep breath, stepped around the gas jug, knelt at the dock's edge, flipped the gun around, and bashed at the skulls below.

The crowd's attention immediately shifted from Carol at the

ladder, and they jumped for Scott, grabbing the ledge, swiping at his gun. He pounded back the hands, smashed in the teeth.

"You fool!" Death's voice rang over the groans. He swept past Emily and snatched the gun on Scott's next upward swing.

"Let go!" Scott yelped.

Death pulled the gun back, dragging Scott with it away from the edge.

Releasing the barrel, Scott stumbled and fell against the wall. "Stop *doing* that!"

The gun clattered to the floor at Death's side. "You risk your life."

"What do you care?" Scott stammered. "If you're not going to help, leave me alone."

What do you care? Phantom tingles pricked Emily's flesh. She asked the very same thing yesterday when Death yanked a gun out of her hand too.

Death swept an arm over the crowd. "Do you think I want them to have you?"

Ah. There it was. Of course. *Idiot.*

Did Death think pulling her from the zombie pile would make her forget what he admitted in the truck? For all Emily knew, he let these zombies out of the semi himself. She was *positive* that door was still locked. She felt her insides clench to steel.

"He doesn't care." She pushed to her feet and picked up the shotgun, stalking past Death to return it to Scott. She'd stalled long enough. She wasn't going to let Scott be suckered in like she was. "He's just saving you for himself. *That's* why he's following us. Scott, the only reason he's here is because he is waiting for you to die."

"What?" Scott gaped at her. "But. What?" He shook his head, his arms twining around the gun. "Then why did he stop me from killing myself?"

"What?" The steel inside Emily poofed into sawdust. "He—what? When?"

"Just now. Right before he dove down there and rescued you."

He *stopped* Scott? Emily twisted to look at Death. He leaned against the rolling door, poking at his screen thing like they weren't surrounded by attacking undead, like Carol wasn't still tearing into them one by one, like he didn't give a damn about anything in the world.

Seriously, what the hell?

His face lifted, but he stilled when he met Emily's stare. The screen changed colors in his hands.

"Stay behind me," Carol said to Scott.

"How much power do you have left?" he asked her.

When Emily didn't hear an answer, she turned around. Carol was pulling at the jaw of a zombie climbing over her lap. It wasn't ripping off like the ones before.

"She's fading," she whispered.

"The fuel!" Scott jumped from behind Carol and rushed to the jug.

"What?"

"Let's— We can splash it over them! Set them on fire."

Yes! If they soaked the ones in front and lit them up, then it could spread to the back when they pressed forward. But wait. "I left my matches in my other pants," Emily said. The ones she didn't have. "I hope you've got some."

Scott shook his head. "But Carol, your laser. Do you have enough power for just one shot?"

She fell silent for a calculating moment. "If I draw from everything."

"Okay!"

"But then I'll shut down."

"If it works, that's okay. Once they're all burnt, I'll get you back to the charging station and—"

"But will it work?" Emily interrupted.

"Probably not."

They both turned to follow Death's voice.

"She wasn't asking you," Scott snapped.

Emily frowned, not wanting to listen either, but Death's doubt increased her own. If they risked it and lost Carol, that would be it for Scott. But what other option did they have?

"Why don't you do something then!" Scott pushed away from the jug and waved his gun at Death. "Huh? You had no problem down there a minute ago."

Death shook his head, tucked his screen away. "They are undead. I have no power over them."

"Emily's undead! You pulled her out of there like it was nothing."

"She wished to be pulled out. She allowed me to do it. They will not allow me to affect them."

"Scott, stay back." Carol knocked another zombie off the ladder.

"Well, can you get the bags?" he snapped. "You have power over bags, don't you?"

"The bags?"

"The bags!"

"Do you mean these bags?" A man's voice rose from the yard. Emily's head snapped to look over the crowd. It took her a moment, but then she saw him, standing atop the forklift as if he were there the whole time. Not at man at all. A goddamn vampire.

And not just any vampire.

The night on Suncrest Hill came flooding back to her. It was the same vampire she witnessed running from the other factory. The one who gave her the idiotic hope her team had the upper hand. She would have recognized that obnoxious pasty smirk and ridiculously arched eyebrow anywhere.

He held Scott's backpack aloft in one hand and the duffel bag in the other, as if he might open his fingers at any moment and drop them into the writhing mass on either side of the forklift. His pale hair wisped, unnaturally elevated, as if full of static electricity. When the orange light spun over him, it looked aflame, like a halo from hell. It glinted off of a belt buckle between the flaps of his long dark coat, pooled in the glossiness of his shoes.

Emily clenched her fists at her sides.

"You!" Scott sprang from his corner.

The vampire smiled. "Me."

"What do you want?" Carol gave a particularly violent kick to the zombie before her.

Emily imagined her hitting the vampire square in the face with her last laser blast. Would it be worth losing her? It just might.

"Why, it's nice to see you again as well, Carol, my dear. Fine weather we're having tonight."

The zombies around the forklift lifted their faces to search for the source of the voice.

Scott aimed his gun at the vampire. "Give me my bags."

"Oh, these bags? Hmm… I suppose I *could* give them to you. Why? What's in them?" He jiggled the duffel against his ear before smiling at Scott again. "You point it very nicely, but your empty rifle is not going to do you much good."

"What do you want?" Carol snapped again.

Emily backed up until she stood at Death's side. "Can't you take them from him?" The way Death jumped onto the dock with her was vampire fast. Couldn't he whoosh over to the forklift the same way?

"I have no power over him," he answered in a low voice.

"Not even physical power? You're huge. Just push him over and take them?"

"None."

The others had gone silent.

The vampire was staring at her. "Oh-ho, what's this? You're not one of them at all, are you?"

"Fuck you," Emily spat.

He smirked his stupid smirk, then gazed past her to Death. "And hello there, tall dark and mysterious. Fancy seeing you here. It's been a while, hasn't it?"

"Tell us what you want for the bags," Carol demanded.

"Oh! A trade? Hmmmmm…" He flicked a shoe at one of the zombies that managed to crawl up the forklift's rung to swipe at his feet. It flew across the yard as if hit by a baseball bat, its head exploding on the wall like a pomegranate.

"What about a bite out of your scrumptious human? Just a little one. A taste."

"No!" Emily jumped forward. "You can fuck all the way off."

The reaction stemmed from pure instinct, but the instant it left her lips, she regretted it. So soon after her new resolution? She took a shaky step back, her hand covering her mouth.

But it was too late; Scott hesitated, looking to her. And the vampire expelled an exaggerated sigh.

"Well, that is a pity." His gaze drifted down Scott's body to the gas can at his feet. "Though I could just take him." He swung the bags over one shoulder and disappeared from the forklift in a blur.

Emily was too shocked to move for a crucial moment as he landed on the dock, inches from Scott. By the time her feet obeyed her, he was gone again in another dizzying rush. But Scott stood there still.

They all looked to the forklift.

The vampire had their fucking gas can.

"But I suppose this is all I really need." He flipped the full can into the air and caught its handle between his fingertips as if it weighed nothing. "Much obliged!"

Another pasty white grin and an absurd wink, and then he dropped backward off the forklift and zipped through the crowd with speed that made it almost impossible for Emily to track his disappearance around the driveway's corner.

"Wait!" she shouted after him. But he was gone. "Bitch!"

Scott's gun drooped to his side. He stared out at the night beyond the yard walls, his mouth hanging open. "He… He…"

"I'm sorry, I—" Emily pressed her palms against her eyes. Had she just cost Scott his only chance at escape? "I shouldn't have spoken for you. I…"

"He…"

"Who is that guy? I've seen him before. He…" No, she should probably keep those details to herself. But could they get him back? Emily's blood was useless, but could she offer him anything else? *Offer a vampire*. The realization grazed her, a muffled blow amid the storm of the moment, and it seemed so simple she could almost laugh. She'd do it. Of course she would. Just like Rosa said, *you do what you gotta do.*

The climbing zombies kept Carol too busy to answer Emily's question, and Scott just gaped, in some kind of shock.

Emily turned to Death. "How does he know you?"

His screen was in his hands again, his gaze fixed on it, but it was dark, off. "He is a killer."

The image of the vampire running up Suncrest Hill with fear in his eyes replayed in Emily's memory. Now he'd showed up here with the zombie truck. How? Why? Not that Death cared. She ground her teeth as she studied his downturned face. "Why did he take our stuff? What the hell does he want?" There had to be a way out of the factory. Something Death could do.

"Did he not make it clear he wants to kill Scott?"

"No." He just said a taste. "Is he going to?" *Something*. Death could move as fast as the vampire. For short bursts, anyway, as far as Emily had seen. He could go after him, *talk* to him if nothing else, tell him she'd negotiate. Or—or could he get more fuel from the generator tanks for the zombie fire?

"Not tonight," he answered with a sigh of resigned disappointment.

Emily's focus zeroed in on that remark. Death's defeatist tone made her want to grab him and shake him until his bones rattled. "How do you know?" she snapped.

He stared at her for a moment, looked down at his screen, then back to her.

"Don't give me that! You said yourself your bullshit schedule changes sometimes."

"*Rarely—*"

"The truth is that you don't know. You can't! You can't know *anything*." Anything... "Just like Manhattan. You can't know they're all going to die! You can't know it's hopeless."

"I've told you. If they don't die, they will un-die."

But no. No. *Yes.*

Emily's voice dropped as a queer calm washed over her. "You can't know that either."

"I know what's going to happen."

Death wasn't cold and unfeeling. No. Not entirely. If he were, would he need to dwell on the worst possible outcome to avoid being surprised by tragedy? He was just lost and afraid. Just...

desperate. Emily knew desperate. Emily could work with lost and afraid.

"And what is going to happen exactly?" She took a careful step toward him. "You made it sound like the fortress is going to get bombed or something."

"No, no bombs. Battle."

Who could attack Manhattan without bombs? Even when several communes banded together a year ago and tried an assault from multiple sides, the LPI decimated them. Did any commune out there exist with the kind of resources now to wage such a battle?

What could they possibly have that would be enough to get through Manhattan's defenses?

Besides the element of surprise, of course.

Emily's eyes widened.

"Well, we can prevent the battle! You said we have twelve days." If they could get out of the factory. "We have time to warn them." If they could get Scott there safely so he could get her past the gates. Then Death's schedule would change, right? It would be direct meddling with his precious balance. Even if he were there. The people scheduled to die would live, would have time to be saved instead. "We have to!"

"We?"

"Yes, we. It's not impossible."

"The only thing *I* can do, Emily, is reap life when it ends."

"Or you could, you know, *not* do that."

He looked utterly disgusted by the suggestion.

"What? You *just* did it with Scott. You're clearly capable! Why did you do that, huh? And why did you pull me up here? Why did you stop me from shooting myself yesterday? You can pretend you don't care about anything but reaping, but you're fucking lying to yourself."

"Do not presume—"

"Oh, no, buddy. I'm presuming. I'm presuming all over the place."

He shook his head, took a step back from her. "If Time does not unbind me, the lives lost *will* fall to undeath. But if he does unbind me, there is nothing to stop me from taking them."

"*You* can stop you! You *can* refrain from reaping. Apparently sometimes you even want to. It doesn't have to be they all die or they all un-die. Listen to yourself. There can be a third option."

"Emily, I am *starving*."

"Deal with it!" He was as bad as the communes with their utterly unsustainable model. "Think about how hungry you'll be later. You'll feast there, but then what? If Manhattan falls, so does the cure. So does the LPI and every last effort to stop the communes. A few years down the line when the last human is gone, what will you do?"

"End."

"Is that seriously what you want? Do you think that's right just because you're 'natural' and undeath isn't?"

"The balance—"

"Fuck the balance. It doesn't have to end your way or theirs. It could *not* end. I'm trying to help you. Work with me here!"

He sighed, turned to look out over the groaning swarm. "It would just be a waste of time."

"Time's the one who did this to you." Her hand caught the long part of his sleeve to draw him back, the midnight fabric soft and thick between her fingers. "So let's fucking waste him."

Silence. Emily's ears were ringing. The noise of Carol fighting on the ladder behind her sounded lifetimes away.

Death stared down at her for a long, grave moment before he spoke again. "But how?"

"Well, who's behind the attack?"

"I don't know."

"Then let's find out. Or *something*. We've got twelve days. We have to try."

"Time has never..." He tucked his screen away, pulled it out again. "I have never... My brethren..." Wind from nowhere blew through him. His robe sank and swelled. He lifted a hand as if to grasp something that wasn't there, ended up clutching dead air. "It would be entirely unprecedented."

"Yeah." Her fingers wound tighter into the material over his arm. "It would." Just like Emily. "Just like us."

The fire deep in Death's eyes flickered, and his mouth actually opened.

But whatever he was about to say was cut off by the guttural roar of a diesel engine. Emily let him go as her attention whipped to the driveway beyond the yard. Scott jumped up from his cowering corner.

Emily strained her ears. Was it receding? No, it was coming closer. A minute later, shrieks rose from the zombies at the far side of the crowd as the back end of a flatbed truck rammed through them. A flatbed truck filled with rectangular bales of hay to the top of its slatted sides. Bodies caught under its wheels, and the howls grew piercing and anguished. It swerved around the forklift and rumbled up to the dock. Bones cracked, flesh squelched. The floor under Emily's feet jolted as its end hit.

Catching herself against the control panel, she looked to Scott. He was shaking his head in disbelief, his mouth moving, but she couldn't hear him.

The flat top of the hay lined up a foot above the dock's floor. The zombies not mowed over or pinned to the wall attacked it, wringing their fingers into the slats, climbing the sides.

The driver side window whirred down. A white hand thrust the nearest zombie far from it before the vampire's face leaned out.

"Well?" he called to them. "Hop on then."

Scott hopped. Emily would have cheered if she possessed any air for it.

"Scott!" Carol cried as he scrambled to the front of the hay. Her eyes flashed red, matching the frantically blinking light on her chest, and she abandoned the ladder to follow him.

Emily dug her fingernails into her spongy palms and faced Death. His hood hid his down-turned eyes, his arms folded across his chest.

Well, she would do it. With or without him.

She turned her back, tucked her hair behind her ears, took a breath, and stepped off the edge.

The truck lurched forward, making her fall to her knees. The hay hit her harder than she expected. And it stank. She flattened against it, twisting her fingers in as it bucked and jolted with each thud of the bodies beneath the tires. Ahead, Carol anchored Scott while they knocked the last of them off the slats as the truck escaped the yard.

Emily craned her neck to look back at the dock, but her hair blew into her face and she couldn't see anything. By the time she shook it from her eyes, the truck was around the corner, the dock long out of sight.

So that was it, then. Fine. Whatever.

"Idiot," she whispered to herself, her voice catching.

"I'm right here."

Emily jerked and rolled over to see Death crouched at her side. A laugh burst past her lips as the weight of the past forty-eight hours took off from her shoulders like a great black bird thundering into the night.

It shouldn't matter, but it did. And Emily could work with that.

"To option number three?" she asked. "Let's save the world?"

"Hm."

"Just say yes." She felt like she could laugh for years. "You know you want to."

He folded an arm over his knee and cocked his head at a thoughtful angle. As the speeding wind whipped his cloak, Emily caught a glimpse of dusty bone feet on the hay. His balance was perfect, effortless while her aching fingers clung to the bales for dear life. Dear undeath. Every muscle tensed. How long would she be able to hang on? If the truck didn't slow soon…

As if reading her mind, Death leaned over to put a hand on the center of her back. The pressure was just enough to make Emily feel like she wouldn't go flying off into oblivion if she ever let herself relax.

She took a long, deep breath, and for once, her chest felt fine. "So, yes?"

"Indeed."

To Be Continued

ACKNOWLEDGMENTS

Erin Wright, if nobody else in the world but you loves this book, I'll still die complete. Thank you for being my biggest fan from the dawn of morbidity and the sweetest spooky friend a girl could ever hope to squish. And Wanyi Jiang, you relished darkness with me in my most formative years. This book would not exist without the two of you making me believe I could write.

Paul Schuler, your unconditional love and support of my macabre weirdness makes me reach for the super blood moon. 'Til death do us part.

Thank you to Linda Jacobs for raising me to be a reader. Your Edgar Allen Poe bedtime stories, Gothic horror pop-up books, and sci-fi indoctrination planted strange and unusual seeds I can't appreciate enough. No, I never wanted a "normal" mom.

To my awesome and bogglingly smart beta readers, thank you all for giving me so many amazing ideas to steal—John Skylar, Katey Garrigan, Lindsay Ellis, Antonella Inserra, A. F. Linley, Stephanie Kroll, Holly Brown, Nick Hansen, Andie Biagini, Serina Young, and Matt Gallo, who was there that night in 2010 when this story first seized my brain and has been giddy about it ever since. So many other incredible people provided feedback on parts of this book through writers' groups and friends that I can't even begin to list you all, and I am eternally grateful.

Thank you, Lindsay Ribar, the query letter queen, for all your industry insight and generosity.

And lastly, thank you Michael Shulman and Emily Streetz for each making me haaaaate zombies so many years ago. They say write what scares you, so I picked zombies. I'm the last person I ever thought would fall for a zombie protagonist of my own making. Thank you, thank you for terrifying me to new nightmare horizons.

ABOUT THE AUTHOR

Elisa Hansen is a recovering musical theatre major who enjoys graveyards, haunted mansions, gothic fashion, decorative skulls, black tea, and red wine. Born and raised in Southern California, she lived fifteen years in New York City before settling in Charlotte, NC.

When she's not reading or writing books, you can find her on YouTube as her alter-ego, The Maven of the Eventide. Her humorously analytical video essay webseries, Vampire Reviews, examines the evolution of vampire tropes and allegories in media and pop culture through a feminist lens.

ElisaHansen.com
twitter.com/ElisaInTime
youtube.com/mavenoftheeventide
facebook.com/mavenoftheeventide
patreon.com/mavenoftheeventide

FALSTAFF BOOKS

Want to know what's new & coming soon from Falstaff Books?

Join our Newsletter List
& Get this Free Ebook Sampler
with work from:
John G. Hartness
A.G. Carpenter
Bobby Nash
Emily Lavin Leverett
Jaym Gates
Darin Kennedy
Natania Barron
Edmund R. Schubert
& More!

http://www.subscribepage.com/q0j0p3

CPSIA information can be obtained
at www.ICGtesting.com
Printed in the USA
LVHW101628220522
719441LV00014B/87/J